THE
MAYFLOWER
REVELATIONS

A NOVEL

Andrew Cameron Bailey

A Cameron/Baxter Book

Cameron/Baxter Books, LLC
P. O. Box 592
Woody Creek, Colorado 81656

Publisher's Note: This is a work of fiction. Names, characters, places, and incidents are a product of the author's imagination. Locales and public names are sometimes used for atmospheric purposes. Any resemblance to actual people, living or dead, or to businesses, companies, events, institutions, or locales is completely coincidental.

Book Layout ©2013 BookDesignTemplates.com
Author photograph: Jonny Marlow Photography

Ordering Information:
Quantity sales. Special discounts are available on quantity purchases by corporations, associations, and others. For details, contact the "Special Sales Department" at the address above.

The Mayflower Revelations/Andrew Cameron Bailey. 1st edition.
ISBN: 978-0-9887547-4-4

Here under cover of darkness the fast dwindling company laid their dead, leveling the earth above them lest the Indians should learn how many were the graves.

—MOURT'S RELATION, London. 1622

First Impressions

Is *The Mayflower Revelations* the first Great American Novel of the 21st Century? Here's what people are saying:

Greatly enjoyed the novel. It holds together well. It will be one of the more original takes on the Pilgrim heritage associated with the year 2020. Well done!
James W. Baker; Pilgrim Scholar; Author, *Thanksgiving: The Biography of an American Holiday*; Editor, *The Cry of A Stone*, by Robert Cushman

I'm not a reader, but I couldn't put it down! The story is fascinating and unique.
Gregory Thompson; Deputy Governor-General, Connecticut Mayflower Descendants

I read the first 400 pages at one sitting. The history is extremely accurate.
John Bradford Towle; Board of Directors, Alden Kindred; Registrar, Society of Myles Standish Descendants

Preface

Pilgrims and Indians on the island of Barbados in the year 2020. What on Earth? Why Barbados? Because that is where boatloads of New England Indians were shipped as slaves in 1676, at the end of the disastrous bloodbath known to history as Metacom's Rebellion or King Philip's War. It makes sense that a Native American ghost might make an appearance on the island three and a half centuries later, especially if she had some vital information to impart. Barbados was the site of the earliest slave rebellions in the British Empire in the 1760s, the beginning of the end for the worldwide slave trade. As unlikely as it might sound, those rebel slaves very likely carried New England Indian blood.

Why 2020? Because November 2020 marks the 400th anniversary of the arrival of the *Mayflower* Pilgrims in the New World. It is also the 399th anniversary of an inter-cultural celebration known to history as the First Thanksgiving.

A little background is in order. *Mayflower* passenger Priscilla Mullins (c.1602 – c.1685) is the mysterious PM, the author of a long-lost diary. The blank, leather-bound journal was a 12th birthday gift from her wealthy merchant father William Mullins, who was a contrarian well ahead of his time. Unlike most of his contemporaries, Mullins believed that, in the future, women would be taught to read and write, and decided that his daughter was going to be one of the first to do so. The idea was controversial, so he had the gift fabricated to look exactly like a Geneva bible, the first bible ever printed and widely distributed in the English language.

When the girl was seventeen, Priscilla and her family, although they were not religious separatists, joined the *Mayflower* passengers and sailed to the New World. Priscilla lost her father, mother, brother and manservant to the 'general sicknesse' (probably scurvy compounded by unfamiliar micro-organisms in the water they drank) that first bitter, disastrous winter, then went on to marry the ship's cooper, John Alden.

Their marriage was immortalized in Henry Wadsworth Longfellow's epic poem *The Courtship of Myles Standish*. Longfellow was a direct descendant of John and Priscilla, who produced ten or eleven children. Today there are literally millions of Americans who are Alden/Mullins descendants. The 21st Century Alden family depicted in this novel, however, is entirely fictitious. The characters you are about to meet are products of the author's fertile imagination. Any resemblance to persons living or deceased is entirely accidental. The contents of the fictional 'PM diary,' on the other hand, are drawn directly from primary source material actually written and published in the 1600s by eye-witnesses to the events described. It is not fiction. Any student of early New England history will recognize the passages.

As one of the wealthiest and best-educated 'first comers' to Plimoth Colony, Priscilla may have served as a letter writer for her less literate fellow colonists, and may have assisted Winslow, Bradford and other Plimoth journal keepers with their publications, such as *Mourt's Relation* and *Good Newes From New England.* As the mystery deepens, we learn that, along with her more personal notes, Priscilla kept a written record of virtually everything that happened to the Pilgrims, from Old England in mid-1620 until the outbreak of King Philip's War in New England in 1675, at which point the journal abruptly ends. The hasty final entry was penned on June 19th, 1675, when the writer was a 73-year-old great-grandmother, and it reproduced an urgent note from a neighboring settler - a dire warning of the bloody disaster that was about to overwhelm all of New

England. A half-century of friendship was over. The Indians were on the warpath.

Despite the foregoing, this is a story of inter-cultural amity. In 1624, Priscilla develops a lifelong friendship with a young native woman, one of Hobomok's five wives, a Patuxet cousin of the famous Squanto, and one of the very few surviving members of that individual's once-powerful tribe. The girl, whose native name was unpronounceable to the Englishwoman, adopts the name Alice, after Priscilla's deceased mother. In June 1675, after fifty four years of peace and friendship, the Indians launch all-out war on the English settlers, committing a series of gory atrocities that give the English no alternative but to organize and fight back.

Alice's granddaughter, who had grown up in and around Plymouth Colony, tries to warn her English friends, but it is too late. The family is slaughtered and the house set on fire. The distraught girl rushes into the flames and emerges clutching a treasure – the family bible. After the war, the Indian girl and her young son are exiled to a Barbados tobacco plantation aboard a slave ship. The only possession she is allowed to take with her is her bible. Her bible, however, is not a bible. It is a handwritten journal, the PM diary.

More than three centuries later, a 93-year-old

descendant of Alice's friends John and Priscilla Alden lies dying in the family's 17th Century Barbados plantation manor. The dying man begins to 'see through the veil.' Apparently, he is talking to someone from the other side. That someone turns out to be a ghost, the spirit of the Indian girl who had run into the flames centuries earlier and rescued the bible. She has an urgent message for Alden's granddaughter, who has flown down from Maine to sit with the old man during his dying days.

The Mayflower Revelations is a work of 21st Century fiction, but it is based upon carefully researched historical fact. The novel accomplishes things that no Mayflower-related book, fiction or non-fiction, has thus far attempted. Firstly, it shines a light on the positive nature of the Pilgrim/Pokanoket relationship between 1621 and 1675. Secondly, it addresses widely held contemporary misbeliefs, the inflammatory historical absurdities that Plymouth scholar James Baker kindly calls 'gratuitous nonsense.' Leyden-based Mayflower expert Jeremy Bangs prefers the more evocative term 'roast bull with cranberry sauce.' Finally, the novel not only revises revisionist history and restores the historical record, but it provides a credible explanation for the greatest unsolved mystery of early American history; to wit, the origin, nature and mode of transmission of the disease pandemic that devastated the native population of coastal New England between the years 1616 and 1618, a few short years before the arrival of the *Mayflower*.

Had it not been for the forgotten, decade-long Tarrantines War and the devastating epidemic which accompanied it, the *Mayflower* would have arrived in Plymouth to find a fiercely defended village fully occupied by the Patuxet tribe, which was estimated by Captain John Smith to number about 2,000 warriors as recently as 1614. Instead, six years later, the Pilgrims found the area abandoned, and the rest is history.

The famous Squanto was one of the very few surviving Patuxets. He had been kidnapped in 1614 by Smith's devious associate Thomas Hunt, and sold as a slave in Spain. He did not return to New England until late 1619, the year the brutal Tarrantines War ended with the murder of Massachuset sachem Nanapashimet by his implacable enemies from the north. Paradoxically, Hunt's treachery saved Squanto's life. Without Squanto's friendly attitude toward the English, his grasp of their language, and his pivotal role in the treaty with Massasoit, could the Pilgrims have survived at all? It is highly unlikely.

The Mayflower Revelations is set on the Caribbean island of Barbados in the weeks leading up to Thanksgiving Day in the year 2020. It is the story of a moneyed, dysfunctional family of Mayflower descendants, some of whom are riddled with shame and guilt at crimes they erroneously believe their ancestors perpetrated on the Indians. Things like bringing them gifts of smallpox-infested blankets. Things like massacreing seven hundred of the harmless and innocent locals before sitting down to a three-day Thanksgiving celebration with the survivors. Things that a remarkable percentage of Americans, native and non-native alike, believe to be historical fact. Things that are utterly, absurdly untrue. The widespread guilt and shame accompanying these misbeliefs has fragmented the fictional Alden family to the point where the current generation has repudiated its early American heritage and legally changed its name from Alden to Alten, claiming to be of German ancestry instead.

Our principal character has no idea that she is a Mayflower descendant, until the ghost intervenes, courtesy of the dying patriarch, and the missing 'bible' comes to light. Even then, it takes a long time for the penny to drop. Once the family learns the truth about their ancestry, and about the Pilgrim/Indian relationship, an enormous burden drops from them, and a profound psychological healing occurs.

The remarkable history of Plimoth Plantation is America's most important origin story. It is a wildly dramatic and much-misunderstood adventure. What has been entirely forgotten - and in fact supplanted by negative misinformation - is the historical certainty that the so-called Pilgrims and the neighboring Pokanoket Wampanoags lived together in peace and harmony for more than half a century, as did the English settlers and their native neighbors to the north in Sagadahoc (also known as Norumbega or Mawooshen) - the area today known as Maine.

This was remarkable in light of the Jamestown settlers' ghastly experience with their Indian neighbors in 1622. In the Jamestown Massacre, over four hundred unsuspecting English settlers were murdered. Another four hundred were besieged in the fort and starved to death. That carefully planned and executed massacre took place one year to the day after the Pilgrims and the Pokanokets met for the first time and crafted their mutually beneficial agreement. As in Jamestown, the Plimoth colonists and the Indians were frequently in and out of one another's homes. Their children played together. Their womenfolk became friends. They exchanged everything from recipes and farming techniques to ideas about the nature of the universe and the shared concept of a supreme deity. Unlike the Jamestown Indians, however, the Pokanokets were pretty much impeccable in the way they honored their mutual-protection agreement, as were the Plgrims.

Here is a fragment from the old diary, which our heroine '*tranfcribes*' to her utter bewilderment. She has no idea what it means.

> *Yea, an Isle at sea, which we never saw, hath also, together with the former, yielded willingly to be under the protection, and subjects to our sovereign lord King James, so that there is now great peace amongst the Indians themselves, which was not formerly, neither would have been but for us; and we for our parts walk as peaceably and safely in the wood as in the highways in England. We entertain them familiarly in our houses, and they as friendly bestowing their venison on us. They are a people without any religion or knowledge of God, yet very trusty, quick of apprehension, ripe-witted, just. The men and women go naked, only a skin about their middles.* (from Mourt's Relation, London, 1622)

The lamentable fact that Plimoth Plantation's fifty-four years of harmony ended in bloody war, when the next generation of Pokanokets undertook, too late, to drive the English settlers back into the sea, does not change the reality that the two cultures found much in common. Out of that commonality emerged the phenomenon that independent scholar Connie Baxter Marlow calls the 'American mind and spirit.'

It was a combination of the Mayflower Compact, written aboard the *Mayflower* in November 1620, before the Pilgrims set foot on American soil, and the Iroquois Confederacy's Great Law, combined with some of the most progressive ideas in Western history, that resulted in the 1787 United States Constitution.

It all started with the English Separatist movement, a late 16th Century religious rebellion with its roots at Cambridge University during the waning years of Queen Elizabeth's reign, and which signalled the beginning of the end for absolute monarchy. The Mayflower Pilgrims were the first group of Puritan Separatists to plant a colony in the New World. It is no exaggeration to say that the *Mayflower* carried the seeds of American democracy across the Atlantic, where they found fertile soil. And here we are, four hundred years down the road... Are we there yet?

*****

1

Barbados, Mon Amor?

There was just the hint of a fading reddish glow in the western sky. Dr. Elizabeth Alten Nicholson gave a deep sigh and settled into the luxurious first-class seat. The aroma of new leather surrounded her. Liz was a tall, striking woman with aristocratic English bone structure and startling blue eyes, although one would not think of her as conventionally pretty. The word handsome would be more appropriate. Detractors might use the term 'horsy.' She adjusted her belted, ankle length off-white skirt, undid the top few buttons of her tartan checked shirt, slipped out of her beaded, high-heeled Santa Fe-inspired boots, fastened her seatbelt, and took in the aroma of newness and the exquisitely retro-futuristic design of the aircraft. The passenger cabin resembled something out of *2001 - A Space Odyssey.*

Tossing her head to shake the shaggy mouse blonde hair out of her face, she inserted the high tech, noise-canceling Bose thingamabobs into her ears. Along with the current issue of *Time*, she had just purchased the ear-buds – for $299 mind you, they had better be good – at a booth in the terminal, along with another compact electronic device that would come in handy in the not-too-distant future.

Liz cued up her favorite collection of 1960s music - the Beatles, the Rolling Stones, Bob Dylan, Simon and Garfunkel, Cat Stevens, James Taylor, Pete Seeger, and Joan Baez. Sixty years down the road, those were still the best songs ever written, she thought, despite the fact that she was, in theory, a Nineties or even a Millennial girl.

Instead of really listening to the music, however, Liz found herself hearing something completely different: a beloved voice from a much earlier and infinitely longer airplane flight; a man instructing his young grand-daughters on how to vanquish a marauding lion, should they encounter such a beast as they hacked their heroic way through the steaming, malaria-infested jungle

2

during their upcoming explorations of Kilimanjaro, the Serengeti, Dar Es Salaam and Zanzibar.

"Should you ever be attacked by a lion," the well-remembered voice said, "here's what you do, girls. Listen carefully now. Wait until the very last moment. Freeze. Don't do a thing. When the lion's mouth is wide, wide open, he can't see you. Are you listening? Wait, wait, wait... Now! Reach down the lion's throat suddenly, all the way to the back, in through his stomach. Quick like a bunny, grab him by the tail and pull really, really hard. FLIP him inside out! WHUMP!!!"

The JetBlue flight attendant materialized in Liz's blurred peripheral vision, bearing a small bottle of a rather fine champagne and a silver platter of tiny gourmet hors d'oeuvres. This was a celebratory flight, a first for the company, even though it was officially just an experiment, and even though the aircraft was terribly slow by 21st Century standards. The hybrid electric airliner was utterly silent. You hardly knew you had left the runway.

Noticing the tear running down Liz's cheek, the kindly, balding, middle-aged steward rummaged in his apron and handed the passenger a pack of Kleenex facial tissues. The passenger nodded gratefully. Grandpa Jack had been an immutable fact of life from the moment of

3

Liz's birth, and now, inconceivable as the thought was, he lay close to death. It had been decades since she'd last thought of old Jack Alten's untested lion repulsion technique, and the memory hit her so hard it took her unawares. Liz burst into tears, and simultaneously let out a much-too-loud shriek of laughter. Loud music and earphones will do that to you. She couldn't help it. The other first-class passengers turned disapprovingly, but Liz was oblivious, lost in *The Times They Are A-Changin'* and a succession of idyllic girlhood memories.

Actually, it is not quite accurate to refer to the 'other first-class passengers.' Let me explain. The flight-list consisted entirely of well-connected 'first-class passengers,' but not one of them was paying a penny, not even His Royal Highness the Prince of Wales. JetBlue's historic Flight 2020 was a promotional excursion, modeled upon the similar debut, back in 1977, of the Anglo-French Concorde and its supersonic flight from London to Barbados and back with a glittering contingent of English royalty. But enough of aeronautical history. Back to Liz Nicholson and her idyllic memories.

Liz's birthday was just two weeks away. She was a Thanksgiving baby. At the ripe old age of thirty-nine-going-on-forty, however, her life was anything but idyllic. Money can't buy you love. It can't buy you happiness, either. Ask any billionaire. The woman was living testimony to that. The decades between the Kilimanjaro climb – the iconic mountain had been hundreds of feet taller back then, before global warming melted the snowcap – and this melancholy journey to the West Indies, had not been kind to her, and the cruelty showed itself in the subtle and not-so-subtle tire-tracks that lined her face, in the downward turn at each side of her large and lovely mouth, and in her recently acquired but ever-expanding broadness of beam.

Why me, Liz wondered? What did I do to attract so much attention from the Grim Reaper? Sarah, my poor, beautiful mother, dead. Ridiculously, inconceivably, unconscionably dead. My first love, cousin Adam, dead, and Adam's mother, Aunt Lizzie, dead just a week later. A brilliant, funny, loving, but troubled husband, dead, gone before his time, abducted by aliens, according to the Montreal newspapers. A beloved firstborn daughter who has not spoken to me since the funeral. Layla might as well be dead, Liz thought with a tinge of bitterness.

Could there be a more screwed-up family anywhere on the planet? The interior monologue continued: the absentee father Liz had rejected after the alleged accident that killed her mother back in 1988. No contact with her famous grandfather since the well intentioned but futile

5

attempt she'd made, ten years ago this month, to recon-cile the splintered clan.

Liz thought about that most unsuccessful of events. Against extremely long odds, she had persuaded every-one to gather at the New Harbor house for Thanks-giving – and her 30th birthday, incidentally – back in 2010. What on Earth was she thinking? The family reunion had been an unmitigated disaster. It was cold comfort to say to herself; "Well, at least I tried."

Grandpa Jack had made a valiant effort, leaving his captain and crew in charge of the America's Cup cata-maran right before the Hobart race. Amazingly, Papa Jack and his fey and somewhat ethereal life-companion, James Walker, Australian walk-a-thon champion and ladies' hairstylist nonpareil, had relented at the last moment.

They had flown all the way from Sydney to Maine, reluctantly abandoning golfing reservations in Dubai that had been confirmed a year earlier. Notably, father and son had traveled on separate flights, despite the fact that they were both in Australia at the time and were heading for the identical destination on the far side of the planet. Jack Sr. took one of the company jets, while the poor long-suffering lads had to settle for a private upstairs suite on an antiquated Quantas Boeing 747.

Liz's three small children had attended the abortive reunion, needless to say. They were too young to object. Their now-deceased father, the history professor, could not get out of his academic obligations at Cambridge, a fact for which he gave sincere thanks to the powers that be.

With one notable exception, everyone else showed up. They might just as well have stayed home, however. The spirit may have been willing, but, sadly, the flesh fell short of the challenge. Far short. Within hours of arrival, heated arguments broke out in all directions. Some hard words were muttered, several of which should not have been deployed in mixed company, nor in the presence of small, alert children. A display of icy, pigeon-like strutting ensued. Liz felt the tiniest smidgeon of sympathy for her father's rather gorgeous companion, who seemed horribly out of place, but there was no way she was going to acknowledge the bastard, attractive and polite and Australian as he might be. Not after what he had done to her mother.

By mid-afternoon on Thanksgiving Day, instead of talking about the weather and Tiger Woods and the upcoming yacht race and stuffing themselves in the traditional manner and then watching the game while drinking themselves into sozzled oblivion, her father and her grandfather were back in their chauffeured limousines, speeding off in opposite directions at maximum velocity, putting as many miles between one and the other as possible. A mortified Liz and her befuddled, jet-lagged offspring had sat down to a large but lonely dinner, and then she had set about directing the caterers and the plumbers as they cleaned up the mess and closed up the big old waterfront house for the winter. Liz got the overfed children to bed and then polished off Grandpa Jack's abandoned unfinished bottle of Johnny Walker Black Label.

Horribly hungover the next morning, Liz herded her sleepy brood into the waiting taxi and flew back to Heathrow and told Professor Nicholson that he hadn't missed a goddamned thing.

"Happy birthday, darling," James had responded gently, driving them home from the airport in the rusty but trusty old Rover 90 - the 'Rust Mobile' as he affectionately called it.

"I'm so glad you're back in time, Lizzie. I have a bit of a surprise lined up for you."

And he had, against significant odds. Beside the last-minute babysitter, there had also been an unexpected cancellation at Ristorante Il Piccolo Mondo, Cambridge's most elegant restaurant, but Liz had been so distracted, hungover, upset and jet-lagged that she was barely present. James was disappointed, but he hid it well. Not the slightest quiver disturbed his moustachioed upper lip. He was, after all, an Englishman.

The other family member attending the abortive reunion *in absentia,* aside from the ill-fated historical epidemiologist James 'Nick' Nicholson, was Priscilla, Liz's younger sister, the skinny, fresh-faced little tomboy she'd always thought of as 'Pissy.' That was the way the three-year-old Lizzie had pronounced the new baby's name, and it still came out that way from time to time. Embarrassingly.

"I'll be there in spirit," Priscilla had promised, "but I have somewhat sexier plans for my body." Now, if Facebook was to be believed, Pissy had officially changed her name. No more Priscilla Alten. She was henceforth to be addressed as Scilla, Scilla Barnes as a matter of fact, having adopted the surname of her new spouse, and having abbreviated her old-fashioned Christian name to the much hipper Scilla. Ten years ago this month, Pissy (or Scilla, rather) had – sensibly as it turned out – skipped the family Thanksgiving, preferring to spend the holiday with a new friend on a trip to Hawaii. That friend's name was Maryah Barnes, and the rest was history. None of the family had responded to the last-minute wedding invitation. They were too taken aback to know what to think.

The nuptials had, apparently, been a clothing-optional New Age affair conducted by a gaunt, naked, tattooed, dreadlocked, bearded and be-feathered Universal Life Church minister chanting a tantric Urdu mantra and brandishing a Lakota Indian peace pipe. The ceremony had taken place at 'magic hour' in a secluded cove somewhere on the Pacific island of Maui. Liz mailed a congratulatory card to the RSVP address on the invitation, and was rewarded two months later with a glossy 8" by 10" photograph of a radiant sunburned Priscilla, as waiflike as ever, her nose peeling, demurely wrapped in a Balinese sarong, accompanied by a topless grinning African-American nightmare with a topknot of bleached-blonde dreadlocks and enormous white teeth. The latter image had brought up a strange, jarring memory – a notorious graffiti painting of a Negro cannibal wearing a crown. Liz had seen the God-awful thing at a Jean Michel Basqiat exhibition with her mother in Switzerland. She put the photograph back in its Fedex package, placed it carefully in the family archives, and had not looked at it since.

Arriving two hours early at Logan International, Liz had time for a leisurely catch-up with Scilla. It was their first real conversation in years. It was not that they disliked one another. In fact, they had never exchanged an angry word. It was just that they lived in entirely different universes, so different that they might have been members of two independent primate species, which had evolved concurrently on two separate planets. Liz's hectic existence as a widowed soccer mom from an illustrious New England family, holding down a full-time job while raising three precocious children at the big old family farmhouse near Gorham, Maine, interspersed with summers in the Hamptons, Cape Cod and Europe, and at the other end of the societal spectrum, Scilla's drug-infested, polyamorous, nocturnal East Village underground art-world reality.

Scilla was a marginally-talented School of Visual Arts sculpture graduate, whereas Liz had finally completed her early-American literature PhD, begun years ago at Cambridge, courtesy of Barnard College's online graduate program, just a couple of years back. That's what happens when you become a mother at nineteen. Hey, nineteen is better than sixteen, at least. Besides, another abortion would have... Liz did not want to think about it. She switched mental tracks.

Scilla, it must be said, was of the opinion that Liz, her big sister, was as homophobic as she was uptight about recreational drug use. There was an element of truth to each of the charges. Liz was the conservative one. Despite the family wealth, she held a steady but low-paying job. The benefits were good. She worked as the antiquities librarian at the Baxter Memorial Library in Gorham, Maine. Fortunately, she was able to live rent-free in one of the family's numerous and far-flung homes, and to take annual holidays in some of the others.

Scilla, on the other hand, had consistently refused to take one penny of the family money, determined to be her own person and to make her own way in the world, come what might. She built websites for the occasional low budget startup company, and worked nights as a waitress - and occasionally as a graveyard-shift dish-washer - at a popular Mexican restaurant in Lahaina, on the west coast of Maui.

Maryah, Scilla's husband (or was it wife?) was a musician, as far as Liz could make out. She had once toured the world with a famous but short-lived rock'n'roll band, but these days she played bass or guitar in various local reggae bands, bouncing from island to island. Between the two of them, Scilla and Maryah were able to scrape together the rent most months. Offspring from the same loins, each of them heiresses from a very wealthy family, the sisters Elizabeth and Priscilla Alten could hardly have been more different. Never the twain shall meet, as the saying goes.

An hour before takeoff, a watery sun broke through the ominous clouds. Turning orange under the influence of its low-angled trajectory through the soot-laden, lens-like atmosphere surrounding planet Earth, the light completed its 8-minute, 93-million mile journey, travel-ing, according to those who claim the ability to measure such things, 186,000 miles each and every second of the way. The light wended its refracted way through the colossal glass walls of the terminal, dodging tall columns of rough, unfinished concrete, and graced Liz with the special illumination that photographers and filmmakers call 'magic hour.' Liz could have taken a perfect selfie, but she wasn't sure that was possible while talking on her enormous iPhone. There was the promise of a colorful sunset, after a late-autumn day of implacable gloom.

A figure in black head-to-toe Middle-Eastern garb followed Liz up the narrow escalator, trying without success to push past her. The woman (presumably it was a woman) glared through the slit in her headgear at the elegant, expensively dressed American talking loudly to herself as she proceeded distractedly up the escalator.

13

At the top, Liz half-leaned on her rolling luggage cart, standing first on one leg and then the other, all the while speaking animatedly, oblivious to the fact that she was obstructing traffic.

The crowd of hurrying travelers parted to move around her. The burkha'd woman favored Liz with a lethal dose of the evil eye and a terse but poisonous statement in an ancient and incomprehensible language, then hurried on her way. Liz quite failed to notice either the withering look or the verbal message, which, given her delicate emotional state, was probably just as well.

After a while she moved on to wait at the gate, all the while vocalizing just a little too loudly for a public place. She took the Bluetooth ear-bud out of her left ear, examined it carefully, then replaced it in the opposite aural orifice. She went on, quite unaware that everyone within a fifty-foot radius could overhear her every word. The heavily armed soldier leaning against the terminal wall eavesdropped for a while. He concluded that she was harmless, then went back to whatever he was doing on his own smartphone.

"I know. Can you believe it? November already? I swear time accelerates as you get older. 2020 is almost over. 2020? Does that sound ridiculous or what? Do you remember when 1984 was the title of a science fiction

14

novel?" Liz stopped and listened. She continued. "No of course you wouldn't. What was I thinking? You were born in 1984. What? Oh. You didn't miss a whole lot. It was a pretty wimpy fall. We have yet to have our first real frost. Global warming, I guess. Anyway, the leaves are gone, such as they were. The Nor'easter last week took every last one of them down. It's totally bleak out there now. Brrr. I'm going to be glad to be back on the island."

Liz listened, looking down at the beaded patterns on her brand-new boots.

"The boys are, as a matter of fact. They're wildly excited, actually. All they think about these days is surfing. Apparently there are good waves in Barbados. Layla on the other hand, bless her icy little heart, hasn't responded to my communications. It's highly unlikely she'll show up. How about Mary - I mean Maryah. Is she planning to accompany you?

"Oh goody. I get to meet her at last," Liz continued. "While the rest of the country's thinking about the election results, the First Thanksgiving, Pilgrims and Puritans and Indians, turkey, cranberry sauce, football...

"Massacres? What massacres? Smallpox blankets? What are you talking about, Prissy? That was a long

15

time ago. I don't think anyone's thinking about massacres or smallpox-infested blankets anymore." Liz frowned, wrinkling her forehead in distaste.

"The National Day of Mourning? In Plymouth? No, I've never been. Why on earth would I? It sounds depressing. Come on. Can't we talk about something a tiny bit more cheerful? Listen, girl. This will be our last Thanksgiving. We should call it that. 'The Last Thanksgiving: a Zombie Comedy.' We should make an iPhone movie, just for the halibut."

Liz paused and squinted up at the banks of electronic displays showing the various arrivals and departures. "When will we ever see each other again, Scilla, once Grandpa Jack's gone? Do we have..? Anyway, as I said in the email, time is of the essence. If everybody fires up and starts packing right away, we might just make it in time." She listened. "What? Oh. I meant, he's seeing things." She listened. "What kind of things? Ghosts. Spirits. He's talking to people who aren't there. At least that's what the hospice nurse says." Liz listened, then went on. "I know. That does NOT sound like our dear old Grandpa, does it? He doesn't believe in mystical horseshit, being the hard-core material science guy of the family. The quintessential MIT engineer. Just like Dad, minus the Indians." She listened. "You're breaking

16

up, Prissy. What? I'm sorry. Say again? What does the hospice nurse say? She says, they see... they do that... when it's getting close to the time." She listened. "What time? My point exactly. That time!"

As Liz alternately listened and spoke, she meandered gradually in the general direction of Gate 34. The echoing sound of the airport public address system interrupted her. She extracted the phone from her jacket pocket and checked the time. The incomprehensible announcement ended and the canned muzak resumed. Realizing that she had not actually noted the time, she took the phone out once more before continuing, and once more, absent-mindedly, put it back in her pocket without actually checking the time.

"We just have to take this seriously, Priscilla," she continued. "Prissy. Sorry, I mean Scilla. It's our last chance. This is it. After all, he's ninety-three years old. Grandpa's had a good long run. Anything over the regulation threescore and ten is a bonus, as he always used to say. Can you believe that was twenty-three years ago?" She listened. "What was twenty-three years ago? Grandpa Jack's 70th birthday. The family gathering at Alden House? We all went down to Barbados, remember? Gran'ma had just been diagnosed. Do you remember how old they seemed to us then? I mean, it's amazing when you think of it. He just keeps on keeping on. He came in second in the Transatlantic as recently as September. Of course he was bummed that *Weetamoo IV* didn't win...

"*Weetamoo?* Actually I have no idea. *Weetamoo.* It's a pretty weird name for a sailboat, isn't it? Remind me and we'll ask him when we're down there. If he's still *compos mentis* that is.

"Say again? *Compos mentis?* Oh. It means having full control of one's mind; sane. At least I'm pretty sure that's what it means. Unless it means thinking about recycling the vegetable scraps. OK, never mind. I was trying to make a joke.

"I do wish you'd have called him on his birthday, deah, but anyway, the old bastard sounded perfectly fine at that point. Sharp as a tack, gruff as ever, even though he's a little slurred since the stroke. Sometimes you have to ask him to repeat himself, but I tell you... What?"

"Dementia, apparently. Is that the same as Alzheimer's? I don't know either. Anyway, apparently, the Parkinson's has come back with a vengeance. Dr. Ginsberg says...." Liz's voice was obliterated by the boarding announcement at the gate.

This is the last call for JetBlue's historic Flight 2020 from Victoria, British Columbia to Buenos Aires, Argentina, with

18

stops at Boston, Massachusetts and Bridgetown, Barbados. The gate will be closing in five minutes.

"Listen, Pissy. Goddammit. Will I ever stop doing that? I'm sorry, I mean Scilla, my flight is boarding. I'm kind of excited. It's my very first flight on the new hybrid electric airliner. Kinda like the QE2 – remember that? You met that snooty English kid… He's Lord what-ever-his-name-is now? Are you still in touch with him?

"Anyway… I'll call you as soon as I get down there and get the lay of the land. Meanwhile, be thinking about what I said in the email. OK? Call Dad. Just do it, as it says on the billboard. Just do it. You were always his favorite. He won't mind, under the circumstances.

"No, you really were. I used to mind a tiny bit but I don't anymore. This might be the chance we've been waiting for. It won't be easy, but we have to try. 'Bye. Give my love to Maui. Mary. I mean Maryah. I mean both of them. I'm really looking forward to meeting her. I hope you know that! 'Bye."

Liz barely made the flight. She was the very last passenger to board, but fortunately her seat number was 1A, right at the very front. The granddaughter of Jack Alden had certain privileges, needless to say, as did the families of the other board members.

The James Taylor song ended. She could never

19

listen to *Sweet Baby James* without crying. Wiping her eyes, Liz reached down and rummaged in her carry-on bag. She had picked up a copy of *Time* magazine at the airport, and hadn't had a moment to look at it yet. The front page was all about the contested election results, needless to say. The re-count. There was a good chance that the electronic voting system had been hacked, yet again. By the Russians, yet again. The Democrats and the Republicans pointed accusatory fingers at one another, failing, as usual, to acknowledge the three fingers pointing back at themselves. It looked as though, despite (or possibly thanks to) the fraud, the Independent candidate was a shoo-in. Democracy, Liz thought. What a goddamned mess. But I'm glad I voted for her, ridiculous as it seemed at the time.

An insert near the top of the magazine cover caught her eye. It read: *This Day In History: November 11, 1620. The Signing of the Mayflower Compact.* Turning to page 36, she read about the covenant the *Mayflower* passengers had crafted and signed exactly four hundred years ago today, a few days before they set foot on the sandy beaches of Cape Cod for the first time. After sixty-six days at sea, the storm-battered, overcrowded little ship had made landfall a long way from its intended destination at the mouth of the Hudson River, and there was a hint of mutiny in the air.

"Mid-November. God! What a ridiculous time for a bunch of religious fanatics to arrive in New England," Liz muttered aloud. "What were they thinking? No wonder the goddamned Indians had to take care of them."

*****

2

Meanwhile, Back At The Plantation

Thursday, November 12, 2020

Through the aircraft's window, the Milky Way was brighter and milkier than Liz had ever seen it. She closed her eyes. The tiny blue planet revolved imperceptibly against a vast background of stars. Part of the sphere was illuminated, and part of it was invisible, lost in utter darkness. A dimly lighted speck with flashing red and green lights whispered slowly under the stars and through the darkened atmosphere. Southward and eastward it crept. Liz must have dozed off. The eastern horizon had lightened imperceptibly. Suddenly it was dawn. The tropical sun prepared to rise out of a cloudless sky over the little West Indian island known as Barbados. The almost silent hybrid aircraft from America, its wings set back like those of an osprey snatching its prey, touched down at last, spurts of white smoke issuing from its landing gear, as its photovoltaic skin began absorbing solar light from the rising sun and converting it into electricity to be stored in the enormous array of ultra lightweight Tesla batteries in the vessel's underbelly.

A gathering of reporters and photographers jostled out on the runway in a carefully roped-off area. The glittering science-fiction apparition stopped momentarily at the end of the runway, just short of the Caribbean Sea, its enormous gossamer wings drooping. It turned slowly and taxied silently up to the newly remodeled high-tech terminal. The building reminded Liz a little of the airport at Denver, with its series of mysterious tent-like configurations. Perhaps the same architectural firm did the design? I shall have to Google it, she thought. I wonder if there's wi-fi at the house?

She pictured Alden House in her mind's eye. She had tried to spot the old plantation manor from the air as they approached the island, and thought she'd caught a momentary glimpse of its white columns among the trees near a headland jutting into the dark blue ocean. She couldn't be sure. The flight had been uneventful, and the takeoff and landing as smooth as silk. It was only later that she discovered that the aircraft's pilot was a robot, and that the actual human pilot sat in front of a computer screen somewhere in Silicon Valley. There was an article on the subject in the *Time* magazine in her shoulder bag.

Out of sight just a few miles away, approaching Grantley Adams International Airport as rapidly as the narrow, bumpy, potholed road would allow, a long, shiny, oversized 1956 Mercedes Benz convertible limousine murmured along the narrow, winding East Coast road. The impeccable beige top was up. It was the kind of vehicle that Adolph Hitler had been so fond of, in its earlier incarnations in the late 1930s and early 1940s. At the wheel of the beautifully maintained antique sat an elegantly greying man who looked to be of African American descent. He was singing along with a Bob Marley song as he drove. There was a sense of muted joy and excitement in his deep voice. *'...these songs of freedom ...are all I ever had. Redemption songs,'* he sang.

The driver rolled down his window and saluted a group of brightly dressed, dark-skinned ladies walking in single file along the grassy verge of the narrow, undulating road. The three women carried colorful bundles on their heads, African style. They each raised a hand in greeting. The vehicle disappeared around a bend in the road.

Moments later, it seemed to the women, the familiar Mercedes reappeared. The ladies were perhaps half a mile closer to the airport, and were still talking about the same subject, the huge bull shark that one of them had watched in the harbor lights down by the Bridgetown sea-wall the previous evening. Each of them had a related story to recount, and they arrived at the same general conclusion. Skinny-dipping at night was not recomended, if you valued your life and your limbs, or those of your lover. The limousine, as it came speeding toward them, was traveling in the opposite direction this time. The top was down. The women waved once more, noticing that the gleaming vehicle now carried a passenger in the front seat, her unruly mousy-blonde hair whipping in her eyes.

"It Missy Lizabet', she gran'father he dead."

"Who tell you that? Ol' Jack Alden ain't dead yet, ah hear from ol' Gladys, but he surely not long for this world."

"He a good man, that ol' Massa Alden. He jus' gettin'

25

too old to keep on keepin' on."

The classic old convertible growled softly around the curves in the coast road, along a tree-lined tropical beachfront. Antique weather-beaten buildings, painted in a variety of primary colors, mostly single-story, flashed by from time to time. The tires protested, just a little. Liz sat in the front passenger seat, gazing through the rolled-up window at the well-remembered ocean views of her teenage years. Her hair was blowing in her face, and she held up a hand to control it. The sun flashed on and off through the tall Australian ironwoods lining the seafront. Jarrah trees, the locals called them. Looking ahead suddenly, her eyes widened. A large school bus, bright yellow, was coming the other way. It was all the way on the wrong side of the narrow road. Liz shrieked, then sagged back into the butter-soft beige leather of her seat.

"Oh. Right. I forgot! You crazy Barbadians drive on the wrong side of the road. You crazy Bajans, I mean. You're as bad as the bloody English. That scared the bejeezus out of me, Washington. Whew!"

Liz gazed back out at the ocean, a few puffy white clouds on the horizon, the waves rolling in, in serried ranks. An albatross soared overhead, gazing intently down at the passing vehicle. Seeing nothing immediately edible, it swooped off to the right and disappeared out to sea. The adrenaline in Liz's bloodstream subsided and she recovered her breath.

"It feels so good to be back on the island, Washington. I love the air! I can't believe it's been twelve, no, fifteen years. That's what happens when you become a mother. A single mother at that."

Washington Franklin IV was an elegant man in formal livery, silver at the temples. He must be sixty-five or seventy years of age, Liz thought. Dad's age. No, Dad must be at least seventy-five, isn't he? Washington could pass for the Hollywood actor Danny Glover, or that other actor, what's his name? Samuel something or other. When Washington spoke, Liz noticed that his familiar but largely forgotten mode of speech was an interesting blend of Caribbean island patois and aristocratic Queen's English. It was not even vaguely American. She was aware of a strange feeling of unreality, as though she were a confused character in a film playing the part of a mental patient coming home after a long time away. She had never been able to sleep on aeroplanes, and last night was no exception. She was half asleep and grateful to be driven. Washington's voice came though as in a dream.

"We heard about your poor dear husband, and we

sent you our deep condolence. I trust you received the card over there in the UK? My wife and myself were very, very sad when we heard the bad news. It reminded us of your auntie and your cousin. But the Good Lord..."

My auntie and my cousin? Adam. My God, I haven't thought of Adam in years. Liz almost spoke, but no words came out. Washington paused, not wishing to go too far. He continued on a different tack.

"I am delighted to see you again, Missy Elizabeth. It brings back so many good memories, although I do wish the circumstance could have been happier."

"I too am happy to see you, Washington. How *is* my poor grandfather?"

"I have barely seen Master Alden for the past month. Six weeks, perhaps more, truth be told. He took to his bed in September, right after coming second in the Transatlantic. *Weetamoo* almost won, but no... I fear the stress was a bit too much for him. Not to mention the subsequent festivities." The driver hesitated, glancing across at his passenger. "I hate to say this, Missy, but I do fear the worst. My wife say Master Alden may not be too long for this world. He is already speaking to his people on the other side. They are coming to greet him."

"That's what the hospice nurse said on the phone. I'm almost afraid to see him. Although... he is ninety-three, you know. He has had a good long life. An amazing life, to be honest. By the way, Washington, on a completely different subject, *Weetamoo*, do you know why my grandfather named it *Weetamoo*? My sister and I were just wondering about that. On the phone."

"Wee-ta-moo." Washington rolled the three syllables around in his mouth, testing each for its exotic flavor. "It is a funny name for such a fierce and aggressive sailing vessel," he replied at last, "but I have no idea what it means. Sound to me like it come from them Australian aboriginals, maybe? Why don't you ask your grandfather? Or your daddy. He lives over there, does he not?"

"Weetamoo. Australian? That never occurred to me. Maybe it's a cross between Weetabix and didgeridoo."

Washington chuckled warmly. He covered his mouth with his free hand - the characteristic coyness that Liz remembered so well.

"Ooh. I don't think so, Miss Lizzie," he said. The car slowed in the narrow uphill road as it wound around a steep bend and came to a modest hilltop, waited for an oncoming pickup truck loaded with landscape workers to go by, then turned in towards the tall iron gates. The workers waved and shouted out a greeting and were gone. Washington and Liz each raised an arm and waved a reply. Liz mused, half to herself…

"I had forgotten how friendly the local people are, Washington. A far cry from New England, I tell you."

"How well I remember, Missy. I spent many, many years in that part of the world, and I never could understand how people could…"

The security sensor recognized the Mercedes' digital sticker and opened the gates, revealing a long winding driveway of crushed coral. A carved stone set into the mossy, eroded left-hand gatepost said: 'Alden House 1659.' The gleaming vehicle pulled up in front of the white colonnaded mansion at the top of the little hill.

Liz took in the familiar view through the jarrah trees. The deep blue ocean beyond. The car slowed and crunched to a halt and the engine died, its powerful growl replaced by the distant hissing roar of the ocean. Liz closed her eyes, filling her being with the sound and the smell of the sea. After the chaos of the Boston traffic it felt a lot like heaven.

There was a sudden loud cry of joy, and the inner vision of a familiar figure stumbling down the curving verandah steps just as fast as she could move - which wasn't very fast. Liz did not have to open her eyes to know who it was. The housekeeper Gladys, Washington's blushing bride of fifteen years, an ample, motherly

30

woman, had stood there before the imposing ten-foot-high entry doors, watching the Mercedes approach, her heavy arms folded contentedly across her ample bosom. Then, unable to contain her joy, Gladys waddled awkwardly down the broad white-painted wooden stairway and opened the passenger door of the limousine, emitting little squeaks and shrieks of happiness as she did so.

*****

3

Catatonic Is As Catatonic Does

John Bradford Alden, Senior, ninety-three years and one month of age, an ancient, skeletal and beak-nosed effigy, familiar but strangely alien in the way that impending death can make even one's own grandfather unfamiliar, lay on his back in the precise center of an enormous bed, propped up on impeccable white pillows against a broad Chinese-red headboard inlaid with mother-of-pearl, staring intently at the ceiling. A thin line of translucent drool ran from his open mouth and

down one side of his freshly-shaven chin. The bed-
clothes were tidily folded back and he was dressed in
perfectly ironed tartan pajamas. The old man's thin hair
was combed back from his craggy forehead. It stuck
straight up like a young schoolboy's, or a punk rocker's.

The large overhead fans paddled the air lazily. The
soft susurration of the nearby ocean was the loudest
sound in the enormous, elegant room, with its enviable
collection of antique European furniture. There was art
on the walls, a hundred million dollars worth of art.
Nineteen Sixties folk music emanated from invisible
speakers, barely audible, and diaphanous off-white lace
curtains swirled gently in the huge open French doors
leading out to the balcony overlooking the view to the
east, where, far beyond the treetops, the dark blue line
of the horizon intersected with the lighter blue of the
tropical sky.

Alden did not react when the clatter of fashionable
high-heeled ladies' boots and the excited voices of
Gladys and Liz echoed along the wood-planked hallway.
If it weren't for the glitter in the open eyes, one might
have thought the old man a cadaver laid out for viewing.
Liz's first impression was similar to the surreal one
when, as a young teenager, she had gone to the Brunswick mortician's chapel with her mother, to view the

carefully prepared corpse of an old family friend. Gladys dropped her voice and spoke softly, as one does in the presence of the dear departed.

"I will leave you with your grandfather, Missy Elizabeth. Miss Liz. Please ring if you need anything. The electric bell is working again, at last. Washington fix it just yesterday. The electricity in this old house leave something to be desired, let me tell you. The button is right there by the bed. Next to the baby monitor."
The large Bajan woman looked at the relatively slender American.

"Did they feed you on the aeroplane, Missy? Breakfast will be ready in half an hour or so, if you are hungry. I will serve out on the verandah."

"Feed me on the plane? What planet have you been living on, dear Gladys? The airlines stopped doing that years ago. They just give you some potato chips and bottled water. Although I have to say, this time it was a rather good champagne and a fair number of delicious little French things I don't know the names of. Fortunately, I had picked up a wrap in Boston. I ate it at midnight. But thank you, Gladys. I'll be on down."

"You picked up a rat? Ugh. You can't be eating rats at midnight, Missy. Oh my. What is the world coming to? I fear those Americans...they not feeding you right.

34

Jus' look how skinny you are."

"Skinny? I'll take that as a compliment," Liz giggled.
Her tone was droll. It had been a while since anyone had
accused Liz Nicholson of being skinny. It had something
to do with so-called 'comfort food.' Gladys stopped, then
left the room. Her vast derrière barely made it through
the doorway, and the doorway was not exactly narrow,
having recently been modified to accommodate a large
electric wheelchair. Liz watched her old friend go, then
turned to the bed.

"Grandpa? Grandpa Jack? Hi! It's me, Liz."
Alden did not react. Liz raised her voice, realizing that
the old man was no doubt hard of hearing. She had not
yet noticed the hearing-aid on the table next to the bed.
A week or two later, Alden would shout at her "Why are
you yelling at me, Lizzie? I'm not deaf, goddammit,"
despite the fact that he was not wearing his hearing aid
at the time. For the moment, however, there was no
indication that Old Jack had heard a word his granddaughter said. Alden seemed entirely oblivious to her
presence.

"Grandpa? Grandpa Jack? Can you hear me? It's me,
Liz. Lizzie. Elizabeth. I came all the way from Gorham.
As soon as I heard..."
The old man did not react or respond. Liz moved to the

foot of the bed, into his field of view, and stood there, taking in the spectacle of her once indomitable but much diminished grandfather, who lay motionless, eyes wide open, staring intently at the ceiling. It was unnerving. In the absence of anything better to do, Liz took out her smartphone, and composed a photo of the perfectly symmetrical tableau. She would send it to Scilla, if she could ever figure out how to do that. From the invisible speakers, a favorite old song, Simon & Garfunkel's 1965 *I Am A Rock* played softly. Liz took in the familiar lyrics, hearing them, really hearing them, for the first time.

A winter's day, in a deep and dark December
I am alone, gazing from my window to the streets below
On a freshly fallen silent shroud of snow
I am a rock, I am an island
I've built walls, a fortress deep and mighty that none may
penetrate
I have no need of friendship, friendship causes pain
It's laughter and it's loving I disdain
I am a rock, I am an island
Don't talk of love well I've heard the words before
It's sleeping in my memory
And I won't disturb the slumber of feelings that have died
If I never loved I never would have cried
I am a rock, I am an island

I have my books and my poetry to protect me
I am shielded in my armor, hiding in my room,
safe within my womb
I touch no one and no one touches me
I am a rock, I am an island.
©1965 Paul Simon

That is the perfect theme song for Grandpa Jack in his former life, Liz realized. How appropriate. The rock. The island. The larger-than-life international business-man, politician, and world-class racing yachtsman, John Bradford Alden, the man whose immigrant German grandfather had Anglicized the family name to match that of Alden Yachts, his favorite New England sailboat manufacturer. Old Grandpa Jack was a one-man island if ever there was one, a dyed-in-the-wool loner. Old Jack, as everyone out of earshot had called him for the past decade, had never needed anybody. He had barely even needed Gran'ma Priscilla, his long-suffering wife of fifty-two years, may she rest in peace. Or his only son, John Bradford Alden, Junior, for that matter.

For more years than Liz could count, Master Jack, as she half-humorously thought of her grandfather, had stood tall at the helm of his own invincible ship, lord of all he surveyed. However, that was then and this was now. The independent, self-sufficient Alden was no longer self-sufficient. No longer independent. He needed 24/7 care. He couldn't even wipe his own bottom.

Liz wrestled a heavy, ornate, high backed 18th Century French chair closer to the bedside. She sat down, breathing hard, then stood up again and tentatively reached for her grandfather's bony hand. It was a stretch in more ways than one. Alden's bed was large enough to accommodate the most enthusiastic and well-attended orgy. Half as wide again as a California King, he had had it custom made at one of his manufacturing facilities in Hong Kong. The mattress and even the bedding had to be specially fabricated. The cadaverous figure was artistically arranged along the central axis of the huge bed, as far as possible from the nearest human being. How Gladys single-handedly accomplished such symmetry and perfection was a mystery.

"How on Earth does she do it? I shall have to ask her," mused Liz out loud. Once she had succeeded in reaching the old man's hand, she took the liberty of gently rotating his left arm at right angles to his body, so that she could sit, leaning forward more or less comfortably, while holding the grizzled claw in her two hands. Sitting there staring wide-eyed at her beloved but moribund grandfather, Liz let the feelings and the memories flow, drifting in and out of one dreamlike reality after the other. Adam. Maine. New York. San Francisco. London. Cambridge. Mykonos. Sweet Baby James. The *menage a trois*. The wedding on Easter Island. The home births of each of her three children. Puerto Rico. Adam again. And of course, Grandpa Jack in a wide variety of settings.

Alden's was a challenging, confusing and contradictory character. Out in the world at large, he was thought of as the sweetest, kindest, most generous man anyone had ever met. Closer to home, however, Liz remembered the cutting edge to his voice, his emotional unavailability, the secretive love affairs that he thought nobody knew about, his loner lifestyle. He was known as a tough, unyielding businessman. He attributed his spectacularly successful career to a set of very specific business techniques - the way he managed people. The only way to get the optimum performance out of an employee, he repeatedly told the teenaged Liz as he trained her for her anticipated future as the chief executive officer of International Business Machines, Incorporated, was to keep them off-balance and in a state of constant trepidation. Only if your staff existed in unending terror of losing their jobs would they deliver their best work. Even as a fifteen year old, Liz could not have disagreed more, and in any event, she had not the slightest intention of ever becoming the CEO of IBM. While she adored her grandfather, she had mixed feelings about the man. She had no doubt about Grandpa Jack's profound and enduring love for her, but his unpredictable behavior had sliced her heart into ribbons so many times it was uncertain whether she could ever truly recover from the emotional damage she had sustained.

"His closed heart no longer serves him - or anyone else, for that matter." Liz spoke the words out loud, quite unaware that she was doing so. She spent a long time just hanging out, as the images and memories came and went, many of them positive, some not so warm and fuzzy.

Adam's iridescent young face floated into view. The handsome teenager had been her first love, and you never get over your first love, do you? Liz had not thought of her cousin in a long time, not until Washington had brought up his name on the drive from the airport. She floated off into a waking dream, and re-lived for the ten thousandth time the most terrifying moment of her life. It was a perfect summer Sunday dawn in rural Maine. She was in the back seat of Uncle Bertrand's sunshine-yellow convertible Impala, and Adam was driving them home from the all-night party in Dam-dam-damariscotta to the waterfront summer camp on Bailey Island. They had been up all night, and if Liz was not mistaken, Adam had lost his virginity sometime in the wee hours. The girl was asleep. She had passed out with her head in Adam's lap. The boy was still very drunk and was driving much too fast. They came to a part of the narrow winding road where the hills undulated wildly.

"Watch this, kids. We're gonna get some air," Adam yelled.

Those were the last words her cousin ever spoke. The sun was rising directly ahead of them. Liz had a sudden prescient moment of terror. She put her head down in Jimmy's lap, to the boy's immense delight. He'd been hoping all night that she'd do that. The impetuous act almost certainly saved Liz's life. As the big yellow Chevy roared up the incline into the rising sun, a huge white bread truck heaved into view from the opposite direction. The Grumman step-van was coming directly at them, and the driver was distracted by his paperwork. Adam screamed and slammed on the brakes. Nothing happened. The Impala was airborne.

A month later, Liz emerged from the coma. She was the only survivor. A week after the accident, she was informed, Aunt Lizzie had jumped off a building in

Portland, leaving a sad little farewell note on her desk at home, and a dark stain on the sidewalk. She could not take it anymore, the note said. Liz was fifteen, and Adam, the unrequited love of her young life, had just turned seventeen. Liz was named after Aunt Lizzie, whose given name was Elizabeth. Two years earlier, her own mother, Lizzie's younger sister Sarah, had been sideswiped by a hit-and-run driver while they were on Spring Break down in Puerto Rico. Sarah had survived the accident, with the help of an emergency blood transfusion. The prognosis was excellent. She would make a full recovery. A year later, she was dead. Inexplicably, the cause of her death was identified as HIV/AIDS. From that point on, Liz might as well have been an orphan. Her father, never particularly present in his daughters' lives, was too taken up with his golf and his Indians out West and his new love relationship to bother much with her or her little sister Priscilla.

After an endless time, in that mysterious vibrating state between wakefulness and dream, drifting in and out of a myriad feelings, memories and images - in the absence of any real connection with the cataleptic effigy of her grandfather on the bed - Liz yawned, rose to her feet, stretched like a cat waking up, and explored the enormous bedroom. Against the far wall stood a large

42

antique cabinet which caught her attention. It was familiar. She remembered it from her last visit - an ornate 19th Century Viennese bookcase with frosted glass door-panels. The cabinet was locked, just as it always had been. Liz peeked behind the cabinet, just in case. There was no sign of a key. She examined the paintings on the walls, whistled softly in recognition of several of the better-known pieces, then went out and stood on the balcony.

The wind whipped her hair back from her face. It felt good, as though a lifetime's worth of cobwebs were being blown out of her brain. Liz couldn't quite make out Indian Point through the treetops, but the surf was definitely happening. The sound of it was loud and seemed to be getting louder by the moment.

"The boys will be excited," she said out loud. "They demanded a daily surf report, on penalty of I don't know what. I mustn't forget to phone them after school," Liz continued. "What time is it in that alternative reality called Concord, Massachusetts, anyway?"

Seeing a familiar figure in immaculate blue work overalls emerging from the garage after washing and parking the old Mercedes, she shouted down to him.

"Hi Washington! I had forgotten how wonderful the view is from up here."

"Ah yes, Missy. But the jarrah trees have grown up so much. Do you remember how it used to be? One could see all the way to the point."

"All the way to Indian Point? You are right. I had forgotten." Liz moved her head from side to side, trying to find a clear sightline though the waving treetops. It was futile. The foliage was too thick.

"Washington," she continued, "I am starved suddenly! Would you mind telling your lovely wife I'm ready for breakfast?"

"Breakfast Missy? It is very nearly lunchtime. But I will tell her. I have been detecting a number of delicious aromas emanating from the kitchen, so I think you might be in luck. Gladys will ring the slave bell as soon as the food is ready."

The slave bell. Liz turned and walked slowly and thoughtfully back into the sumptuous master suite of her grandfather's 16-bedroom winter cottage with its apricot-colored brocaded walls. "That's right," she mused. "I had forgotten." The people who built Alden House had slaves back then, didn't they? This was one of the first successful sugar plantations in the West Indies. The original owners had grown tobacco before that, all on the labor of innocent people stolen from Africa. As Liz turned to leave the room, something caught her eye.

44

She stopped and looked to her left. There was a huge framed black-and-white photograph above the locked bookcase and she had not even noticed it the first time around. It took up the entire wall above the Viennese cabinet. She walked back over to the photograph, which showed a futuristic aeroplane pulled up in front of a 1930s-style Art Deco air terminal. The terminal was vaguely familiar, as was the aircraft, which had a long downward-pointed nose. A group of a dozen or fifteen people was formally arranged in front of the aircraft. The women wore huge floppy hats.

A polished brass plaque was attached to the bottom of the heavy, ornate frame. Liz did not have her reading glasses with her; they were downstairs in her shoulder bag, so she could not make out the plaque's text as well as she would have liked. She stepped back and re-examined the picture. Her stomach rumbled loudly. Wait. The be-hatted woman in the very middle of the group looked a bit like... Was it? Yes it was. Of course it was. Her namesake, Queen Elizabeth the Second. QE2. What? Liz squinted at the plaque. The date and the title were in a larger font than the main body of the inscription. She could just about make out the words.

"Copyright 1977, Patrick Litchfield," she read out loud. "Passenger Contingent. Maiden Voyage of the

BOAC Concorde. Barbados to London."

The slave bell reverberated softly. Liz began to salivate. Ivan Pavlov would have been proud of her. The ravenous woman had something other than sustenance on her mind, however. Why on God's green Earth, she wondered, would Grandpa Jack have this photograph taking pride of place in his bedroom, among the Monets and the Manets and the Van Goghs? Between the two Salvador Dalis? She stepped back and squinted at the figures gathered before the Concorde.

"Oh shit!" she gasped out loud. She put her hand to her mouth. The man three to Her Majesty's left, one over from HRH Prince Philip of Spain, was none other than her beloved grandfather, the handsome former senator from New York, the onetime mover and shaker whose mortal remains, barely breathing, lay ten feet behind her. "And, oh my! It's Gran'ma Priscilla standing next to him. Look how young and elegant they are! God, she was beautiful. I had no idea."

The slave bell rang a second time.

"OK! I'm coming," Liz repeated from the landing, as she descended the curving stairs and made her way out onto the broad verandah with its distant glimpses of the ocean through the evergreens. Triggering a second Pavlovian response, a blend of delicious aromas portended

46

the spectacular brunch awaiting her.

While Liz had occupied herself upstairs communing with Old Jack, Gladys had been busy. She had set the huge verandah table for one. Once she was satisfied that all was good and ready, she made her way ponderously down the sweeping stairs to the old slave bell. When the plantation bell was installed 375 years ago, it had been used to summon the slaves to their duties at the different times of their highly regimented days. Now Gladys, quite possibly a descendant of those self-same slaves, gently rang the bell to summon her beloved mistress. The times they are a-changin'. In fact, the times the times they have already a-changed, have they not? Liz's voice had wafted from Alden's room, out through the French doors and down to Gladys as she puffed her way back up to the verandah.

"I'll be right down, Gladys deah. Thank you."
As Liz emerged onto the verandah through the wide-open double doors, which must have been ten feet tall, the full impact of the astonishing aromas hit her olfactory senses. The last time she recalled smelling food this delicious, she was twelve years old, half dead from hunger, returning to the bush lodge after an endless day descending from the snowcapped peak of Mount Kilimanjaro. She realized she was almost faint with hunger,

and sat down without further ado. Gladys placed a large warm raku-fired platter in front of her, and with a proud sweep of her ample right arm, indicated the sizzling array of food she had laid out. It was enough to feed a small army. So much for my resolution, thought Liz with a wry smile.

"Here, Missy. Shall I help you? I think you will like this a little better than that dreadful rat you were eating last night. Ugh. It is well that you are here. I am planning to put a little meat on them poor bones o' yours."

"Thank you Gladys. Not that these poor bones, as you so kindly call them, need much help in the meat department."

Liz decided not to correct the misapprehension about the rat. I shall have to tell the boys, she thought. They'll get a giggle out of that. It sounds like something their dear departed Daddy would've come up with. Gladys took up a tall decanter of fresh-squeezed iced lemonade and placed a frosted glass in front of Liz. Satisfied, she stepped back and continued.

"Our famous island lemons, fresh from the tree. I picked them less than an hour ago. The salad greens as well. Washington loves his organic vegetable garden." If Gladys's great beaming smile had been any broader, the top of her head might have lifted off in the breeze and landed out on the lawn. She went on.

"Now, your grandfather. As I told you, dear, he has been like that since Sunday the week before last. After three or four days, we thought it best to telephone you. And here you are."

"And here I am, Gladys. Here we both are. Well, it had to come to this, some day. The doctor?"

"Dr. Ginsberg wants him in Queen Elizabeth. So he can be properly fed, through a tube, no less."

"The hospital in Bridgetown? But he has been eating just fine, you said. Nutrition does not seem to be the issue. And you are a qualified nurse."

"Precisely. So is the hospice lady."

"Barbara? Hmmm. It sounds like you've got it cover-ed. So what exactly is the problem, Gladys? Is it the Parkinson's? Is it dementia? Is it just old age? And what's all this about talking to spirits? He falls into a trance. Then he gets all excited, yells out something unintelligible, then he goes catatonic again? What gets him so het-up? Any idea?"

Gladys was thoughtful. This was something she had been pondering.

"I don't know," she began. "Well...I think... It seems to be something about Indians. I was discussing this question with Barbara. Which Indians I do not know, whether the brown ones from India or the ones from your country, the Red Indians, but he keeps shouting 'Indians! The poor bloody Indians!' " Gladys wiped her brow and continued. "There are a fair number of people from India here on the island, so that must be it. That famous writer, I don't recall his name, he is Indian, although of course he lives in Trinidad. He came to visit your grandfather two or three years ago. He was quite flirtatious. Rather fond of the larger specimen of lady, he say. If your handsome husband should ever run off with a skinny one and desert you... But, I digress. There are no Red Indians in Barbados. Obviously. The hospice nurse will be back on duty tomorrow. She can tell you more than I can."

"Barbara told me on the phone... She said he's talking to people on the other side. Could that have anything to do with it?"

"The other side? The spirit world? I don't know 'bout that. Alden House house is haunted, everybody know that. But our ghosts, they never say a word to anyone as far as I know. Them keep a tight lip."

"The house is haunted? Uh oh. I'm not sure I wanted to know that. But Barbara, she said it's a sign."

"A sign that the time draws nigh? It is, indeed. I hear that from the other doulas as well."

50

"Doulas?" Liz had not heard the term before.

"We are like the midwives who bring in the new children, only at the other end of life. Death doulas like us help the old ones to go peacefully to their rest."

"I'll look it up, dear Gladys. Oh, by the way, is there wi-fi here?"

"Wi-fi?"

"Wireless internet."

"Is that part of the television? I think we have it, but I'm not so sure it's set up properly. Doctor Ginsberg was annoyed... He could not find out something about the Stock Market in New York. But Washington, he will know. My husband knows everything."

*****

4

Junior's Lucky Day

Friday, November 13, 2020

Wakey wakey, Junior! It's your lucky day. It's Friday the 13th, and your worst nightmare is on the telephone. Growwwrrr!" A scratchy angry male voice responded from the telephone handset. The woman's voice continued. "Whozat? Whozat, you ask? Who else would it be? It's me, Scilla. Priscilla. Your ever-loving daughter, the one you haven't spoken to in fifteen years. The disappointing kid you named after your dear departed mother, may peace be upon her.

Remember me?"

Day was just dawning over Maui. The sun was already bright on the upper slopes of Mount Haleakala and Scilla Barnes was smoking a marijuana cigarette and speaking on the telephone. Scilla was a scrawny flat chested sun dried thirty-five year-old blue-eyed Iggy Pop lookalike with spiky jet-black hair, a diamond nose ring and multiple tattoos. Come to think of it, she looked more like Lily Tomlin than Iggy Pop. If Lily and Iggy had produced a child, Scilla would have been the result. She was resplendent in a moth eaten black Ramones T-shirt over the paint-spattered sarong loosely tied around her midriff. The sleeves had been carelessly ripped out of the T-shirt, and her exposed arms were a tad too skinny for comfort, as was the rest of her much-decorated body. Her feet were bare and blackened. She had just returned from work, a three-mile walk, after washing dishes all night for substantially less than minimum wage.

Scilla spoke in a teasing singsong voice, sounding alternately playful and exasperated, as she paced around the cluttered backyard of her ground-floor apartment. The enclosed yard doubled as an untidy outdoor sculpture studio. She was on the phone with her father. Her father was not amused. He was in Sydney, Australia and

it was three o'clock in the morning in Sydney, Australia
- tomorrow morning, from Scilla's chronological perspective. The soothing chimes of a Samsung smartphone
had just woken one of the world's highest-paid chief
executive officers from a thrilling dream in which he
was playing the best golf game of his entire lifetime.
The dream faded and the CEO of Alden Enterprises
International was as pissed as a snake.

"Do I know what time it is, Junior?" Scilla sounded
equally annoyed. "Of course I know what time it is. Let
me consult my wristwatch." She was not wearing a
wristwatch. She examined her wristwatch-free left fore-
arm. There was a tattoo of a watch there. In place of the
customary hour and minute hands, the tattoo said,
simply, NOW.

"Hmmm. Two hairs past a freckle. Not! It's six
o'clock in the goddamn morning, Dad. Why would I be
calling you this early? This is an emergency. Unless you
don't see an impending family funeral as an emergency."
She took a toke on the joint, but it had gone out.

"What? Whose funeral? Grandpa Jack. Your father.
Remember him? The old fart's on his last legs. Did you
know that? Liz just flew down there from Maine. He
may be dead already for all I know." Scilla stopped and
listened, taking a deep puff on the joint after re-lighting

it with the barbeque clicker. "Down where? Barbados, of course. Listen Dad, for fuck's sake. Golf? It's your family, not that that means a whole lot to you. Say you'll think about it, please? Can't you change your golf plans? I mean seriously, Junior. Golf plans?"

Highly-structured oscillations in the limpid tropical air, triggered by the dulcet tones of Scilla's voice, were converted into a digital signal by the circuitry in her telephone, an antiquated paint-spattered wireless device which was leased to her and Maryah by a company called Hawaiian Telcom. By some miracle of physics, a unique, never-to-be-repeated series of ones and zeroes ascended into the sky at the regulation 186,000 miles per second, bounced off an invisible satellite up there above the stratosphere, and hurtled down on the far side of the Pacific Ocean into the receiver circuitry of a brand-new Samsung Galaxy something-or-other belonging to her highly agitated and irritable parent. Scilla's voice was then decoded in real time and came out sounding as though she was speaking from the next room.

Johann Bergdorf Alten Jr, also known as 'Johnny,' 'Jack' or 'Junior,' was a fine figure of a man for his age, especially when observed from astern in the absence of clothing by someone who happened to appreciate that kind of view. Old Jack Alden's only son - and onetime heir apparent - was in his late 60s or early 70s, and he was on the telephone with his daughter Scilla, who lived somewhere in America. Junior wasn't sure where. It was an unseasonably hot, early summer night. As a matter of fact, the night was almost over. The bedside clock said 3:02 a.m. and it would be getting light in an hour. Junior stood naked and suntanned in the bedroom window, the soft focus pre-dawn city lights of Sydney visible beyond him. James Alten, *nee* Walker, a younger man, 50-ish, wide-awake now, observed the proceedings from the king-sized bed behind Jack. If James listened carefully, he could make out what Scilla's scratchy voice was saying on Jack's Samsung.

"Dad, come on! Think about it. Isn't that just a bit of a double standard? You have a husband, remember? I'm not the only queer in this wonderful middle-of-the-road family of ours. And, just so you know, Maryah is emphatically not a junkie. She's been clean ever since we moved to Maui. That was the deal and she has honored it. Impeccably."

Scilla squinted at the handset in the bright sunlight, and found the elusive little button she was looking for. She put the device on speakerphone, and holding it at arm's length, listened to the angry male voice emanating from the thing. The voice paused for breath.

"I called because this is a family emergency, didn't I just tell you that? Unless you think Grandpa Jack should put his impending demise on hold 'til after your oh-so-important golf trip to Scandinavia." The handset squawked angrily. Scilla took a deep breath, rolled her sky-blue eyes, and did a weird sort of angry whirling yoga stretch before continuing. "OK, South Africa, not Saudi Arabia, wherever the fuck that is. Would you like me to ask Grandpa Jack whether that would be convenient?

"So, let me get this straight, Dad," she continued angrily. "You don't mind if I call you Dad, do you? It's almost Thanksgiving, after all. Grandpa Jack is dying. I haven't asked you for anything, ever. You're a fucking billionaire, and you're damned if you're going to pay your daughter's airfare. Especially if she insists on bringing that quote-unquote 'goddamn woman' with her. You've got better things to do with your frequent-flyer miles." Once again, the handset squawked angrily.

"OK, so you're no longer technically a billionaire. You're only a multi-multi-millionaire and you just can't afford shit like this. And, oh right. I forgot. You don't get frequent-flyer miles on your own company plane. What's up with that? Can't you just send your spare Lear Jet for us, in that case?" Her voice rose to a scream.

"Your accountant would hack your nuts off with a blunt butter knife? Is that what you're trying to tell me?"

Scilla was beside herself. She pressed a button on the handset, angrily terminating the exchange, and strode stiffly into her apartment, muttering to herself and stumbling over the cat. She crawled into the mussed-up, unmade bed and pulled the covers over her head. Where the hell was Maryah when she needed her?

Junior put the phone down. He stood there pensively, gazing out at the lights and the sparse traffic on the Sydney Harbor Bridge. Behind him, James lay in the king-size bed, propped up on the luxurious pillows, admiring Jack's rear view. James had shoulder-length brown hair. Suntanned and in excellent physical shape, he looked ever so slightly Native American, but he spoke with a strong Australian accent when he broke the silence.

"Nice arse, darling. Fair dinkum. Hand me the Samsung, do you mind? Thanks. Now go back over and gaze pensively out of the window. Nice. Ah look at that, would you. You still look amazing from the rear, just like the first time I spotted you on Fire Island back at the dawn of history. Hmm. I'd better not post this on Facebook. We'd be overrun with applications." James paused and looked at the clock. "Are you coming back to bed,

Johnny? It's three o'clock in the morning, in case you hadn't noticed. 3:17 actually."

Junior did not answer. He was upset and distracted. He made a half-turn sideways and stopped, reviewing the conversation with his distant daughter. In profile, his body was significantly less attractive than the rear view, thought James tenderly and a little sadly. His hunched posture was not what it used to be. The nightly five-star restaurant feasts and the five-course lunches and the finest wines and the endless gins-and-tonics were adding up.

Junior was burdened by a forty pound bale of hay, a barrel of lard and runaway microorganisms, a buffer between the man and the rest of the world. To put it bluntly, James realized suddenly, the CEO of Alden International was a heart attack waiting to happen. His beloved life-partner could drop dead at any moment.

*****

5

The Hospice Nurse

Barbara Ann Masterson, R.N., it said on her plain white no-nonsense business card. The hospice nurse was a dumpy overweight middle-aged divorcee in a shapeless floral dress. Her smudgy complexion left a little to be desired. She smoked more Camels than was good for her. There was a beautiful young girl in there somewhere, but the lovely lass hadn't shown her face in a couple of decades. For the past several months, Barbara had been taking one of the crowded local taxi-vans out from Bridgetown twice weekly, to check old Jack's vitals. Now she was on day duty at Alden House Monday through Friday, and on standby the rest of the time.

Barbara spoke with one of those decidedly upper-crust, anal British accents, the kind that tends to put Americans on edge, the kind that sends Canadians and Australians and New Zealanders and South Africans racing for the pantry to check their stock of carrots. Foreigners may think the snooty manner of speaking is affected, but it's not. It is quite unconscious. It comes with the English public school package. Unsurprisingly, therefore, Barbara did not make a very good first impression on Liz, despite the fact that Liz had lived in England enough years to know better. Fortunately, that, the first impression, would change over the next few weeks. They would become lifelong friends. Liz would see a ghost. And Barbara would quit smoking.

The aroma of fine Jamaican coffee floated on the air. Liz poured a second cup for her new acquaintance, who had a strong ancestral predilection for a nice cuppa tea, but was doing her best to blend in with the locals. The two women relaxed at the verandah table, as Gladys, humming a well-known gospel song to herself, cleared away the debris from their morning repast.

"As I might have mentioned on the telephone," Barbara was saying, "Mr. Alden has started seeing spirits! Engaging in conversations with them. That's usually a sign. They start seeing through the veil."

"Seeing through the veil? Explain, please."
Liz's tone of voice had a subtle, barely-detectable edge to it. Although a fundamentally kind woman, she was accustomed to being in command of those on the family payroll, an unconscious sense of entitlement that comes with being born into money, something she had unwittingly picked up from her arrogant old grandfather, very likely. Command and control. Keep 'em on edge, your staff, Master Jack had taught her. It makes 'em deliver the goods. 'It's a very strange world you live in, Master Jack,' the young Liz had responded in the privacy of her own mind, 'according to Four Jacks and a Jill.' She was referring to a popular British song from the 1960s.

"It's because their loved ones are coming to greet them." Barbara said. "Your grandmother, I wouldn't be in the least surprised."

"My grandmother? But Gladys says... She thinks he's talking to Indians. What could that mean?"

"Indians? Now that might explain it."

"Explain it? Explain what?

*****

6

The Shriek Of The Popinjay

That night after dinner, upstairs in Alden's bedroom, Liz stood gazing down at her grandfather, now neatly tucked in for the night. His eyes were open. A transparent plastic catheter bag trailed out of the bed on its long translucent umbilical cord and rested on the thousand-year-old Persian carpet at her feet. After a while she pulled up the French chair and sat down and regarded the old man sadly. She addressed him in a loud but affectionate voice.

"Life doesn't get any easier as one gets older, does it Grandpa Jack? May I ask you a question? You don't have to answer if you don't want to. What's all this about talking to spirits? You're not getting soft in your old age are you? You know you don't believe in voodoo nonsense like that." She paused. The gentle sound of the surf was indistinguishable from the rhythmic swishing of the wind in the ironwood trees beyond the balcony doors.

"I do wish you'd talk to me, Grandpa. Aside from anything else, I want to hear some of your old stories again. I want to record them for posterity, for your great-grandchildren. Remember? You have three of the little bastards, two of whom are packing their suitcases and their surfboards at this very moment. The boys will be here the day after tomorrow, if I've got the timing right." Her voice trailed off.

Alden ignored her. He continued to examine the ceiling. Simon & Garfunkel's *I Am A Rock* played for the umpteenth time. Liz, noticing that fact for the first time, ejected the CD and examined it. The antique disc was faded and ancient, but she couldn't see anything wrong with it. She put it back in the tray and pressed play. Every time the album came to *I Am A Rock* the player repeated that one song, over and over. Liz took it as a sign, and let the machine play on, based partly on the optimistic (but ill-founded) notion that a favorite song might stimulate the old man into waking up and noticing her. She looked around anxiously, as a trapped animal might.

"This is beginning to get to me," she yawned out loud. She looked at her grandfather for the first time in a few minutes. His eyes had closed and he appeared to be asleep. Liz drowsed there by the bedside, listening to the old man's soft breathing and the shushing of the sea and the uneasy chattering of the nocturnal wildlife through the open doors. It was as peaceful as it gets.

A sudden terrifyingly loud surreal shriek exploded from the trees outside and shocked her into wide-eyed astonished wakefulness. Her skin resembled that of a freshly plucked chicken.

"Goddamn it!" Liz yelped. "There's that insane bird again. I'll have to ask Washington. Is it a nightjar? What the hell is a nightjar? Any relation to a jam jar?" As usual, Liz did her wondering out loud. It had long been an unconscious habit, this talking-to-herself thing. In fact, she had been talking to herself for several years, quite unaware that she was doing so, pretty much as long as she had been living alone. Outside, the manic, be-feathered, winged, warm-blooded, egg-laying verte-brate shrieked again. Its raucous mechanical screech sounded a dire advance warning from the end of the world. Alternatively, Liz hallucinated, could it be some poor innocent creature screaming out its death throes as it was dismembered, molecule by quivering molecule, by some evil grinning predator? Unbidden, the ridiculous term 'purple popinjay' entered Liz's head.

"Popinjay, Grandpa Jack?" she enquired of her catatonic grandfather. "Whatever that crazy thing is, it is definitely not a purple popinjay. It's probably some kind of South American parrot blown off course by the late season hurricane last month, the one that made such a mess of the Grenadines."

The archaic English term 'popinjay' had not entered her conscious thoughts in a couple of decades. The first time she had heard that decidedly uncomplimentary word, it was used in reference to a certain James Edward 'Nick' Nicholson, a person for whom she had a certain attachment at the moment it was uttered, to put it mildly. She was in the process of marrying the man.

Liz had had to look the word up in the oversized Oxford dictionary on the coffee table once they got home from the honeymoon in Patagonia. The occasion had been the young medical scholar's belated marriage to a certain American heiress, a foolish 19-year-old girl who, with a statistical probability of approximately fifty

66

percent, the young Cambridge graduate student had knocked up, as they say in the jolly old UK, roughly four years prior to the nuptials in question. Nick's diminutive three-year-old 50% probable daughter Layla had proudly played the role of ring-bearer in the ceremony. Liz took up her trusty iPad 8S Mini and did a quick Internet search, which revealed the following:

> **Popinjay:** *This deeply insulting word for a vain or conceited person, one given to pretentious displays, is now rather outmoded or literary. A good example can be found in Joseph Conrad's 1902 short ry "The End of the Tether."*
> *"When he looked around in the club he saw only a lot of conceited popinjays too selfish to think of making a good woman happy."*

The living, breathing skeleton on the bed, encased for the moment in loosely-fitting, sun-damaged, blotchy 93-year old human skin, had been the one to avail himself of the deeply insulting term, although on Easter Island, where the wedding was held, not one person in a thousand had ever encountered the archaic term. Even if any of the attendees had, they would probably have thought it referred to some kind of exotic bird, Liz reflected. Hearing her grandfather use the term, she had protested mildly in the privacy of her own mind, not daring to confront the intimidating old international businessman who had deployed the inflammatory word during his uproarious and entertaining wedding address, which seemed to contain career advice directed more at the two dozen or so other young men present than at his errant granddaughter and her somewhat crestfallen new husband.

It was the once and final manner in which Alden expressed his disapproval of the despicable cad who had impregnated his teenaged granddaughter. Liz thought about James, sweet baby James. Unlike everyone else, she never called him by his nickname, which happened to be Nick.

Poor, drowned, fish-eaten James was not one given to pretentious displays. Besides, he had only recently completed his Doctor of Philosophy degree at Cambridge University's notoriously challenging School of Clinical Medicine in some obscure, arcane and unpronounceable academic discipline. Who had ever heard of historical epidemiology, for heaven's sake? If ever there was a time when a pretentious display might appropriately be called for, that was it. James, on the other hand, was self-effacing in the extreme. 'Vain or conceited' did not describe him in the least. In fact, to be honest, he was a bit of a nerd. Thin, you know? With a prema turely receding hairline and horn-rimmed glasses to match? He was a rather well-endowed Elvis Costello doppelgänger, and, significantly perhaps, young Liz had been a diehard Costello fan at the time of the fateful Mykonos tryst.

The nearest thing to a pretentious display on James's part was the rented grey top hat and tails that he had rather absurdly donned for the wedding. Against all odds, her husband had looked fantastic at the wedding, despite the tattered Reef Brasil flip-flops he had insisted on wearing during the ceremony, having quite forgotten to pack any more appropriate footwear. He was the most elegant man there, and that was saying something. In the five years she had known him, Liz had never seen 'Nick' Nicholson, PhD, looking remotely like that. He had even brushed his unruly hair for the occasion. She fell in love with him on the spot, and never fell out again, until death untimely did them part.

Liz thought back on the wedding. It had cost her grandfather a small fortune, a very small fortune, relatively speaking, but still. Thankfully, spending small fortunes was something Grandpa Jack had done time and again, and thankfully he never seemed to run short of funds for such indulgences. She had, rather nervously, asked Alden to give her away, in the absence of her disgruntled and unavailable father, who, from what she had heard through the grapevine, was planning to be off with his Native American buddies somewhere in the Black Hills of South Dakota exchanging gunfire with the FBI. Grandpa Jack had responded to the request with guarded enthusiasm, and agreed, on two conditions or caveats. First, he absolutely would not *give* her away. He was not one to give anything away, he protested, especially his beloved firstborn granddaughter. He would sell her to the highest bidder, preferably by the pound. And secondly, he reserved the right to deliver a concise homily at the high point of the festivities.

Having little idea what the word homily, concise or otherwise, meant, and having no idea that the man was serious, Liz had agreed to the terms. Beggars can't be choosers, and neither can single mothers. It was in that wedding address off the foggy coast of Chile that Liz heard the word 'popinjay' for the first time. Fortunately for her immediate happiness, she had had no clue what it meant. It sounded like it referred to a young and inexperienced boy, which in certain respects James was. It is not at all certain that her grandfather knew the full meaning either. He was an American, after all, although he did claim to have learned his English directly from Her Royal Highness on a flight to or from somewhere or other, back in the nineteen seventies. Grandpa Jack, arguably the world's leading raconteur, was full of such absurd and apocryphal tales. Nobody took much notice of old Jack Alden's endless 'ridiculousities.'

True to his word, Alden really did set up the wedding as an auction, complete with a professional auctioneer. His oft-repeated motto was 'If it ain't fun, I ain't doing it,' and he probably had as much fun at that wedding as at his own. He and Gran'ma Priscilla were still dancing the wild fandango when Liz and James and Layla excused themselves and retired to their private waterfront penthouse overlooking the moonlit row of prehistoric statues.

A word concerning the auction: in light of the deadly dearth of qualified suitors lining up to bid on the young mother and her angelic golden haired blue eyed three-year-old, little Layla, poor indigent James came in as the first, highest, and only bidder for young Elizabeth Alten, certified non-virgin that she was. True, a significant number of handsome young suitors were on hand, Cambridge, Oxford, Harvard, Princeton, Stanford and/or Yale undergraduates each and every one of them, having somehow inveigled themselves onto the all-expenses-paid guest list, but one and all, they seemed more interested in the equally wealthy but presumably virginal and child-free Priscilla 'Prissy' Alten, than in her horse-faced older sister. Liz recalled the auction, which was reminiscent of one of those delightful 17th Century slave sale-a-thons, with just a hint of residual bitterness. They didn't know what they were missing, those pimple faced yuppies.

The wedding was the beginning of a long and relatively satisfying marriage, which only ended when dear James mysteriously but permanently and incontrovertibly vanished in the midst of an archeological research trip across the pond in Canada. The Montreal newspapers had fielded the improbable and unsupported hypothesis that the scientist, one of the world's leading experts on ancient disease pandemics, had been abducted by aliens who wanted to study his brain, a theory that the local Iroquois had concurred with - and had quite possibly initiated.

There had been a major UFO sighting, so the Indians said, directly over the area where James was last seen, on the very night he disappeared. Be that as it may, there was no indication of foul play, and there was no sign of a body. The young scientist and father of three had vanished off the face of the earth. Professor James Nicholson knew more about the New World origin of syphilis, and the nature of the pandemic that wiped out the East Coast Indians shortly before the *Mayflower* dropped anchor in Provincetown, than the rest of his scientific colleagues put together. His research, needless to say, vanished off the face of the earth with him.

That was the situation until the spring thaw, and the grisly discovery later that summer. An avid ice-angler and inveterate devourer of innocent limbless cold-blooded vertebrates with gills and fins, whose only crime had been to swallow his baited hook, James E. Nicholson, PhD, had himself been eaten by fish.

"Revenge is sweet," chanted the little fishies. Only his clean-picked skeleton remained, reclining full fathom five, as James himself would have put it, on the slimy, glyphosate-contaminated bottom of Lake Huron.

> *Full fathom five thy father lies; Of his bones are coral made; Those are pearls that were his eyes; Nothing of him that doth fade, But doth suffer a sea-change, Into something rich and strange. Sea-nymphs hourly ring his knell: Ding-dong. Hark! now I hear them — Ding-dong, bell.*
>
> Ariel's song, *The Tempest.*
> William Shakespeare

7

Alden, or Alten?

Saturday, November 14, 2020

I t was a Saturday morning in the tropics, a day no different from any other day of the week, except for one significant factor. A late-season tropical depression was moving in. It might turn into a hurricane. Liz and Barbara were clearing up the breakfast dishes and taking them into the kitchen. The women were soaking wet. They had elected to eat outside, at one end of the long verandah table, despite the ominous forecast and the towering line of graphite-colored cumulus clouds bearing down on the coastline. They had barely begun their meal when day turned to night and a sudden vicious squall threatened to uproot the trees blocking the ocean view. The horizontal rain drove the new friends unceremoniously indoors. Liz wrestled with the howling wind, and finally got the front doors closed. A blessed silence descended. She was soaked to the skin.

"Whew, was that wild or what?" Liz panted. "I could barely get the door shut. Look at that rain, would you? I've never seen anything like it. What were we talking about? Oh yes..."

"I too have never seen anything like it. Good God!" Barbara handed Liz a folded white towel from the powder room. "And to think there are still people who don't believe in climate change. Your grandfather?" she continued, still breathing hard. "Nothing? Not a word? I'm surprised. He has been quite talkative, although I have to say I have no idea who it is he thinks he's talking to, or even what he's saying, since the series of mini-strokes. It doesn't sound like he's talking to your grand-mother, though. Whoever it is, your grandfather gets highly agitated."

"You know, Barb, this might sound funny, but Gran'ma Priscilla, my grandmother, once told me, in the strictest confidence, mind you, that she wasn't planning to hang out with Grandpa Jack once they got to heaven. I think it wasn't the easiest job in the world, being Jack Alten's wife."

Barbara, being English, and a clever girl, was quite the expert at guessing people's origins from the cadence of their voices. She noticed that the way Liz pronounced the name Alten was indistinguishable from the way an Englishwoman would say Alden. Or was it the other way round? Liz's pronunciation seemed to have an almost imperceptible German inflection, which made sense under the circumstances, if in fact a German accent could have survived three generations of Americanization. Liz paused. She did not want to get too personal this early in the relationship. She went on.

"Well anyway, when I'm with him, all Grandpa Jack does is lie there staring at the ceiling. So far, at least. He's pretty much catatonic. I can't believe the dementia has progressed this much. He tried to say something the other day, at least I think he did, but I missed it. Barb, what does he talk about, when he does get going? Gladys thought you might have some insight into what's going on in that fuzzy old head of his.

"It's hard to tell, Elizabeth."

"Liz. Please call me Liz. Everyone else does."

After a while, the two women went their separate ways. Barbara sat down at the far end of the long dining room table with her laptop, writing up her weekly report for the hospice company, and Liz went upstairs to sit with the dying man, noting as she went the well stocked antique bookcases on either side of the winding mahogany stairwell. Gladys had just finished Old Jack's morning ablutions and was buttoning his fresh pajamas. Liz and Gladys tarried for a while in Alden's bedroom, looking out through the closed French doors at the weather.

The wind was still howling viciously and tearing at the shutters like a Tasmanian devil on steroids, but it looked like the rain wouldn't last long. Old Jack lay exactly in the center of the huge bed, mouth and eyes open, staring at the ceiling. His dementia had certainly progressed rapidly. Liz reminded Gladys that when she'd called him on his 93rd birthday, just a few weeks earlier, he had been as sharp as a tack. Old Jack had been as gruff and brusque as ever, and he was in full control of his faculties. Picking up the phone himself, he had greeted Liz in the classic Jack Alden manner.

"What?" he grunted. No hello. No how are you? Just that one word, delivered in a tone of mild annoyance.

"If you didn't know better, you'd think the old

bastard disliked you," Liz laughed.

"I know," said Gladys, "but he has a heart of gold. He likes to play the tough guy, but he's a big ol' sweet teddy bear inside."

Liz went downstairs and ventured out onto the verandah, a little tentatively. The main body of the storm had veered out to sea at the last minute, barely brushing Barbados before going on to devastate several islands to the north. As she stood there, the wind stopped and the rain ended and the day was suddenly glorious in the magical ever-changing manner of the tropics. A double rainbow was partly visible through the trees. Liz took a walk through the steaming under-growth down to the water, and explored Bathsheba beach for the first time in her adult life.

Barbara was just coming down the stairs when Liz re-entered the house an hour and a half later. She showed the nurse an enigmatic object she had picked up at the water's edge.

"My God! What *is* that?"

"It's a coconut. I found it among the seaweed washed up on the beach."

"A coconut? Are you sure? It looks just like a human face."

"Doesn't it? I looked down and there it was, staring

78

up at me like a voodoo doll. It gave me quite a start. Hey Barb, how about a margarita? It's been an awfully long morning. I'll make them. You look like you could use a break."

"A margarita at lunchtime? Now there's a novel idea. How decadent. Well... Why not?"

An hour later, after two or three margaritas and some light snacks out on the still-wet verandah, Liz looked at her new friend.

"Barbara, I have an idea," she said. "Why don't you bring your things and stay over for a while? It's a long trip out from Bridgetown every day. God knows we have enough room. Sixteen bedrooms at last count, not including the guest cottages. I'm the only one in the house, except for a catatonic old man who's taken to communicating with discarnate spirits, but refuses to say one word to me, *moi*, his long-suffering granddaughter. It's a little creepy, if you want to know the truth. I wouldn't mind a little company."

"What about the factotum and his wife? The house-keeper. Aren't they here?"

"Washington and Gladys? Haven't you noticed? They won't come into the house after dark. They think the place is haunted. They live in the old slave quarters. My grandfather had them converted into guest cottages.

Apparently they, the cottages, are not haunted. Thank goodness for small blessings."

"It only takes me an hour and a half in the taxi-van. The company pays for it, and it's quite an interesting drive. I enjoy it, actually. I get to chat with some of the locals. But let me think about it." Barbara smiled. "Thank you Liz, you are most kind. It might be nice to get out of the city for a bit. I could actually spend some time on the beach, for the first time since I got here. I've got a few loose ends to wrap up, then perhaps…"

*****

8

Still Life With Antique Porsche

After a mostly-liquid luncheon, decidedly intoxicated, and with Washington's collusion, Liz absconded with her grandfather's precious 1959 Porsche 718 RSK Spyder, a rare collector's item. The company only even made ten of them. Washington started the limited-edition sports car, reversed it out of the garage, and parked it at the bottom of the verandah stairs, where it sat, muttering and growling ominously. Liz's plan was to explore the island for the remainder of the day and to be back at Alden House well before sunset.

The silver Porsche was not exactly easy to drive. It had a mind of its own. The high-performance vehicle was race-tuned. It belonged on an autobahn or a race-track. It kept snorting and pawing at the ground like the thoroughbred racehorse it was, shooting up sudden spurts of gravel, and wanting to do a hundred and fifty miles an hour on stretches of ridiculously narrow pot-holed road where twenty was more appropriate. As he saw her off, Washington shouted a reminder.

"Take it slow, Miss Lizzie. Breathe deep. Remember, don't miss the Flower Cave. It is as far north as you can go. Just follow the signs. Oh, and on the way, make a stop at the Wildlife Reserve in Farley Hill. Feeding time is two o'clock. You will be just in time. Say hello to those little green monkeys for me."

Washington watched her go, then fetched a rake from the garage and repaired the damaged parts of the crushed coral driveway, chuckling to himself and shaking his silver-crowned head.

Once she got the Porsche more or less obeying her instructions, Liz jerked cautiously down the driveway, went out through the automatic wrought-iron gates, hung a left, and roared erratically off, all the way to the northern tip of the island, where the Atlantic Ocean and the Caribbean Sea meet, at the base of a forbidding series of five-hundred-foot tall cliffs. Outside the gates of Alden House, it would not have taken a Kalahari Bushman tracker to determine the direction the Porsche had taken. A wiggly line of black tire-tracks disappeared off to the left, down the hill, and around the next curve. The aroma of burned rubber lingered for an hour or more.

*****

9

Nothing $10,000 Won't Fix

The last of the light had faded from the western sky by the time Liz returned in the Porsche. The poor thing was somewhat the worse for wear. The silver bullet looked as good as new from the front, but its bulbous rear end was 'all stove in' as Liz's mother would have put it. Leaving Mullins Beach Bar in the gathering twilight, bombed out of her gourd, she had backed into a low concrete wall that had most unfairly materialized out of the darkness behind her.

As if that wasn't enough, she had become horribly confused on the way home, missed the Alden House driveway, and it was another hour before Washington heard the clang of the electric gates. He was sitting there in the darkness, fifty feet from the house, patiently awaiting her return. He pulled the sports car into the garage, roaring and growling, switched the machine off, got out and walked around to the rear of the vehicle. Liz watched him anxiously.

"Nothing $10,000 won't fix," he chuckled ruefully, "Once we ship it back to the factory in Germany."

"Oh my God, I'm so sorry."

"It is not a problem, Missy. Really. I wouldn't feel too bad. Your father used to do it once a month on average when he was your age, according to your granddaddy. Oh, before I forget, Gladys has left your supper for you, in the kitchen. It will just need a little heating up."

Washington said good night and scuttled off to bed. He did not like being near the main house after dark.

*****

10

A Message For Scilla

It had been a decidedly alcohol-infused day, what with the three-tequila luncheon and one too many Mount Gay sundowners at Mullins Beach Bar. Liz realized she was famished. She had eaten nothing since the aborted breakfast with Barbara. Out on Alden's balcony, balancing her heaped dinner plate in one hand, she called Scilla on the house phone and, getting no answer, left her a long rambling voicemail. The mynah birds were muttering darkly in the mango trees.

"What time is it in Hawaii?" Liz wondered out loud. Hearing a human voice, the mynah birds went silent and eavesdropped on the one-way conversation. Had Scilla had any success with their recalcitrant father? Liz realized that she had no idea what hours her sister worked. Or even whether she worked.

"Hi lil' sister," she continued, slurring just a little. "It's me, Liz, with a long-overdue and slightly intoxicated report from the far Antipodes or the Lesser Antilles or whatever they call these beautiful islands down here. Let's see. Where do I begin? Hmm. I've been sitting with Grandpa Jack mornin', noon and night. Still not the slightest sign of recognition. He hasn't so much as blinked an eye since I got here. Pretty boring company, as you can imagine. It was getting so I needed a break. So, after lunch, with a little help from Washington, I got Old Jack's precious one-of-a-kind silver Ferrari or Porsche or whatever it is, out of the garage and explored the island for the entire afternoon without getting into a single serious accident. Well, I did end up backing into a goddamned concrete retaining wall, but that was later. I drove all they way around the island, and didn't get lost until I was almost home. It took me another hour to find our driveway after missing it the first time.

"That thing has a mind of its own, the car I mean. It's not exactly easy to drive. It kept doing a hundred and fifty miles an hour on stretches of insanely bumpy potholed road where twenty miles per hour and four wheel drive would've been more appropriate. Actually, it was a hundred and fifty kilometers an hour, but I didn't realize that 'till later." Liz took a breath. Her head was spinning. "I'm glad I got that yellow '68 MGA for my 18th birthday, remember it, Prissy? I mean Scilla. At least I had some vague idea of how to drive a European sports car. Remember how I used to scare the bejeezus out of you in France and Spain and Italy? The time you pooped your pants in downtown Geneva? Wow, I had forgotten all about that trip. We had so much fun, didn't we?

"Let's see. Where was I? I can't wait for you to get here, Prissy. It's been so long. We're going to have ourselves some good times. I'm anxious to meet your better half, among other things." She paused. "So, where was I? Hmmm. Oh yes, there's a sea-cave, they call it the Flower Cave, way up at the northern tip of the island. Did we ever go there, back in the day? I can't remember. It turns out the flowers aren't really flowers. They're actually sea anemones, and it also turns out there are no sea anemones in the cave. It's the wrong time of year. Maybe they head south for the winter? Are sea anemones migratory? I'll have to Google them and find out. But it was so beautiful, down there right at sea level with the low sun on the horizon. Some kids were doing yoga, reflected in the water, and I got a great photo on my iPhone. I'll send it to you if I can ever figure out how the hell to do that.

"Then I thought, well, I should go watch the sunset from the West Side. I found this funky little beach bar called the Mullins something or other, it's in a tiny little town called Mullins. They had a really good live reggae band, and wouldn't you know it, I got totally bombed for the first time in years and met these British tourists and danced my butt off. It was the most fun I've had in quite a while. Suddenly it was totally dark and I hadn't the faintest idea where I was. I couldn't even find the headlight switch on the dashboard. Then some dreadlocked local guy appeared out of the gloom and scared me shitless and then showed me where the flashlight was on my iPhone, and then...

"I know I'm rambling a bit, Sis. Let me finish up quickly. Item one: It's been great catching up and reminiscing with Washington and Gladys. They remember every single thing from when you and I were teenagers. Item two: I have assessed Grandpa Jack's hospice situation. Everything seems to be well under control, although Dr. Ginsberg seems more than a little irritable. Was he always like that? Must be all these shitty days in

Paradise, one after the other. I guess he'd rather be trudging through the soot-blackened snow back in New York, dodging the dog poop and the muggers and the crackheads." Liz stopped and took a deep breath.

"What else? Gladys. She's doing a great job. Did you know she's a retired RN? Now she's a death doula – that's a word from the Greek for 'a woman who serves.' Kinda like a midwife for the dying. The English hospice nurse, her name is Barbara, she comes in five days a week. I'm getting to quite like her. She's moving in here in a couple of days. I invited her, because, well, quite honestly it's a little creepy being in this huge haunted house with no one for company but a catatonic dying old man, lying there all night listening to him breathing on the baby monitor. I've been having some really weird dreams...

"Oh, and finally, Washington says it will only cost about ten grand to fix the Porsche, once we get it shipped back to the factory in Germany. Not to worry. Dad used to do it all the time, apparently, so I guess it runs in the family." Liz took a deep breath. "Bye, Prissy. I mean Scilla. I love you. I can't wait to see you again. Oh, I forgot. Let me know what's up with our beloved Papa, would you? Did you ever reach him? Is he coming?"

11

Death By Boredom

A wafer-thin crescent moon ruled the dark crimson strip of sky over the coastal mountains to the west. Liz vaguely wondered whether it was a new moon or the last of the old one. James Nicholson had tried to explain the difference, one evening long ago on the faraway island of Mykonos, but Liz had never quite understood it. It was cooling down out there on the balcony. Returning to the bedroom, she closed the French doors and sat down sadly by Alden's bedside, pecking at the food with her fingers. She had a splitting headache.

"A death vigil can be awfully boring," she mused out loud. "I need something to read. I bet there's a good book or two in those bookcases downstairs. Or a hundred."

Tired of *I am a Rock* – the CD seemed to be permanently jammed on that goddamned song - she turned off the bedroom's built-in stereo system in its little alcove, returned to her chair by the bedside, and located some peaceful classical music on her iPad, which was still on the side-table from her earlier visit. Her favorite, Frédéric François Chopin. Speaking of Chopin, there was a beautiful old Steinway grand downstairs in the music room, she remembered. She had been meaning to try it out, sometime when no one was around, but the moment had yet to arrive.

The evening breeze whispered in the trees and stirred the window curtains gently. Outside, the ocean had calmed down. You could barely hear it. It was high tide. The loudest sound was the last of the mynah birds in the huge mango tree beyond the line of jarrahs, catching up on their day's stories, but they were running out of things to say one by one and zipping themselves into their little sleeping bags for the night. Just their beaks stuck out. Someone, most likely Grandpa Jack, had told little Lizzie that birds did that at the end of the day, and the eight-year-old had decided that that was at least as likely as the absurd fairy tale that they stood on a branch on one leg all night waiting for the sun to return.

Alden continued to stare at the ceiling, unblinking, his mouth open wide. At times his eyes closed and he snored or grunted loudly. How long was the old man going to linger in this state of limbo? Liz found herself wondering whether she'd been out of her mind virtually ordering everyone to drop everything and get their butts to Barbados. She decided to give it one more try.

"Grandpa Jack, you do remember me, don't you? I'm your little Lizzie. Remember? I know we had our differences from time to time, but it would be really nice if you were to look at me and say hello."

The old man continued to stare at the ceiling. Liz realized that she had yet to see him blink. Was that possible? Wouldn't his eyes dry up and..? She sat there quietly, gazing forlornly at the emaciated figure on the bed, barely a shadow of his former self, little more than a scarecrow.

"Grandpa, listen to me. I want to record some of your stories before it's too late. We can record them right on my iPhone, someone told me. Like how your great grandfather made the family fortune. How your father invented the altenator. How you turned the lion inside out in Africa when you were seventeen. How the saber-toothed ostrich came to your rescue at the last moment and chased off the hyena pack. How the Queen took you in hand and taught you to speak English instead of American. How you came up with your complaints department strategy."

There was no response. Discouraged, Liz stood up, restarted the CD player, and wandered, lonely as a cloud, translucent and intoxicated and wraith-like, back to her bedroom. The wind had dropped and the birds had fallen asleep and the vast empty house was utterly silent. It clung to the hillside above the ocean like a sleeping giant. The ancient building creaked and breathed and sighed, but somehow it did so without making a sound.

It was black dark outside. The crescent moon had gone behind the mountains. Washington and Gladys had long ago retired to the slave quarters for the night. "Oops, mustn't say that," Liz mumbled, as she took off her jewelry, slipped out of her no-longer-white denim jeans, and prepared for bed. "I meant to say the guest accommodations."

The shutters rattled suddenly, startling her. The wind was coming up, again, the first signs of yet another change in the weather.

Washington had warned her about it, before saying goodnight and hurrying off into the darkness. Hurricane season was officially over, but ever since global warming, one just never knew any more. That is what he had said.

An owl hooted far off in the distance. "Hoo hoo."

"Hoo hoo to you, too!" Liz replied, conversationally, as she folded the covers back and lay on top of the bed. After a moment she pulled the sheet up to her chin and lay there staring at the ceiling in the light from the bedside lamp, wondering what it was that Grandpa Jack found so compelling in that particular view. The ceiling revealed no secrets. The baby monitor sat next to the digital clock on the nightstand and she could hear her grandfather's gentle breathing. She reached over and put the light out.

Liz was seriously sleep-deprived. "Go to sleep, for God's sake," she muttered out loud. She had been unable to get a full night's rest since her arrival on the island. She stopped trying, and once she did so, she actually fell asleep at last. Aside from a series of disturbing dreams that she could not recall in the morning, she slept through until an hour before sunrise.

She woke with an irrational feeling that something

was amiss. Lying there going over the past month's events, she could not pin the feeling on anything specific. It was almost as if Alden House itself was home to some malevolent spirit.

*****

12

Grandpa's First Words

Sunday Nov 15, 2020

It was overcast and the long overdue tradewinds had arrived at last. They were gusting hard, and the ironwood trees were whipping back and forth. Washington's weather radio called for rain later in the day. It was Liz's first Sunday back on the island, and on Sundays after church, if she remembered correctly, the local Bajans gathered in droves, just down the hill from Alden House at the picturesque Bathsheba Beach, with its mysterious free-standing rock formations and its international surfers and its little restaurants and funky beach bars and expanses of green grassy lawn extending almost to the ocean's edge. There was some kind of special event going on down there. Stepping out onto the windswept verandah, Liz could hear the echoing sound of a public address system and snatches of music and the sound of excited voices coming up on the wind. I shall have to take a walk and see what's going on, she thought. It sounds like fun. Maybe I'll meet someone, you never know. I could use a little human interaction. A good-looking single man would come in handy right about now, for instance. It's new moon tonight. Or was that last night? A time for new beginnings.

Liz had fallen into a routine, spending an hour or so several times each day with her uncommunicative grandfather, morning, noon and night. On the sixth or seventh visit, Alden surprised her by growing agitated and muttering a series of incomprehensible grunts. He was trying to say something, but the words just wouldn't come out. Shortly after his 93rd birthday back on October 13th, Old Jack had suffered a series of transient ischemic attacks, mini-strokes which had affected his ability to speak clearly. The Parkinson's did not help. On the tenth visit or thereabouts, the words came out a little less slurred. Alden seemed to be saying something about slaves. Indians. Something about an old sea chest. The

98

words came out hoarsely, one at a time, the result of an enormous effort. Over a period of several days, Liz was able to piece together the 'message' if that was what it was. A message? A message for whom? From whom? About what?

"Indians... Slaves... Old.. Sea... Trunk... Cellar... Urgent!"

Liz was uncertain whether she had heard the words aright. She could barely make them out, the one time the old man was finally able to string all the words together into a single disjointed sentence. She was standing in the doorway looking out towards the ever-present Atlantic and thinking about the fragmented mess her once-close family had become. She hurried back to the bedside and sat down, but no further words were forthcoming. The old man had relapsed into his habitual silence.

*****

13

Intimations of Immortality

What a depressing afternoon! The wild winds seemed determined to batter away at the island until it capitulated and sank beneath the waves. The torrential, horizontal rain had resumed, and presumably, washed out the planned festivities down at the beach. Liz was house-bound, sitting miserably by Alden's bedside. She looked distinctly pale and haggard, and was wondering about a term that had recently come to her attention.

Was she in the midst of an 'existential crisis?' What could that possibly mean? Getting a good night's sleep had not helped her much. She needed to sleep for a week, but that was hardly an option. In her lap lay the pristine hardcover book she had selected from one of the many well stocked bookcases downstairs. Maybe that would help. The novel had obviously never been read. Flipping the cover open, she read the inscription once again. It was signed *'For John and Priscilla with affection, Stephen'* by the author. John and Priscilla? Why does that ring a bell? Oh, right, Grandpa Jack's real name was John, of course it was. Jack was John B. Alden's nickname, just as Jack was John F. Kennedy's.

For as long as she could remember, Liz had been meaning to read something by Stephen King, a fellow Mainiac, and this seemed like as good a time as any. The old man had not moved an eyelash during the half-hour Liz had sat there holding his hand. Before settling down to read the book, she decided to try again. She spoke loudly and authoritatively, with just a hint of a childish whine.

"Grandpa Jack, listen to me. It's me, Liz. Elizabeth. Please, please talk to me. You're making me uncom-

fortable. Come on, Grandpa. You can do it. What's all this about seeing spirits? I know you don't believe in horseshit like that. I don't either. I don't believe in ghosts, just like I don't believe in God."
She paused, wondering how best to express it.

"At least I don't believe in God in the form of some bearded old Osama Bin Laden lookalike on a diamond studded swing-set up in the sky, reaching his bony forefinger down toward humanity.

"What do I believe?" the monologue continued. "I am certain there is a creator God, but nothing remotely like the authoritarian male anthropomorph the religions would have you believe in, most of them. As far as I'm concerned, the thing people talk about as 'God' is actually the entire universe, or more accurately the consciousness of the entire universe. The invisible part. Of which we are an integral part. Something like that. Do you remember how we used to talk about things like that, Grandpa, before..." Liz lapsed into silence, then went on. "Well anyway, Grandpa, neither of us has ever darkened the door of a church. I don't think we're about to start now. Are we?"

Nothing. Liz abandoned the effort. She sat back and closed her weary eyes. Alden continued to stare at the ceiling. His eyes moved, just a tiny flicker, but Liz failed to notice. She was leaning back in her chair, eyes shut, deep in thought. Simon & Garfunkel's *I Am A Rock*, as descriptive of Old Jack's persona as it was, was reaching the point the ancient Romans called *ad nauseum*. Liz was getting sick and tired of that bloody song, for God's sake. Alden's slurred voice was barely comprehensible.

"Goddammit! You were SLAVES! SLAVES! I...er...aah."

Liz's eyes snapped open.

"Grandpa Jack!" she said. "What did you say?"

Alden lay there, staring at the ceiling, mouth open, a horrified look on his face. Without warning, he jerked up violently, raising himself on his right elbow and staring beyond the foot of the bed. His shaking left hand pointed at one of the large ornate armchairs against the far wall. Liz leapt up, turned, and looked hard in that direction, but there was nothing to be seen. The chair was entirely unoccupied. Alden stuttered, repeating Liz's question.

"Wh-what? Wh-what d-did..?"

"Grandpa Jack!" Liz shouted in alarm. "Who are you talking to? There's nobody there. There's nobody here but me."

"I...I...Aah...a rock! I am a rock."

The old man fell back, exhausted, and closed his eyes.

He grunted loudly. He snored. After a long while, Liz got up and left the room. She stood in the doorway looking back sadly toward the bed. *I Am A Rock* played on. And on. And on. Ad nauseum.

****

14

Lizzie Gets The Message

Back up in Alden's suite after dinner, the room was a little stuffy. The wind had dropped, and the raucous mynah birds had at last declared a moment of silence in memory of their fallen comrades, or at least that's what Liz, in her existentially depressed state, imagined they were doing. Bird by rowdy, squawking bird, a blessed silence descended. The roar of the stormy ocean was barely audible through the tightly closed

French doors leading out to the balcony. After she had opened one of the windows a crack, Liz sat by the bed, her hands on the bedcovers in front of her, staring at her grandfather intently. Something seemed different. The old man was more active tonight, more restless than he had been since her arrival. Were his eyes actually moving? Liz blinked and re-focused her gaze. Grandpa Jack's toothless mouth was moving, soundlessly. His dentures were in their usual spot, in the glass by the bedside.

Suddenly the old man croaked and tried, unsuccessfully, to raise himself up on one elbow. The words came out one by one, slurred, with long pauses in between.

"God... Dammit... Shellar... Urgent... Shea-chesht... Old... Shea-chesht... Cellar... May... Day... May... Day..."

"Grandpa Jack, are you trying to tell me there's something in the cellar?" Liz jumped to her feet and leaned over the bed toward the old man. "An old sea-chest? Did I get that right? In the cellar? Am I hearing you correctly?"

The taciturn Alden did not answer, but the owl seemed to have something to say on the matter. It hooted from one of the jarrah trees directly outside. Hoo hoo. Far in the distance, a second hoot came, faint, but distinctly affirmative. Alden had resumed his wide-eyed

106

catatonic posture. Somehow, Liz got the impression she had received the message correctly - if indeed it was a message. An old sea chest, down in the cellar? Thoughtfully, she wandered down the hall and prepared for bed.

*****

15

The First Nightmare

The digital clock by Liz's bedside read 11:17. Even though it was approaching midnight, it was surprisingly hot and humid. The house had been closed up all day. Liz sprawled on the bed in her white cotton underwear, her eyes wide open, the Stephen King novel, the cheerfully titled *MISERY*, inverted on her bare bosom. The sluggish overhead fan sent a cooling breeze down onto her sweaty, naked skin. She was thinking deeply. After a long while, she put the book aside, rolled over and put the light out. The owl she had been hearing each night had moved closer. It sounded as though it was directly outside her window. She thought she detected strains of creepy music in her inner ear, as she gradually drifted off to sleep and into a frightening nightmare.

Liz Nicholson, PhD, the 21st Century antiquities librarian and rather conservative mother of three, found herself on the outskirts of a 17th Century colonial village, transfixed and helpless. It was a hot, humid day in mid-June. A furtive band of painted Indian warriors emerged from the forest. They attacked and burned a settler family's simple wooden home. The heat from the blazing house was unbearable, but Liz stood there, paralyzed. Whooping joyfully, having the time of their lives, the youthful warriors were killing and scalping the unarmed occupants, who were dressed in Olde English clothing.

Strangely, there were no English men present. Apparently, Liz knew, they were off somewhere on important business. The warriors dragged the women and children out one by one, making sure that no one remained in the house. They left no one alive, not even the three infants, each of whom they picked up by the feet and smashed against the nearby tree trunks, laughing uproariously at the resulting gore. The braves carried gleaming new flintlock muskets, European hatchets and bloodstained scalping knives of shiny metal. When the house was completely engulfed in flames, and all of its former occupants lay dead and bleeding in the courtyard, the shrieking warriors rushed off to burn the neighboring house, half a mile away.

As soon as they were out of sight, a young Indian woman materialized from the forest, an utterly horrified look on her face. The girl ran right by Liz, weeping blindly, entered the burning house, and came out a moment later, choking and sobbing. Her hair was on fire. She clutched a large leather-bound bible to her bare bosom.

Liz felt as though she was being suffocated. Gradually, she emerged from the surreal dream, panting for breath and absolutely terrified. She lay there in the dark, listening to the rain in the trees outside. It was a few minutes after midnight and she was wide-awake. The owl had moved away. It hooted sadly in the far distance. Is there any sound more melancholy than that of a far-off owl in a dripping, rain-drenched forest in the middle of the night? She remembered hearing somewhere that the owl was a portent of death.

110

16

Lizzie Rents A Moke

In the morning, using her iPad to get online, Liz managed to rent a little blue Suzuki 'Moke' from the car rental place at the airport, and Washington drove her into Bridgetown to pick it up. Liz was still shaken by her nightmare, but she said nothing of it. The kindly man who wrote up her information had a nametag on his khaki shirt. 'Jefferson Franklin,' it read. He turned out to be Washington's cousin, the son of his father's sister.

The Moke was more Liz's style than the dented Porsche. The car rental place also offered electric mopeds. She had never heard of such a thing, and found the idea tempting, but she ended up with the cute powder blue Suzuki. Paging through back issues of a glossy tourist periodical back at Alden House, she planned her continued explorations of the twenty-one by fourteen mile Island.

"How big is the island of Barbados?" she had asked Washington a day or two earlier.

"Twenty-one miles long, and one smile wide," was his beaming answer. It was the standard response to that oft-asked question.

*****

17

Aftermath of a Nightmare

The date was Monday, November 16, 2020, her fourth day on the island. Liz was speaking on the house phone, returning Scilla's unanswered collect call, which was in response her own voicemail message two days earlier. The sisters finally spoke in person. Liz sat alone and under-dressed on the verandah, hugging her knees, shivering, gazing out at glimpses of the raging ocean through the furious, wind-whipped jarrah trees.

It was surprisingly chilly, wet and windy as hell. The storm was lifting, though. The worst was over, according to Washington, who kept careful track of such things on his battery-powered emergency radio.

"Scilla, listen to me. I haven't had that nightmare in ages. Not since I was ten. You remember the dreams I used to have? Mommy thought it was a past life memory? Me and you and Mommy being attacked by the Indians, just like in the movies. Of course I woke up every time and there were no Indians. This time it was different, though. It was really, really scary. I mean, it felt so real. I was there. I wanted to help them but I was utterly helpless. I couldn't move." Liz shuddered at the memory. "I still haven't gotten over the feeling I woke up with. It feels as if my world is ending. That's what was happening to the people in the dream. Their world was ending. I wonder what it means?" She paused and listened to Scilla's response.

"Anyway, about Dad. That's great, Pissy," she continued. "Goddammit, I've got to stop saying that. I mean Scilla. I'm so glad. I can't wait to see you. Really.

"You know, it's been a whole ten years since we last got together as a family. For a whole hour. Dumb idea, on my part, but at least we all tried. What a goddammed disaster that was. You didn't miss a damn thing. Next

114

time I'm coming with you to Hawaii." Liz listened, gazing out at the trees. The sun was starting to break through. She inhaled deeply, then went on, exhaling the words in a rush.

"Well, yeah. I know. This will definitely be the last Thanksgiving for this particular family constipation... I mean constellation. It's sad, but what can anyone do? When will any of us see each other again, after Grandpa's gone? Do any of us have anything in common? Maybe my life really is coming to an end? It feels that way sometimes.

"Well, I'd better get back inside. It's freezing out here. Can you believe it? Barbados, freezing? Hey, wait, did I tell you? I almost forgot. Grandpa Jack actually spoke to me last night. Well, not exactly, but he blurted out a bunch of disconnected words. Suddenly. Something about Indians and slaves. An old sea trunk in the cellar. Something like that."

*****

18

The Haunted Cellar

Neither Gladys nor Washington would go near the cellar. The place was haunted, everybody knew that, but the nurse was not afraid of ghosts and neither was Liz. They were made of sterner stuff.

"Why would anyone be afraid of something that does not exist?" Barbara wondered out loud. Opening the groaning, centuries-old mahogany plank door to the cellar, Liz peered in. A musty smell greeted her. It was as dark as Hades down there. The two women inched their way hesitantly down the rickety, creaking steps, Liz in

116

the lead. They stopped halfway down. Liz groped for the light switch. There was no such thing. They didn't have light switches back in 1659. The cellar was pitch dark and musty and dank, and there was no electricity. Even in broad daylight, they'd need a lantern, or an extension cord from upstairs. They went in search of Washington.

Needless to say, the resourceful Jack-of-all-trades had a supply of kerosene-fueled hurricane lanterns on a shelf in the main garage, and it didn't take him long to set up a pair of them. To no one's surprise, once the two women were down in the ancient, dirt-floored cellar and their eyes had grown accustomed to the gloom, there were no ghosts. The cellar ceiling was very low, and it was challenging to move around because of all the old furniture randomly stacked everywhere.

On their first foray the women found no sign of anything resembling a trunk or a sea chest. The nearest thing was a small wooden toolbox. If there was a sea chest in the cellar, it was buried all the way in the back, behind dozens, if not hundreds, of items of dust-and-mould-covered antique furniture. Everything was draped in moldy, dusty old sheets or canvas tarpaulins and festooned with several centuries' worth of cobwebs. Liz was the first to call it quits.

"Ugh," she shuddered. "I hate cobwebs. What the

fuck is a cob, anyway, and why the hell does it need a web? This reminds me of Halloween minus the fun. This is impossible, Barb. Let's get the hell out of here."

"It's going to be a bit of a job," the nurse agreed.

"That's the understatement of the century. We'll have to get everything out onto the lawn. It'll take a crew. I'll ask Washington if he can arrange something."

"No wonder no one's been down here for a hundred years."

"A hundred years?"

"That's what Gladys told me. This cellar is haunted, according to local legend. Something to do with the slave rebellions."

"Hmmm. Slaves? Grandpa Jack was shouting something or other about slaves just last night. Interesting..."

*****

19

Consulting With The Rastamen

Washington backed his pristine 1956 English Ford 'Angular' out of his personal storage barn by the organic garden next to the old slave quarters. He drove into town, and sat down with a group of dreadlocked local island men sitting on a park bench near the marina. They were passing round an aromatic spliff and listening to reggae music on a portable boombox. The men were not exactly tempted by his offer. Apparently, Washington had a nickname among the locals.

"Naah! No way, Wash Cloth! You know dat. You t'ink I crazy? I no going down dat spooky beesment! Not for any moneys, mon! You know what dey got down dere? Skellingtons, dat's what dey got. Skellingtons."

Washington adopted the Rasta patois, and replied, "Skellingtons? Where you get dat idea, Freddie? I ain't hear dat. Some say dat ol' Spanish pirate treasure down dere. Gold doubloons an' stuff. That what them gho-asts be guarding. Me, I don' know. My Daddy say ain't nobody been down in dat hole for a hundred years before he was borned."

"I ain't goin' down there neither. Not for nothin'. You gotta find somebody who don't know..." The second Rastaman stopped in mid-sentence. "Yo, Wash. Listen up, mon. I jus' got a idea. Ah always know I a genius. How about dem crazy new Sout' African fellas?" He pointed toward the nearby marina. A forest of sail-boat masts stuck up above the low rooflines.

"Dey jus' come in last week, got pretty beat up on de crossing. I hear dem outta money. Maybe dem do de job, if'n you don't tell dem nuthin' bout dem go-ats."

"Go-ats? Not go-ats, mon, gho-asts." The first Rastaman reacted impatiently. "Peoples dey die down dere, mon. Slaves. Back in de old day. Dead peoples. Gho-asts. Spooky 'tings. My mama tol' me when I jus' a

120

little pickaninny."

The third Rastaman, the acknowledged Wise Elder of the group, a decade older than the others, chimed in, exhaling a cloud of aromatic smoke as the words came out.

"Get dem Sout' Africans beeg jug-a-rum," he wheezed. "A gallon a Mount Gay. Den dey do de job, no question asked. Yo ho ho a bottle a rum! Go-ats or no go-ats."

Freddie, the first Rastaman, was not amused.

"What I tol' you, mon? Go-ats? Not go-ats, mon! Gho-asts."

"Zackly what I say, mon." The third Rastaman chuckled happily. "Go-ats. I's pullin' yo chain Freddie, I know de difference believe me when I tell you, but I enjoy to see you get all upsettled. Pass dat spliff, mon. What your name? Humphrey Bogart? What? I already got it?" He held the spliff up for all to see. "Oh, I forgotted."

*****

20

The South Africans

I t was getting close to sunset as Washington piloted the dented '59 Porsche down to the Bridgetown yacht harbor. He handled the car effortlessly.

"Got to give this poor baby a little exercise." His eyes twinkled. "And make sure it's still behavin' mechanically after its little adventure the other day."

Liz sat in the passenger seat gazing out, as glimpses of angry ocean flashed by. Another storm was moving in. It would be raining by nightfall. Again. She updated the driver on the recent developments.

"Thanksgiving plans are coming along nicely, Washington. Did Gladys tell you? My father has relented. He's coming, believe it or not. Scilla and her quote-unquote best friend Maryah are on their way. It wasn't easy. Scilla always refused to take any money from the family, now she had to beg our dad for their airfare."

On a once-white, rust-streaked, decrepit 66-foot steel ketch with the mysterious name *Tokoloshe*, the rigging clattering in the gusty wind, Liz and Washington politely declined the offer of a traditional South African libation called a double cane and Coke and talked the rough-and-ready crew into making a few quick bucks. The four friends had earned a bunch of money working in the motion picture industry back home, and had purchased the boat with the pooled proceeds. Now they were sailing round the world, but they were already out of cash. They were less than a quarter of the way round. As they had discovered to their chagrin, the definition of an ocean-going sailboat is 'a great big hole in the water into which the owners pour money.'

"Cash? Of course. United States dollars, if that's OK." Liz stood up, narrowly avoiding bashing her head on the main boom. She smiled and shook hands all round.

"Tomorrow it is, then! As early as you like. I'll have

coffee ready. You'll need dust masks! Can you pick some up? One for me, too. Some big trash bags as well. Those big black construction ones? And some gloves. Keep the receipt. I'll reimburse you. No, wait, on second thoughts." Liz reached into the rear pocket of her white denim jeans. "Here's a hundred dollar bill, American. They'll accept that, won't they?"

"Next stop, the nearest ATM machine, to withdraw some cash for the guys tomorrow," said Liz, as the Porsche growled off into the rush-hour traffic. At the bank, she discovered that she had left her wallet back at the house.

"Ooops," she said. "Oh well, it will have to wait until tomorrow."

*****

21

Discovery Day

The enthusiastic Afrikaans foursome showed up in a taxi-van at the bottom of the driveway just as the sun was heaving itself out of the ocean beyond the jarrah trees and the fragrant frangipanis. Within minutes of their arrival, the sun disappeared behind a huge bank of cumulo-nimbus clouds and it began to spatter with rain. Donning dust masks and goggles and paper painter's hats in the dim lantern-light, with Liz directing the operation, the four men tore into the cellar, moving each and every piece of furniture and re-arranging everything as best they could. The dim light of four smoky paraffin lamps imparted a rather spooky atmosphere to the proceedings. After a while, they all looked like ghosts, covered in dust and cobwebs.

Despite the ominous clouds at sunrise, the rain did not materialize. Liz and the filthy, dusty, exuberant South Africans ate lunch on the verandah. Gladys served the food, after politely turning down an invitation to join them. It was a big meal, with no shortage of Lion Ale, South Africa's traditional beer, to the ecstatic delight of the men. If Liz had understood their private exchanges in their gutteral language, she would have realized that they had not had a square meal in a while.

As they wolfed down Gladys's gourmet concoctions, the men told their stories, the wacky science-fiction movies they had worked on back home, and a tall tale about sharks and crocodiles fighting to the death in the Zambezi River, hundreds of miles from the Indian Ocean. More than anything they wanted to know about the plantation and the Alden family. What was so important about this old sea trunk they were looking for? Did it have anything to do with Captain Kidd, by any remote chance?

"Later, guys," said Liz. "First let's find the famous sea

chest. If indeed there's any such thing down there."

While Liz and the South Africans were focused on the contents of an ancient, dark and musty cellar on the island of Barbados, not far from the north coast of South America, two related events were unfolding on the far side of the planet, events that would soon have an impact on our story.

Two young women were in the process of boarding a crowded American Airlines Airbus 360 at Honolulu International Airport on the Pacific island of Oahu. The morning sun was high over the ocean. As Scilla and Maryah Barnes buckled themselves into their seats, the African-American girl remembered something. She got up, opened the overhead bin, and sat down again holding a book she had just purchased to read on the long flight ahead. Scilla took the book and examined the cover. It was a paperback edition of Nathaniel Philbrick's best-selling non-fiction work "Mayflower."

At precisely the same moment, two well-dressed men, a generation older than the girls, were busy boarding their plane on the outskirts of Sydney, Australia. The outer circumstances were quite different, but a phenomenon that Carl Gustav Jung would have called a 'synchronicity' was unfolding. As the gleaming private jet rolled out of the hangar, John and James Alten buckled themselves into their seats and prepared for takeoff. The rising sun was reflecting off the Opera House. The steward brought the over-weight, balding older man his gin and tonic. James remembered something suddenly. He reached below his seat, rummaged in his backpack, and straightened up with a newly purchased book in his hand. The older member of the couple reached over and took the book from his companion's hand. "What the fuck?" he muttered, making a sour face. "Couldn't you find something a little more interesting, Jimmy?" The book was a paperback edition of Nathaniel Philbrick's bestselling work 'Mayflower.'

*****

22

A Waste of Bloody Time

Back down in the ancient cellar with its low, cobweb-festooned beams and uneven earthen floor, it was getting late. With a little help from Washington, who spent the afternoon outside on the lawn, the men had managed to open a grade-level window and had hacksawed the padlock off the old wooden hatch to the outside world. The light was much better, and the air a lot less musty. The weather had cleared and the low sun was preparing to go down behind the mountains to the west.

For the past hour or more sunlight had penetrated the cellar, for the first time in how many centuries? Everything had been moved, dusted off, examined for any resemblance to an old sea trunk, and covered up again with the same yellowed old linen sheets, after the latter had been handed outside to the dust-masked Washington for a long-over-due shaking.

There was now a clear path between the stairs up to the kitchen and the wide open hatch to the outside world and the setting sun. Washington had peered in through the hatch from time to time, but he would not come down into the cellar itself. He shook out the linen sheets as the men passed them up to him, and handed them back down, sneezing profusely all the while.

Gladys, as far as Liz could tell, had spent most of the day hovering around the cellar door up in the kitchen. All afternoon the excitement had been palpable, but gradually the sad truth had dawned on Liz, and the others were not far behind her. There was no sign of anything remotely resembling a sea chest. What a let-down. Frustration reigned. It was time to give up, pay the men, give them another Lion Ale each and send them on their way with the unopened gallon jug of Mount Gay rum as a bonus. What a waste of time and money!

Liz took off her dust mask and goggles and shook her hair free of the scarf. The goggles left a white impression in the midst of her filthy, frustrated face, giving her a somewhat reverse raccoon-like look. If one were to project a negative photograph of a raccoon onto a freckled brick wall, it wouldn't look in the least like Lizzie, but you get the general idea.

"That's enough, gentlemen. There's nothing here. I'm so sorry. What an absolute waste of time. What was I thinking? Let's get out of here, for God's sake. I can barely breathe."

The four men, cobweb-encrusted and covered in grime, needed no further encouragement. They moved as one toward the cellar stairs. They couldn't wait for payday and half-a-dozen beers to wash down the grit in their throats. As an afterthought, Liz said,

"Gerry, before you come up, would you mind closing the hatch to the outside world? It might rain again, and we don't..."

*****

24

It Came Over With Columbus

Liz slouched up the creaking steps to the kitchen, profoundly disappointed, embarrassed even, at the futility of her ridiculous mission. Gerry turned and made his way back across the cellar, stooping low to avoid hitting his head. He closed the window and bolted the ancient wooden hatch, turned, and followed his mates, anxious for a beer. Suddenly, he stopped in his tracks, his eyebrows rising above his goggles and into his receding hairline.

"Hey! Wazzat?" he whispered hoarsely. "You hear that? Shhh!"

Fritz, halfway up to the kitchen, stopped. He started back down the stairs. Liz hesitated, then turned and followed him. The other two stopped, crammed into the narrow stairwell, uncertain as to what they should do.

"Stomp again, Gerry," called Fritz. "Shhh! Listen blokes! It's blerry hollow, hey?" Fritz held up a hand and everyone fell silent. "Hear that? Look! There under the rubble – See that? It's a blerry trapdoor, I swear, just the very edge of it. Shit man... Sorry Miss. Someone get a blerry spade, hey?"

"Did you got a shovel anywhere, Missus?"

"How about the dust pan?" Liz suggested.

"That'll do, Miss. Ag, look, there's a blerry crowbar, hey. Perfect. Move over, man."

Once the sand covering the trapdoor had been scraped off, the rusty old crowbar did the job. The heavy wooden slab came up with a loud creak, to reveal an utterly black void below. A waft of cold musty air exploded into the cellar, accompanied by the distinct sound of dripping water. There was an unpleasant aroma, the kind one might encounter down in the catacombs under Paris or Rome. Hesitantly, Fritz lowered himself down the rotting wooden ladder. Gerry handed one of the kerosene lanterns down to him. Everyone gathered round the hole, including the other two members of the crew, who had returned to the cellar to see what all the fuss was about. They stood in a circle, peering down into the darkness. Fritz's eyes took a few moments to adjust, then he yelled.

"Bingo! Ah sees it! Jesus H. Christ, man, I think this blerry box musta came over with Christopher Columbus on that blerry *Mayflower* ferry-boat, hey?"

Fritz's pronunciation of the word 'Christ' came out sounding like 'Kraas.' Liz's eyebrows went up at the Columbus/Mayflower conflation. And, for those cultur-ally-deprived readers who don't know, the mild English curse-word 'bloody,' when spoken by an Afrikaner, comes out sounding like 'blerry.' The original derivation (the author apologizes to those already in the know) of the British colloquialism 'bloody' was 'by Our Lady,' as in the blessed Virgin Mary.

"Thou shalt not take the name of the Lord thy God in vain," said Moses. As to taking the Virgin's name in vain, the prophet was silent, which was entirely reason-able, considering that Moses died some two thousand years before the Virgin Mary was born. It would be a little unfair to accuse the poor fellow of gender bias.

On a ledge carved into the earthen wall of the hole,

barely visible in the gloom filtering down from above
and the flickering light from the smoke-blackened
lantern, Fritz gazed at a decrepit old leather-bound sea-
chest, amid untidy stacks of moldy, moth-eaten blankets
and boots and miscellaneous objects whose purpose was
not immediately clear. The place smelled like a mausoleum, the reason for which would gradually become
clear, as Fritz's eyes adjusted to the darkness. Fritz yelled
up at the four silhouettes gazing down at him.

"I'll start passing stuff up, hey?"
Liz thought about it for less than a second.

"Just the trunk, for now, Fritz," she said. "We'll look
at the other things later."

The heavy sea chest came up, an ancient leather-
bound steamer trunk with rusted iron corners. It wasn't
easy. The thing creaked and twisted, threatening to
disgorge its contents prematurely. It was literally falling
apart at the seams. Once it was safely in the hands of his
mates, Fritz stepped back into the dungeon-like space
and took one last look around. His blood went cold. He
let out a deafening shriek of terror and dropped the
lantern, which promptly went out. His eyes had adjusted
to the darkness and for the first time he had discerned
the stack of skeletons piled against the far dirt wall. He
leapt up out of the hole in a single bound, the ancient

wooden rungs disintegrating one-by-one as he ascended. Pushing his mates out of the way, he scrabbled his way back to the relative safety of the cellar floor, and hastily dragged the trapdoor back over the gaping hole, his face ashen, although it was hard to tell with all the dust. Wordlessly panting, his eyes wide with panic, he pulled a heavy dresser over the trapdoor.

"What? You OK, Fritzie boy?"

"You see a ghost down there, or what, hey?"
Fritz got his voice back.

"Skeletons, man," he panted. "A whole *donderse* pile of blerry skeletons. Staring right at me. They's alive, man. One of them's got blue eyes, even."He stopped. "Ag shit okies, I think I has pooped my pants."
Frikkie wrinkled his nose.

"So that's what that awful stink is, hey?"
Fritz was breathing hard.

"Please, lady, can we just get paid and go home now?"
Gerry turned to Liz.

"It's helluva heavy, hey? Shall I open it up, Missus?"
Liz wiped her bleary eyes with the backs of her filthy hands, adding a layer of black to the white outlines. She looked like an extra from one of Michael Jackson's famous zombie videos.

"No, no, thank you," she sighed, holding her nose and hurrying up the stairs to the kitchen. "Sufficient unto the day. Enough is enough. Just leave it there on the table. Let's call it a wrap, clean up and get out of here, shall we? It's been a long day." She wrinkled her nose. "Fritz, there's a bathroom at the top of the kitchen stairs, if you'd like to make use of it."

Liz hurried to the far side of the kitchen, exhaled at last, and took a deep breath. She let out a burst of joy.

"Well done, gentlemen! Can you believe it? It's time to celebrate! Let's open that jug of Mount Gay. I make a mean piña colada if anyone's interested. You have certainly earned your keep. And by the way, gentlemen, Columbus did not sail the ocean blue on the *Mayflower*, in 1492 or in any other year. For the sake of hysterical accuracy, you know."

The four men stopped, jammed into the cellar doorway. They stared at Liz uncomprehendingly, then swarmed clumsily into the kitchen, glad to put some distance between themselves and that god-awful hole in the cellar floor. It had indeed been a long day. Gladys backed off in alarm at the sight of the four figures, who really did look like ghosts.

"Piña contada? Whazzat? A stiff blerry rum and Coke is what I needs right now. Two doubles, asseblief!!

Please! One for each hand," Fritz called from the bathroom, his voice still shaking. Liz didn't have any Coke. Coca Cola is not organic. Emerging from the bathroom a few minutes later, Fritz helped himself to two double Mount Gay shots and downed them straight, as Liz went about preparing the piña coladas.

*****

25

Liz Gets Plastered

Alone at last. Whew. What a day! The sun had gone down behind the coastal mountains, the colorful sunset was fading, and the men were gone. The landscaper had happened to stop by to pick up his monthly check, and was kind enough to offer the filthy, aromatic South Africans a lift back to the marina. Perfect timing. Unfortunately, Liz had been unable to pay the men. She had yet to make it to the bank, having completely forgotten about it. The poor fellows had to take it on trust that Washington would indeed deliver the cash to the *Tokoloshe* the following day. They were, after all, illegal aliens with no work permits, and had no alternative.

Liz was sitting out on the verandah, bombed out of her gourd on the fresh state-of-the-art Mount Gay piña coladas she had prepared for the men, before they suddenly ran out on her. It would have been a terrible waste to pour the precious mixture down the sink. Her New England upbringing proscribed such displays of extravagance and waste. Her hair was still damp from the shower. Gladys brought the tea tray, then hovered at the top of the verandah steps, waiting to see if Liz wanted anything else. The last of the light was fading from the western sky. The melancholy owl was back, hooting from half a mile away.

Barbara emerged from the house. She had settled her patient down for the night, after spending the previous night and day in town and returning to Alden House while everyone was still down in the cellar. The nurse stood for a while gazing out at the luminous sky, then went down to the lawn and lit a cigarette. Five minutes later she came over to the table and sat down.

"That was my last cigarette," she announced, firmly, in her prissy English way. "I'm quitting."

"Siddown, Barb." Liz's voice was slurred. "I've saved you a piña colada or three. The ice has all melted, so it's not quite as strong as it used to be. Ooh, that has the makings of a poem, doesn't it?" She giggled.

As Barbara helped herself to a generous glass of the cream-colored concoction, and the aroma of coconut wafted through the evening air, Gladys said suddenly,

"There he is again. The owl. Hear him? He has a message for us. Someone is going to die." They listened. The owl did not repeat his call. Liz broke the silence.

"Well, that makes sense under the circumstances, does it not? That's what the American Indians say, as well." She looked up at the big Bajan woman. "Goodnight Gladys. Don't worry about the mess. Barbara and I will clean up. Won't we, Barb? Say goodnight to Washington for me, and oh, tell him we found the trunk. The old sea-chest. Right after he left."

Somehow, Gladys had not realized that the trunk had been discovered. She tried not to seem surprised, but her eyes lit up like catherine wheels against the golden brown of her face. The owl hooted again.

"The old treasure chest? The Spanish doubloons? My husband will be so excited. Oh, by the way. Hear that? The owl. It can also be telling us to expect a visitation. A ghost is coming."

"Treasure chests? Owls, skeletons, and now ghosts? The plot thickens," muttered Liz, under her breath.

"A ghost?" she said out loud. "Just what we need to complete the mix. Sounds like a Stephen King thing. Thanks for everything, dear Gladys. Go get some sleep will you? We've got a busy week coming up. You need your beauty rest, just like the rest of us."

Liz couldn't wait to share her discovery with someone who might just understand its significance.

"Barbara, you won't believe it. We actually accomplished something on your day off. We found the bloody sea-chest. It was in a cunningly concealed sub-cellar that nobody knew anything about. That old trunk must have been down there forever. It's an old leather sailor's chest that looks like it came over with Columbus. That's what one of the workers said. On the *Mayflower*, no less. Can you believe it?"

"The trunk came over on the *Mayflower*? Is that what you said?" Barbara was puzzled. "What was in it? The famous pirate treasure?"

"I don't know yet," Liz laughed. "Either Spanish doubloons or a bunch of old bricks. It's heavy enough to be either. But the goddamn thing's locked. There's a huge old rusty padlock on it. Good luck finding the key. Unless... No. I'll go back down and break it open tomorrow. There's no rush, now that we've actually found the goddamned thing." Liz poured tea for each of them. Teacup in one hand and piña colada in the other, Barbara looked tired. So did Liz.

"Speaking of the *Mayflower*, what are you doing for Thanksgiving, Barbara?"

"What am I doing for Thanksgiving? What does that have to do with the *Mayflower*? You lost me there. I'm English, in case you hadn't noticed. We don't have Thanksgiving in Nottinghamshire. We have Harvest Festival. We have Michaelmas. We just had Guy Fawkes Day. I don't even know what your Thanksgiving's all about, really. Turkeys and Indians or something. Something about the *Mayflower*? Or did you say that was Columbus? I really haven't paid much attention to American history. It's all very confusing."

"Oh right. You poor thing. Thanksgiving's my favorite holiday, or at least it used to be back when..." Liz hesitated, remembering. "When I was a little girl, the whole fam damily used to gather down here each and every year. We'd come in from wherever we were, all over the world, and... Here at this beautiful old house. On this beautiful stretch of tropical coastline. It was literally my idea of paradise. Please join us, if you don't have other plans."

"I don't know, Liz. Really. I'd feel like an outsider. But thank you all the same."

"Well, guess what, Barbara dear? You're family now, like it or not. Oh, and by the way, this is a very special Thanksgiving. The *Mayflower* arrived exactly 400 years ago and there's a huge kerfuffle going on up in the States."

"Actually, I saw something about that on the Beeb the other night, believe it or not. The BBC. They're making quite a fuss back home in England. The royal family has put up a huge sum of money. My sister lives in Plymouth, Plymouth England, that is. I hear you Americans have a Plymouth of your own these days. She, my sister that is, she's been on some kind of committee for the past... May I think about it? That's next Thursday if I'm not mistaken. I'll be here anyway."

"Well, you're invited, Barb. You'll be very welcome, if you'd like to join us. The family's coming together for the first time in I don't know how long. Probably be the last time, too.

"I get the impression..." Barbara thought better of it. She did not finish the sentence. She drained her second piña colada, slurped down the rest of her tea, said her goodnights, and a little unsteadily, disappeared into the house. A few minutes later, Liz followed her up the stairs, more than a little inebriated. She was whacked.

26

We Found It, Grandpa Jack

Liz sat half-asleep by Alden's ultra-king-sized bed. The piña colada had knocked her out. It was 9:58 p.m. on the bedside clock. The dim antique lamps glowed on the priceless inlaid end-tables on either side of the bed, barely illuminating the thousand-year-old Persian rugs on the floor. Simon & Garfunkel's *I Am A Rock* provided a gentle but repetitive and increasingly annoying soundtrack. Alden lay there, neatly tucked-in, his arms over the bedcovers, in exactly the same position as always. He must have moved, for Heaven's sake. How did he eat, drink, perform his bodily functions? Do Gladys and Barbara place him in exactly the same position every day, in the perfectly-made bed wearing the same perfectly-ironed pajamas? To the highest standards of theatrical perfection? With his thinning hair always perfectly pomaded? Or was she imagining it?

"Remind me to ask Gladys," Liz muttered to herself, as her head nodded on her chest.

Alden was dozing. His shallow breath came and went softly. A long time passed. What was going on in that once-brilliant old mind of his? Where was he? Was he dreaming, Liz wondered, half-dreaming herself.

Suddenly the old man jerked convulsively. He spoke in a slow, jerky, slurred, but urgent voice. "God... dammit!" he croaked. "Mayday! Sea chest. Old sea chest. God... dammit! Now! Not... one... moment... to lose." Liz snapped awake and gaped at the old man drunkenly.

"We found it, Grandpa Jack. We found it. We found the sea chest. It was so deeply buried, we almost missed it. There's a whole 'nother cellar down there. Containing a pile of skeletons as an added bonus, mind you."
Alden turned his head and glared at Liz. It was the first time he had looked at her since her arrival almost a week earlier. His rheumy eyes bored into her. They were

146

manic under the bushy eyebrows. They brought to Liz's inebriated mind the epic Coleridge poem.

It is an Ancient Mariner,
and he stoppeth one of three.
By thy long grey beard and glittering eye,
now wherefor stopp'st thou me?

The Simon & Garfunkel song was suddenly loud enough to rattle the walls, although the volume could not possibly have changed. Could it?

"I'll go back down and open it tomorrow, when it's light." Liz had to raise her voice over the thunderous music.

"No!" the well-dressed cadaver gasped, raising a bony claw and pointing his crooked, commanding forefinger at his intoxicated granddaughter.

"No! Now! Urgent. May...Day... Not one... God...Damned...moment..." Alden subsided onto the pillows, exhausted. He panted like a drowning man. The music resumed its normal volume. The building stopped shaking.

"Grandpa, I said I'll get to it first thing in the morning. It's been a long day. You have no idea. I'm exhausted. Exhausted and drunk!" she muttered out loud.

Alden stared at the ceiling as though reading some

147

profound revelation inscribed there. His expression was frantic. After a while he gradually let go and relaxed and closed his eyes. His breathing slowed down, and he seemed to have fallen asleep. *I Am A Rock* started over, softly. The song played on, incessantly. Liz planted a kiss on her grandfather's outstretched hand, folded the exposed arm under the bedcovers, and headed for the stairs. Before leaving Alden's room, Liz went over to the stereo system, planning to take the CD player off repeat. No such luck. The little door-thingy refused to cooperate. Finally, she pressed the power button and a blessed silence descended. On cue, the owl hooted outside.

"Hoo hoo!"

Out in the dimly lit hallway, Liz could see that Barbara had gone to bed. The light under her door was off, and the house was as still as the grave. The grave? Liz's mind went to the skeletons, allegedly not twenty-five feet beneath her. The house *was* a grave, for fuck's sake. She stopped and stared down at the floor. She had not given the skeletons a thought since the terrified South African fellow, what was his name, had slammed the trapdoor shut and pulled some heavy furniture on top of it - as though that would keep the ghosts from filtering up through the cracks.

The owl hooted again. There was another owl, afar

148

off, answering the first. Hoo hoo. Hoo hoo. Resisting the temptation to head straight for bed and collapse, Liz staggered back down to the living room, hanging onto the curving mahogany balustrade for dear life.

*****

27

Relax, She Cried

Liz plonked herself down on one of the luxurious red Spanish leather sofas in the expansive living-room with its mahogany-paneled walls and its 14-foot ceilings, picked up the remote control for the giant-screen television, and stared at the device as though it was the first time she'd ever seen such a thing. The world was rocking alarmingly. Instead of putting on the electric lights, for some reason, Gladys had lit three large candles in tall glass containers covered in religious iconography, and lined them up on the glass-topped coffee table, before abandoning the house to the spirits of the night.

"Relax, Goddammit!" Liz instructed herself, at the top of her voice. She took a deep breath and relaxed - for all of thirty seconds. She exhaled forcefully, letting out a loud exasperated sigh, then bounced back up, dropped the remote onto the coffee table, and walked swiftly into the kitchen. Her stride, although it would fail a drunk-driving test, had a sudden sense of purpose to it. She rummaged in a drawer, found some matches, rekindled one of the kerosene hurricane lanterns, and opened the creaking door to the cellar.

For the first time since Liz's arrival on the island, the house phone rang, loudly. Ignoring the insistent sound, she made her way carefully down the rickety steps, hung the flickering lantern with its soot-blackened glass on a bent nail in the low cellar ceiling and stood there, suddenly uncertain, looking down at the decrepit old sea chest which the men had placed on a rusted wrought-iron garden table before they had beat their hasty retreat. The trunk smelled awful. The mold-encrusted leather was cracked and curling, on the very verge of disintegration. Hesitantly, Liz reached out a hand and touched the ancient trunk, half expecting an electric shock. Nothing happened. Emboldened, she rattled the heavy antique padlock, but it was either locked or it was rusted shut. She remembered the skeletons, just a few feet beneath her silly slippers, the ones Layla had given her years ago. Were they really alive, the skeletons, as Fritz had imagined in his terror?

There was a sudden distinct sound behind Liz. She froze, the little hairs on her neck standing on end. The stairs creaked. A scuffle. Rats? A ghost? A footstep at the bottom of the stairs. The skeletons, come to life? Liz was not alone. Slowly she turned, hand to mouth, glancing from side to side in the impenetrable darkness, wondering which way to flee. There was no way out, other than the way she had come. She fought an overwhelming urge to pee her pants. Slowly, the silhouette at the bottom of the stairs came into focus.

"Oh it's you." Liz exhaled in a long sigh of relief. She took the lantern from its hook. "I thought you'd gone to bed. You startled me. In fact you scared the living be-jeezus out of me. What are you doing down here, for God's sake?"

Barbara, the English nurse, was holding up the hem of her ankle-length nightgown to keep it out of the dirt. Her knees, Liz could not help noticing, were red and chapped, like those of a Mexican religious mendicant she had once watched in Chiapas.

"Sorry. The cellar door was open," the nurse said. "I thought you were going to wait until the morning."

"Well, I'm curious, Barb. Actually, I'm sort of excited, for some unknown reason. It's not every day that one comes across an ancient treasure chest, is it? This thing is really, really old. It belongs in a museum. It's literally old enough to have come over on the *Mayflower*, I think. Except the *Mayflower* never came anywhere near Barbados. Needless to say." Liz paused for breath. She had been hyperventilating. She went on, gushing a little. "I can't help wondering what's in it. Washington says, well, he thinks it might be a lost treasure chest. There's an old legend. Pirates, Spanish doubloons etcetera."

"I know. You've told me a dozen times, Liz. I was the first one down here with you, don't you remember?" Barbara paused. "This is an exciting discovery indeed. Be that as it may, I came looking for you. Didn't you hear the telephone ring? It was... Your sister, Scilla, she phoned a moment ago. She reversed the charges. I accepted the call. I hope that was the right thing to do? She and her friend, what's her name, Mary? Maria? They're on their way. They'll be here tomorrow. And your father's on his way, too. She'll email you their itinerary from the airport in Atlanta."

"Thank you, Barbara. That's all good news. Well, it looks like I'm going to need some tools to open this thing. Or a goddamned locksmith. Perhaps Washington will help me, if I can ever persuade him to come down here. These locals are so superstitious. Although, having found those skeletons... I'm not sure I blame them. Oh well, I'm going up to bed. It's been a long and dusty day. My sinuses are still..."

"Skeletons, Liz? You didn't say skeletons, did you?"

"I'll tell you all about it in the morning, if that's OK with you. I'm going to bed."

Liz followed Barbara back up the creaking steps. The light of the lantern disappeared as the cellar door closed behind them. Impenetrable darkness resumed. Had this been a Hollywood movie, the reader would have heard a burst of ominous music, but as it was, Alden House was silent, as still as the grave. Liz blew out the candles in the livingroom and crept slowly on up the winding stairs to bed.

*****

28

The Bedside Clock

The time was 11:17, according to Liz's bedside clock. It was the second night in a row that she had noted the identical digits. While the clock's digital readout said 11:17, 11:17 also happened to be today's date. It was 11:17 on 11.17.2020, coincidentally, if there is any such thing as coincidence. Today's date, Liz realised, was November the 17th, James Nicholson's birthday, may the poor, sweet, dead epidemiologist rest in peace. Liz had completely lost track of the days.

James, sweet baby James, would have been...how old? Try as she might, she couldn't remember how old James would have been today, had the evil fish not stripped the flesh from his skinny bones in that icy lake somewhere northwest of Rochester, New York.

Liz could not get off to sleep. She rolled over and put the light back on, tried to read the *Misery* book, gave up miserably. She just couldn't concentrate. In frustration, she flung the book across the room. It lay where it fell, the shiny embossed title on the cover reflecting a sliver of light from the wall-sconce in the hall outside the open bedroom door. Misery, indeed.

"No wonder I've never read anything by Stephen King," she muttered to anyone within earshot. She closed her eyes and lay there, wide awake, fulminating against she knew not what. She felt as though she were being sucked backwards into a black hole that smelled like a mausoleum.

"Fuck," Liz Nicholson said. She spelled the word out loud. "P-h-u-q-u-e! Fuck. Goddamn, Henry, this is getting ridiculous. Beyond ridiculous." Rather than talking to herself this time, Liz was addressing her life-long imaginary friend, Henry David Thoreau, the 19th Century American tiny-house-dwelling transcendentalist of *Walden* fame. She sighed, swung her bare feet off the bed, pulled on the silly pink slippers with the bunny-rabbit ears, after fishing one of them out from under the bed where it had done its best to escape, proceeded downstairs in her flapping, flowery chiffon nightgown to the kitchen, rummaged about in the capacious drawers below the granite counters, and came up with a large, murderous-looking butcher's knife. She refilled and rekindled the kerosene lantern.

"God, that glass needs a good cleaning," she said to herself. "Later for that."

Liz turned, armed and ready for action, and caught a glimpse of herself reflected in the glass cabinet windows opposite the sink. Her hair was a mess. She looked absolutely ridiculous, nothing like the intrepid female Indiana Jones of her fevered imagination.

*****

29

A Slave's Pitiful Possessions

Back down in the musty cellar, Liz stood there looking down at the ancient sailors' trunk. The light was lurching about dimly, as the lantern swung on its hook. She took a deep breath, then awkwardly but determinedly had a go at the latch with the heavy butcher's knife. No luck. She tried again. Nothing doing. She looked at the knife, bewildered. It was the wrong tool for the job. Stabbing a padlock? What was she thinking?

"Dumb bitch," she chastised herself.

Her eye fell on the old toolbox. A small, rusty crowbar came to hand, the kind that comes in useful for getting nails out of horses' hooves, if you happen to have a horse with an unwanted nail in its hoof. She pried clumsily, and *voila!* The latch itself almost immediately crumbled to powder and broke apart in a sudden cascading shower of disintegrating ferrous oxide. The heavy iron padlock, unopened, fell to the earthen floor with a dull thud and rolled noisily over onto the edge of the trapdoor before coming to a rattling halt, an inch from her unprotected right foot. She looked at her hand, realized she was shaking. Her thumb was bleeding, though she did not remember cutting herself. She dropped the crowbar, narrowly missing her slipper-clad toes.

"Calm down, you silly girl. Breathe. It's only a couple of million dollars worth of Spanish doubloons, after all. I mean, really. What's all the fuss about?"

With some difficulty, Liz managed to open the creaking lid and wrestle it into the upright position. There was the faint aroma of ancient organic material, long decomposed. Needless to say, Murphy's Law was in operation. The Law states that when you have a 50% chance of being correct, you have a 100% chance of being wrong. Such, sad to say, is the luck of the Irish.

159

Your toast will land butter-side down, every single time, statistical probabilities be damned. The lantern was on the wrong side of the trunk and the lid shadowed its contents. There was absolutely nothing to be seen.

Closing the lid again, her hands shaking uncontrollably, Liz rotated the heavy chest a hundred and eighty degrees, very nearly tipping it off its precarious support. Taking a deep breath, she opened the lid once more. Five minutes later, the interior of the trunk was lit by the dimmest of flickers from the smoky lantern. What was in the trunk?

Liz blinked and rubbed her eyes. The uppermost item looked like an old sailor's peacoat. A very old sailor's peacoat. Once black, it was grey with mold, and tightly folded. Trembling violently, Liz lifted the heavy wool coat and set it aside. What glittering sight met her bloodshot eyes? Hundreds and hundreds of shining gold coins, gleaming in the flickering lamplight.

Well no, not exactly. There were more items of clothing, completely rotten. They fell apart as Liz lifted them and set them aside. Three mismatched antique woman's shoes. A pair of decrepit old boots, desperately in need of soles. A small collection of rusty iron tools. Two battered clay tobacco pipes. A mouldy rectangular package, roughly a foot square, wrapped in

160

stiffened, moth-eaten oilcloth. A water-stained, rolled-up old parchment, flattened and jammed up against one side of the trunk. The kinds of historical artifacts an antiquities dealer might get all excited about, with the emphasis on the word 'might.'

"So, idiot fool! What did you expect, Elizabeth Alten? Did you really think you had found Captain Kidd's long lost treasure trove?" Upstairs in the living-room hall, barely audible, the grandfather clock struck midnight. Liz realized she had been talking to herself again.

"The first sign of insanity, talking to yourself," she said out loud. She remembered her mother telling her that when she was a little girl. She took the lantern off its hook and dragged herself disconsolately back to bed. What a let-down. The famous trunk contained nothing more than some long-dead slave's pitiful possessions.

Lying in bed with the moonlit trees weaving their mysterious reflected shadows across the walls and ceiling, Liz heard the owls talking back and forth. Hoo hoo. Hoo hoo.

"Oh God, I drank too much," she muttered. "I'll be a basket-case tomorrow." Drifting into sleep at last, she was sucked down unwillingly into an awful dream.

161

30

Abducted By Aliens

Liz shivered uncontrollably. It was deepest winter and she was numbingly cold in her flimsy summer nightgown and decrepit bunny-rabbit slippers. The latter had been a Christmas gift from Layla, almost fifteen years ago. Somehow that comforting fact seemed as important as the unsettling sight that met her eyes. A stealthy band of five or six Indian warriors, their faces striped in greasy red and black war-paint, crept up on a huddled figure seated far from the shore of a frozen lake. They seemed familiar. Oh! It was the same group that had slaughtered the English settlers in her earlier nightmare, despite the fact that the two events were clearly separated by several centuries.

The hunched-over figure was ice-fishing in the moonlight, apparently, but he seemed to have fallen asleep on the job. The fisherman's body language reminded her of someone. Liz tried to warn the doomed man. She shrieked soundlessly and ran slip-sliding across the ice in agonizing slow motion, but it was too late.

The Indians encircled the fisherman, and stopped. Silence. Nothing moved. After an endless microsecond, one of the warriors bounded forward, and with a single blow from an ornately carved war-club, crushed the bowed skull of the seated man. Whooping triumphantly, his companions rolled the figure over onto its back in the moonlight and broke into a circular dance of victory. Suddenly Liz found herself directly over the scene, looking down. To her utter dismay, she recognized the dead man. It was her late husband, the controversial Cambridge epidemiologist James 'Nick' Nicholson. She screamed her lungs out, but nary a whimper emerged.

As the warriors hastily stuffed the corpse through the hole in the ice and pushed it down into the icy water with the help of the man's fishing pole, Liz woke in a cold sweat and lay there in her grandfather's Barbados villa, staring at the ceiling. The last thing she had witnessed before she opened her horrified eyes was a huge elliptical shadow descending over the circle of warriors, the Indian braves staring up at it in terror.

The moonlit trees outside shifted and sighed. The owls hooted close by. A shuddering revulsion took hold of Liz. The entire house was haunted, inhabited by a thousand disenchanted spirits echoing uncounted generations of unconscionable human behavior.

Nauseated, she staggered up, vomited into the bathroom sink, and very nearly made it back to the bed before she collapsed to her knees, moaning pitifully, and passed out cold on the luxurious Afghani carpet in the Islamic position of prayer.

*****

31

Invasion of The Surfer Dudes

The bedside clock said 7:15 AM. It was unbearably hot, and it was painfully, dazzlingly bright. The sun streamed in through the open windows, directly onto Liz's face. Liz fought her way back to consciousness through a suffocating haze. She had a blinding headache. Every muscle in her body ached. She was on the carpeted floor next to her bed and she had a serious hangover. Her mouth tasted like the bottom of the vulture enclosure at the San Diego Zoo.

In her delirium, Liz had been hearing voices all

night, well-known voices. There they were again. Hearing the excited, strangely familiar sounds through the open window, she groaned pitifully, pried herself carefully off the carpet, spat a mouthful of Listerine into the bathroom sink, and staggered down the stairs and out of the house, unkempt and barefoot in her dressing gown, to confront two virtually identical teenage boys out on the lawn, the one just a little taller than the other.

They were Liz's sons. Jason and Jonny were dressed in matching black Ocean Pacific board-shorts and white Rip Curl rash guards. They carried identical surfboards under their arms and were heading off to Soup Bowls without another moment's delay. They had not been in the water since late August in Bridgehampton, and they were desperate to get wet.

Their flight from Massachusetts, where the boys were boarding students at the Concord Academy, had been delayed by the tropical storm. They finally arrived at Grantley Adams well after midnight. Fortunately, the driver of the last lingering taxi-van had taken pity on them and spirited them to the east side of the island. In her comatose state, Liz had not heard their rather noisy arrival, but Barbara was sufficiently conscious to let them into the house and direct them to their large double bedroom. They had no idea that their mother was comatose on the floor in the next room.

Bouncing out of bed at first light, the boys hadn't taken the time to say good morning to their mother. The thought had not crossed their adolescent, surf-obsessed minds. Gladys fed them an early breakfast, which they inhaled with alacrity. Now they had other priorities, specifically surfing. Followed by surfing. Followed by yet more surfing. The aspiring world champions had not been on the island since they were little boys, and they were wildly excited. Alden House was within walking distance of world surfing champion Kelly Slater's favorite surf break, a little promontory in Bathsheba mysteriously known as 'Soup Bowls.'

"Hey wait up, you guys," Liz yelled hoarsely, her voice cracking. She stumbled down the verandah steps. "What's the big rush? How about a good morning hug? Did you forget we haven't seen each other since August? This is November, for God's sake."

Jason stopped and turned around. He examined his disheveled, hung-over mother with a mixture of affection and disapproval. She was a mess. She reminded him of one of those bedraggled old Salem witches on her way to the hangman.

"Hi Mom! We're going to Soup Bowls," he said.

"Soup Bowls? What are you talking about? Didn't Gladys give you something for breakfast?" Liz winced at the jackhammer in her forehead.

"It's the best surf break in the world, Mom," young Jonny piped up. "Kelly Slater says so. One of the three best, anyway. And it's right there, behind those stupid trees. Half a mile from great-grandpa's house." He pointed eastward.

"Stupid trees? How can trees be stupid?" Liz was confused. Holding his surfboard to one side, Jonny gave his mother a tentative hug. Ugh. She smelled of rum and vomit and Listerine and decomposed corpses.

"You can't see through them to check the waves," he explained.

"Oh. Right. I shall have to have a little talk with them. And Kerry Stater is..? I'm sorry. I forget."

"Kelly Slater, Mom. He's the world's greatest surfer. Everybody knows that."

"He's been world champion fifteen times. Remember all the videos you watched with us?"

"Mom, it's great to see you," Jason said, "but we gotta go, before the wind comes up and it gets all blown out. The waves are perfect. I just know it."

"Are you sure it's safe? Is there a lifeguard on duty this early in the morning? What about the sharks?"

"Mom! Surfers don't use lifeguards. We save each other if someone gets in trouble. We gotta go, Mom. Come on Jonny. I'll race you. Last one to catch a wave is a gormless twit."

"That would be you, you chinless wonder! Come on! Catch me if you can! 'Bye Mom."

Gormless twit? Chinless wonder? Those had been two of dear James's favorite British insults. At least they had gained something of cultural value from their prestigious Cambridge father.

The boys sped off toward the ocean. Liz watched them go in a combination of admiration and trepidation. Someone had spotted a huge bull shark in the moonlight a few nights back, she remembered, right in by the sea wall in Bridgetown. Gladys had pointed out the article in the local newspaper. Bull sharks are the most dangerous sharks in the world. They are responsible for more fatal attacks than any other species, the article had said. Liz's headache was blazing. She groaned, turned and lurched back toward the house, muttering pitifully to herself.

"Oh God. My head is going to explode."
As she started up the verandah steps, there was a sudden soft crunching sound behind her. It was a gold-colored Toyota Prius, pulling up in front of the house.

"Fuck!" Liz cursed, for the second time in as many days. "Not Ginsberg. He's the last person I want to..."

*****

169

32

The Bedside Manner

The ensuing day was going to be a rough one, no question about it. A busy one, as well. Liz was sluggish, sleep deprived, semi-present, as though she'd been drugged the night before, which of course she had. Mount Gay rum is a very powerful intoxicant. She found barely a moment to collect her scattered wits.

Arthur Ginsberg had been the family's general practitioner for almost forty years. His prognosis was not encouraging, and his attitude was even less so. His tone of voice had the usual superior edge to it. The know-it-all, lecturing condescendingly to the ignorant child.

"Your grandfather is fading fast, Priscilla," the doctor intoned in his resonant, self assured voice. "I have never seen Parkinson's move this fast. Or dementia for that matter. I'm not in the least happy with his vitals. He might not last until Thanksgiving. That's less than a week away, so it's just as well that the family is gathering..."
Ginsberg glanced at the disheveled woman disapprovingly. His communication was clipped and just barely short of rude. Liz's hackles rose, but she was careful to control her tone.

"My name is Elizabeth, in case you were wondering. Priscilla's the other daughter. The skinny one." Liz said, coolly. Ginsberg stared at her. She could see herself vaguely reflected in his thick-lensed spectacles, which were in need of a good cleaning. "Less than a week, did you say?" she continued. "How about a week from tomorrow? That would be, let's see? Eight days, last time I checked. It looks like the family will get here just in time."

"Well, I need him in the hospital in Bridgetown sooner rather than later. The day after Thanksgiving at the very latest - if he lives that long. This is not good."

Liz had about had enough. This was the last thing she needed to deal with right now.

"Are you suggesting my staff is not looking after him properly? That he's not getting proper care?" Her voice had a definite edge to it.

"I want him on a drip."

"A drip, Arthur? A goddamned drip? So? You can do that here. Can you not? I mean, this is 2020, not 1620, in case you hadn't noticed." She took a deep breath, blinking in the blinding sunlight. "We have two certified nurses in the house. And you know... Should I tell you what my grandfather told Barbara, when she told him you wanted him in the hospital? Did she tell you?"

"No, she did not. What did he say? And what the hell would your sister know about it?"

"Barbara is not my sister, goddamn it. Barbara is the hospice nurse you've been working with for the past six months. Grandpa said... he said the hospital would kill him in a week. He's not going near any goddamned hospital. He's still got a lot of living to do."

"Well... We'll see about that."

Ginsberg grumbled off down the driveway, scratching his sweaty, balding skull and muttering into his scraggly beard. The gold Prius meandered slowly and erratically back into Bridgetown, where Alden had rented him an oceanfront condominium for the duration. The good doctor spent the remainder of the day, as he did every day, seven days a week, three hundred and sixty-five days a year, hunched over his battered old Dell laptop, working on his stock portfolio. He had a system...

*****

33

The Maui Contingent

As Liz started, painfully hallucinating Tylenol and harder drugs, up the stairs to the verandah, she heard the metallic clang of the electric gates at the entry to the property. The Mercedes came crunching up the driveway and stopped at the foot of the curving verandah stairway, just as Liz reached the top step. She had not realized that the vehicle was not in the garage. She turned, her head reverberating like a slave bell on steroids, and went dutifully back down to the driveway.

Scilla and Maryah had arrived on the morning flight from Atlanta, and the faithful Washington had been there at Grantley Adams to greet them.

There was an exchange of hugs. The two new arrivals were dreadfully jet-lagged.

"Sister, are you OK?" Scilla whispered. "Look at you. You need to brush your teeth. And your hair."

Maryah had a decidedly outrageous Southern accent and a bushy mop of bleached-blonde dreadlocks tied up on top of her head, but she seemed basically friendly as the sisters-in-law shook hands, meeting for the first time. While Gladys showed Scilla and Maryah to their suite, Liz helped herself to a cup of strong black coffee and went up to her bedroom, wincing at each painful step. She swallowed a trio of extra-strength Tylenols. As she did so, she happened to catch a glimpse of herself in the bathroom mirror.

"Oh God," she gasped in horror. "Did I really go out looking like that?"

In the shower, she reviewed the events of the previous day. It was a blur. There had been no time to have a further look at the old sailor's trunk and its contents, although Liz suddenly recalled seeing an unidentified rolled-up object stuck against one of the sides. For some reason, the scroll, if that was what it was, now piqued her interest. She was almost desperate to know what it was.

Her iPhone chirped on the nightstand next to the bed. Her father had texted in from Miami. They'd be on the island by sunset, although they had made a reservation at the Hilton. Don't wait up for them. They'd take a taxi out to the house mid-to-late morning the following day, after a quick round of golf. Liz found herself wondering about James. Not her James. Her James was dead. It was her father's James she was wondering about. She could not recall ever meeting the man. Was he, like her father, a golf fanatic, or was he, as she had so often felt during her childhood, more of a golf orphan? In any case, who gave a shit? The bastard had murdered her mother.

*****

34

Hanged In 1776

Once Scilla and Maryah were snugly ensconced and fast asleep in their suite, and the boys had come home for lunch and a quick nap, before calling a taxi to take them to some of the West Side surfing spots, Washington drove Liz into Bridgetown in the Mercedes. The Tylenol and the coffee had kicked in and she was feeling almost semi-human. She had to go to the bank and the post office, both of which were closing early today. It was some kind of local holiday. Last but not least, they should make a stop at the local bottle shop to replenish the piña colada fixings.

"Might as well stock up for Thanksgiving while we're out and about," Liz muttered, half to herself.

Washington, needless to say, wanted to hear all about yesterday's big discovery. He'd been both incredulous and profoundly disappointed at Gladys's description of the trunk's mundane contents. The news could not possibly be true.

"They say you found that old sailor's sea-chest, after all, Missy, down in the haunted place. Them Sout' Africans dug it up?"

"They did. It wasn't exactly easy, but they found it. It was extremely well hidden. We almost gave up. Did you hear what was in it?"

"Clothes? Old shoes? Boots? More boots. Nothing but ol' boots? No! I don't believe it. I was certain it would be that long-lost pirate's treasure chest, full to the brim with gold doubloons. Shinin' in the dark. Everybody knows about it. My daddy used to tell us stories, when we were little..."

"No doubloons, sad to say, Spanish or otherwise. Not even one. There might be some valuable historical items, though." Liz paused. How much should she say? There was a question that had been troubling her. "One more thing, Washington. There are some skeletons down there in that hole. Apparently. I haven't actually seen them yet. Would you know who they might belong to?"

"Excuse me? Skeletons? Who might they belong to?" Washington's silver eyebrows went up as he pondered the idea. "I have never in my life thought about such a thing. Skeletons belonging to people? But wait! Skeletons? Aha! That is exactly what my friend said, down at the docks. Freddie. The gho-asts, he said. The skellingtons. They must be from the old slave days, when my great-great grandfather..." Washington paused and drew a breath, then went on.

"Miss Lizzie, I am going to tell you something. I have never told Master Alden this. I don't know why. It is a matter of public record. My great-great grandfather was hanged by the neck in the year 1776, because of leading the slave rebellion at the old Bayley plantation, the same house where the great reggae musician Eddy Grant have his recording studio right now."

"Hanged in the year 1776 for leading a rebellion? Somehow, that brings to mind George Washington..."

"Exactly, although it turned out better for the father of your country. Here, it took our people a little bit longer. They call it the Bussa Rebellion these days, put up a statue of Bussa in the town park and everything.

179

You have heard of Bussa, right? But it wasn't no Bussa. It was Washington Franklin, my great-great-great grandfather, same name as myself. The slave rebels used to hide down there, the old stories say. In the bottom of our house."

"Whoa, I did not know that, Washington. That is a lot of information. But first, what are we supposed to do about the skeletons? Call the police, I suppose."

"I will find out what to do about the skeletons. The chief of police is the cousin of my wife."

"Perhaps we should... What do you think? Is there such a thing as a Barbados historical society?"

"I think... I shall make the necessary inquiries, Missy."

"And I will Google it. I believe we have made an interesting historical discovery, Washington. Between the two us..."

"Google? What is a google? It sounds like some kind of flightless bird in the Galapagos Islands."

Liz giggled as Washington pulled the gleaming old car into a shady spot in the bank parking lot, under a spreading coral tree covered in bright-red blossoms. The asphalt was still wet from a recent squall, but the trade winds had blown the storm clouds away and Father Sun was sending his rays down to Earth as enthusiastically as ever. The sounds of songbirds and the wind in the trees returned as the engine died. The last wisps of steam rose from the heated tarmac and evaporated back whence they had come. The humid air was exquisitely clean and fragrant.

Acting on force of habit, Liz opened the passenger door herself and swung her feet out. She was not accustomed to having car doors opened for her, not since sweet baby James... Washington stopped in the midst of his high-speed race around the vehicle, turned around on his heel, and walked instead to the bank door. Perfect timing. He bowed.

"You're thinking of a booby, not a google, Washington." Liz laughed as the handsome older man opened the bank door for her. "And speaking of birds, have you heard that crazy thing that shrieks outside my window in the night? I swear it is cursing at me in Spanish. Is it really a popinjay? I won't be long."
Washington ambled back over to the parked Mercedes, shaking his head in disbelief.

"No Spanish doubloons? That is simply not possible," he said, softly but emphatically..

*****

35

Baxter de Waal

In the queue at the bank, Liz found herself standing behind an American woman, a tall, slender, forty-something dressed in Paisley hot-pants, a beige tank-top and flowered chartreuse flip-flops. She was the only other customer in the place, and they got talking, as expatriates often do. It was tea time, the traditional English obligation that is as strictly observed in Barbados as the five-times-a-day prayers are observed in the Islamic

182

world. As far as the mystified Americans could tell, the building had been abandoned. There wasn't another soul in sight. The tellers had all disappeared backstage, and nothing seemed to be happening. Perhaps a bank robbery was expected, and the staff had fled for their lives like rats abandoning a sinking ship.

The American woman turned out to be a graduate student and research assistant at the University of California in Berkeley. Her field was early American history, and she was staying at an AirBnB rental out near the old plantation estate on the East Side. In Bathsheba.

"You mean Alden House? That's our family place. It belongs to my grandfather," said Liz.

Baxter, as the American called herself, hailed from the great state of Maine. That is what she called it: the great state of Maine. Her father was, she went on to say, a South African yachtsman who had sailed across the Atlantic and landed here in Barbados back in 1969. She was here on the island to perform historical research into the possible presence of New England Indian slaves in Barbados back in the 1670s.

"South African, did you say? What's up with that? We had some South Africans helping us at the house just yesterday. Very interesting," said Liz, having little to no idea what her effusive new acquaintance was talking about. "It looks like we have a few things in common. What fun. My family has deep Maine roots, and my father's a sailor too. Not to mention my grandfather, although Grandpa Jack's sailing days are over." She paused and put out her hand. "I'm Liz Nicholson. What's your name?"

"Baxter de Waal. It's a Dutch surname. South African, actually, but..."
Baxter stopped and stared. Liz was having trouble keeping a straight face. Backs to the wall? Where had Liz heard that phrase before? Bax was about to continue, but noticed that Liz had gone red in the face.

"Are you all right, Ms Nicholson? What's going on?" Liz nodded in the affirmative, but then broke into a paroxysm of choking splutters. She was clearly on the verge of a heart attack. Baxter looked around anxiously. Was there a doctor in the house? They were still the only people in the building. At that moment, the outer doors slid open and three customers entered, two young black men in their mid-twenties and a little black boy about seven years old. None of them looked like a doctor. They looked more like bank robbers, or at least the older ones did. There was still no sign of a bank employee. It took a few minutes, but Liz finally calmed down and wiped her eyes. She tried to explain, still

184

gasping for breath:

"I... I've never met a girl named...ah... Bax... Baxter. Ah ah... It's... very unusual, isn't it? I have a friend in the Ha..hamptons who named her son...ah... Baxter. I thought it was a lovely name for a little boy."

"You're right, of course. I'm the only female Baxter I've ever met. But what's so funny, for Heaven's sake? You're not making fun of me, are you?"

"I'm sorry. I really am. Let me explain. It's an inside joke. There is, or at least there was, another Baxter Duval, a male one. He was extremely obscure, so I'm sure you've never heard of him. In fact he was entirely fictitious. He's an icon in my inner reality. That's what I was laughing at."

"I'm sorry. I just don't get it." Baxter de Waal examined Liz Nicholson suspiciously.

"I don't blame you. How could you? Baxter Duval was the name of a South African superhero - a fictitious character in one of my late husband's nutty bedtime stories. There we go again. Another South African, um... Baxter's sidekick was a midget Japanese martial artist named Kung Fuji, who, being his sidekick, kept kicking him in the side. He was a very, very silly man, my late husband was, not Baxter Duval. His stories were hilarious, if you happen to be a fan of the theatre of the absurd. James was a Brit." Liz explained her reaction as best she could, breaking down repeatedly and gasping for breath. After a moment, Bax got over her initially negative reaction and the two women ended up spluttering and laughing together.

"Oh. I see," chuckled Bax. "You were married to a Brit. Well, that explains it, doesn't it? You poor thing, you."

"We lived in Cambridge for nine years. Cambridge, England, not Cambridge, Massachusetts, but I never did adapt to the humor. I tried, I really did. I even listened to re-runs of the bloody Goon Show, for God's sake. James, everyone called him Nick but I always thought of him as James, I used to introduce him as my late husband because he was never on time, but now he really is late, permanently." Liz was barely coherent. She was on the verge of hysteria again. She went on. "In fact, he's so late these days, he's dead. He used to walk around muttering 'Always on time, tick-tock,' but I never quite got it. The explanation 'I'm going steady with half-past three' only made the matter more confusing. British humor! No wonder we had to have a goddamn revolution."

"You'll have to straighten all that out for me some-time..." Bax began.

The bank teller interrupted Baxter.

"Next customer please!" There was a slight hint of impatience in her voice. The bank was closing early today and there was not a moment to waste. The line of customers now extended out of the lobby and as far as the eye could see into the parking lot. As fortune would have it, there were now two tellers open side by side, so the women were able to continue the conversation as the bankers peformed their mysterious rituals on the far side of the bulletroof Plexiglass.

"So, Baxter? Bax, did you say? I love your name. I really do. What brings you to the island? Business or pleasure?"

"A little bit of each, really. I was ready for a break from the endless El Niño rain in California, and the ridiculous heat wave in New England. I've never been to Barbados before. Of course it has rained every day since I got here, but at least it's warm. Sort of. I was born on Grenada, less than a hundred miles away, but... I'm here working on a little historical research. I'm looking into the possibility of there being descendants of New England Indian slaves among the black population here."

"Grenada? You said you were born in Maine."

"Wrong. I said I was *from* Maine. I grew up in Maine, among other places. I was conceived in Maine, as a matter of fact. Nine months later I was born in

187

Grenada. That's what happens when your parents are nomadic, a.k.a seasonal. But yeah, there may be some interesting history here, if I can prove there really were New England Indian slaves in Barbados."

Liz was confused. New England Indian slaves? What did that mean? Native American slaves from New England? She had never heard of such a thing, and she was from New England. She knew pretty much everything there was to know about New England.

"New England Indian slaves?" she asked. "That's a very strange thought. There aren't any Indians in New England. The goddamned Pilgrims killed them all off."

"The Pilgrims did what?" Baxter's voice was sharp. Her eyes were like gimlets. Liz did not notice. She considered for a moment, then took the plunge. She just couldn't keep her mouth shut.

"Listen Bax, do you mind if I change the subject? Just for a minute? I have something that might interest you, something we found just yesterday. Actually it might have to do with slavery. An old, old sea trunk down in our basement. I think it may have belonged to a slave. An Indian slave, who knows? I doubt it. That would be too much of a stretch." Liz went on. "Anyway, did I tell you? We have an old plantation house out on the East Side, with a history of slavery and all. First tobacco and

188

then sugar. We still produce sugar on a small scale for my grandfather's boutique rum business." She paused, looking at the line of fidgety customers behind them. The bank would close in twelve minutes, and there was no possible way... "Why don't you come over for lunch one of these days, and I'll show you the trunk."

"That would be interesting. I'd love to," said Bax. "Did I tell you? Just to complete the thought, I'm in the midst of my doctoral thesis on the history of slavery in the West Indies. The role of the Native Americans. It will be coming out as a book, with a bit of luck, in a couple of years."

"That is really interesting, although I still don't get the connection between the West Indies and Native Americans. Columbus thought he had landed in India, which is why everyone calls them Indians to this day." Baxter looked at her new acquaintance, but did not interrupt. Liz continued. For some reason she was excited.

"We need to talk, Bax. Would you like to meet for coffee some day soon? Or better still, wait. Wait! I have an idea. Are you done in town? Do you have a car? No? Why don't we give you a ride back out to Bathsheba? There's a funky little espresso place, right on the beach. It's all made of driftwood. I've been meaning to check it out. It says ESPRESSO on the side. We could grab a cappuccino, if the place is open. Assuming the sign means what it says."

Baxter had wrapped up her banking business, which had merely involved the depositing of a check. She moved over and stood next to Liz as the teller counted out the Bajan equivalent of ten one-hundred dollar bills. The two black men and the child took Bax's place. They watched the teller as she counted out the money. They couldn't help themselves. Liz stuffed the cash into her purse, and the two women turned and left. As they departed, they heard the child say in a loud whisper:

"Two 'tousand dollar. You see dat, Daddy?"

"Oh, you a good little counter, William. A good little counter. How you do that? Maybe one day you get a job right here in dis bank counting out de money for da wealthy tourist peoples."

*****

36

Indian Point

Washington, resplendent in his formal livery, held the rear door of the gleaming Mercedes open. Liz and Baxter clambered into the spacious rear of the vehicle, which had two rows of seats facing one another, one forward, one aft. Liz performed the introductions.

"Glad to meet you, Washington. Wow, this is a beautiful vehicle, isn't it? I've never been in such a..." Baxter stopped in mid-sentence and picked up where she and Liz had left off in the bank. "Liz, I know the place you mean, the espresso place. Something about a witch, isn't it? Or a ditch. Let's do that." Baxter went on. "Meanwhile, I have a question. Did you just say you found evidence of Native American slaves in your cellar? You mean you knew there were Indians here, way back then? Nobody knows that. I'm just in the process of discovering... My book won't be published for two more years. I haven't told anyone except my thesis advisor..."

"I didn't say that, Baxter. I'm just beginning to wonder about the old slave days, myself. It's a long story, a story that might just interest you, given your research project. As long as you're not afraid of ghosts. D'you know the name of the area where you're staying? It's called Indian Point. Ever wonder why?"

"I know. That's one of the things I'm doing here. I've been looking for places with the word 'Indian' in them, in their names, and trying to figure out how they got their names. And why. There are several. Indian Point. Indian Hill. Indian Pond. Indian Hollow. It's interesting, isn't it? I had no idea, but I was doing some online slavery research back home in Berkeley, and a major clue suddenly dropped into my lap. I found a post about an old Barbados law forbidding the importation of New England Indian slaves to this island, dated 1676. The year King Philip's War ended."

"King Philip's War? You mean King Charles, don't you? I've never heard of King Philip. Forbidding the importation of..? But that would mean... I'm sorry, Bax, but you've lost me. Let me ask you a question. It's probably not related, but you never know. My grandfather, he's ninety three and he's not long for this world, he's pretty much catatonic these days, but every so often he gets all druv up. He yells out something about Indians, although for the life of us we can't figure out what he's talking about. Sometimes he also says the word slaves. "

*****

37

A Voice From The Shadows

That night, after a light supper with the subdued, jet-lagged Scilla and Maryah before they crawled sleepily back into bed, and after sitting for an hour with a remarkably peaceful but silent Alden, Liz went back down to the cellar, singing to herself, a tad nervously, it must be admitted. Simon & Garfunkel's *I Am A Rock.* The song had been going through her head incessantly for the past several days.

"I can't get that damn song out of my head! How

annoying. Can we switch channels, please? Right now I'm more in the mood for something by John Denver."

Opening the trunk by the dim, flickering light of the kerosene lantern, she examined the crumbling contents item by aromatic item, and carefully stacked the objects on a nearby dresser, which she had dusted off for the purpose and covered with a faded old blue and white striped beach towel. The motley, mildewed collection of oddities was obviously old, very likely hundreds of years old. Sadly, it was nothing more than some long-deceased slave's few possessions, as far as Liz could tell. She picked up the brittle rolled-up parchment, held it up to the dim light without attempting to unroll it, and set it aside. The last thing Liz had examined the previous night was at the very bottom of the trunk; a heavy, stiff oilcloth-wrapped package, roughly a foot square and three or four inches thick.

"Now this..." she began.

The packaging material cracked and crackled and partially disintegrated as she opened it. She set the wrapping aside and stood there gazing at the ancient object in her hands. She held it up to the smoky flickering light. Her eyes widened. It was a battered old bible with a worn, tattered leather cover, secured by a stiff leather thong tightly tied in a sailor's reef knot. She held the book higher and scrutinized it by the intermittent lamplight.

"Hmmm," she said out loud. If the skeletons beneath her feet were truly alive, they could hear every word she said. "Now, this could be interesting. Looks like an original Geneva Bible. This is the first one I've ever seen. Pre-dates the King James version by half a century, if I remember correctly. This might be worth a pretty penny at Sotheby's. More than the rest of this old house put together, I wouldn't be surprised. Wow! How on earth...?"

Liz worked, it should be remembered, as an antiquities librarian back home in Maine. She was in charge of the Baxter Memorial Library's collection of antique books and manuscripts, so she had a rough idea of what she was looking at. She replaced the old bible reverently in its package on top of the pile, picked up the scroll and turned to go. She unhooked the lantern, deep in thought, walked to the bottom of the stairs, then changed her mind and stopped. Talking to herself , she muttered.

"Wait a goddamned minute. This doesn't add up. That can't be a slave's bible. Slaves didn't have bibles, for God's sake. Did they? At least not ones like that.
I wonder whose it was, originally? The old families often

kept their marriage records... What if..?"

Excited suddenly, Liz turned and retraced her steps. Replacing the lantern on its overhead hook, she picked up the bible again and carefully tried to undo the stiff leather thong. The tight, flattened knot would not come undone. She tried harder. The thong disintegrated in her hands, much to her chagrin.

"Dumb bitch!" she cursed. "Why would you do that?" She hadn't meant to damage the precious artifact. Very, very carefully, she opened the cover. If this had been a Hollywood movie, this would have been the cue for some appropriately dramatic music. In fact, if Liz had held her breath and listened closely enough, she would have noticed that the Simon and Garfunkel in her head had been replaced by a heart-pounding piece of Beethoven.

"Hey, hang on a goddamned moment," she squeaked, loudly. "This is not a Bible. It's...it's hand-written. In ye Olde English. By someone with the initials... um... P.M. Fascinating. It even has the year it was written, if I can figure out the Roman numerals. M-D-C-C-X-V..."

Liz's vocal ponderings were interrupted suddenly.

"Correct, Elizabeth. Not um Bible."

The ethereal voice emanated from the shadows off to

the left. Liz whirled around, terrified, and banged her forehead on the heavy lantern between her eyes and the source of the voice. She was barely able to control her bladder. The woman's voice had an old-fashioned Native American accent, the kind Liz remembered from the cowboy movies during her childhood. There seemed to be a diffuse glow back there in the gloom, but Liz, dazzled by the lantern and seeing stars, could not make out a thing.

"Wha? What?" She was finally able to speak, her voice shaking. "Who's there? Who is down here?"

"Gran'mother bible," the disembodied voice replied. "No bible. Story. English people story. Me think bible. Run gran'mother house. Fire. Rescue bible. Brothers burn house. Kill your mother... my mother friend... Knock head. Even baby children. Scalp everyone. My own brothers. You family. English friends. Oh! Oh!" Liz's eyes widened.

"Now hold on, dammit, that's my dream. You're talking about my dream? How could you..? What are you talking about? Who's there? I can't see you. Show yourself, goddammit!

"Come gran'father room. Explain, if can. Need gran'father. Gran'father know truth."

"The truth? Grandpa Jack? But..."

"Do as gran'mother bid. Soon possible. Important. No time. Gran'father die. Too late Gran'father die."

"Who are you? Are you a ghost? I do *not* believe in ghosts."

"Ghost nation, yes. Daughter you gran'mother friend. Anice. Patuxet friend. Fifteen minute gran'father room."

"My grandmother? She died twelve years ago. This bible, this book, it's hundreds of years old."

"You gran'mother friend. Gran'mother Anice. Patuxet friend. Weetamoo."

"Weetamoo? Grandpa Jack's sailboat? Come on! This is getting ridiculous. What's that got to do with anything?" Liz had recovered her composure, as far as that was possible under the circumstances.

"You're messing with my head. I told you, my grandmother died twelve years ago. This bible, this book, it's hundreds of years old. You said Patuxet? You mean the Indians that the Mayflower Pilgrims...?"

"Gran'father room, now! No time!"
The ghostly voice was not taking no for an answer.

"Yes M'am. I'll be right along! As soon as my god-damn head stops spinning."
Liz's forehead was bleeding from a nasty cut. The blood trickled into her left eye. She rubbed the eye impatiently

and made a gory mess of the entire left side of her face. She stood there for a long moment, shaking, uncertain as to what her next move should be.

*****

38

What The Hell?

Liz, her hands shaking, set the water-stained packaging aside, carefully put the old book back down
on the dresser, then hurried upstairs and sat, wide-eyed
and expectant, with the sleeping Alden. She sat for a
long while. Her face was smeared with dried blood.
Nothing happened. No ghost. No mysterious voices.

The silence continued. No sounds came in from outside. Not a breath of wind in the trees. No crickets or
tree frogs. No owls, no mynahs, no surf. Someone must
have switched off the CD player. It was as though the

entire universe had stopped in its tracks.

Suddenly, Alden opened his eyes and whispered something, the words slurred. It sounded like...

"Oui. Oui..."

"Oui? Grandpa, are you speaking French? Say that again, please."

Alden turned his head and looked at Liz. His red-rimmed eyes glittered disconcertingly under the bushy eyebrows.

"Oui. Wee... Wee... ta... moo," he gasped.

"Grandpa Jack, what did you say? Weetamoo? Your sailboat?"

*****

39

The Doctrine Of Discovery

Thursday, Nov 19, 2020

It was dawn, first light. The morning birds were loud. Liz lay in bed listening to the sound of the ocean coming in through the open windows. She was wide-eyed and wildly excited. There was no question about it; she had found an artifact of some historical significance, not to mention economic value, and was boggled by the fact that it had, apparently, taken a dying old man with a foot in each of the worlds to receive a communication from the spirit of a Native American woman from the 'other side.' Without that communication, the old sea trunk would have remained hidden forever, and if Grandpa Jack had passed away before Liz had decoded the message, well, that would have been the end of that.

The identity of the 'ghost' was a mystery, but one thing was certain – she had known details from Liz's nightmare that no one could possibly have known. Was the disembodied voice that of the Indian girl she had seen in the terrifying dream, the one who had run howling into the burning Colonial farmhouse and emerged with her hair on fire as the building collapsed behind her in an explosion of sparks? Wasn't she clutching something to her bare bosom as she screamed and sobbed? The dream had faded from her conscious memory, but Liz seemed to remember that the Indian girl had rescued something from the flames.

Liz knew enough about archeology and the academic world to know that she needed to be circumspect with regard to her discovery. It would not do to blab about the old 'bible' to everyone she met, especially as the book was definitely not a bible. In fact, she realized with sudden alarm, she would be well advised to get back down to the cellar as swiftly as possible and remove all traces of the discovery.

"Does anyone, other than our family, have a claim on this extraordinary artifact?" she wondered out loud

Interestingly, the issue of *TIME* that she had picked up at Logan Airport had contained an article on the Papal Bull of 1494, a Vatican proclamation which was the subject of an ongoing series of protests by Native Americans and other indigenous people around the world. The so-called 'Doctrine of Discovery' was put forth by European monarchies between the mid-fifteenth and mid-seventeenth centuries to justify the colonization of lands outside of Europe, thus allowing countries like Spain and Portugal, and later, France, England, Holland, Denmark and others, to claim lands already inhabited by indigenous peoples, under the guise of discovery. Essentially, according to the Vatican, if the land was occupied by anyone other than Christians, it was yours for the taking. Just send any gold you happened to find to the Pope.

"A Papal Bull? A load of bull indeed," Liz had muttered out loud, reading the article on the flight to Barbados. Suddenly, however, the shoe was on the other foot. Was the decrepit old journal hers to keep, or did it actually belong to the nation of Barbados? After all, it had been in Grandpa Jack's home for centuries, long before Barbados became an independent country in its own right. Long before Grandpa Jack had bought the house. What was the ethical thing to do?

"I found it, goddammit. And I'm keeping it. It's mine!" she said out loud.

She bounced out of bed like a Jack-in-the-box, hastily brushed her teeth and threw on some clothes, then went down to the kitchen, said good morning to Gladys, and continued on down the cellar stairs guided by the flashlight on her iPhone. Furtively, she returned to the kitchen, clutching the old journal and the rolled-up scroll, waited until Gladys was busy out on the verandah, then scuttled back up to her bedroom. The top of the tall antique wooden wardrobe seemed like as good a hiding-place as any. Still shaking, she jumped into the shower and stood there in the hot deluge, awaiting some earth-shattering revelation. None came.

*****

40

The Locked Bookcase

The early morning sun came in at the open French doors, filtered by the sheer chiffon curtains. Alden reclined silently in the middle of the enormous bed, as usual, staring unblinkingly at the ceiling. The customary trail of translucent drool trickled down one side of his bristly, unshaven chin, a result, according to Barbara, of the Parkinson's disease, which was inexorably escorting the old man to his grave. Alden's days were numbered.

"Well, you know," Liz had said to Gladys a few days back, "Something has to take him out."

Liz was down on her knees attempting to peer through the frosted glass into the locked Viennese bookcase. She had no idea why. The English nurse stood watching her.

"It's locked. As long as I can remember, it's always been locked. Why would anyone lock a goddamned bookcase?" Liz was exasperated, and made no attempt to conceal the fact.

"Can you make out anything in there?" asked Barbara.

"It looks like books. What else would be in a bookcase? The frosted glass makes it impossble...Goddammit! I bet Gladys or Washington - or both of them - know exactly where he keeps the key. I'm tempted to find a brick and just smash the glass."

"That bookcase is worth a pretty penny. I wouldn't do that, if I were you."

"Hey! You are not me, for one thing, and I'm about to inherit the fucking thing, for another. I'll do what I goddamn well like with it."

The nurse was offended, and she turned to leave.

"Well," she retorted stiffly. "I'm sorry I spoke."

"No, I'm the one who should be sorry, Barbara. You

have no idea how stressed-out I am." Liz got to her feet, laughing. "You Brits aren't used to such florid language, are you? I'm from Maine, you know. Back home, we use words like fuck and shit for everyday punctuation."

"Well yes. I have noticed that," said Barbara, somewhat mollified. "Your grandfather's language was... shall we say, colorful, before he... We Brits, on the other hand, tend to save those fine old Anglo-Saxon four-letter words for special occasions, on the theory that they might lose their flavor with overuse. As does the chewing gum on the bedpost overnight." They giggled, and the tension dissolved. Despite their differences, the two women were in fact becoming good friends.

"By the way, Barb. I met an interesting woman at the bank yesterday. She's going to come over for lunch one of these days."

"What sort of woman?"

"American. She's from my neck of the woods, Maine, of all places. She's some kind of academic. Historian, as far as I can tell, but not in the least stuffy or boring. Dresses like a hooker. She's a hoot. You might get a kick out of her. Anyway, she's at an AirBnB at the other end of the beach."

"An AirBnB? What on Earth is that? It sounds like a bed-and-breakfast where you sleep on an air mattress."

"Never mind. I keep forgetting. You locals have never heard of Google or Alphabet or AirBnB. Things we Americans take for granted."

"Wait a motherfucking minute, Liz. Of course I've heard of Google. I use it all the motherfucking time." Barbara wanted Liz to know that, despite the veneer of English gentility, she could give as good as she got when it came to foul language.

*****

41

Burying The Dead

After a solitary breakfast, Liz took her second cup of coffee up to her bedroom and took her first good look at the old bible, which she was now certain was not a bible at all. It was someone's diary, a journal, and if she could decipher the spidery old handwriting, she might be able to determine who the writer was, and when it was written. She would need a notebook.

Where could she find such a thing? Rising from the little desk, she looked out of the window, hoping to spot her elusive boys, or failing that, Washington. There was no sign of any of them. Shutting her door carefully, she hurried downstairs to her grandfather's office, and returned with a ballpoint pen and a wad of eight-and-a-half by eleven paper out of the Brother printer. Sitting down once more, she took a deep breath and set about the task of transcribing the mysterious document.

Liz was bewildered. She was also strangely moved, emotionally. In fact, she was elated. Why had this precious manuscript come into her possession at this moment in time? Remembering something from her early life, she had a sudden moment of intense gratitude. The most useless elective she had ever suffered through at Cambridge, an utterly boring course in Elizabethan calligraphy, taught by the dullest professor she had ever had to tolerate, was suddenly coming in handy.
The universe works in mysterious ways, she smiled.

Her immediate task was to decipher the date of the manuscript. It was spelled out in ornate Roman numerals, each of which was embellished with dozens of little leaves and flowers. There were suns and moons, and tiny elves and goblins lurking in the foliage. It took her a while, but after consulting with the Internet, courtesy of her iPad, she figured the date out and wrote the number down. The author's initials, elaborate and decorative as the shaky, child-like lettering was, had been were much easier to make out: P.M. Liz sat back in her chair and took a deep breath. She exhaled.

"OK, let's see what we've got here," she mused, as she consulted her notes. "The author's initials are clear enough: P.M. Peter or Paul somebody? Percival? Patrick? Perry? The date? Hmmm. M-D-C-C-X-V. That's Latin for, um... Sixteen, no seventeen... Seventeen fifteen. This house was built in 1659, so that makes sense. The house would have been forty-six years old back in 1715, when this book, this journal... Well, this *is* going to be a fascinating little detective story, isn't it?" she muttered. "Thank God I read so much Sherlock Holmes as a teenager. So, let's see. What do we have so far? Hmmm. We're looking for an 18th Century colonial guy with the initials PM. Right? Elementary, my dear Watson."

Satisfied at last with her transcription of the title page, she carefully opened the stiff old book to the very end. She could never resist the temptation to find out what happened, before plunging into the full text of any book she picked up. It was a habit for which dear departed Nick had berated her time and again, but she just couldn't help herself. The back page was blank, as were the last fifty or so sheets of yellowed paper. She turned to a random point twenty or twenty-five pages from the beginning. The rough-cut pages were brittle and brown around the edges.

She set to work, and began to scribble, letter by laborious letter, word by laborious word, mistake by laborious mistake. She made no attempt to understand the transcription. It was enough just to get the words written down in the correct order. After almost an hour, Liz sat back, closed her burning eyes for a long moment, then reviewed what she had written. There were twenty seven words on the sheet of printing paper. She read the sentence out loud, very slowly and hesitantly. One word at a time.

"Here... under... cover... of... darkness... the... fast... dwindling... company... laid... their... dead... leveling... the... earth... above... them... lest... the... Indians... should... learn... how... many... were... the... graves...

"Indians? Graves? What on earth *is* this, Henry?" Liz spoke out loud, although there was no one in the room and her door was shut tight and the latch bolted. If Henry David Thoreau, one of America's earliest ethnographers, was paying attention, he gave no sign of such. Liz went on. "Indians? What's up with all these Indians, Oliver Sardine? As James would have put it? All of a sudden, for anyone in their right mind. There *are* no Indians in Barbados. There never have been, at least in historic times. What were the island's original people

214

called? The Cro-Magnons? No, that was us, wasn't it, back in Europe? Arawaks? Maybe. I don't remember. Wait. No! I knew it began with a C - the Caribs! Weren't they the same as the ones Columbus encountered? The ones who gave their name to the Caribbean Sea?

"Well, one thing we know for certain – this book, this journal, was written by someone with the initials PM, a man, obviously. Women did not write back in 1715. Well, some did, I guess, Jane Austen, when was she..? But... is it a diary? Could it be fiction? An early attempt at a novel?" Liz sat back and closed her eyes.

"What did the so-called ghost call it? 'Not bible. Story? English story.' Is that what she said? The other thing we know, it begins in the year 1715, so that should give us some clues. What was going on in Barbados in the year 1715, I wonder? Slavery, I'm certain of that. Ummm... I wonder whether my new best friend Baxter Duval might have any idea? I should text her."

Liz realized that it would probably be best to begin the work of transcription at the beginning, as there were no page numbers or dates in the journal, if that was what it was. It would be all too easy to get horribly lost. She returned to the elaborate title page once more. The following several pages, eight or ten of them, were filled

with odd little doodles, childish stick figures interspersed with strange malformed letters that made no
sense at all. Forgetting her decision to begin at the
beginning, she reverted to her initial approach. She
ploughed on, randomly choosing a section about sixty
pages in.

"But alass!" she transcribed, *"this remedy proved worse
then ye disease; for wthin a few years those that had thus gott
footing ther rente them selves away, partly by force, and partly wearing ye rest with importunitie and pleas of necessitie, so
as they must either suffer them to goe, or live in continuall
opposition and contention. And others still, as yey conceived
them selves straitened, or to want accomodation, break away
under one pretence or other, thinking their owne conceived
necessitie, and the example of others, a warrente sufficente for
them. And this, I fear, will be ye ruine of New-England, at
least of ye churches of God ther, & will provock ye Lords dis-
pleasure against them."*

Completely losing track of the fact that the house
was rapidly filling with incoming family members, Liz
spent the remainder of the day sequestered in her room,
puzzling over the arcane document that for some reason
had landed in her astonished hands. It was only when
the cacophony of mynahs and the failing light at last got

her bleary-eyed attention, that Liz remembered where she was. Her back was aching. She was starved. She wandered downstairs, feeling like a time-traveler from an earlier century.

*****

42

A Message From The Other Side

After dinner, a distracted Liz excused herself and went back upstairs and sat with Old Jack, as had become her custom. She closed her burning eyes. There was a lot to think about. Her grandfather was uncharacteristically calm, although he continued to ignore her. It might have been Liz's imagination, but Grandpa Jack seemed to have the faintest vestige of a smile on his craggy, sunken face. The owl hooted from the tree outside, and its companion replied from afar.

218

To many indigenous cultures, the hooting of an owl signified a message from the other side, apparently. A warning. Someone is going to die. Liz pondered the notion. Who? Grandpa Jack was the obvious answer. If it's not Grandpa Jack's turn, then whose is it? Somehow this morbid, owl-induced train of thought brought up a long-buried memory.

*****

43

An Ancient
Mediterranean Dock

S itting by Old Jack's bedside, befuddled and half-asleep, Liz re-lived one of the last times she and Prissy had sat with their grandfather, just the three of them, watching the fading sunset over the sea. It must have been 1994 or 1995, on the edge of an ancient stone dock on one of the islands in the Mediterranean. Which one, she could not recall - there were so many. Grandpa Jack's four-masted Alden-built schooner, *Metacom,* was moored out there somewhere and Junior had gone off in the Zodiac. Their father had disappeared again. Alden called his son and heir Junior, and, to the latter's chagrin, his daughters had picked up the habit. He'd either meander back across the harbor in the pitch darkness, drunk as a skunk, or they'd hire one of the local fishermen to row them back out to the *Metacom*. There was no rush.

Liz remembered one of the puzzles of her teenage years. For some mysterious but presumably cosmic reason, the inflatable dinghy with its little outboard motor was called the Zodiac. The outboard motor itself was called a Seagull, although the girls could not, for the life of them, figure out the connection. The tiny motor was entirely lacking wings or beak.

The huge red sun had set into the Western sea and it was warm and they were heartbroken teenage virgins and Grandpa Jack suddenly asked them something so strange and so sudden and so unexpected that they both turned and looked at him and saw the tears in his pale blue eyes. He asked a question which was incomprehensible to Lizzie and Priscilla, something that made no sense at all to their young, immortal minds.

"Have you cried much lately, you girls?" he enquired softly. His moist eyes gazed out at the last glow of the sunset. "It's OK if you have not, but know this. By the time you get to my age, if you find yourself repeatedly breaking down and crying, know that this is not necessarily a bad thing. In fact, it might well be a sign of success. A good thing. It is a sign that you are living fully. You are actually alive. Actually human. On the other hand, if you have not cried for a long time, there is a problem. How do I know this? Because I have not cried for a long time, and now here I sit, a silly, somewhat inebriated old man with two lovely granddaughters who have just lost their beautiful young mother, crying my stupid eyes out."

Somehow, that moment, decades ago, in another time and place, on another island, was alive again in Liz's mind. Sitting by her grandfather's bedside a quarter of a century later, holding the dying man's gnarled old hand, the recollection brought tears to her eyes. Needless to say, at the time, Grandpa's insensitivity and selfishness had infuriated her.

"What do you mean, have I done any crying lately? What are you talking about? I haven't done anything *but* cry since Mommy's death. Not to mention Dad's treachery. Correction. Junior's treachery. I'm never going to call him Dad again," she had said under her breath.

"Grandpa Jack," Prissy had asked. "Why are you crying?"

"Well, sweetheart." He paused. "I'm getting to be an

old man and I find myself crying a lot these days."

"But Grandpa." Liz was insistent. "Why now, this very moment? What happened?"

"Do you know where we are right now?"

"On this old dock?"

"Yes."

"No."

"Yes. We're in the Greek islands."

"That is correct, Elizabeth. The island of Corfu, to be precise. Do you know what happened here on this dock during the Second World War?"

"No, Grandpa," the girls chorused.

"Good. I hope you never find out. It's better that way."

That was the last word Jack Alden had uttered on the subject, but the unanswered, almost-forgotten question had haunted Liz ever since, in a strange subliminal way. The incident on the dock was somehow intertwined with the surreal news of Sarah's death, which had arrived in the form of a ten word telegram out of the clear blue sky while Liz was off at finishing school in Switzerland the previous December. Not even the freezing funeral with its endless mind-numbing speeches in the soot blackened New York snow had convinced Liz that her mother was really gone. It just made no sense.

The dock they were sitting on and waiting for Junior to come back with the goddamned Zodiac, if he didn't mind, was situated on the Greek island of Corfu. The dock had been been built by the Persians, or the Phrygians, or by the inhabitants of either Tyre or Sidon or both, to defend themselves against, or to trade with, the Persians. Or was it Helen of Troy? During the Crusades? The Ottoman Turks and the Byzantine Empire were in there somewhere. The girls were confused, as, to be honest, was their young American social studies teacher, who was spending the summer on the *Metacom* with them. History was not the latter's strong point.

The ancient granite dock at Corfu was one of the dozens of similar quays on similar islands they would visit that long and lovely summer, gradually getting used to the fact that Sarah was really, really dead and that their father was really, really crazy. He, their father, had suddenly taken up the formerly despised game of golf with a passion amounting to obsession. He was drinking far too much, and smoking a lot of hashish, and talking about moving the family to Australia, of all the god-forsaken places on the planet. He was spending a great deal of time out west with the Indians. He had flown in

224

four nights ago from South Dakota to spend a week on the boat, and the girls had barely seen him.

Junior had sat in on one early morning breakfast meeting with the girls and the teaching staff, and had then made himself scarce. He spent most of his time on his father's sailboat talking on the satellite phone with someone called Jimmy, back in New York. His new vice-president, apparently. There was something going on between Grandpa Jack and Junior. After a lifetime of close companionship, they did not seem to be getting along any more. Although no one was talking about it, there was a new and uncomfortable tension in the air.

The summer home-schooling cruise had begun on the Bosphorus and would end on the volcanic island of Tenerife in the Canary Islands, after further educational sojourns in Rome, Beaulieu, Spain, Gibraltar, Tangiers and Fez, at which point the girls would fly back to New York to rejoin their father. Their grandfather would then try to beat his own transatlantic monohull sailing record to a place called Barbados, which was yet another island somewhere in the Caribbean Sea, wherever that was. Geography was not Liz's strong point.

Of all those docks on all those islands, however, it was only the one on Corfu that had reduced their grandfather to tears. There was a good reason for that. While his son had been off on a motor yacht the size of an ocean liner, getting sloshed on gin and tonic and smoking hashish with a gaggle of fellow billionaires and their polyamorous, bisexual, international jet-set hangers-on, and his under-age granddaughters had been flirting, harmlessly enough, with four of the local Greek lads - it would be good for their language studies - Jack Alden was sitting in a quayside *taverna* getting to know an elderly local named Cristo. The wizened 70-year-old Corfuan had evidenced a remarkable capacity for both ouzo and retsina, alternating the shots, and had related to the American, himself busy with his bottle of Johnny Walker Red, a series of events that had unfolded right here on this peaceful dock on the 27th of December, 1940. Cristo was twelve years old at the time. His birthday had been two days earlier.

"Merry Christmas, amigo," Jack interjected, raising his shot glass, a touch of irony in his tone.

"That why they give name Cristo," the man had responded. Two days after the holy day, the unholy Italians, abetted by the unholy Vatican, had bombed the ancient, undefended island, killing more than fifty unsuspecting and unarmed civilians, including Cristo's mother and sister, and injuring hundreds more. The last-minute warning had come on the secret radio.

226

Cristo's mother had propelled the boy and his four-year-old baby sister deep into an ancient cave under the dock, and told them in no uncertain terms to remain there until she came for them. It was the same cave Ulysses had hidden in, she told them cryptically, as she handed them half a loaf of stale bread and an almost empty bottle of olive oil. She disappeared into the impenetrable darkness.

Nothing happened for a long time. It was utterly dark. It was silent, except for the gentle susurration of the sea. Cristo fell asleep, little Marina in his lap. Then the world exploded. He remembered nothing further until he woke up in total darkness with the water lapping at his feet. There was no sign of Marina. She had gone to look for her mother before the bombs fell, he concluded at last, and was never seen again. Neither was their mother. Their father was off on the mainland fighting in the war.

Emerging into the brilliant moonlight, Cristo beheld a world that he had never seen before. The Mediterranean Sea was as tranquil and lovely as it had ever been, but the little town, thousands of years old, was a pile of shattered rubble. It was utterly deserted. Then the rusty grey Italian warships came. They were there for a long time, but the Italians were lazy and incompetent, and

Cristo lived by his wits among them. Then the Germans came. They were neither lazy nor incompetent. The Jews of Corfu were shipped off to Dachau on December 25th 1944. From this very dock.

"Merry Christmas," Jack interjected for the second time, raising his bottle in an ironic toast.

"Christmas. The Nazis were doing the Church's work, God's work, and they knew it with perfect certainty." Cristo went on, ignoring the interruption. He was among the captives. Although his body contained not one corpuscle of Semitic blood, he had found refuge in the oldest part of town, the ghetto, which the Italian bombs had somehow missed. The Germans could not tell the difference between a Jew and a Greek, and they weren't taking any chances.

In the midst of Cristo's rambling and increasingly inebriated tale, Alden remembered something, suddenly. It was annoying, but there was nothing to be done. Life in those days, luxurious and leisurely as it might appear from the outside, was full of interruptions and responsibilities and unfinished stories. Where were Elizabeth and Priscilla? Good God. It's been hours!

Before Cristo had time to relate his miraculous escape from the Nazi death train, and the chance reunion with his freedom-fighter father in the moun-

228

tains near the border, Alden had looked at the storyteller suddenly, as though seeing him for the first time. Cristo's age-creased face was lit by the last of the sun. Alden was an enthusiastic amateur photographer, and the lighting was as good as it gets. There was something else on Alden's mind, however. His granddaughters. His son. His yacht. It was about to get dark and he was sloshed.

"Hold that thought," he said, not unkindly. "I'll be right back." He staggered to his feet, put a $100 American banknote on the table, grabbed his Leica and his half-empty whiskey bottle and hurried outside. Liz and Prissy were sitting on the dock of the bay, watching the tide roll away. They were big girls and they were used to such abandonment by now. In fact they rather liked it. It made them feel grown-up.

Priscilla had just paid a solo visit to the ladies' facilities next to the dock-master's hut. Among the ragged inscriptions there in many languages, Greek, Russian, Italian, German, Japanese, there was one in rather elegant English calligraphy. It read:

"Here I sit, broken-hearted. Paid my penny, and only farted."

"Sarted," corrected Liz, loudly. Little Pissy, Prissy rather, had always said 'I sarted' instead of 'I farted,' until

229

she was four or so, and Liz had adopted the turn of phrase permanently. Just for the fun of it. If anyone challenged her, her excuse was that she always got her s's and her f's mixed up, just like the old Elizabethan calligraphers did.

Speaking of old Elizabethan calligraphers, one of the more irrational things Liz would do, a few years later in life, would be to enroll in a Cambridge University course in Elizabethan handwriting. How anomalous was that, for God's sake? The course would serve her in her later career at a variety of New England libraries, but at the time the decision had puzzled her. At one of the countless faculty parties in Cambridge, she had engaged in conversation with an interesting (well, not really – he was a crashing bore if you want to know the truth) Australian academic whose specialty was, you guessed it, Elizabethan calligraphy.

The professor's name was James something or other. They had embarked on a convoluted conversation that had something to do with James the First, who was the King of England at the time of the Mayflower Pilgrims. James the Elizabethan handwriting expert and Liz were pretty inebriated, and Liz's husband James Nicholson, the historical epidemiologist of rising fame, had stepped outside for a quick smoke with two of his medical colleagues.

"That makes your husband James the Second, doesn't it?" the Australian was saying. "Perhaps I'll be James the Third. I would rather like that."

Liz had looked at the Australian suddenly. Her attention had been wandering. She was more interested in the exotic manner of his speech that in the content. The randy bastard was actually trying to seduce her, wasn't he? She had politely declined his kind offer, but for some reason allowed him to sign her up for his ridiculous handwriting course. Perhaps the Lebanese hashish and the rather good cognac had something to do with the absurd decision.

Unaware that they had grandfatherly company looming above and behind them, Priscilla and Elizabeth had resumed their attempt at deciding to which of the four willing Greek boys, if any, they would prefer to lose their virginities. Alden interrupted the conversation by sitting down between them and bursting into tears. It wasn't merely Cristo's story, but the entire sweep of human history, that had triggered the outbreak.

*****

44

Goodnight Henry

L iz stood up, whispered goodnight to old Grandpa Jack, who was sleeping peacefully, shut the door carefully, wandered down the hallway and went to bed. Her eyes were too bleary and she was too emotionally disturbed to do any more work on the old diary. After lying there for a while, listening to the gentle rain in the trees outside, something made her bounce up, put the light back on, and check her email. There was a message from Baxter de Waal.

"Have you been hearing the owls?" it read.

"According to the Native Americans, an owl means someone is going to die. I guess that makes sense given your grandfather, but please be extra careful. OK?"

"I don't believe in crap like that, Bax," Liz wrote back, "but I'll be careful all the same. I've been having some scary dreams. Thanks. Liz." She went back to bed.

A sudden powerful gust of wind roared through the trees. The horizontal rain slammed against the house, and she remembered feeling a few stray drops at the table where she had just been sitting in front of the window.

"Please don't get my laptop wet," she begged. Or the precious PM Diary. She leapt up again, slammed the windows shut, and went back to bed.

"Goodnight Henry," she muttered to her invisible friend. Her eyes were burning. Abandoning her resolve to read some more of the *Misery* novel, she closed her eyes. It took her a long time to get to sleep.

*****

45

Liz Ponders The Encounter

Friday, November 20, 2020

Washington had, very kindly, made a run for Liz. He had picked up half a dozen those little black and white school composition books, and a pack of bright yellow pencils, at the decrepit little convenience shop down by the waterfront, and Liz had already transferred yesterday's notes into the first of the books. Sitting on the verandah nursing her morning coffee, reading through the notebook with its enigmatic series of entries, Liz found herself distracted. She was thinking about Baxter de Waal. Backs to the wall? Liz chuckled to herself, recalling her hysterical reaction at the bank.

The two women had quite a lot in common. Like herself, Bax was from Maine. Her father was a yachtsman, like Liz's father and grandfather, even though Andre de Waal was South African. Bax's ex-hippie mother was, apparently, a Mayflower descendant from an old New England family.

"The *Mayflower*. That's right." Liz gazed out to sea. "This is 2020. It's the 400th anniversary of the *Mayflower* landing, isn't it? I had forgotten all about that."

Baxter de Waal was the name of a South African superhero character in one of her late husband's nutty childrens' stories. Dear crazy James – or Nick as everyone else called him – had made up dozens of spontaneous, wacky bedtime stories for the kids. It was the only way to get them to sleep, although, truth be told, it was often James himself who fell asleep in mid-story. On such occasions, Layla would come into the study and find her mother hard at work on her master's thesis.

"Mommy, he fell asleep. The boys are fighting. Can you come and finish the story? Please?"

Leaving Bridgetown, Liz and Washington had given Baxter de Waal a lift back to the East Side of the island, eventually dropping her off down the road from the little cottage she was renting. On the way to the East Side, Washington had made a suggestion, a reminder rather, so they stopped at a bottle shop by the side of the winding coast road and bought several cases of Lion Ale, which, as Baxter redundantly pointed out, just happened to be made in South Africa. Liz added another gallon jug of Mount Gay rum, and half-a-dozen cans of a sweetened coconut product called Coco Lopez, plus two half-gallon jugs of pineapple juice. Washington looked on approvingly, then indicated the stack of fresh pineapples next to the check-out counter. As the store proprietor helped them into the car with the boxes, he asked Washington about the ghosts. The word was getting around.

Opening her eyes and draining the last of her coffee, Liz recited a passage from the school composition book. Gladys stood in the doorway, pretending not to eavesdrop.

"As touching our correspondence with the Indians, as our dear Governor told us after prayer, we are friends with all our neighbours, namely, those of Cohasset and Massachusetts to the north, with the great king of Pocanocket to the southwest, with those of Pamet, Nauset, Capawack and others to the east and south. And notwithstanding that those of the isle Capawack are mortal enemies to all other English, ever since

Hunt most wickedly stole away their people to sell them for slaves, yet are they on good terms with us of Plimoth, because as we never did any wrong to any Indian, so they will put up no injury at their hands.... True it is that Narragansett, situate to the west of Pocanocket, sent our Governor a snake's skin full of arrows in token of hostility and defiance...

"Massasoit hath a potent adversary to the south – the Narragansetts – that are at war with him. It was Samoset related that, the very day we first met him."

"Wait a moment." Liz yelled. "Massachusetts? Plimoth? Narraganset? This is not about Barbados. It's about New England. What on earth? I don't get it. This is just plain weird." Her train of thought was interrupted by the sound of the telephone ringing. Gladys turned and disappeared into the house.

*****

46

They're At The Hilton

Gladys brought the portable handset out to the verandah. She stood there, panting a little, until Liz noticed her and looked up expectantly.

"Someone from the hotel in Bridgetown with a message for you, Missy," Gladys explained. Liz's father and James had arrived at the Hilton. They'd be out later, after golf. Hanging up the phone, Liz wondered what it would be like to see her absentee father again. What would James be like? She could not recall ever meeting the man. Or wait, didn't he come to New Harbor ten years ago? Maybe. Would Junior and her grandfather get along? The last time they'd encountered one another, ten years ago this week, the reunion had been an absolute, unmitigated disaster.

Liz closed the composition book, put it in the hippie purse slung over her shoulder, and made her meandering way down to the beach to keep her appointment with Baxter de Waal. On the way, for some reason, she experienced a sort of flashback. There had been a pivotal day in the family's history, back in 1995. She had not been present, physically, but she had often imagined the unpleasant and violent confrontation that now unfolded in her inner consciousness.

*****

47

Wall Street Flashback

The images came to her in a sequence of vignettes, rather like a slide show or a PowerPoint presentation. 1995. Wall Street. The Alden Building. The top floor Corner Office. The view of Staten Island and the Statue of Fliberty. Did you say 'Fliberty?' Liz had heard it that way as a little girl, and she still pronounced it that way, just for the halibut. Alden and Junior were twenty-five years younger. Jack Junior had just come out of the proverbial closet. Jack Senior was less than happy.

"You are an insult to our ancestors, John." The older man spoke softly but firmly. "You have besmirched the family name."

"Besmirched the family name? Our goddamned ancestors besmirched the family name hundreds of years before you or I were born. In any case, I don't give a shit about our ancestors, Jack. They're dead and gone."

"Well then, if you can't respect the people who made you what you are..." Alden's face was turning an alarming shade of beetroot. He was apoplectic. His voice rose. "Get out of my goddamned office."

"This is all just homophobic bullshit, you know that, don't you? You hate faggots. Fuck you, Jack! Not only that, you're a goddamned Indian hater. You're a bigot. You despise anyone whose skin is a different color from yours, just like your goddamned Puritan ancestors. I'll see you later, Mein Führer!"

"I said, get out of my goddamned office."

"Yes sir! Right away, sir! And by the way, it's not *your* office, Mister Alden. It's *our* office, just in case you'd forgotten. I'm the CEO of this goddamned corporation, according to the Board. But yes, I'll get out of *your* office, permanently. I'm moving to the Sydney plant full-time. See you later, dickhead." Junior turned to leave.

Alden was on the verge of a heart attack, but he took a deep breath and gradually regained his composure. He shook his head in feigned wonder.

241

"Dickhead?" he said. "You children have such a wonderful way with words."

Junior stopped and turned on his father violently. He did not like being called a child, and Jack Senior knew that all too well. "Oh and one more thing before I go," Junior said, his voice rough at the edges.

"I don't know how to tell you this." He got his emotions under control. "I changed my family's name. Legally. Back in 1985."

The older man breathed deeply, recovering his balance. His facial color changed from deep purple to a somewhat healthier bright pink.

"So I heard," he said at last. "The walls have ears, you know. I have seen my granddaughters' report cards. Did the name change have anything to do with your angry Indian friends, by any chance? All the crap they were feeding you, in return for your oh-so-generous financial support? Sarah was not exactly happy about that, was she?"

The father stopped and regarded his red-faced son. There was weariness and sadness and even a hint of compassion in his look. He went on.

"Alten, huh? John Bradford Alten. Or is it Johann Bergdorf Alten? That certainly has a fine Teutonic ring to it. German, you say? Well, perhaps you're the Adolph

Hitler of the family, not me. Good riddance to you, Johnny-boy. You did not turn out the way your mother and I hoped. Too goddamn permissive by a mile, we were." The father's voice rose again, while the son watched him icily. "You are not only an idiot and a selfish fool, John, you're a goddamned liar. I do not like what you have done to my granddaughters. I shall henceforth consider myself childless, and you... you may consider yourself disowned from this moment forward. I'll have my lawyers get the paperwork to you at the Sydney office. I wish you well. I truly do. Goodbye."

John Bradford Alden, Senior turned on his heel and left the building. Johann Bergdorf Alten stood staring blindly out of the window at the Statue of Fliberty.

*****

48

The Ditch Witch

There was not a breath of wind, and it was hot. The new friends sat on the sand in the shade of a palm tree, hoping not to be hit on the head by falling coconuts, tentatively sipping their dreadful machine-made cappucinos. The steaming concoctions tasted like rancid artificial milk laced with a sugary dash of sulphuric acid. Liz made a sour face.

"How's your coffee, Baxter?" Liz pronounced the word cawfee, Long Island style, just for the fun of it.

"I've had worse, although I can't remember when. But what can you expect from a beach shack made of driftwood?"

"A beach shack called the Ditch Witch, to boot."

"To boot? I haven't heard that term since Thoreau, back in my undergraduate days."

"Henry David Thoreau is my all-time hero. He was my invisible friend when I was a little girl. That's how we met. I'd have married him in a New York minute if we hadn't lived centuries apart." Liz did not mention the fact that she still maintained a daily conversation with the Concord transcendentalist. For obvious reasons, it was one of her better kept secrets.

"Thoreau never did marry, did he? Must have been the neck beard." Bax giggled. "Anyway, for what it's worth, it turns out the Ditch Witch belongs to a surfer couple from Long Island. I was just chatting with the husband. The original is at a surf spot in Montauk called Ditch Plains. Hence the name. "

"A surf spot in Montauk? You mean Montauk, Long Island? Well that explains everything, doesn't it? Not! There's no surf in Long Island, is there? I'll have to ask my boys. They know everything there is to know about surfing."

"Speaking of surfing, look at that." Baxter pointed

out at the headland, where a longboarder was manoevring gracefully up and down the leading edge of a beautiful, shoulder high wave. Beyond the surf line, a large white sailboat moved slowly against the dark blue horizon.

"Oh look! Look at that beautiful yawl. It looks just like the boat Andre came over on. My dad."

"That's right. Your father was a sailor, wasn't he? Tell me about him."

"Correction. My dad *is* a sailor. He's still doing it, every chance he gets."

"Sorry. I was..."

"No worries, Liz. My dad, Andre, he... You'd like him. He's fun. Let's see. Andre sailed the ocean blue back in 1492. Not really, but that what he always told me when I was a kid. He actually came over in 1969, part of the delivery crew that brought *Gitana* over from Europe. He arrived in the Americas on Thanksgiving Day, so he claimed he was a latter-day Pilgrim. Then he met a real Pilgrim - my mom."

"Hang on a sec. *Gitana?*"

"She's a sailboat. Gitana means gypsy in Italian. An appropriate name for my father if ever there was one. She's a beautiful 90-foot wooden yawl from the nineteen fifties - still going strong. She's based in Antigua, last I heard."

"You mean, all these years later? A wooden boat?"

"Those old racing yachts are so precious. They are usually perfectly maintained. There are plenty of even older ones, still in perfect condition. You're from Maine, right? Ever go to Camden in the summertime?"

"Of course. We used to have a house there. We still do, actually. My first job out of college was interning at Camden Public Library. But I haven't paid a lot of attention to sailboats lately. Speaking of sailboats, you seem to know a lot on the subject. Here's something that's been puzzling me. Have you ever heard of *Weetamoo?*"

"Weetamoo?" Baxter turned and stared at Liz. "Boy, you do change subjects, don't you? But hey, I was raised by hippies. Some of my parents' friends used to change subjects five times in a single sentence. I can roll with the punches."

"I didn't change the subject." Liz said, defensively. If there was one thing she hated, it was to be unjustly accused of something she did not do.

"Yes you did. One minute I'm telling you about my father. Out of left field you ask about an Indian princess from back in the day. Tell me that's not changing the subject."

"An Indian princess? A princess from India? Now

wait a minute, Bax."

"Weetamoo was Wamsutta's wife. She and Philip always believed the Pilgrims poisoned him. She was the one who kidnapped Mary Rowlandson."

"Kidnapped Mary Rowlandson? The woman the Puritans kicked out of..? Whoa, Bax. Hold on. You're getting way ahead of me. I asked you whether you had heard of my grandfather's sailboat, and suddenly you're deep into early New England history. Talk about changing the subject."

"Your grandfather's sailboat? I didn't know he had one."

"Weetamoo? Weetamoo IV? America's Cup?"

"Hi Mom!" The double cry issued from two teenage boys trotting along the beach, surfboards under their arms.

"Jonny, Jason, come here a moment."

"But Mom!"

"There's someone I want you to meet."
The surfers reluctantly stopped and dutifully came over, looking longingly out at the waves all the while.

"This is my new best friend Baxter. Everybody calls her Bax."

"Hi Bax," the boys chorused politely.

"Bax, these are my sons, future world surfing

champions Jason and Jonny Nicholson. Ta-rah!"

"Mom!"

"You're not supposed to tell anyone."

"It's back luck, Mom."

"Pleased to meet you, Bax. Can we go now, Mom?"

"Just answer me one question." Liz replied. "There's no surf in Montauk, New York, is there?"

"Mom, what have you been smoking? You're sitting in front of the Ditch Witch."

"I noticed that. So?"

"Ditch Plains is one of the best breaks in Montauk. Aside from the Ranch, when it gets really big. Ditch closes out when it gets that big."

"You remember when we used to go to Tortola?" Jason asked. "That's where we started surfing."

"Tortola? What's Tortola got to do with anything?"

"Do you remember the Bomba Shack?"

"Well yeah. I do, actually."

Baxter de Waal watched this exchange with amusement.

"Well, Mom, you're at Bomba South."

"Well, now, that explains everything," Liz laughed. "Thanks a lot, guys."

"No Mom, you don't get it." Jonny said. "What he's trying to tell you is the Ditch Witch guys bought this shack from Bomba, after he died."

"They bought this shack from a dead person? Wow. You guys better get in the water. Your brains are over-heating."

The boys needed no further encouragement. Ten seconds later they were paddling for the horizon, ducking under the incoming waves, then popping up and paddling on.

"What handsome young men. They're going to break a few hearts."

"Thanks."

"I didn't know that, about Bomba Shack. That explains it."

"Explains what? You know the Bomba Shack on Tortola? It's probably the most obscure place on the planet."

"Well yeah. My dad used to skipper sailboats, remember?"

"So?"

"So we spent a whole lot of time at Bomba Shack when I was a kid. He was running a charter boat that spent the winters in Road Town and the summers in Camden. I did my first mushrooms there. The shack was made entirely of driftwood, just like this one. I didn't know Bomba had opened another one."

"Boy. Can we hit the pause button for a moment?

My brain is getting a cramp."

"Bomba served mushroom tea for free every full moon." Bax was on a roll. "Remember? I was thirteen or fourteen, but my parents had no problem with that. I was conceived on MDA, apparently. Or at least that's where the Katahdin idea came from."

"The Katahdin idea? Baxter, stop! You're freaking me out. One thing at a time, please. Would you remind me, one more time, how your folks came up with your name? You told me, but..."

"A girl named Baxter? You thought that was pretty funny, didn't you? But that's me, Baxter, the one and only." Bax stopped in mid-sentence. She had lost track of her thoughts. "Where was I? Oh. Andre, my dad, he made his first landfall in the New World right here on Barbados, on his 25th birthday, back in 1969. Oh, by the way, my parents are threatening to come to Barbados. It is his birthday next week after all, and I'm here already."

"Are they really? I'd love to meet them. And just so you know, it's my birthday too. The day after Thanksgiving."

"No! You're kidding. The 27th? That's my father's birthday. How cool. I sense a party coming on. Will they actually show up, that's the question? It's fifty-fifty. My Mom's been having some health challenges. Maybe they'll go back to Maui from Maine via Barbados? Take the scenic route. That's what I'm hoping, anyway." Baxter had grown up on sailboats in the Caribbean, Hawaii, and Maine. "My dad was a nutty Goon Show fan. He would make up surreal bedtime stories, and ask impossible questions like 'What's the difference between a duck?' See what I had to live with, Liz? You're not the only one." Bax gazed out at the ocean thoughtfully. "Andre and Sally are retired. They spend their summers at the cottage in Camden, and the winters living on their boat in Maui."

"Maui? My little sister Prissy lives on Maui. She's here on the island at this very moment. Right up there at Alden House." Liz pointed up the hill. "She and her, um.., they just got in from Hawaii."

"Anyway, Liz, can we hit the reset button?" Bax continued. "Do you mind? Weren't we going to talk about Pilgrims and Indians? I was just at Plimoth Plantation, did I tell you that? Two weeks ago."

The conversation had veered off on yet another tack. Liz picked up the Plimoth Plantation thread.

"Plimoth Plantation? I haven't been there since I was a kid. What on earth were you doing there?"

"My mother is... Well, there's just so much misinformation. This Indian kid is sitting there in the wetu,

252

the wigwam, telling the Japanese tourists and the busloads of schoolkids stuff about the English settlers, the Pilgrims. Most of what he said, it's historically untrue. It's just not right. They need to be trained."

"Stuff? What kind of stuff?"

"Oh, you know, like, the Pilgrims didn't know how to hunt. Or fish. They didn't know any of the local plants or trees. The Wampanoag had to feed them, show them how to build wigwams, then teach them farming or they'd have starved to death the first winter. Oh, and they were kicked out of Provincetown for grave-robbing."

"The wampa what?"

"The Wampanoag. It means people of the dawn. That's what the Cape Cod Indians call themselves these days."

"Hmmm. OK. I know they, the Pilgrims, stole the Indian's corn, right? That could get you kicked out, if you got caught. But wait. There was no Provincetown back then, was there? How could they be kicked out of a place that didn't exist yet?"

"They paid for the corn, later, but yeah, that wasn't the most diplomatic move on their part, I agree. At least they've given up on the smallpox blanket story. Last time I was there... Someone must've complained." Bax returned to her original thread. "I saw the Indian kid later, in the cafeteria. I went up to him and asked him where he got his information about the Mayflower people. He said, 'I don't know much about them. It's just what I hear on the rez. All I know is I don't like them.' " Bax paused for breath. "So I asked him, do you respect your ancestors? The kid said: 'Of course I do. It's the Native way.'"

"Tell me something, Baxter." Liz interjected. "Are you a Mayflower descendant?"

"Didn't I just tell you that? My mom? Anyway, hang on, Liz. I'm getting there. So I said to the Indian kid, I said, tell me, do you think I should respect my ancestors, or is that strictly a Native thing. He said, of course you should. Everybody should respect their ancestors. So I said, well, I'm a Mayflower descendant. The people you were talking about down there are my ancestors. You were saying a lot of things about my ancestors that are historically untrue. Negative things. How should I respond to that in a respectful way?"

"So you are a descendant?"

"A Mayflower descendant? In fact I am, on my mother's side. Four or five lines. How about you, being from New England and all?"

"I don't think so. We're German on my grandfather's side. I have a feeling my mother might...but she's dead. I don't know much about her ancestral background. It's a closed subject in my family, for some reason. All I know is, my great-grandfather Anglicized the family name from Alten to Alden, something about a sailboat."

"Alden makes some of the finest sailboats ever built. My dad... Is that where..?"

"Then my father changed it back again, our family name, back to Alten. My dad, just so you know, has a serious aversion to anything concerning the Pilgrims and the Puritans. If you ever want to rouse his ire, just bring up the subject." Liz thought for a moment.

"Hey, you might know the answer to this, Bax. When we get a chance, I want to talk to you about... You just mentioned the smallpox blankets the *Mayflower* brought over. I've never understood... how the heck did they pull that off without infecting themselves?"
Bax stared at her new friend, her mouth open. Liz went on. "But first, listen to this, Bax. Can I read you something I'm working on?"

"Smallpox blankets the *Mayflower* brought over? You're shitting me, Liz. You don't really believe that, do you?"

"What? Of course I do. Everybody knows that. It's

an established fact. It's what I was taught in high school, in college. My dad was the first one to tell me about it. He knows everything there is to know about the Indians. Growing up in New York City, we always had Indians in the house, you know, the AIM guys. They told us everything we had been taught in school was a lie. It was pretty sickening. How the first Thanksgiving was actually to celebrate a massacre. How the white invaders came over and wiped the peaceful Indians out, using the first form of biological warfare in human history."

"Oh dear."

"What do you mean, oh dear? Are you saying you know something I don't?"

"I mean, oh dear! Everything you just said is the biggest crock..." The new friends were on the verge of an argument. Liz was, however, more interested in sharing her transcription with Baxter, than in dredging up irrelevant and ancient English crimes. She interrupted Bax in mid-sentence.

"Anyway, Bax, we can sort that out later. Is that OK? First, can I read you something I'm working on? It's only a rough draft, it's probably full of mistakes, but it might be germane to your research. It's about American Indian spirituality, as far as I can tell. I want to know what tribe you think it might refer to. Listen."

"I know where that garbage comes from," Bax ignored Liz and went on. "I just had an email, two or three days ago, from my colleague in Berkeley. She sent me a link to an article about Angelina Jolie, the actress, who hates Thanksgiving because she thinks it's a celebration of murder. You can look it up. She quotes the whole God-awful Susan Bates thing as though it was the Gospel."

Liz took no notice of Bax or her obvious passion. She took the composition book out of her shoulder bag and started reading.

"*Further, observing us to crave a blessing on our meat before we did eat, and after to give thanks for the same, he asked us what was the meaning of that ordinary custom? Hereupon I took occasion to tell them of God's works of creation, and preservation, of his laws and ordinances, especially of the ten commandments, all which they hearkened unto with great attention, and liked well of: only the seventh commandment they excepted against, thinking there were many inconveniences in it, that a man should be tied to one woman: about which we reasoned a good time.*"

"Go on," said Bax, still fuming, but feigning politeness. "This is definitely interesting. It sounds an awful lot like... Where did you say this came from?"

"Let me finish this part, and then tell me what you

think it's about." Liz went on.

"*Also I told them that whatsoever good things we had, we received from God, as the author and giver thereof, and therefore craved his blessing upon that we had, and were about to eat, that it might nourish and strengthen our bodies, and having eaten sufficient, being satisfied therewith, we again returned thanks to the same our God for that our refreshing, etc. This all of them concluded to be very well, and said, they believed almost all the same things, and that the same power that we called God, they called Kiehtan. Much profitable conference was occasioned hereby, which would be too tedious to relate, yet was no less delightful to them, then comfortable to us. Here we remained only that night, but never had better entertainment amongst any of them.*"

****

49

Flashback To Plimoth Plantation

It grew even hotter as the day wore on. There was still not a breath of wind to rustle the trees, and the soft hiss of the ocean was clearly audible in Liz's bedroom. The late afternoon light poured in through the open window and lit the small, ornately-inlaid table where Liz sat upright, staring bleary-eyed at the old 'bible.' For two hours straight, she had been busily '*tranfcribing*' the diary's contents. It was an extremely challenging undertaking. Little did Liz suspect, the transcription was about to occupy the next three years

259

of her life, and that would be just the beginning. In fact, the perplexing discovery in the Alden House cellar would change the entire course of her existence.

Liz's eyes were stinging. As she worked on the transcriptions, she talked to herself. Everything that went through her mind came out of her mouth in real time. It was an old habit.

"My eyes," she muttered. "I need some eyedrops. That will take another trip into town."

She leaned back in the chair and exhaled, closing her lids against the burning sensation. In her inner mind, she experienced a sudden golden flash of blinding light, which resolved into a pleasant dreamlike out-of-body experience in which she was both observer and participant at the same time.

Somehow, Liz knew that the year was 1625. It was a drowsy summer afternoon. Priscilla, a young, slender, mousy blonde, blue eyed English woman in her early twenties, with Dutch braids in her hair, and a black haired, dark eyed woman of a similar age named Alice - or Anice, rather, as the Indians never could pronounce the English letter 'l' - were sitting in Priscilla's tiny wattle and daub house at Plimoth Plantation. A contented baby gurgled somewhere in the background. Outside, through the open back door, a group of women could be heard softly singing an old English hymn as they weeded the communal vegetable garden, accompanied by the enthusiastic humming of bees and the occasional squawk of an alarmed hen pursued by an amorous rooster. The English girl was sitting at her spinning wheel, eyes closed, thinking deeply, while her Indian friend placidly stitched a pattern of colorful glass beads of Venetian origin onto a pair of buckskin leggings for her husband, the Pilgrims' trusted friend and ally, Hobamok.

The women had been exchanging notes on the history of the area. As Anice's English improved, she had been able to give her friend more and more information, but of course, her grasp of the history of Massachusetts Bay was extremely limited. Anice had rarely traveled more than twenty miles from the spot where she was born, which was roughly three hundred yards from where the women sat. On the other hand, she had learned a great deal simply by listening to the well-traveled men of her community. Her husband had journeyed as far north as Mawooshen, and as far south as the island of the Manhattees. He had recently accompanied some of the English men on a trading journey across the water to the country of the Massachuset.

As their relationship slowly deepened into a warm, trusting friendship, Priscilla was able to piece the story together, by combining what she had learned from her English menfolk with the new information she was hearing from Anice. She was beginning to understand the apocalyptic nature of the series of events that had shaken the entire Eastern seaboard, the area her people called New England, just a few years before the storm-battered *Mayflower* finally dropped anchor less than a mile from the Plantation.

The original name of Plimoth, as Priscilla had heard from Samoset, their very first Indian visitor, was Patux-et. The lovely bay, with its pristine, park-like surroundings, was the former home of Anice's tribe, the Patuxet band of Massachusetts Bay Indians. A decade earlier, as Priscilla had gathered from a conversation between her husband John Alden and their friend and shipmate Edward Winslow, the Patuxet had been estimated to be some two thousand warriors strong. So wrote Captain John Smith, the English explorer of Pocahontas notoriety. And yet, when the *Mayflower's* passengers stepped ashore that bleak and icy December afternoon almost four years ago, the place had been utterly deserted. It was an abandoned and haunted place. Something awful had happened since Smith's 1614 visit. There were unburied skeletons in the woods and weathered, sea-weed-festooned human skulls along the rocky shoreline.

What Captain Smith did not know, when he submitted his map and his report to his employer back in London, was that the Massachuset federation of tribes had become embroiled in a brutal war between their northern allies - the Mawooshen - and the Mawooshen's fearsome enemies, the Tarentynes (or Tarrantines) of faraway Nova Scotia.

The conflict had erupted over control of the fur commerce with the French, who maintained their trading posts some four hundred miles to the north of the Patuxet village. This remote and unprecedented war, which had nothing whatsoever to do with the Massachuset people, was about to unleash a relentless reign of terror upon all of the coastal communities Smith had encountered, followed in short order by a devastating epidemic of disease. A deadly combination of war and plague was about to wipe the Patuxet off the face of the earth.

Priscilla was aware that Captain Smith had given the English name Plimoth to Patuxet Bay. Before departing from England, the *Mayflower's* passengers had purchased a copy of Smith's detailed map. Priscilla had examined the complex document carefully as the ship lay at Cape Cod, while the men explored the shoreline in search of the best place to plant their colony, endeavoring at the same time to establish contact with the local Indians. Back in Holland, the colonists had declined to employ Smith himself, choosing instead the fierce red-bearded Catholic, Myles Standish, as their military captain.

As to Alice, or Anice, she was one of the very few survivors of the doomed Patuxet tribe. The reader has quite possibly heard of the other Patuxet survivor, the famous Tisquantum or Squanto. Anice and Squanto, it transpired, were first cousins. Squanto's father, the powerful Patuxet sachem, and Anice's mother, had been brother and sister.

Squanto himself, a well-traveled local man who Priscilla had known rather well and had regarded as a friend, had met his end under sudden and mysterious circumstances a few years earlier, in December, 1622. Squanto was the Pilgrims' indispensable Indian guide and interpreter, but, as they slowly came to realize, he had a hidden, manipulative side to him. Sentenced to death by the paramount sachem Massasoit for allegedly conspiring against him, Squanto had taken refuge with the Plimoth colonists, who refused to hand him over for execution. Governor William Bradford had not the heart to so reward their stalwart friend Tisquantum, despite all that had emerged concerning the sinuous survivor and his subtle, serpentine ways. Besides, they desperately needed his ongoing services as translator and negotiator. On a trading expedition to the other side of Cape Cod, however, Squanto had suddenly taken ill. According to Governor Bradford's account, he had begun 'bleeding at ye nose,' and soon died of the 'Indian fever.' Was Squanto poisoned? If so, by whom? Certainly not by the English, one must agree.

Was Squanto's death the result of witchcraft, as the Cherokee researcher Betty Booth Donohue proposes? It is not impossible. To this day, African witchdoctors or sangomas know how to dispense with their enemies, and their client's enemies, for a suitable fee, by purely psychic means. It seems likely that the powers of the Pokanoket pow-wows were no different. Why should they have been? They inhabited a similar world of primal animism dominated by powerful and dangerous spirits, not too different from certain parts of Africa in the 21st Century.

What does Nathaniel Philbrick, the author of the bestselling book *Mayflower,* say on the subject? He proposes that poisoning was indeed the cause, and compares Squanto's death with that of Massasoit's son Wamsutta a half-century later.

The baby cried, emitting a loud and desperate plea for sustenance. Priscilla stopped her spinning, stood up,

265

and went over to the crib, picked up the caterwauling eight-month-old, and put the baby girl to her fair white breast. The English girl's voice was gentle, her Middle Country diction clearly from an earlier era.

"Why did the Pokanokets not trust Squanto, Alice? He was such a Godsend to us."

"Trust? Massasoit no trust Tisquantum. Me no trust Tisquantum," the Indian girl replied, struggling for the right words. "Not since little child. Tisquantum think he big sachem when small boy. Tell every people what do."

"Although I do remember the men talking," recalled Priscilla. "Well, without him, and of course Samoset, we would never have survived this long."

"Samoset? What Samoset?" Alice was puzzled. She had never heard of Samoset.

"Samoset walked naked into our town one morning before it was so much as a village. It was the day of the spring equinox. I had never seen a man unclad. It...it was quite a revelation. He was... beautiful. Tall and beautiful. Samoset greeted us in English. 'Welcome, Englishmen,' he said, clear as daylight. His deep voice had the elegance of an English count to it. You could have knocked us over with a feather."

"Count? Knock a feather?"

"Never mind, dear. Samoset told us much about the

country hereabouts. Of Massassoit, and his enemies to the south, the Narragansett. He spoke of the war that came down from the north, and of the plague that had taken so many of your people before our landing here. Then a few days later, he introduced us to Tisquantum, the one we called Squanto. He spoke much better English than Samoset, having previously lived several years in our country, and who had many friends among the English."

"Samoset?" Anice was puzzled. "Not Algonkin name."

"Samoset comes from an island a day's sail to the north. Mohiggen, I think he called it. He knew the names of all the English fishing captains up there."

"Ah, Mawooshen. Samoset English name? Me English name Anice, that man English name Samoset?"

"Hmm, come to think of it, my husband and Edward were speaking of him. They wondered whether the name Samoset could in fact be derived from the English name Somerset. Perchance his English friends gave him an English name, just as we have done with you. Now tell me this, Alice, I still do not understand. Why did you not trust Squanto?" Priscilla looked down at little Lizzie, who was falling asleep, a contented smile on her pudgy face. Her thin strawberry hair stuck up like a

Mohawk's. Was the indigenous spirit already beginning to infiltrate this latest wave of migrants? Priscilla continued. "I have not forgotten your request. First, speak to me of Squanto, and then we shall talk about your desire to learn to read and write."

"Tisquantum bad mad man. Mad bad man," said Alice. "Come from far country with bad English captain, Captain Hunt, steal many Patuxet boy. Long time go. My brothers. Steal Nauset boys as well." Anice was a pretty girl, about five months pregnant. You might meet her like in the hills of Andalucia at a gypsy fair over there. She held up both hands, pushed them forward twice, then held up a single hand. Five and twenty. Twenty-five local men stolen by the treacherous Captain Hunt. This was not news. Priscilla had heard it before.

"No wonder your people were loath to meet with us when first we arrived. We met no Indian for four long months."

"No boy come home. Brothers gone. When Tarentine come no more, Tisquantum return. Tisquantum only. After plague finish. Too late. People gone. Patuxet dead. All dead. Sachem dead. Father dead. Mother dead. Only Anice and small baby sister. Hobamok take, make wife. Now five wife. Live with

English at Patuxet. How say? Neighbor?"

Priscilla shook her head. Tarentine? Five wives? This was a lot of information all of a sudden.

"That's right, Alice. Neighbor. You and I are neighbors. That is your first important word in my language, English. Now, tell me, what is your Patuxet word for neighbor? For friend? I will write this in my book, my bible as you call it. Your language and my language."

Priscilla looked into Alice's eyes. They were impenetrably dark pools. Infinite sadness resided there.

"But first, tell me dear, did you say your husband has five wives? I could not imagine sharing my dear John with four other women." Priscilla spoke these words out loud, while simultaneously thinking, 'Oh dear God. You lost your whole tribe? I did not realize that.' Priscilla had lost her mother, her father, her brother and almost fifty more of her compatriots, fully half of the original Mayflower community, but Alice had lost everyone, literally her entire tribe, thousands of them. How did she feel? She seemed so peaceful.

"I did not know that," she continued gently, "and I want to know more. But first, I would be impolite not to answer your request."

"Is good have help. Lazy man have no help. Many wife much help. Correct?" Without waiting for an

269

answer, she returned to her original subject. "Anice learn English write."

"Really?" Priscilla asked. The idea had surprised her. "English? Why on Earth would you want to learn to write?"

The Indian struggled with the unfamiliar language, although she had made remarkable progress in the few months of their friendship. Alice could not pronounce Priscilla's name. She called her Scilla.

"Scilla write English people, Anice write Patuxet people. Write story. In bible."

"You mean in my diary?"

"Write story. That, what you call? Bible? That bible you write? Here when Scilla gone ancestor? When Scilla breathe no more? Bible here?"

"What? I have never had that thought. It's not really a bible, you know. It's just an empty book with several hundred blank pages. My dear departed father had it made for my 12th birthday. I call it my diary." Priscilla hesitated. How could she explain a phenomenon that was rare even in her own culture to one who depended upon oral history for her sense of continuity in the world?

"I am really just writing it for myself, dear Alice. When I am an old woman, when my memory is fading away, perhaps I will be able to remember the things that happened when I was young. Perchance my grandchildren will be interested in such foolish old memories."

The Indian woman was persistent. "Bible, Scilla?" There was a point she was determined to get across. "Still here when Scilla go ancestor?"

"It's called a book, not a bible, Alice, although those words actually mean the same thing. Our English language is so confusing, I'm afraid. Well... I do suppose the book will still be here, as long as I don't lose it, or as long as it doesn't burn up in a fire, or wash away in a flood, or as long as the Governor doesn't catch me writing in it and take it away from me."

"No stand?"

"Understand. We English goodwives are not supposed to know how to read or write. That is man's business, although an exception is made when it comes to the Bible. Certain of our men, however, dear Edward for example, they like me to help them with their writings. But my father - oh how I miss him - my dear father thought it a most ridiculous rule. He began to teach me reading and writing when I was just five years old."

"I beg thee, teach me."

"Alice, methinks I begin to understand your request.

You want to write the story of your people, before it is lost forever. Is that correct?"

From the fort up on the hill, there came the distant sound of a bell. It was the call to prayer. The sound was reminiscent of the old slave bell ringing outside Alden House four hundred years later. The dream was fading. Liz shook her head. Priscilla stood up, holding the naked baby girl on her hip. Little Elizabeth stood up bravely, her stocky legs stiff.

"It is time for evening prayers, my dear Alice. Followed by supper. Would you deign to sup with us? You would be most welcome."

The Indian woman stood up and prepared to leave. "Food make. Men come home from hunt. No deer. No fish. Men hungry. No food, angry husband. No good." Anice rubbed her stomach gently, and Priscilla realized for the first time that her Indian friend was pregnant. How could she not have noticed?

The bell rang again, closer now. It was the slave bell. The sound of the ocean returned. Gladys's melodious voice wafted up from below.

"Dinner time, Miss Lizzie. Your new friend is here. Come and get it, before it gets cold..."
Liz opened her eyes. The old bible lay on the little table before her, her hands open beside it.

"What?" She asked herself. "Was that a dream? Where am I? Who am I?"

She closed her eyes again and sat there deep in thought. She was between worlds. After a while she re-read the bewildering transcription she had made an hour earlier. There it was, that unfamiliar word - Tarentine.

"...the Warre growing more and more violent between the Bashaba and the Tarentines, who (as it seemed) presumed upon the hopes they had to be favoured of the French that were seated in Canada their next neighbours, the Tarentines surprised the Bashaba, and slew him and all his People near about him, carrying away his Women, and such other matters as they thought of value; after his death the publique businesse running to confusion for want of an head, the rest of his great Sagamores fell at variance among themselves, spoiled and destroyed each others people and provision, and famine took hould of many, which was seconded by a great and generall plague, which so violently rained for three yeares together, that in a manner the greater part of that Land was left desert without any to disturb or appease our [English] free and peaceable possession thereof..."

Liz wandered down the stairs in a daze, and sat through dinner feeling disconnected from reality. It was a very quiet dinner. Scilla and Maryah had gone to town with the boys, and Barbara had excused herself. She had quit smoking, and had decided to fast instead of giving in to the hunger pangs.

Liz said barely a word to Baxter de Waal, her dinner guest. The phrase 'the Tarentines' kept going through her mind. Who or what were the Tarentines? As soon as she had eaten, Liz excused herself and went back up the stairs, leaving her guest with a puzzled look on her face.

"I will ask Washington to walk you home if you like, Miss Baxter," offered Gladys. "It looks as though Miss Lizzie is off in another dimension, and there is a nice half- moon shining."

*****

50

Liz Puts Her Vigil To Use

It was dark outside. Liz sat with Grandpa Jack for a couple of hours, as was her custom. There was a difference this time, however. Two differences, as a matter of fact. Old Alden slept like a baby, snoring gently, while Liz sat distractedly by the bedside with the ancient, crumbling diary in her lap, carefully opening brittle page after brittle page, and continuing to wonder what on earth she was looking at.

Her father and his Australian consort had arrived at

last, while she was sitting there with the sleeping Alden. She heard their weary voices through the open door to the hallway, and prepared for company, but the two men continued on down the hall and, presumably, went straight to bed. She considered running out to greet them, but decided she would see them in the morning.

Sometime between nine and ten o'clock, Liz wandered back to her room, where she stayed up most of the night, transcribing various sections of the hand-written text. Getting into bed at last, she found herself wide awake, so she picked up the book she'd selected from the well stocked library downstairs - a Stephen King novel with the uplifting title *Misery*. King, as has been mentioned, was a fellow Mainiac, but Liz, for some reason, had yet to read any of his books.

It was a different kind of night in another regard. Sometime in the wee hours, Liz turned over and put the light out. Moments later, it seemed to her, she woke up from a deliciously erotic dream. Lying there trying to hold onto the heavenly feelings, she recalled the still-packaged device she had purchased at Logan International. It was in her carry-on suitcase.

"Well, Henry," she sighed to the world at large, "There's no time like the present."

51

The First Encounter

Saturday, November 21, 2020

Liz and James strolled slowly along the lovely tropical shorefront, their bare feet splashing through
the warm shallow water as it ebbed and flowed around
them. Birds sang from the palm trees overhead. The surf
hissed quietly. A dozen surfers sat on their boards out in
the relatively calm water, praying to Davey Jones, the
deity of surfing, to send them a little action.

James walked stooped over, his shoulders hunched,

his hands clasped behind his back. His straight, shoulder-length brown hair hung over his face, as he gave Liz's question his full attention.

"But Elizabeth... Think about it." James's voice had a strong Australian inflection. "It's just not possible. Johnny has never had HIV. I would know, if anybody would. He got tested, back in the late 90s. So did I. I was one of the lucky ones, and as for your father... he never... I was..." They walked in silence for a while. Liz picked up an eroded conch-shell, examined it and put it to her ear. James glanced at her and went on.

"I mean, that's right when we met. 1994. We didn't... you know... for over two years, for God's sake! After your mother died, John was absolutely devastated. So guilty. He should have been there, but he was too busy being the millionaire playboy in New York. You poor girls! I can barely imagine."

Liz stopped and took the shell from her ear. James turned, took a step back, and looked at his stepdaughter with a mixture of compassion and wonderment. The family resemblance was eerie. Liz looked exactly like a female version of her father. She was...alluring. And intimidating. Just like her father. The woman challenged him suddenly, her eyes blazing, her voice low and intense.

"So tell me this, James. My mother, Sarah. She goes out grocery shopping, leaving us girls at the villa. The next time we see her is in the fucking hospital in San Juan. She could have been killed, but, oh no, she's going to be OK. Just fine. A routine blood transfusion has saved her life. A year later she's dead. Dead, as in terminated. Kaput. Dead of fucking AIDS compounded by pneumonia. It's pretty obvious isn't it? Our father turns out to be gay. He's having an affair with you. He's part of the whole West Village fag scene, and God only knows what else. Our mother's dead of AIDS. Come on."

They walked on in silence for another fifty yards, then sat down in the sand at the foot of a huge weather sculpted rock formation, gazing out at the sparkling ocean. James looked at Liz, his face lit by the moving reflections off the water. There was a glisten in his soft, brown eyes. He opened his mouth to respond but changed his mind. Liz went on.

"I was fifteen. Pissy was twelve or thirteen. Our life was over."

"Pissy? Oh. Priscilla. Your younger sister."

"Scilla. She was eleven."

James hesitated, a tear glistening in his eye.

"I understand. I..." he stuttered.

Liz leapt to her feet. She turned on him like a ferocious

279

she-bear defending her cubs. James sat there in the sand, looking up at the furious woman, helplessly.

"You understand? Understand? Bull fucking shit. Don't give me that. You haven't the faintest idea what you did. You and that asshole quote-unquote husband of yours. What a joke. Fuck you! Fuck both of you!"

James burst into tears. Liz glared at him scornfully, then turned and strode stiffly back down the beach in the direction of the house. James sat there, his face wet, gazing blindly out at the out-of-focus surfers.

"You're right. I'm sorry," he said. "I shouldn't have said that."
Liz did not hear him. She was too far away and the sound of the surf swallowed up James's humble whisper.

*****

52

'Tranfcribing' The Old Diary

Back in the kitchen at Alden House, Liz calmed down gradually, and stopped sobbing. She thought about the encounter with James. Perhaps she had misjudged the man, unlikely as that might be, but she just couldn't give it any more attention. She had other fish to fry. She was anxious to get back to work on the old diary. She took a carafe of cold coffee and went up the stairs and sat down at her desk. She was *obfeffively*

bufy tranfcribing segments from the PM Diary, as she
wrote in an email to Baxter, apologizing for her anti-
social behavior the previous evening.

The days went by. Nobody had seen Liz for a week,
or at least that was how it seemed to Scilla when James
inquired about her sister. Liz was skipping meals, and a
concerned Gladys had taken to putting a covered tray of
food outside her closed bedroom door a couple of times
a day. More often than not, the food went untouched.

In the bathroom, Liz consulted with the mirror to
see whether her red-rimmed eyes were as crossed as
they felt. They were, indeed. She returned to the little
table under the window, and reviewed what she had
written in the now dog-eared, almost-full composition
book.

"OK, so where are we?" she mused out loud. "Let's
go over the evidence, for the umpteenth time. The
writer's initials are PM. That much is clear. The big
question is, who the fuck was PM? Peter somebody?
Paul? Peter, Paul and Mary? He was definitely English.
He was a sailor, or at least he was someone who spent a
lot of time on boats. Some of the material seems to be
from New England, which makes sense. There was a lot
of commerce between Barbados and New England back
then. What if PM was a slaveship captain? The date is

1715, no question about that. That's over three hundred years ago, three hundred and five years, to be exact. That makes this a very significant historical discovery. The English had tobacco plantations in the West Indies as early as the early sixteen hundreds, as I learned on the plane ride.

"The questions of the moment are," she continued. "One, who is this guy PM? And two, how did PM's journal get into our cellar? Along with a pile of skeletons? I wish I had Sherlock to talk to. He'd figure it out in a moment, wouldn't he, Henry?"

Liz reviewed the most recent fragment she had transcribed. She read it out loud.

"This day before we came to harbour, obferuing fome not well affedted to vnitie and concord, but gaue fome appearance of faction, it was thought good there fhould...

"Oh God," she protested. "This guy's handwriting is preposterous. Didn't they teach these people anything? The best 18th Century handwriting is tricky enough, but this is impossible. Half of it is so faded and water damaged. God! I still get mixed up with all the s's looking like f's, and vice versa, and the spelling, there's no consistency, but... Oh my God, this is...this is... definitely interesting. The guys at the Maine Historical Society will know what to do with it when I get it home.

Perhaps I'll write an article for the Journal once I finally figure out who the hell wrote this."

Taking a deep breath, Liz ploughed on.

"*Says Mafter William Bradford, after prayers, I (hall a litle returne backe and begine with a combination made by them before they came afhore, being y« firft foundation of their govermente in this place; occafioned partly by y« difcontented & mutinous fpeeches that fome of the (hangers amongft them [i.e. not Ley- den men, but adventurers who joined them in England] had let fall from them in y« (hip, That when they came a (hore they would ufe their owne libertie; for none had power to command them, the patente they had being for Virginia, and not for New-England, which belonged to an other Government, with which y« Virginia Company had nothing to doe.*

"Wait a Goddamn minute," she yelled, startling the birds in the trees outside her window. "What the hell? Did I just say Master William Bradford? Didn't William Bradford have something to do with Plymouth Plantation? But that was a hundred years earlier. That can't be." Astonished and confused, Liz continued. "Unless this is a novel. Am I looking at one of the earliest works of American fiction?"

"*It was thought meet for their more orderly Carrying on of their Affairs, and accordingly by mutual confent they entred into a folemn Combination as a Body Politick, To fubmit*

284

to fuch Government and Governours, Laws be an aflbciation and agreement, that we fliould combine together in one body, and to fubmit to fuch government and governours, as we fliould by common confent agree to make and chofe, and fet our hands to this that followes word for word.

"IN the name of God, Amen, We whofe names are vnderwritten, the loyall Subiedls of our dread foveraigne Lord King Iames, by the grace of God of Great Britaine France and Ireland, King, Defender of the Faith, &c.

"King James? What? He was... No! It's... This is about... What's it called again? The Magna Carta? No, the Mayflower Compact? It has to be. A hand-written original? No! This is NOT possible. *Having vnder-taken for the glory of God, and...*

"This is crazy, girl! It can't be. But it is. It's different, the wording, but this is... the Mayflower Compact. It's a bit mixed up compared with..." Liz was boggled. "I was wrong! I must be. This thing was *not* written in the seventeen hundreds. It was written in the sixteen hundreds, the year sixteen twenty, to be precise. I was a hundred years off! What the fuck? How could I get the date so wrong? Dumb bitch! So much for the information you get on the Internet." Taking a deep breath, she read on.

"Having vnder-taken for the glory of God, and advancement of the Chriftian Faith, and honour of our King and Countrey, a Voyage to plant the firft Colony in the

285

Northerne parts of Virginia, doe by thefe prefents folemnly &
mutually in the prefence of God and one of another, covenant,
and combine our felues together into a civill body politike, for
our better ordering and prefervation, and furtherance of the
ends aforefaid; and by vertue hereof to 'enadl, conftitute, and
frame fuch iuft and equall Lawes, Ordinances, conftitutions,'
offices from time to time, as fhall be thought mod meet and
convenient for the generall good of the Colony.

"OH MY GOD! THIS IS INSANE! WHAT IS
THIS?" Liz shrieked at the top of her voice. The flock of
mynahs in the tree outside her windows flew up in
alarm, circled the house a few times and then gradually
settled down again. James, her poor maligned stepfather,
sitting out on the lawn in one of the weathered Adirondack chairs, glanced up from his book for a brief
moment, then went back to reading about the Pilgrims
and the Indians. Neither he nor Liz knew it, but James
was busy reading virtually the same words that she was.

A week later, Liz would get together with James to
solicit his opinion on the Roman date. Liz was not
wrong, it turned out. The writer was! PM, whoever he
was, had apparently intended to write the Roman
numerals for the year sixteen fifteen, but had added an
extra digit, thereby making it seventeen fifteen.

53

The Pandemic

Liz Nicholson and Baxter de Waal were each involved with early New England history, although in very different ways. What were Liz and Bax's relative degrees of historical expertise? Were they equally well informed, or was one significantly more knowledgeable than the other? If so, which one? It is clear that, despite her doctorate, her marginal proficiency with Elizabethan handwriting, and her antiquarian job at the library in Maine, Liz carried a lot of historical misconceptions, as did her father, with whom most of them had originated.

Did the women's different bodies of work perhaps complement one another, and add up to a more comprehensive picture? What misbeliefs did Liz and Bax each carry? Liz was convinced that the *Mayflower* had carried a load of smallpox-infested blankets for distribution to the Indians, and believed a number of the other widespread misconceptions about the Pilgrims, despite the fact that she was a certified historian with a PhD to prove it.

Baxter was outraged to hear such inflammatory misinformation from an otherwise intelligent person, but she had kept her cool. This was not the first time she'd heard nonsense of this nature. Did Liz fail to take Prof. James Nicholson's theory seriously? She hadn't even read the article, it turned out. What? Why ever not? Because her father had taught her differently and her father wouldn't lie to her. Would he?

After returning well after sunset from a solitary stroll on the beach, Bax sat out on the patio in the moonlight. She opened the frosted bottle of rather decent New Zealand chardonnay that she had purchased on her first day on the island.

"Mmmm. That's good," she thought to herself. "Liz would like this."
An owl hooted softly and silently glided overhead, its ghostly moon-shadow causing Bax to look up in wonder. She opened her laptop and checked her email. As her new best friend had promised, there was a message from Liz, and an attachment titled simply:

'Pandemic.' It was a portable document file or .pdf of Liz's deceased husband's article about the pre-Mayflower New England Indians, for her information. Liz had confessed that she had never read the thing, and vowed to correct the omission once the dust settled.

Bax thought about Liz and her absurd beliefs concerning the Mayflower Pilgrims. It was a problem she was well aware of, having encountered the phenom-enon from coast to coast. It disturbed her deeply. Three years earlier, in fact, she had drafted the rough outline for a proposed book called 'Ten Common Mispercep-tions about the Pilgrims and the Indians.' The project had been sitting on a back burner ever since, awaiting the moment when her doctoral thesis was complete and her Caribbean slave book had been published at last.

Yesterday, as they picked their way though the washed-up seaweed at the ocean's edge, Liz had told her about James Nicholson's *Vanity Fair* article and the storm of controversy it had engendered. The academic denials. The anonymous threats. Liz had promised to email Bax the article, and there it was...

Bax wrote a swift thank you email to Liz. She had been thinking about the woman and her sheer igno-rance, but did not want to offend her new friend. It wasn't her fault. After all, an amazingly high number of Americans shared the same misbeliefs. They had been misled by an intentional campaign of misinformation, she suspected.

"About the Indians, Liz" she wrote. "Don't get me

wrong. I think they carry something really important for humanity. When I first heard a Native elder express his reverence for all life as sacred and conscious, it opened my mind and heart to a new reality. Just like that! The four-leggeds, winged-ones, creepy-crawlies, standing ones, the two-leggeds. *Mitakue Oyasin* is how they say it in Lakota, meaning 'all our relations.' There's just something about it, the way they put the words together, that changed me. That was twenty years ago.

"Now my treasured elders are all gone - those rare ones who saw all of humanity as brothers and sisters and cousins. Grandmother Bertha Grove, she was a Southern Ute. Grandfather Wallace Black Elk, Lakota, Grandfather Arnie Neptune, Penobcscot. Those are a few who blessed me as their friend. I miss them, and honestly, I can't help wondering, where is the next generation of wise elders.

"Anyway, I'm sipping on a nice glass of white wine, and getting ready to read your husband's article. Take care! Bax."

She started reading Nicholson's paper, moved inside after a while, poured herself another glass of the chardonnay, and did not stop reading until she was done and the bottle was empty.

THE PANDEMIC THAT TRANSFORMED
AMERICA (AND THE WAR THAT CAUSED IT)

By James E. Nicholson, PhD

Four centuries ago, in the sultry summer of the year 1614, the indigenous population of the northeast coast of the continent which the inhabitants called Turtle Island caught their first glimpse of the troubles to come. An English sea captain with a marvelously generic name - John Smith, no less - sailed his open pinnace into Cohasset harbor on the coast of today's Massachusetts Bay. His welcome by the Cohasset locals took the form of a shower of arrows. You have very likely heard of John Smith as a result of his legendary (and probably apocryphal) 1607 rescue in Jamestown, by a young Indian maiden named Pocahontas. Seven years later, having escaped a lingering and painful death at the hands of the Powhatans in Virginia, Smith was back in the American North-East, engaged in an exploratory mapping expedition in the service of one Sir Ferdinando Gorges, the visionary and wealthy Englishman who was determined to plant the first colony in the part of Turtle Island that Smith was about to re-name New England.

Sailing with Captain Smith were several other men who were destined to play a part in the impending

291

colonization of New England. One of them was, notably, a local native of the nearby Patuxet band, a group which could muster about two thousand warriors, according to the detailed report that Smith presented to Gorges upon his return to England. The Patuxet man's name was Tisquantum, or Squanto, as his English shipmates had nicknamed him. Also on the vessel was a young sailor named Thomas Dermer, and one part of Smith and Dermer's mission was to return Squanto to his home at Patuxet. Squanto had, willingly or otherwise, spent the previous several years in England as the guest (or captive, depending on your perspective) of Sir Ferdinando. Squanto seems to have liked and trusted the English, and had learned their language. Now, at last, he was being delivered home to his people.*

[* Author's Note: For those readers who would like to read Professor Nicholson's article in its entirety,** the complete document is reproduced in the appendix at the end of this novel. The article contains information which is essential to a full understanding of the circumstances in New England immediately prior to the arrival of the *Mayflower*. It dispenses with a number of widespread misbeliefs, including the notion that the Mayflower settlers arrived with a load of smallpox-infested blankets for distribution to the native population of New England. **Please note that the article was actually written by this author, not by Dr. Nicholson, who is entirely fictitious.]

It was close to midnight when Baxter came to the end of the dissertation. She had read each and every paragraph twice. The owls were hoo-hooing softly back and forth in the moonlight. Bax's eyes were burning, but she was strangely elated. The material she had just read confirmed her own tentative conclusions about pre-Mayflower Native America, and had filled in some important gaps. Nicholson's paper answered a number of her most intractable questions. She had never heard of James Nicholson, or his work, or of the 2014 discoveries in London, until she serendipitously encountered the deceased researcher's wife in the line at a bank thousands of miles away from either New England or Cambridge, England. Providence does indeed move in mysterious ways, she thought. Thank you, Providence.

Baxter de Waal put on her nightgown and brushed her teeth and went to bed and lay awake a long time, pondering the enormity of the deception that had been perpetrated on Americans from every ethnicity and walk of life. She was well aware of the fraudulent, plagiaristic publications of a certain fake Native American academic at a Colorado university. His poisonous work had very successfully triggered the smallpox blanket hoax, but this was an entirely different kettle of fish. This was the historical truth emerging through a series of apparent coincidences. If what Liz had said in the cellar was true, a Native American ghost or spirit had guided her new friend to yet more critical information, although Liz had yet to tell her exactly what she had discovered. Baxter's maternal ancestors had trusted in the guidance of divine providence, and it looked as though the process was on-going, even in the 21st Century. Bax got out of bed and composed an email to Liz.

Your poor husband was truly amazing. What a loss to humanity. He totally confirmed my theory about pre-Mayflower New England. You might want to read the thing. It's great! See you tomorrow? Love, Bax.

*****

54

Frank And Ernest

Should a young couple be frank and earnest?
Or should one of them be a girl?

James wandered down to the waterfront in the dazzling early morning light. He reached the water's edge just as a strangely familiar, cockily self-assured young man came strutting through the shallows from the opposite direction, like some slender embryonic Greek hero emerging new-born from the ancient Mediterranean at the dawn of time. The boy carried a sleek white surfboard under one arm, and he had a certain unmistakable something about him. The French have a term for it.

James recognized the teenager from the photograph by his bedside back home in Sydney. The apparition was James's - what would one call him, his... his... step-grand-son? A hundred feet beyond the boy, a second, almost identical figure came speeding toward the shore, chest down on his surfboard. It was, or rather, they were, Junior's grandsons, Liz's two sons.

"Good morning Jason," James called to the first boy.

"Hi. Do I know you?" Jason was puzzled.

"This is the first time we've actually met, although ten years ago we... In Maine. You were about five. I'm your grandfather's ..."

"Oh. You must be Frank. Or is it Ernie?" Jason interrupted. The boy didn't really mean to be rude, but that was how the siblings had always referred to their deviant grandfather and his notorious Australian consort. They called them Frank and Ernie. And to be perfectly frank and earnest, the kid did have a bit of an attitude. James squinted at the boy. The sun was right behind his head. The younger brother, what was his name again, jumped to his feet and joined them.

"Is that what you guys call me?" James asked. Jason was embarrassed. He looked down at his feet. James continued. "So, if I get the gist, your question is...?" The boys looked at him. Jonny had no idea what the stranger with the bizarre accent was talking about, but Jason had blushed red.

"Well, first things first, gentlemen," said the Aussie. "Please allow me to introduce myself. The name's Alten. James Alten.

"Hi I'm Jonny. Jonny Alten. Wait. James Alten? Are you Grandpa's...? You must be... Ummm?"

"I have been accused of worse things, to be frank," James said, "but you can call me Ernest if you prefer. How about Frankenstein?" The boys glanced at one another, guiltily.

"Look," continued James. "I know this is sort of difficult. The answer, or rather the rest of the question is, shouldn't one of them be a girl? And if so, which one? Right?" James laughed out loud. After a moment's hesitation, the boys joined him, Jason actually getting the joke, and Jonny pretending to, so he would not appear foolish. They had made it through the worst of it.

"Anyone got room for a smoothie?" James indicated the Ditch Witch. The shutters had just opened and the place was open for business. The trade winds were coming up. A sudden squall slammed one of the weathered driftwood shutters shut. There was the sound of breaking glass from within, followed by a muffled curse in a strong Long Island accent.

"Sure, I'm starved," came the chorus.

Sitting sucking on their thick, smooth drinks made from fresh tropical fruit puréed with milk, yogurt, and vanilla ice cream, Jason was the first to speak.

"So we've been wondering, James. How did you and our Grandpa wind up together? I mean... Our mom refuses to... She won't..."

"How did we meet? We were introduced by a cross-dressing Russian hairdresser, needless to say. Her name was Ivana, like the Donald's first wife. Ivana Hakitov. In New York."

"A hairdresser named Hack-It-Off? You're shitting me."

"Well, that's true, but there's more to the story. Are you sure you want to hear it?"

"Go on."

The boys would give this weird guy with the strange accent the benefit of the doubt. Barely.

"Ivana Hakitov wasn't a real person."

"You coulda fooled me." Jonny giggled, or was it Jason?

"Ivana was a fictitious character in a screenplay. She was the founder of the infamous Club for Hairy Men. You've heard of it, I'm sure? I was cast in the lead role."

"The lead what?"

"So, you were Ivana Hakitov?"

"Yup. I was the leading lady. I was twenty-two. I was gorgeous."

"So, Ivana, what has this got to do with our grandfather, if anything?"

"OK, so the story in the screenplay went as follows: Ivana Hakitov was this angelic transvestite vampire drag queen. She would seduce an unsuspecting man every night. In the morning the unfortunate fellow would wake up as bald as Yul Brynner. Ivana would be nowhere to be found, of course, having returned to her coffin before the sun came up. As the story went on, and the plot thickened, you learned that Ivana was hundreds of years old..."

"Yul Brynner? Is that a person?" Jason was too young to have heard of Yul Brynner.

"And that's where baldness came from?" Jonny interrupted with a sudden giggle.

"Exactly, John. True story, I swear. Ivana Hakitov made a huge fortune in the hair-replacement industry. She became the richest vampire in undead human history."

"Everybody calls me Jonny."

"Right-o then, Jonny it is. And everybody calls me Jim." He pronounced the word Jeem.

"OK, Jeem."

"Do you know why you should call me Jeem?" Having made friends, the trio shook hands. In the midst of the three-way handshake, a shadow fell over them.

"Because that is his name," came Liz's voice. "Well, good morning, boys." It was the boys' mother, out for her morning walk. She was on a mission. "I see you three have met. Good morning, James," she said, making a valiant effort to be friendly.

"Mom, that's not James. His name is Ivana. I mean, her name... Ivana Hakitov."

"No, it's not. It's Ernie."

"Just call me Frank. It's short for Frankenstein," explained James, compounding the confusion. "Just don't ask me what the 'N' stands for."

"Frank N. Stein? I get it." Liz did not smile. "Well, you boys are having fun, I can see that."

"Mom, we're trying to find out how Jeem here and Grandpa..." He stopped. James took up the story.

"They asked me how your father and I met. I was telling them."

"You met in New York. In the West Village gay scene. Fire Island, maybe?"

"Well yes, but are you aware of the circumstances?"

"Spare us the details, please. I'm sure it was not

300

something my boys would want to know. And before I forget, I told Gladys I'd come and get you boys out of the water for breakfast. Shall we go?" The men heaved themselves to their feet and dusted the sand from their board shorts.

"Ivana Hakitov? Did I hear that correctly?" Liz couldn't help herself. She giggled.

"So, Liz, you probably don't know this, but *Ivana Hakitov* was the title of a famous movie."

"It was? I've never heard of it."

"That's because the film never got made, but the screenplay was the buzz of SoHo and Christopher Street for a couple of years. It was the darkest days of AIDS and we were losing friends left right and center. We desperately needed something to laugh about. As importantly, it's the reason we're all here together on this beautiful beach on this beautiful morning."

"How so?"

"Boys, do you mind if I start at the beginning? So your mother won't think we've completely lost our minds."

"It's too late, Jeem. She thinks that already."

"Jeem," muttered Liz. "Jeem?"

They walked up through the trees in the direction of the house. A flight of parrots erupted in noisy airborne warfare above them. The gusty tradewinds whistled through the jarrahs. A troop of green monkeys chattered somewhere in the undergrowth.

"It's totally blown out," complained Jason. "We'll have to get an Uber around to the West side." Needless to say, he was talking about the surf.

Over a sumptuous Gladys-style breakfast the Ivana Hakitov saga finally came out in all its marvellous absurdity. The story even had a South African component. Scilla came down and joined the party halfway through, so James, after the appropriate introductions, had to start all over again.

"A whole mob of us downtown New Yorkers took the subway out to Brooklyn to see the famous cross-dressing comedian Pieter Dirk Uys, who happened to be South Africa's most famous woman at the time. He was performing at BAM - the Brooklyn Academy of Music. He also happened to be a man, a man named Evita. With me so far? Anyway, after the show - which was absolutely hysterical, by the way, you should have seen his Bill Clinton impersonation - we all went back into town and out for dinner and sometime during that meal, the idea was born. We'd write a mad comedy about a downtown transvestite hairdresser and it would be an underground hit, like *Priscilla, Queen of the Desert*. The idea started out as a play, a theatre piece, but then we realized..."

"Hold on, Jeem." Jason was losing patience. "What has any of this got to do with Grandpa John?

"Bear with me, Jason," said James. "Bear with me. I'm getting there, me lad. So, what's the first thing you do when you have an idea for a movie? You write a screenplay. You start thinking about who you're going to cast in the lead roles. They all looked at me and said you're her! I said 'no bloody way.' 'You're perfect,' they insisted. So I became Ivana, at least in our little circle. We got the first draft written. We started having rehearsals every Tuesday night at Big Mama's. The script was really funny. In fact it was completely insane, sort of like Dracula meets the Matrix, meets, I don't know, the Sound of Music or the Wizard of Oz. As performed by Monty Python."

"OK, fine, but I'm with Jason." Liz butted in impatiently. "Where does my father come into all of this?"

"He was the money man."

"The money man?"

"One of the group, it was a straight woman actually, what was her name? Monica? No, Mallory something or other. She brought up the name Jack Alten. She knew him from the Met. She was on the Board. We'd all heard

303

of him, of course, and so we decided to approach him about financing the movie."

"So let me get this straight, James. You approached my father and asked him to fund your wacky film?"

"We did. Four of us went down and met with him at Alden Enterprises. Down on Wall street."

"What did he say?"

"He thought we were absolutely nuts."

"He was absolutely correct."

"Of course he was. But everybody who has ever mounted a play or made a successful first film was nuts. It's par for the course. Think about Monty Python. Who'd have thought America would end up loving them?"

"Speaking of par for the course, where is my father? I haven't seen hide nor hair of him yet."

"He went off golfing before the sun came up."

"Ah so. Did he fund your film?"

"He did not, sad to say. As I said, it never did get made. Sadly. *Priscilla* went on to be a huge underground hit, and our idea, well..."

"But it sounds like our father did get a little something out of the film?" Scilla said.

"Yes, he got the star, Ivana Hakitov. No money down. It was a helluva deal."

"Grandpa John got a gay cross-dressing man out of the deal?" Jonny was intrigued.

"He did. And free haircuts for life. Think about it. I do his hair to this day, what little is left of it, and I have yet to charge him a bent penny."

"Helluva deal for sure," said Scilla. "Are you still a cross-dresser, Jim?"

"Allow me to demonstrate. Liz, pass me that sarong of yours, do you mind?"

Liz clutched the sarong to her otherwise-bare bosom, triggering an outbreak of laughter. The ice was broken and the boys had bonded with James, which was a good thing. Liz had started the conversation icily, doing her haughty Queen Elizabeth impersonation, but she was beginning to like James, despite herself. The frost around her wounded heart was melting by the moment.

"My grandfather?" Jason had a final question.

"Yes, Jason?"

"Is he bald?"

"Under the wig? Well, you'll just have to wait and see, won't you?"

*****

55

Jack Meets Jack

After his golf game, Junior came back to Alden House. He was driving the dented Porsche. He left the vehicle at the foot of the verandah steps, and hurried up and into the deserted kitchen. It was high noon. Being a man of fixed habits, he mixed himself a gin-and-tonic, downed it in a single gulp, made another, and proceeded upstairs with the drink. He stood by Old Jack's bed, looking down at his unmoving father. Simon & Garfunkel's *I Am A Rock* played softly. *I've got my books and my poetry...* The French doors were closed against the wind.

"Well, Mr Alden, it's been a while, hasn't it? You gonna say hello?" There was no response from the addressee, not so much as a quiver or a twitch. "I guess we're still not talking, are we?" Junior took a brisk turn around the room, examining the art as though the bedroom was a New York gallery. Downing his drink, he deposited the empty glass on top of the priceless bookcase, stopped in front of the Matisse, took out his smartphone, and moments later the appraisal was done. Nodding approvingly, he walked back over to the bedside.

"If you change your mind, Jack, do let me know." His tone was curt. "I've come a long way and it's not exactly cheap, you know? The Airbus A380, the crew, the hotels. Elizabeth's idea was that we might have one last go at being a family. Admirable idea on her part, but I'm not so sure you give a damn about the family. I know I don't. Have yourself a wonderful day."

*****

56

Happiness Is A Kosher Pork Sausage

Liz was balanced precariously on top of a tall craggy rock on the eroded cliffs above Soup Bowls, waving her arms for balance and looking out at the surfers. She was trying to pick out her boys, and she was thinking about James. They had a date. Right on cue, James materialized below Liz, gazing up at her.

"How are you, Jeem?" she asked, looking down at the Australian.

"Not too worse. Could be bad. Are you coming?"

"Coming? Oh, right. Coming for a walk."

James was gone. Liz clambered carefully down and turned and tried to catch up with the man. It was the first walk of the rest of her life. On the flight down from New England, Liz had made a solemn resolution. "Enough of sitting cross-eyed in front of computer screens," she had said out loud. She was determined to turn over a new leaf and get herself back in shape. Needless to say, she had forgotten all about the resolution the moment she had arrived on the island. Gladys's delicious cooking didn't help much. Now here she was, panting like a dog and perspiring and striding as swiftly as she possibly could, but it was impossible to keep up with James. The man wasn't nicknamed 'Speed' Walker for nothing.

Eventually Liz just had to give up. She was completely out of breath. Her heart was pounding. There was a bench up ahead, under a tree overlooking a deserted arc of white sand beach. An elderly tourist couple was just getting up. She sat down, breathing heavily. Her armpits were sweaty. There was no sign of her handsome step-father. After ten or fifteen minutes, she got her breathing under control and there he was standing in front of her like the man in the Bob Dylan song, how did it go? "*Why wait any longer for the one you love?*" James wasn't even breathing hard. He looked as though he'd just stepped out of the shower.

"Hey, luv, I lost you. You OK?"

"I thought we were going to walk quote unquote together. "

"Excuse me? Oh, I see. Oops! I'm sorry. Force of bloody habit."

He sat down next to Liz and gazed out at the horizon. The tops of some distant cumulus clouds were just visible over the dark blue horizon. They were silent for a good few minutes.

"So James, are you happy?" Liz asked, out of the blue. James jumped up. He turned around and stood in front of Liz looking down at her. He was taken aback, and stuttered...

"Happy? Me? Ummm."

"No seriously, I don't mean to pry, but I've been watching you and my father. Not that I ever see the two of you together. I have to say, I'm a bit worried about him. He's seventy-two. He's carrying a lot of extra weight. Is he drinking too much? It certainly looks that way."

"One thing at a time, girl. Am I happy? Or is your father happy?"

"OK, let's get right to it. Is my father happy? We'll come back to you in a moment." Liz had a way of getting right to the point.

"Is Johnny happy?" James thought about it. "Truly, deeply happy? You know, probably not."

"Are you two happy together?"

"Well, that's a different question, isn't it? I would have to say yes, we are." James hesitated. "He's... He treats me very well. I care very much about him. In fact I adore the bastard. I would call that happiness."

"So, my dad. What's up with him? You know what's been going on in the family these past how many years? Twenty?"

"Twenty five years. I know. It's been a rough ride."

"My father. You wouldn't say he's a happy camper, then?"

"Your father does not believe in happiness. He calls it a kosher pork sausage."

"A kosher what?"

"That's what he calls it. It's one of his nuttier sayings. 'Happiness is a kosher pork sausage.' I think he got it from a Beatles song. He wanted to make a bumper sticker saying that."

"A Beatles song?"

"The original lyric went *happiness is a warm gun* if I remember rightly. He changed it..."

"A kosher pork sausage? There's no such thing. How

could..."

"Exactly, my dear. That's the whole point."

"Oh. Duh." Liz got it. There is no such thing as happiness, just as there is no such thing as kosher pork. However there is such a thing as a warm gun, if she had understood John Lennon's *double entendre* correctly as a teenager. But, she thought, we'd not better go there. Not tonight, Josephine!

She dragged her eyes away from James' surfer style board shorts, which were precisely on her line of sight. The shorts were a dark navy blue with a lightning-bolt of brilliant orange down each side. They looked brand-new. Oh God, she thought. I hope he didn't... Was she...? James turned and looked out at the ocean, then sat down again. He turned to Liz.

"Listen," he began. "About yesterday...".

"It was the day before yesterday, wasn't it?" she interrupted. "I've been thinking. I was terribly rude."

"No you weren't. I understand..."

"Let's not go there again, James. That's the word that got us in trouble last time. So look, firstly, I want to apologize. It's an emotional issue, my mother's death. Secondly, I really appreciate your inviting me along on this walk."

"If only I'd bloody well slow down," he laughed

ruefully.

"There is that," Liz allowed herself a tight smile.
"But, I do appreciate your reaching out to me. I'd really
like us to be friends."

"You have my word on that. Scout's honor."

"So let's see. I think you said you and my father
never... I mean..."

"Look Liz. We met. We liked one another. You girls
and your mother were out of town, but he was a married man. With children. There was no way..."

"OK. I believe you. What I want to get at is her exact
cause of death. There's no question it was AIDS. Can
you get AIDS from a blood transfusion?"

"That is something that your father investigated
very thoroughly, Liz. The answer is yes. There is no
doubt. In fact, your father actually met someone else that
it happened to, out in the Hamptons. The husband of
the woman it happened to, rather. A blood transfusion
after a car smash. Their two kids were born HIV positive, and then the mother died. It's been a nightmare for
their father ever since."

"Oh, my God. I can only imagine." She looked at the
man with new tenderness. "So... it wasn't you?"

"It wasn't anyone else either. Jack told me he'd
always been attracted to the gay scene. He found the

313

men gentler than the macho... More like the American Indians."

"Hmmm. So James, you're saying he never..."

"Now look. I can't vouch for it, Liz. But as far as I know I was his first."

"And that wasn't until..."

"1997. Your mother was... Well, he was still mourning. Then, at some point, it was time..."

"Thank you, James. I needed to hear this. Shall we walk as we talk?"

"Walkie-talkie? OK. If you insist."

*****

57

The Conditioned Mind

As they walked, they talked, or more accurately, James talked. The Australian speed-walker adjusted his pace, more or less, to Liz's, and continued where he had left off earlier in the day. He had the remarkable ability to remember exactly what he had been saying twenty-four hours earlier, although, she thought, he does have a bit of a tendency to lecture. Not that she minded, really. She just loved listening to the sound of his voice. His delivery was gentle, but enthusiastic and persuasive. He could have been reciting

315

excerpts from a Julia Child cookbook, for all she cared.

"We have all been conditioned to accept, as un-
contestably real," James was saying, "the agreed upon
consensus reality that governs our present existence. As
a result, many of us have great difficulty accepting the
possibility of a different world. Have you ever seen one
of those figure ground paintings which depicts two
completely different scenes?"

"Like the one with old woman and the girl?" Liz
could see the painting in her mind's eye.

"Exactly. When you are focused on either one of the
two scenes, it is impossible to see the other one, and vice
versa. When we are immersed in this reality, we cannot
see, or even imagine, another. Fortunately, once we
make the shift to a higher reality, we cease to see this
one. It simply ceases to be real. It evaporates like the
illusion it is."

"Fair enough. But..." Liz panted.

"The big question is," interrupted James, "how do
we de-condition our minds? In a profound sense, we
have all been brainwashed, all of us, by countless generations of now-outdated thinking. Imagine if it were
possible to unplug our minds and send them in to the
deprogrammers, kind of like updating the operating
system of our computer? We would emerge reborn,

with a brand-new, fresh reality."

"Careful now, Jeem. That sounds like something out of *1984* or *Brave New World*." Liz gave vent to a merry laugh. She couldn't help herself.

****

58

Pheromones In The Wind

Being, apparently, the only family members with any interest in personal fitness, Liz and James took to going on regular daily beach walks together. James, as much an obsessive walker as he was a talker, had already explored much of the surrounding area, and told her about a beautiful, isolated cove that could only be reached at low tide. The moon would soon be full, and maybe the tide would be low enough, he said as he drove. It was another windy afternoon.

The new friends had taken the little powder blue Suzuki Moke and bumped and bounced into town on a minor shopping spree, making sure the house was properly equipped for the rapidly approaching Thanksgiving feast. James was thinking of music, and Liz was thinking of liquor. At the World Electronics shop in Bridgetown, purchasing the tiny portable Bose sound system that James had been researching online, there occurred a surprising incident that stopped Liz in her tracks. As they stood at the checkout counter, the young Bajan clerk asked how long she and James had been married.

"You tell me," responded James, playfully. He twinkled at Liz out of the corner of his eye.

"I don't know, but I can tell you've been married for a long time," responded the girl, her white teeth gleaming in her friendly brown face. "It's amazing how married people start to look like one another. You're down here having a second honeymoon, aren't you?"

"That is amazing. You're absolutely correct. It's been thirty years this month," said James with a sidelong wink at his befuddled companion. Walking out of the shop with the package and swinging their legs into the open-sided Moke, they broke into hysterical laughter, cracking up at the riduculous thought.

"Hey, that would have made me seven years old at the time, you evil bloody cradle-snatcher," protested Liz, subconsciously snipping a couple of years off her age. They glanced at one another with sudden new eyes, then looked away.

"Give me a break," Liz muttered under her breath. Utterly out of the question, for obvious reasons. James and her father had been together for decades, and anyway, James was as queer as... as an Offenbach cantata.

Driving home, the new friends were strangely silent. Liz wondered about the incident. She and her father were unmistakably Altens. Did that account for the alleged similarity in looks that the sales clerk had claimed to see? Was it a similarity in vibrational essence? Did married couples actually grow to look alike, or was it something else?

"Remind me to have a good long look at you and my father," Liz commented, as the electric gates swung open. "The next time I catch the two of you together. If I ever catch the two of you together."

*****

320

59

Washington's Story

The last glow in the western sky had faded. It was as dark as it was going to get. There was an almost full moon reflecting off the ocean through the gently swaying ironwoods and bathing everything in an ethereal flickering light. A shadowy figure emerged from the house and stepped out onto the verandah and headed for the stairs.

"Ullo, Maryah. Where are you off to in such a bleedin' hurry?" The voice came from James, who was sitting in the shadows. It had grown too dark to read and he was quietly sitting there, Mayflower book in lap, contemplating his navel. He had much to think about. Somehow Liz's living presence had become an integral part of the four-hundred-year-old Pilgrim story he was devouring so avidly.

"Oh hi there, James. What are y'all doing, lurking in the shadows like that? Got a few minutes? Y'all should come along."

"Sure. Where are we going?"

"Come," Maryah replied, seductively. "Y'all won't regret it."

She turned and made her way down the stairs to the driveway and disappeared off to the right. James eased himself to his feet, left his book on the armrest of the Adirondack chair, and followed her. When he got down to the driveway level there was no sign of the woman.

"Hey Maryah. Wait for me."

"Come on, slowpoke," came a laughing voice from the shadows fifty feet ahead. "I hear tell y'all are the fastest walker in town, and you can't even keep up with a little ol' girl from Georgia?."

James headed into the diffuse gloom among the trees. He had never been this way before, but he found himself on a winding pathway of crushed seashells that was easily discerned in the misty moonlight. Accelerating, he soon caught up with the black girl, whose disembodied blonde hairdo was the only moving thing in sight, except for the whites of her eyes and the luminous teeth when she turned and grinned at him. Maryah was wearing black tights and a black tank-top, and was otherwise quite invisible.

"Hey, what's the rush, girl?"

"They're serving their special rum punch. They only do it once a year, for Grenada Thanksgiving. I don't want to be late."

"They?"

"Come on."

The smell of wood-smoke reached James's nostrils. Moments later, a string of decorative lights appeared though the bushes and he made out the silhouette of a low building set among the tall dark trees. A familiar voice came out of the darkness. The voice belonged to Gladys, old Jack Alden's housekeeper.

"Is that Miss Maryah I hear out there in the under-growth, beating about the bushes? Fightin' off the tigers?"

"You almost missed it. But we saved you a sip. Just a tiny little taste." Washington's deep voice was jovial and friendly.

"I've brought a friend. I hope that's all right?"

"Who is that? Step into the light, please. Ah, Master

James. Welcome to our humble abode, my dear."

"Good evening, Gladys. Evening, Washington. Please, forget the Master James bit. My name is Jim."

"Well, good evening, Jim," the two of them chorused. "Would you like to sample an Island Special?"

"An Island Special? Why certainly. I'll try anything twice. It's one of my guiding principles in life."

As it transpired, the elderly islanders had saved more that a mere sip of the punch. On the battered wooden table, fitfully illuminated by the flickering fire-light, rested a huge beige ceramic jug, at least two gallons in volume. It was full to within an inch of the brim. The shimmering contents reflected the moon as the radiant orb emerged between the trees. The vessel contained a mixture of three different kinds of rum, Washington explained, one of them distilled on that very property, plus fresh coconut water, fresh pineapple juice, sliced island limes and lemons, and half a dozen spices. Gladys carefully dunked a large, long-handled metal scoop into the jug and filled a mug with the liquid. She handed the container to Mary-ah, then turned and went into the building in the shadows behind her.

"One moment, Master James. Jim. I'll get another cup. Or a Mason jar if we are out of cups. Would you mind?"

324

An hour later the moon ruled the sky, the stars had dimmed, the fire had burned down to a mound of glowing red embers, and the four of them were distinctly mellow and pleasantly sozzled. Maryah had given an account of her adventurous upbringing in the surprisingly non-racist Atlanta music scene, and her subsequent life on the road. Gladys had just finished an extended review of her life to date. Surprisingly enough, she was a New Yorker, although her mother was originally from the Island. Her parents had met in Hempstead, Long Island, which her mother had always called 'Wrong Island.' She had never stopped longing to go 'home' to Barbados, even though she had been absent for more than half a century. Gladys had had a long professional career both as a nurse and as a midwife, a 'doula,' as she called herself.

"And you two? How long have you two been hangin' out together?" asked Maryah.

Washington picked up the story. "I was born right here on the Island, but my father got a job in Canada when I was ten. Brrr. Those winters. The Washington Franklins go back a long time here. I am the fourth Washington Franklin in my line, but I was gone for a long time. Most of my life, in fact."

"Canada? You didn't meet Gladys in Canada, did

you?"

"Oh no. We met in New York. Believe it or not I was working for my present employer, Master Alden."

"In New York?"

"I was his driver. He traveled a lot, so I had plenty of time off so I could pursue my passion."

"Which was?" James asked.

"Oh I thought you knew. Music, of course." Gladys chipped in. Her husband could take forever to get to the point.

"Let me explain, before you start thinking Washington was some kind of rock star."

"No no. I was just a humble driver even back then."

"He was the driver for my husband. In fact that is how we met."

"Your husband?" James and Maryah spoke almost simultaneously. The result was a bit of a confused babble. "I thought Washington was your husband."

"No no. I will explain. First, Washington Franklin the Fourth, this fine gentleman sitting right here, pretending to be the famous American actor Danny Glover, is the biggest music fan you will ever meet. He can describe each and every note any jazz musician ever played. Second, Washington Franklin is not my first husband. He was the limousine driver for my first husband. And for some other unsavory characters who shall remain anonymous."

Washington chuckled. "Baby, you make it sound like Sammy was an unsavory character. She is referring to the time I was the chauffeur for one of the big Mafia boss men. But I got out of that with my skin intact, most of it. Then I got the job driving for Dizzy."

"Dizzy? Dizzy Gillespie? Gladys, do you mean to tell me...?" Maryah stopped in mid-sentence. There was a sudden sound off in the woods. Scilla's voice came floating into the circle of firelight.

"Yoo hoo. Hey, Maryah. Where are you?"

"Over here, baby. Follow the lights."
The rustling in the shrubbery grew louder. Scilla appeared out of the shadows.

"Aha, so this is where the party's at? I got your note, sweetheart. I've never been down here, or at least not since I was a teeny tiny girl, the time I got lost when the wind blew the door shut and locked me into one of the old slave..."

"Welcome, Missy Priscilla," said Gladys. "Would you care for a little libation? There is some left, if we squeeze the jug a little. I'll get you a cup."

"Thanks Gladys. I'll have whatever you're having. Hello, Washington, hello, James. You guys having fun?

This is so nice. I'm glad I found you. It's like a morgue up there. Oops, I shouldn't talk like that."

"What's your big sister up to?" James asked.

"Her door's shut. She's got her nose buried in that old bible-thing she dug up. You can't even talk to her anymore. Oh, Jim, I almost forgot. My dad's back from town. He's wondering if you've run off and left him."

"Is he in a good mood?"

"Not exactly. In fact he's a bit, you know..."

"Sloshed?"

"That's the word I was looking for, sloshed. Exactly. Nodding out in front of the television with Fox News blaring. The election news back in the States. The Supreme Court has ordered them to do a re-count. Hmm, I see my illustrious father's not the only one who's sloshed."

"Miss Priscilla, here." Gladys handed her a miniature Mason jar. It had a little glass handle. "You have some catching up to do."

"Thanks Gladys. Please call me Scilla. Cheers everyone." She drained the jar in a single long guzzle. "Mmmm, that's good." She handed the little jar back to Gladys, who refilled it to the brim.

"So what did I interrupt? Please continue."

"Just exchanging life stories, y'know." Maryah

moved her plastic lawn chair closer and put her hand on Scilla's knee. "You won't believe it. This handsome gentleman sitting here so quiet-like is none other than the famous Dizzy Gillespie."

"No no no!" cried Washington. "We are now officially completely mixed up. But I put the blame on the notorious rum punch. One glass and you can't keep your story straight. Two glasses and you're lying on your back talking to the Man in the moon. The correct story is that once upon a time, many years ago, I was the driver, the chauffeur you could say, for Mister Gillespie."
Gladys took over.

"Priscilla, Scilla, that was back in the late 1970s, before my husband got the job with your grandfather."

"I was..." Washington began.

"Washtub dearest, let me tell it. Otherwise we shall be here all night."

"Which is very pleasant by the way," said James. "I for one don't mind staying here all night. I don't mind in the least." He was trying to focus his eyes on the label printed on his Mason jar. It seemed familiar, somehow. He leaned back and gazed up at the moon, which was wobbling erratically across the sky. The Man in the Moon winked down at him, conspiratorially.

"To get back to your original question, Maryah,

which was, how did we get together? We met in New York during the time when my first husband was playing the drums with Dizzy Gillespie's orchestra. We had a big old Greyhound bus for the equipment and to sleep in - the motels would not accept people of color at that time - and the long black limousine for the band. Actually it was an old black hearse. The oh-so-handsome driver of that hearse was a fine young gentleman named Washington Franklin. That very person sitting right there. I liked him because he had the same way of speaking as my mommy."

"Aha. The plot thickens. Did I catch your husband's name? Sammy?"

"That is exactly right, James. I was Mrs Sammy Walters."

"A fortunate man, that Sammy Walters," said James.

"A fortunate fellow indeed, but Sammy had a few less than desirable habits," said Washington. "Which was a good thing for me, as things turned out."

The conversation went on until almost midnight. James summarized the bits that Scilla had missed. The Franklins had moved to Canada when Washington was ten. In his twenties, he ended up in New York, spending as much time as possible at jazz clubs like the Village Gate and the Half Note. Gladys's husband, Sammy the drummer. Chauffeur duties for some unsavory Mafia characters, then Mr. Alden's ugly brown Maserati.

In the meantime, Sammy came to the conclusion that heroin was more important to him than Gladys was. He died in a cheap motel room in New Hampshire. Washington came back to Barbados with Alden after the latter bought the old plantation house for a song. Gladys was working as a nurse/doula on Wrong Island. They stayed in touch, and finally, she came to Barbados for a holiday. They got married. The 1955 Ford Angular was a wedding present from Mr. Alden. Actually, it's a Ford Anglia, but Angular is more fun, isn't it? Especially with that backward sloping rear window. Alden purchased Alden House in 1983, during the Reagan invasion of Grenada, as his retirement home. He got a helluva deal. October 25 is Thanksgiving Day on Grenada.

These and many other snippets of information floated around in the moonlit clearing in front of the converted slave quarters. The conversation turned to the elections in America. Maryah looked at her huge designer wristwatch.

"Oh my God. It's after midnight. How time flies."

"It is?" asked Gladys. "I completely lost track. I have to be up before the sun. Please stay as long as you like, but I must get to bed."

"Scilla?"

"I'm ready, babe. Good night Gladys. Good night Washington. It was fun getting to know you both." Maryah stood up, wobbling unsteadily. "My, my. I'm seriously bombed. I had no idea until I stood up. Good night, everybody," she went on. "My answer is this, James. Give me a gay black woman to vote for and I'll vote for her. Otherwise I take no notice."

"Do you vote, Washington?"

"I do. Down here one vote can make a difference."

"James?"

"I'm a bloody alien. Little green antennae and all. They wouldn't let me vote if I wanted to."

"You mean back home? Or in America?"

"I'm with Maryah." James realized that he was slurring his words. "I pretty much ignore politics as usual. I'm so far to the left, I actually believe in the founding documents of my country. And your country. Can't have that, y'know. They'd lock me up before letting me vote. Which means, basically, there's no one worth voting for. The lesser of two weevils principle doesn't much appeal to me."

The women wandered off into the moonlight, hand-in-hand, leaving James and Washington to solve the world's problems by themselves.

"What about your friend? Master John?" Washington asked.

"Republican to the core, despite the fact that the party barely exists anymore. My party right or wrong. We have avoided the subject since... Do you follow American politics?"

"You know, strangely, old Mister Alden and I would talk forever on the subject."

"Another dyed in the wool Republican."

"You might be surprised, my friend. Do you know who Mr Alden voted for in '08 and again in 2012? Barack Obama, that's who. He voted for Mrs. Clinton in 2016, however reluctantly. This time he missed the election, unfortunately, but I am certain he would not have voted Republican. Donald Trump..."

"Now that's a surprise indeed."

"He thinks the Republicans went off the rails back in the days of Ronald Reagan."

"Well, he wouldn't be the only one, would he? Personally, I think Reagan was the most un-American president in US history. Except for Donald Trump, needless to say."

"What do you mean un-American? Everybody talks about Ronald Reagan like he's the great American hero."

"I mean pro-big-money, pro-corporation, no matter

what it might cost the American people. Government of the people, by the corporations, for the corporations. I'm not sure that's what your founding Fathers had in mind."

"They weren't *my* founding Fathers, James. Neither were they yours. Well, you sound pretty political to me, my friend. And I have to say, I have no problem with that. You appear to be on the same side of the Great Divide as I am."

"Let me ask you something, Washington." James held up his empty Mason jar in the moonlight. "Do you have any idea where this came from?"

"That little Mason jar? Well yes, I do as a matter of fact. It is a souvenir. We picked four of them up on our honeymoon in the United States."

"Are you telling me..?" James held the jar out for his friend to see. "Are you telling me you and Gladys went to Jerome, Arizona on your honeymoon?"

"As a matter of fact, that is exactly what we did. After the Grand Canyon and Las Vegas. Gladys wanted to experience a ghost town out in the Wild West, and Mr. Alden suggested..."

"Mr. Alden suggested Jerome, Arizona?" James interrupted.

"He did indeed. Why do you ask?"

"Because I recognize this jar. It's from a little restaurant called the Haunted Hamburger."

"So it is, my friend. How on Earth do you know that?"

"We went there on our own honeymoon. Johnny wanted me to experience the American Southwest, and that was part of the trip."

"You didn't stay at the Grand Hotel, by any remote chance?"

"Oh come on, Washington. This is ridiculous. We certainly did. The old hospital, dating back to the copper mining days. We slept in separate hospital beds. It was so romantic."

"As did we. The most uncomfortable night's sleep in my entire life. The next day poor Gladys and I moved into a bed and breakfast down the mountain."

"Good heavens. That is exactly what we did."

*****

60

Hanky-Panky At Thoreau Spring

Monday, Nov 23, 2020

Baxter and Liz were strolling northward along Bathsheba Beach, one of the more beautiful stretches of oceanfront on our beautiful, endangered planet. The pre-dawn rainstorm had given way to a glorious sunny morning. The surf had dropped, but a new swell was on its way. This was going to be a big one, according to the boys. Just in time for the contest.

Liz had a question for Baxter. "We get interrupted every time you start telling me about your name.

Baxter?"

"Baxter Thunderbird, no less. Can you imagine being saddled with a name like that? At least it wasn't Rainbow Tofu. With hippies for parents, one never knows what they'll come up with. Why, one of my childhood friends was named Pumpkin Pie... That's actually what it says on her birth certificate. She hated it. She changed it to Blueberry Strudel when she was five. That's her Facebook name to this day. Everybody calls her Blue. If we were spending Thanksgiving with her, the last thing she would serve would be pumpkin pie. She hates the stuff with a passion."

"Out with it, girl! Baxter Thunderbird. That's an unusual name if ever there was one. Explain."

"So, OK. And remind me to tell you more about the Thunderbird thing. I've got a lot of information on that subject."

"Roger. Go on, please."

"You've heard of Baxter State Park?"

"Ummmm. Maybe. I'm from Maine, remember? Are you telling me you're named after a state park?"

"Close, but no cigar. Answer me this, Liz. Where were you conceived?"

"Conceived?" Liz stopped in her tracks. "You mean, where did..? I haven't the faintest idea. I know the timing - one year and nine months before my first birthday, but where... I wasn't there at the time. I was hanging out in... what do the quantum physics people call it? The indeterminate field? What's that got to do with anything?"

"Everything. Listen. Baxter State Park. My Mom and my Dad met in Camden..."

"We used to have a house in Camden. In fact we still do." Liz interrupted. "And, come to think of it, I know exactly where my daughter was conceived... But how would I know anything about my own conception?"

"Great, but listen, Liz. I want to know about your daughter's conception..."

"No you don't. You really don't." Liz's response was oddly emphatic. They continued their stroll. The sun was beating down on them, and it was getting hot.

"Yes, I do. But Liz, please... My dad was crewing on a 100-foot sailboat. My mom had a summer job flipping burgers at the Camden Yacht Club."

"And the rest is history!"

"Liz! What have you been smoking? I'll never get this story told if you don't shut up and listen."

"Smoking? Nothing. I... I don't..." Liz was duly chastened. "Sorry," she muttered. "Why am I suddenly being accused of smoking, by every..."

She dropped her head and tucked her tail between her legs, metaphorically speaking.

"So they meet at a party, Andre and Sally. He takes her out sailing. They fall in love. With me so far?" Liz did not reply, looking down at the two pairs of bare feet as they moved swiftly along the wet sand in their colorful, flapping sarongs. Bax's toenails were painted a sparkly purple. Hers were plain Jane pink.

"She, my mom, asks Andre, my dad, have you ever climbed Katahdin? He says, Katahdin? What the hell is Katahdin? Wait. I've heard of it. It's a mountain in the Himalayas, isn't it? My mom straightened him out, and the rest *is* history, as they say."

Bax stopped for breath. They had been walking hard. They stood with their legs in the rushing white water. The first hint of the new swell was in the air, and the tide was coming in.

"Go on, Bax. You've got my undivided attention."

"Whew. I'm out of breath. Give me a minute."

"OK. Should we turn back? What if the tide came in and we couldn't get back around the point?"

"Good thinking."

The women started moseying lazily back in the direction of the Ditch Witch.

"So, I was asking you about Mount Katahdin. Have

339

you ever climbed Katahdin?"

"As a matter of fact I have, a number of times. My dad and I used to... but please go on."

"OK. So. This is a story my parents love to tell. It used to embarrass me as a kid. But I got over it." Bax was puffing and panting again.

"C'mon Baxter. Cut to the chase. This is about how you got your name, remember?"

"Right. So here are my folks, they've known each other less than a month. Three weeks, in fact. They take some MDA."

"MDA?"

"Methylene deoxy amphetamine, also known as the love drug. Similar to Ecstacy, although somewhat more focused. The instructions when taking MDA were as follows; be careful who you take MDA with. You'll very likely end up married to them. It blasts the heart wide open, and..."

"Again, interesting," Liz interrupted. "But what has that got to do with your name?"

"I'm getting there, Liz. Let me finish. So, they, my parents, take some MDA, fall even madlier in love, and during the experience, they decide to have a baby. That would be me."

"Is madlier a real word?" began Liz. She stopped,

hearing a sound behind them.

"'Ullo, Lizzie. Who's yer gorgeous friend?"

Dang! Interrupted again! James's resonant Australian voice came from behind them. He had been sitting in the shade of a rock reading *Mayflower* and saw the women walk by. He decided to intercept them and here he was. A line from a Bob Dylan song echoed in Liz's mind. *Why wait any longer...*

"To be continued, Bax. James, this is my new friend Baxter. Bax. She's from Maine. Are you going up to lunch?"

"I am. I'm ravenous. How about you?"

"Momentito, Jeem. Bax, would you like to come up to our house for lunch? Aside from some very good food, there's something I want to show you."

"Anything to do with an old slave trunk?"

"That, and a rolled-up broadside from the 1700s," said Liz. "You could even meet my beloved but catatonic grandfather, if you like. Maybe he'll talk to you. He always had a thing for pretty women. Let's go. I'm starved suddenly and it's brunch time. I haven't eaten anything today, just that dreadful coffee."

"Speaking of catatonic grandfathers, Liz, how is Old Jack?" James voice was respectful, despite the lightness of his phraseology.

"Your father-in-law, James? He's getting chattier by the day. He won't say a word to me, *moi*, his faithful long-suffering granddaughter, but he's having an ongoing conversation with an imaginary friend. A woman, needless to say. One can eavesdrop if one has the patience. He says about three words per day, on average."

They continued their stroll back down the beach. The incoming tide rushed up, the warm, clear water soaking the women's sarongs. They shrieked happily. Bax listened, intrigued, to the exchange between Liz and James. The chemistry between them was obvious to her. Tiny electric thunderbirds hovered in the air like those annoying floater-things in your eyes.

"So James, you don't sound particularly American," Baxter asked. "How do you fit into this picture?" James and Liz looked at one another. How did James fit in? That was a complicated question if ever there was one. Especially now, with the pheromonal chemistry that was suddenly fizzing and bubbling between the two of them.

"He's Australian," Liz said, as if that explained everything. "It's a little complicated. Umm. James is my stepfather," she said finally.

"Oh. He's married to your mom. I get it. That's not so complicated."

"Well no. My mother died a long time ago, back in the nineties."

"Oh. I had no idea. I'm so sorry."

They walked on in silence for a hundred yards. The powerful roar of the surf made them realize that a big ocean swell had come up while they weren't looking. They stopped and looked out to sea. There was a lot of energy out there, suddenly. The beach was infested with surfers carrying surfboards, each of them gazing intently out to sea. Several photographers were setting up tripods by the water's edge. Their cameras had the longest, most phallic lenses Liz had ever seen.

"I told you it was complicated. But here goes..." Liz began. James was more adept at this. He interjected.

"Actually Baxter, I'm Liz's father's husband. We're in a same-sex marriage."

"No worries, mate. Why didn't you say so, Liz? I have a whole bunch of LGBT friends back in Beserkeley."

"LGBT? What are you talking about, Bax?"

"Lesbian, gay, bisexual, and transgender," James explained.

"Whew, the plot thickens," Liz laughed. "Methinks I see the steam beginning to rise."

"As Maryah would say," said James. "What were y'all

talking about, before I so rudely butted in?

"We were talking about Mount Katahdin."

"That's a mountain in Maine, if I'm not mistaken. The sacred mountain of the Wabenakis."

"Didn't my father tell you?"

"Tell me what, Liz?"

"How the two of us, he and I, we used to climb Katahdin every summer, all through high school. It was pretty much an annual ritual with us, until..."

"You know, it's a bit puzzling to me, but John really doesn't like to talk about his earlier life. His marriage. Maybe there's lingering guilt about your mother. I don't know."

"I know. He just says 'I don't give a shit,' doesn't he? Same when it comes to the family."

"Yeah. Speaking of the family, you know, I've been trying to track down your family ancestry."

"Have you tried ancestry dot com?" Bax butted in, enthusiastically. "I love it. Ninety-nine dollars and you just send them a swab from inside your cheek. I found my father's lineage going all the way back to Holland in the early fourteen hundreds."

"Right. Now I'm jealous. My cousins back in Oz and New Zealand have only tracked us down to the jolly old UK in 1540."

"God, I'm jealous too. I barely even knew my great-grandparents," said Liz. "So James, tell me. Actually, this is interesting. My boys have been wanting to know more about our family history, and I really don't have that much information. Like, how did we come over as penniless German refugees and get so rich?"

"I've had that same thought. Your dad said, how do you know they were penniless? Good point. What if the Altens go back to old money back in Europe?"

"Hmmm. I hadn't thought of that. Of course Grandpa Jack's father, my great-grandfather, invented the altenator. It's named after him, the altenator. Whatever it is, there's one in every vehicle on the planet. He gets a royalty on each unit sold."

"I've heard that theory. There's one minor problem, however. I think someone's been pulling your leg, Liz."

"Oh?"

They were ascending the stairs to the verandah, where Gladys stood waiting, her large arms folded maternally across her ample bosom.

"The word is not altenator, Liz. It's alternator with an 'r.' The word comes from electrical engineering, as in alternating current. Alternating with an 'r.' Arr!"

"Oh."

"And by the way, Jeff, just in case you were

wondering, I was born in Grenada, right over there."
Bax waved a manicured hand in the general direction of
the western horizon. "I was conceived in Maine, but I
was born in Grenada."

"It's James, girl, not Jeff," Liz whispered to her new
best friend as they sat down and Gladys began to serve
the food.

A gusty breeze sprang up from the east, bringing
with it the sound of the rising surf and stirring the
jarrah trees into a sudden frenzy. Jason and Jonny,
catching a whiff of the food coming in through their
bedroom window, materialized suddenly from the house
and joined them.

*****

61

The Pursuit Of Happiness

James Walker Alten, a reasonably intelligent and observant Australian, who had spent a number of his formative years in New York, had developed a theory about Americans - Americans and happiness, to be precise. Finding himself with a captive audience, and never one to miss an opportunity to enlighten the masses, he decided to share his theory with the lunch party, all of whom were Americans. After all, this is at heart a story about Americans, mostly, and a story about happiness, or, more accurately, the absence thereof, so

James's thoughts on the subject seem pertinent.

"If I'm not mistaken, one of the most fundamental assumptions of you Americans," James said between dollops of Gladys's mouth-watering quiche, washed down with a crisp pinot grigio, "is your inalienable right to the pursuit of happiness. It's written into the founding documents of your society. Therefore, one would as-sume, the Americans are the happiest people on Earth. Correct?

"However, think about this. If one is forever pursuing something, can one ever actually possess the object of that pursuit? Think about it. As the 17th Century French philosopher Blaise Pascal put it, *instead of living, we hope to live. Forever preparing for happiness, it is inevitable that we should never know it.* Is it possible that Americans are no happier than anyone else?"

Surprisingly, for teenagers, Jason and Jonny paid rapt attention. They were beginning to like this guy.

"Is happiness, in fact, something to be pursued?" James went on. "If we do so, it is fairly certain, we shall never possess it. We will find ourselves in a state of eternal waiting – waiting for outer circumstance to align itself with our inner expectations.

"The key to happiness, of course, is to be content, no matter what our outer circumstances might look like.

Happy and grateful when things are going our way. Equally happy and grateful when they're not, because that is precisely where we learn the most. Why are things not going my way? What can I do to change them? As the 1960s guru, Swami Satchidananda - remember him, he opened the Woodstock festival? As the swami once said: *Make no appointments and you will have no disappointments.*" James enunciated the foregoing phrase with an exaggerated, fake, Bombay accent. "In other words, have no expectations, and you will never have your expectations dashed. But how can one live in the real world without expectations?

"What can one do? It's basically about acceptance. If we can accept every circumstance in our lives with gratitude, without judgment, we will be a lot happier than if we resist the things we don't like. It's as simple as that. The word 'acceptance' is possibly the closest synonym in the English language for the much-misunderstood word 'love.' In other words, if we live in a state of acceptance, we are in love. We are happy. What a concept!

"To some, this may not sound easy. Wishful thinking, you say? However, once our fundamental assumptions are aligned with the quote-unquote true, expanded or higher nature of things, the shift becomes a whole lot easier to accept, and to put into practice. There is a

349

profound difference between living life with a positive set of assumptions and the opposite. Ultimately, it's all about attitude. Isn't it?"

*****

62

Atilla The Hun

Gladys had outdone herself once again. Over a long and luxurious luncheon and several bottles of white wine, James and Bax and Liz and her boys plunged deep into the question of ancestry, once James had completed his monologue on the subject of happiness. The boys were surprisingly interested in such arcane matters. Why not simply savor the present moment? Who gives a tinker's curse who begat whom, when, and on top of what mountain? No, Jason and Jonny really wanted to know where they came from.

Afterwards, James went up to his room and read a little, before falling asleep with Nathaniel Philbrick on his suntanned chest. The boys went back down to the beach to check the waves again, wondering whether they could really be descended from Attila the Hun, as their crazy new Aussie friend had suggested.

Jason was quite excited at the possibility. He had just completed a semester of early European history at Concord, and while he could not recall every one of the names and dates of the countless battles, he somehow remembered what the fearsome warrior had looked like. In fact Jason had made a detailed pen-and-ink drawing of the dreaded Hun, thereby emblazoning the image upon his soul. Following a memorized description attributed to Priscus, standing there gazing out at the wind-confused surf, Jason ad-libbed a paragraph for his enthralled little brother, who had loved the drawing to the point where Jason had no alternative. The drawing, appropriately framed, now occupied pride of place on Jonny's dormitory wall.

"Our dreaded ancestor, the notorious Atilla the Hun," declaimed Jason in a deep and wildly dramatic tone, standing atop a craggy rock overlooking Soup Bowls, "Our ancestor, Atilla the Hun, was a man born into the world to shake the nations. He was the scourge of all lands. He terrified all mankind by the dreadful rumors noised abroad concerning him. He was haughty in his walk, rolling his eyes hither and thither, so that the power of his proud spirit appeared in the movement of his body. He was a lover of war, yet restrained in action, mighty in counsel, gracious to supplicants and lenient to those who were once received into his protection. Short of stature, with a broad chest and a large head; his eyes were small, his beard thin and sprinkled with grey; and he had a flat nose and tanned skin, showing evidence of his origin."

"Hey!" retorted Jonny. "We don't have flat noses and tanned skin. We have long straight noses and our skin's as white as the driven snow. What's up with that?" Jonny asked, rolling his eyes hither and thither, all the while marching haughtily on the spot.

*****

63

The Ancestors Are Watching

The women sat at the verandah table for almost an hour after the males had gone about their business. Baxter, as Liz had discovered, was a Mayflower descendant on her mother's side. Bax mentioned five or six different bloodlines - Hopkins, Brewster, Billington, and various other names, none of whom Liz had ever heard of. Liz's knowledge of the Mayflower passengers was limited to what she had gleaned from *The Courtship of Myles Standish*, Henry Wadsworth Longfellow's epic poem, back in high school. Even then, she could not for the life of her remember any of their names, with the single exception of William Bradford, whose name had come to her attention very recently.

Bax's maternal ancestors had, apparently, staggered ashore at Plymouth exactly four hundred years ago this month, and the current anniversary was a big deal to her. For years, Bax had planned to spend a couple of weeks in Plymouth over Thanksgiving in 2020, but it was going to be such a mob scene. Every hotel, motel and bed-and-breakfast had been sold out two years before the event. Besides, Bax said, hundreds or even thousands of angry Indians from all over the Americas were converging on Plymouth for a huge protest rally. They had declared a national day of mourning, which had the potential to turn violent. Discretion being the better part of valor, Bax had decided to come to Barbados instead. Much safer, not to mention a whole lot more pleasant, weather-wise! And more directly relevant to her current research.

Baxter explained that she had nothing against the American Indians. On the contrary, she was a supporter and proponent of their spiritual ways, having endured more sweatlodges, vision quests, shamanic journeys and pow-wows than she could remember. She maintained close connections with the Hopi, the Navajo, the Zuni, and the Lakota, and with several leading Native American elders and academics out west. However, she had been struggling for decades to develop a trusting relationship with the New England Indians, who tended to distrust and dislike white people. They had lost King Philip's War back in 1676, after which the Indians had pretty much disappeared from history. They still resented that fact. It had not been easy for Bax, and for all her efforts, she had few native friends on the East Coast. She sighed and continued on a lighter note.

"I spent three years at Wheaton before transferring to Berkeley for my final year. I fell in love with the weather, and stayed out west. I've been a recovering New Englander ever since. I just love the fact that we have spring in February. What about yours?"

"What about my what? My ancestry? As James just confirmed, my great-great grandfather Johann Wilhelm Alten emigrated from Prussia sometime in the 1880s. That's all I know for sure. I seriously doubt Atilla the Hun had anything to do with it. My mother's side of the family is from old Maine stock. 17th Century, I'm pretty sure, but not necessarily Mayflower. My grandfather and my father were born in Brunswick, Maine. I was born in New York City, so strictly speaking..."

Liz took Baxter down to the cellar and showed her the decrepit slave trunk and its pitiful contents, but for some reason she said nothing about the secret sub-cellar under the trapdoor. Or the skeletons, rattling about, just beneath their feet. Or the scroll, or the diary, both of which were safely upstairs in her bedroom on top of the armoire. Her intuition told her to wait. She had quite forgotten that she had told Bax about the scroll within minutes of meeting her at the bank. The skeletons could be legal trouble, and as to the diary, Liz knew with certainty that she had made a profound historical discovery. She was not about to share it with a stranger, an academic stranger at that, knowing what she knew about academic behavior. Not until she knew a bit more...

*****

64

But, Are You Happy?

Baxter and Liz were still talking. They had just emerged from the cellar and were standing at the head of the verandah steps when James came sleepily back down the stairs. He picked up where he had left off. Bax extricated herself and went on home to work on her writing. She borrowed one of the electric mopeds, promising to bring it back in an hour or so.

"I've been thinking about your question about your father's happiness," James yawned. He was still in philosophical mode. "Unhappy humans are unhappy for one reason and one reason only, because they fail to accept

358

things exactly as they are. Happiness is an attitude, a state of mind.

"A dozen people presented with exactly the same circumstance will have a dozen different responses, based on their attitudes, which are in turn determined by their basic belief systems. Are they happy? If not, why not?"

"I don't know," said Liz, distractedly. "Tell me."

"May I offer an analogy? Let's say I present you with a freshly minted one-hundred dollar bill. Are you happy?"

Liz looked at James without answering. She had other things on her mind. He was the best looking man she had ever been this close to.

"That depends on who you are, what your frame of reference is, and so on," James continued. "Let's take just two cases. You are a homeless beggar on the street. You haven't eaten in days. A hundred dollars is an enormous fortune, and you dance for joy." He stopped and looked at her. His brown eyes were sparkling. "In the second case you are a millionaire, and I owed you a hundred thousand dollars. Owed, past tense. The bankruptcy judge has just ruled that all you get is this measly cheque for one hundred dollars. Are you happy? Probably not. It's exactly the same amount of money, but your attitude toward the hundred dollars is likely to be very different from the beggar's."

Liz was starting to pay attention. She was able to get a word in edgeways.

"The first, gratitude and joy," she said. "The second, resentment and bitterness."

"Exactly," James smiled. "In each of the above scenarios, happiness is an option, isn't it? It's a choice. One's happiness depends on one's fundamental assumptions, one's view of the world. The beggar may have boundless trust in the abundance of the loving universe, knowing that his needs will be met at all times. The hundred dollars proves yet again that he is correct in his assumptions: the universe is abundant. It loves him! He loves it."

Liz leaned against one of the tall white columns that supported the roof over the verandah. She was feeling feelings that she had not felt for a very long time.

"The millionaire, on the other hand," James continued, "trusts only his own ability to make and to hang on to money, and so lives in anxiety and the not unreasonable fear of losing what he has. The loss of his $99,900 proves yet again that he is correct in his assumptions - we live in a world of scarcity. What has the universe got to do with it, for God's sake?

"Are beggars happier than millionaires, then? In the story about the hypothetical beggar and the hypothetical millionaire, to what degree is their happiness or unhappiness dependent on outer circumstances? It's not hard to be happy when things are going our way, and it's pretty easy to be miserable when they're not.

"The challenge is to maintain one's equanimity no matter what is going on in one's outer world. The little story I just told you gives us no information about either of the fictitious characters and how they might handle their very different situations in life. There is a third character in the scenario, the hypothetical 'me,' the person blessed with the opportunity to present a hundred dollars to the other two characters. Am 'I' happy? What is 'my' situation in life?"

Liz wandered over to the long verandah table and sat down again. Was she happy? It certainly felt that way, for a change.

"Let's look at that." James was saying, waving his well-tanned hands in the sultry air. "I might be happy, I might not. What if that hundred dollars was all I had in the world? What if I gave the money to the beggar at gunpoint, who was in fact a mugger?

"In the case of the beggar, it looks on the surface as though I am doing a good deed. I am helping the poor fellow, and that is a good thing. I am generous. I should be happy, knowing this. The second case is more complex. I am doing a bad thing to the millionaire. As I hand the hundred dollars to the unhappy bloke - or more likely, to his well-paid attorney - I am confronted with a number of conflicting feelings. Firstly, I am deeply relieved that the judge ruled on my side. I no longer owe the man the $100,000. So, am I happy? Well, what if, despite my triumph, I feel guilt at my failure to honor the debt? How do I feel about myself? Was I generous? Was I honest? Am I happy?

"Don't forget that the judge in this situation was a bankruptcy judge. It sounds like I have problems beyond the immediate situation. How am I handling that? The answers depends entirely on my understanding of the nature of the universe, which in turn depends upon my fundamental assumptions, my core beliefs."

"You should write a book, James," said Liz, her heart thumping for reasons other than the exciting concepts James was presenting. "That could actually help people, you know that?"

"Funny you should say that," said the handsome Australian. "Guess what I'm working on, back home in Sydney?"

*****

65

Thunderbirds To The Left Of Me

James raced off on one of his high-speed solo walks. He called it his daily stagger. 'Give me this day my daily stagger' was the mantra of the new religion he was in the process of developing, apparently. That is how he expressed it to Liz, tongue firmly in cheek. Liz was having difficulty knowing when to take this gorgeous being seriously, but at this stage in the proceedings, it mattered not a whit. Happiness had hit her firmly and deliciously, right in the heart. Nothing physical could possibly come of it. After all, James was married with children, and she was one of those children.

Baxter de Waal had expressed a desire to explore some of the hilly back roads around Indian Point, so she and Liz had made a date to take two of the electric mopeds and do so. A few days back, Liz had reserved four of the sleek, solar-powered machines for the duration, and Washington had set up the rented, sun-powered charging station in an appropriate spot next to the garage.

As good as her word, Bax returned to the old plantation manor just as James left, and the two friends set off down the driveway on their little adventure of exploration. The only discovery of any interest was a weathered, almost undecipherable wooden road sign saying 'Indian Grove,' but it merely indicated a winding, unpaved cul-de-sac that terminated at the crumbling gates of a once-elegant private home. The rusty wrought-iron gates were locked and the place felt overgrown and abandoned. A battered metal notice, half-buried in the brambles, read: 'No Trespassing.'

"I bet there's a story here," said Liz. "This place is as old as Alden House. We should come back and do a little trespassing when we get a chance."

On the way back to the beach at Bathsheba, they stopped at a pull-out above the cliffs, dismounted, and took a breather. Baxter shared another part of her recent Massachusetts experience.

"By the way, there was an interesting aftermath to my Plimoth Plantation visit last month. We were in the middle of a late-season heat wave. Indian summer, with a vengeance."

"I remember. I was in Maine and it was unbearable. I could barely function. I took most of the week off work. All I could do was lie on my goddamn bed with the fan blowing on me."

"Ninety five degrees Fahrenheit and one hundred percent humidity in late October. It was Hell, wasn't it? And they're still denying that the climate is changing? Anyway, after visiting the Wampanoag home-site and the 17th Century English Village, I was just soaked in sweat. I stopped in at the bookstore and the gift shop, partly to dry out and cool off, and partly to see what books they might have, related to my thesis. I saw this large Indian man speeding by in a powered wheelchair, so on a whim I followed him. Long story short, we ended up becoming fast friends and exchanging emails. Answer me this: Have you ever heard of the Thunderbird?"

"Well of course. It's a famous Ford sports car. I desperately wanted one for my 18th birthday, but I'm willing to bet that's not what you're talking about. In fact, Thunderbird being your middle name, I have a sneaking suspicion there's more to the story. Unless you're named after a sports car?"

"I'm talking about the original Native American legends. Shall I tell you what I know?"

"Please do."

Bax flipped into lecture mode, launching into a learned dissertation. Liz was having quite a day of it, listening to her eloquent and erudite new friends and learning as much as she could keep track of.

"The thunderbird was a legendary creature in certain North American indigenous cultures. It was a gigantic bird of supernatural power, frequently depicted in the art and oral histories of the Pacific Northwest Coast people. It was also found in various forms among the tribes of the American Southwest, not to mention the Great Lakes and the Great Plains."

"Question, Bax. Why was the creature called a thunderbird, pray tell?"

"The thunderbird's name came from the belief that the beating of its enormous wings caused thunder, and stirred up the wind. The Lakota name for the thunder-bird was *Wakį́nyąn*, from *wakhą́*, meaning 'sacred,' and *kįyą*, meaning 'winged.' The Kwakiutl had many names for the thunderbird, and the Nuu-chah-nulth or Nootka called it *Kw-Uhnx-Wa*. The Ojibwa word for the thunderbird was *animikii*."

"Whew. I have no idea what all of that means, Bax, but go on, please." Liz was fascinated. She looked at her friend with a new level of respect. How on earth do people remember all this stuff? Bax looked out at the ocean, and went on. For the first time, Liz noticed that her new best friend had a rather beautiful profile.

"In many North American indigenous cultures, the thunderbird was described as a huge bird, capable of creating entire storm systems. It thundered as it flew. Clouds were formed by its wing-beats, the sound of thunder was made by its wings flapping, sheet light-ning came from its eyes when it blinked, and lightning bolts were created by the glowing snakes that it carried in its claws. In masks, it is depicted as multi-colored, with two curling horns, and, often, teeth within its beak."

Liz sat back, closed her eyes, and tried to visualize the fearsome creature. Somehow, in her fevered imagi-nation, the bird looked a lot like James, a devilishly handsome, red-skinned James, with the addition of some horns and a pair of black, leathery wings.

"Dang!" she exclaimed. "I'm glad I never met one. Presumably they're extinct? If they ever existed."

"Apparently not, but let me finish, and then I'll address that question. Depending on the people telling the story, the thunderbird is either a single entity or an entire species. In each case, it is intelligent, powerful, and wrathful. Everyone agrees that one should go out of one's way to keep from getting a thunderbird angry at you."

"You're not kidding. I'll keep that in mind, next time I hear the rumble of thunder."

"The thunderbird was said to reside on the top of a mountain. It was the servant of the Great Spirit. Have you ever heard of the giant Roc?"

"The giant rock? Are you talking about the one out near Joshua Tree? The one where the UFO people..?" Bax turned and looked at Liz. "Wait. Um.. maybe. You mean..? Oh. The Roc is a gigantic mythical bird, isn't it? I remember it from a children's story I used to read to the kids back in the UK."

"That's it. The thunderbird mythology is remarkably similar to stories of the giant Roc from around the Indian Ocean. Like the Roc, the thunderbird is thought to be based on a real, though mythically exaggerated, species of bird, probably the bald eagle, which is very common on the Northwest Coast."

"Interesting. You really know your stuff, don't you? You started out telling me about this Indian man in his wheelchair. Is this thunderbird stuff related to him?"

"I wrote my master's thesis on the thunderbird legends. I teach an elective on the subject at Berkeley. But, let me cut to the chase. Do you know where the thunderbird is right now?"

"Right now? As in Thanksgiving, 2020? I have absolutely no idea." Liz closed her eyes. Bob Dylan's raspy voice echoed in her imagination. *He's standing in front of you, ooh ooh.*

"I'll tell you. Inside Mount Katahdin."
Liz snapped her eyes open.

"Inside Mount Katahdin? Come on, Bax. You mean the mountain is hollow?"

"Apparently."

"A giant bird living in a hollow mountain? That reminds me of a tall tale I was told up on Mount Shasta in California when I was thirteen or so. Except, in that case, there were a bunch of twelve-foot-tall ascended masters living inside the mountain, not a giant bird. So tell me Bax, what does any of this mean for us 21st

369

century mortals?"

"I'm coming to that. That is what this Abenaki gentleman wanted me to know, the one in the wheel-chair. He got quite excited. I might have been the first person who'd ever understood what he was talking about.

"Firstly, he said, there's more than one thunderbird. There are ten of them. Ten. Secondly, they are waiting for us, humanity that is, to get our act together, to reach a certain point in our evolution, at which point they will return."

"Hmmm. Ten thunderbirds. I'd like to see that. That would be an impressive sight, indeed. But tell me this, Bax. Why don't they just get it over with, and come back now, before we completely destroy this beautiful planet of ours?"

"As I understand it, there's a sort of non-interference policy. They can't come back until we wake up and invite them."

"Sounds like something out of Star Wars. What did they call it? Umm..."

"You mean Star Trek. The 'Prime Directive.' It does sound like Star Trek, doesn't it? I wonder if that's where Gene Roddenberry got the idea from? Could it be an ancient indigenous concept? Be that as it may, the

Native Americans have a lot to teach us. It's time we stopped ignoring them."

"I think that applies to all of the indigenous cultures," Liz responded. "Think about the Australian aborigines. My father does a lot of work with them, bless him. It's his one redeeming feature, trying to preserve and restore their traditional culture, to rescue their languages. There were four hundred and fifty distinct aboriginal languages when the white settlers first arrived. And then there are the bushmen of the Calamari. You know, I think we actually live in an amazing time. We *are* starting to pay attention. Ever since the Sixties, when the hippies started growing their hair and taking part in sweat lodges..."

"The bushmen of the Calamari? Don't you mean the Kalahari?" Bax giggled at the mental image. Little brown people dressed in loincloths made of squid. "The *Gods Must Be Crazy* people? Anyway, Liz, I totally agree with you. Don't forget the peyote ceremonies, and Carlos Castenada. If you want my not-so-humble opinion, the cosmology of the indigenous people is vital to humanity, if we are going to survive and evolve."

*****

66

Who Can You Trust?

J ames and Liz strode vigorously along the beach. The wind whipped the words out of James' mouth as Liz struggled to keep up with the man. James was still in his philosophical mode.

"The re-programming tools are simply a set of alternative assumptions," he continued. "Change your assumptions, and the world changes with you. It's like looking at the world through a different lens. The big question is, how much internal resistance will we encounter as we embark on the shift? Free will allows each and every one of us to remain exactly as we are, or to change as radically as we choose, or dare. It takes courage to launch oneself into the unknown, and most people seem to prefer the security of the status quo, illusory and dangerous as that may be.

"On the other hand, perhaps there is no alternative, if our species is to survive. The time has come, the walrus said. The year 2020 is upon us. Our world is clearly in the midst of a profound and fundamental shift. We live in challenging times, there is no question about it. Hanging on to outdated beliefs is highly unlikely to serve anyone. People used to think money bought them security. Not any more. The equity in most peoples' homes has gone away. It went away back in 2007. It never was real. No amount of believing in it will make it come back. So, where do we put our trust? Ah, that's the question!"

James is quite the original thinker, thought Liz, sincerely fascinated. Not to mention being one of the most gorgeous men I have ever seen, outside of a movie theater. Her mind and her body were responding to the Aussie in equal measure, and her face was radiant.

"Can we depend on our society, our elected leaders, our friends, our partners, parents, mentors and teachers?" James went on. "Are they not all basing their reality on the same outdated assumptions and beliefs as everyone else? If so, they are not going to be much help, are they? Most importantly, can we trust ourselves? Is there such an entity as a 'higher self,' which is divinely guided and therefore utterly trustworthy? If so, and we could let go of our insecurities and trust that, we'd no doubt find ourselves in much better shape. Alternatively, can we trust God, the omnipresent entity that one might call the Conscious Loving Universe? Clearly, if such a thing really existed, and we could truly know that, then trusting that would be the best of all solutions.

"Does it all come down to faith? What is the difference between trust and faith? Between faith and belief? Is there any difference? These are not simple questions. They are the great mysteries which have been pondered by the world's greatest thinkers for thousands of years. We are unlikely ever to be able to answer them definitively, because it all comes down to our individual core beliefs, which differ greatly from person to person and from culture to culture."

Liz had quite lost track of him by this time, but James plunged on rewardless. He stopped momentarily to let her catch up, changed his gait to a Michael Jackson-like moonwalk, then resumed his monologue.

"All is not lost, however. We have the right and the

freedom to choose our beliefs and to craft our assumptions based on the best information available to us. Here in the opening decades of the 21st Century, one thing we have in abundance is information. Right at our fingertips, we now have most of the wisdom and knowledge ever gathered by the human species. We can study and compare everything, from ancient Vedic science to aboriginal cosmology, to the religious writings of all ages, to the most advanced speculations in the field of quantum science. Using a combination of intelligence and intuition, left and right brain thinking, we can begin to imagine things in ways previously impossible.

"We can ask ourselves un-answerable questions. Do UFOs really exist? If not, why not? What about parallel universes? Anything we can imagine is possible, and we can imagine more and more as time goes on. Is this the only inhabited planet in the universe? Not impossible, but statistically, I think it's highly unlikely. When we die, are we simply erased from existence, leaving no trace? Again, not impossible, but highly unlikely, given what we are learning about the nature of consciousness and the Quantum Field.

"We could go on forever, asking ever-more arcane questions, but this is the realm of philosophy and academia. What is philosophy, really? Have you ever heard of the Sufi master, Pir Vilayat Khan?" James plunged on without waiting for an answer. "Pir Vilayat was fond of saying, tongue firmly in cheek, 'A philosopher is a blind man in a dark room searching for a black cat that isn't there!'

"Far more relevant than studying the fusty old philosophers, from our present standpoint, is the fact that we can now construct a highly coherent individualized picture of the Universe based on the knowledge and wisdom I just mentioned, choosing aspects or elements with a high statistical likelihood of accuracy, and rejecting the less-likely possibilities as we encounter them. As long as the end result contains no blatant contradictions or obvious absurdities, we can choose to believe our personal construct, until better information comes along.

"Again, this is our right as sovereign beings. We do not have to believe anyone else's cosmology, nor should we try to impose ours on others. This goes far beyond freedom of religion as it is currently practiced, and offers a fascinating new possibility: we can custom-build our own Universe."

"Whew, Jeem. You've really got me thinking," Liz lied, completely lost.

She had lost track of his stream of verbiage at least

ten minutes back. It did not seem to matter in the least. They had come to the end of the beach. In front of them was a sheer face of grey, weathered granite, with the surf pounding against it. They turned around and started back in the other direction. With a quick, dazzling smile at her, James picked up where he had left off.

"We all do our best to construct our reality on the basis of observable facts, don't we? Needless to say, that is not always possible, so we have to use our best guess, based on the best information available. There are certain things we may never know, but as we move out of the left-brain-dominated era of rational materialism into a more balanced apprehension of reality, it seems certain that we will come closer and closer to a true understanding. Both science and religion, as they have come down to us, contain untruths and absurdities, partial truths and just plain fantasies. We now know the world is not flat, that the Earth orbits the Sun, that Santa Claus, the Tooth Fairy and even the Easter Bunny are imaginary. God is not an elderly middle Eastern gentleman seated on an ornate throne somewhere up in the sky, stroking his long white beard as He doles out clusters of white-clad virgins to each martyr as endless ranks of discarnate spirits arrive in Heaven.

"What we know for certain is this: the Universe is

expanding. It is evolving, it is unfolding even as we speak. It has been gushing into existence for something like fourteen billion years, and will continue to do so for the foreseeable future, long after our species, our planet and even our sun have ceased to exist in their present forms.

"Is the human species important in the big picture? Again, it is impossible to know, but for the moment we know of no species more conscious, with more potential. Consciousness itself, human consciousness, may be extraordinarily important. Self-realization is a uniquely human phenomenon, and may be contributing in extraordinary ways to the unfoldment of the living Universe, the great awakening of which we are part.

"One problem in pursuing such thoughts is this: we unavoidably give the impression of separation, speaking as though such a thing, separation I mean, could be real. When we speak of our higher and lower selves, or of our relationship to a higher power, of circumstance guiding us, think about it. The very words imply separation. It seems impossible to analyze the situation while at the same time maintaining a state of undifferentiated oneness. Perhaps there is only one truth, but which truth would that be? The Oneness of Creation? The Conscious Loving universe?"

378

By the time James reached the end of his discourse, they were back at the house, sitting out in the deck chairs sipping margaritas on the rocks. These kinds of thoughts underlay the increasingly profound one-way conversations that unfolded between James and Liz, as their friendship deepened. It did not matter to Liz that James did most of the talking. She just loved the sound of his resonant southern hemisphere accent. She paid rapt attention, noticing how the sounds of the surf and the cries of the sea-birds wove themselves into the music of his voice. The words he spoke simply did not matter.

"You can't have this kind of conversation with just anyone," James said, holding his margarita up to the light. "It's been years since your father and I last communicated like this. We used to go on forever, but lately we seem to have run out of things to talk about..."

*****

67

What's That Rattling Sound?

The afternoon was still and hot. Liz and Bax sat in the shade of the large beige umbrella on the patio at Bax's little AirBnB rental cottage, gazing out at the sea in the middle distance. Liz's sleek electric moped leaned against a nearby picket fence. The fence was perfectly painted in bright shiny white. Some thoughtless bird had pooped a purple and white streak down the side of one of the slats. The streak had dozens of tiny black dots in it. The dots were the seeds of future generations, of what plant Liz did not know.

"Bax, do you mind? Can we get back to the genesis of your name? I'm actually rather interested. Not just the Thunderbird part. The Duval surname is French, I know that, but it's the Baxter part I'm interested in, mostly. Being from Maine and all."

"De Waal is not French, Lizzie. It's Dutch, actually, or in my case, South African. It's pronounced 'duh vahl,' not 'da wall' as most Americans pronounce my name." Bax spelled out De Waal. "D-E W-A-A-L."

"Oh. Got it."

"So where were we? Did I get to the part about the thunderstorm?"

"The thunderstorm? Thunderbirds, yes. I don't recall a thunderstorm. You were talking about Baxter State Park, last I remember."

"That's right. The thunderstorm on Baxter Peak when I was conceived."

"Wait. I'm totally confused. You were *not* conceived on Baxter Peak, unless your parents were masochists. Baxter Peak is a jumble of huge rocks that look like they just rained down from the sky. It's cold up there, no place to make a baby. Could we begin at the beginning?"

"Sure. I'm sorry. Deep breath! Where was I? They, my parents, took the love drug, MDA. Did I tell you that? They fell even more deeply in love and decided to have me. With me so far?"

"Tell me about AMA one more time. I'm not sure I got it the first time around."

"MDA. So, Ralph Metzner, you remember him, he was one of the three Harvard professors?"

"Bax, I am totally lost. Ralph who? Which three Harvard professors? There are hundreds of them."

"My goodness, Liz. You *have* led a sheltered life. All right. Let's start at the beginning. Have you ever heard of Timothy Leary?"

"Well yeah! My late husband was very interested in Timothy Leary. Turn on, tune in, drop out! Lucy in the sky with diamonds."

"That last was the Beatles, but yeah that was Tim. How about Richard Alpert?"

Liz looked at her blankly.

"Ram Dass?"

"Rum what? Is that some kind of tropical drink?"

"Ram Dass was a guru. He had a stroke, but he's still…"

"I'm sorry to hear that, Bax, but what in the world does any of this have to do with the AMA?"

Before Bax could reply, Liz's cell phone rang, deep in her hippie purse. She fished for the elusive device.

"First phone call on my iPhone since I arrived on the

island," she said in surprise. "They've tracked me down at last." Digging the phone out with a struggle, she listened. "Oooops, sorry Barb. I'll be right there. Tell 'em ten minutes." She turned to Bax.

"The police are there. It's about the skeletons."

"There? Where's there? Which skeletons?"

"At the house. This could be trouble. I'll catch you later, Bax. I'll text you!"

Liz vaulted onto her moped and silently high-tailed it back along Bathsheba Beach and up the hill to Alden House. Bax watched her friend go in some consternation. Trouble? Liz did not seem terribly worried. Skeletons? Well, every family has a few of those rattling about in their closets. But it wasn't every day the cops came over to check up on them.

Bax went into the cottage and sat down at her laptop. She had been steadily working on the slavery book, but suddenly another subject had leapt to the forefront of her awareness. She hit Command 'F,' typed in the word 'pilgrim,' and found the Microsoft Word file she was looking for. It was a rough draft for another book she had begun three or four years earlier. She hadn't given it a thought for quite some time. She reviewed what she had written back in 2017.

PILGRIMS AND INDIANS - Ten Common Misbeliefs

Question:

What do Jennifer Lawrence, John Quincy Adams, Franklin D. Roosevelt, Marilyn Monroe, Richard Gere, Ulysses S. Grant, Clint Eastwood, Sarah Palin, Alec Baldwin, Orson Welles, Ralph Waldo Emerson, Henry Wadsworth Longfellow, Humphrey Bogart and George W. Bush have in common?

Answer:

1. They are all descendants of the Mayflower Pilgrims, and

2. Their Mayflower forefathers have been dishonored, maligned, vilified, and disparaged by widespread misinformation. How? And why?

'Politically correct' falsehoods have been spread about the Pilgrims, by people as diverse as Hollywood actress Cher in her 2013 Thanksgiving Day 'Tweet,' the fraudulent Native American academic Ward Churchill, revisionist historian Howard Zinn in his bestseller *A Peoples' History of the United States*, the United Native Americans of New England, and many others.

Countless Americans believe these untruths and distortions, which are now deeply ensconced in the national psyche through our school and college textbooks and curricula. Google 'The Real Story of Thanksgiving' for more...

Let's look at some of the current assumptions* about the Mayflower Pilgrims and the Indians.

An assumption is a belief that we take to be true without question. Our assumptions color our perceptions and our attitudes and affect our feelings and our actions.

Bax deleted the word 'affect' and replaced it with the word 'determine.' After saving the file, she read on:

Fiction vs Fact

1. **Fiction:** The Pilgrims gave the Indians smallpox-infected blankets, wiping out 90% of the indigenous people of New England.

Fact: The *Mayflower* landed in November 1620, several years *after* the inter-tribal war and disease epidemic that decimated the New England tribes in 1616-1618. There is no historical evidence of smallpox aboard the *Mayflower.* The first recorded smallpox epidemic in New England occurred in Boston in 1633.

The epidemic that decimated the New England coastal tribes in 1616-1618 was almost certainly not smallpox. It was most likely either measles or bubonic plague from French fur traders in Nova Scotia and present-day Maine. The disease was probably brought from the north by seafaring Mi'kMaq warriors, who destroyed a large percentage of the coastal native communities from Maine to Cape Cod during the Tarrantines War (1615-1619.)

2. **Fiction:** The Pilgrims and other Europeans were welcomed with open arms by the friendly Indians.

Fact: At the 'first encounter' on December 6, 1620, Nauset warriors attacked a group of Pilgrims exploring the Cape Cod shoreline. The Indians fired some 30 arrows at them, before being driven off by musket fire. Fortunately, no one was killed or even injured.

Two years earlier, two French fishing vessels had been attacked, burned, and their crews tortured to death. While Plymouth Plantation was under construction, the Pilgrims were under constant threat of attack and annihilation by the neighboring tribes, with the notable exception of Massasoit's Pokanoket band and a few other friendly groups.

3. Fiction: The Pilgrims would have died of starvation during the first winter if the Indians had not taken them in, housed them, and fed them.

Fact: The *Mayflower* anchored at Provincetown on Nov 11, 1620. Other than one brief, violent encounter, they did not meet any Indians for over four months, during which time half of the passengers died of the 'general sickness' (probably scurvy) not of starvation. The Pilgrims met their first Indian, Samoset, on March 16, 1621, and then Squanto, Massasoit, and the Pokanokets on March 22, 1621. On that date the Pilgrims and Massasoit signed a peace treaty that both sides honored for fifty-four years. The Pilgrims had adequate supplies of food, and in fact fed their frequent Indian visitors on numerous occasions.

4. Fiction: The Indians lived in universal peace and harmony before the coming of European settlers.

Fact: There are hundreds of first-hand reports showing that many of the Indian tribes were in a state of perpetual war, building federations and empires, competing for territory, exterminating trading competitors, taking slaves, sacrificing and eating humans, and torturing captives.

5. Fiction: Indian society was completely egalitarian and democratic.

Fact: Like the Europeans, the Indians recognized royal and noble bloodlines, such as those of Nanapashimet, Massasoit, Powhatan and hundreds of others. Only persons of royal lineage could marry one another or succeed a sachem or sagamore. In Virginia, Powhatan was an emperor, and Pocahontas was a royal princess. In New England, 'Squaw Sachem' and Weetamoo were queens, and King Philip was a royal prince. Philip declared that he was the equal of King Charles II of England, which is why the settlers nicknamed him 'King' Philip.

6. Fiction: The Pilgrims came ashore in 1620 as an invading army, raping and pillaging. They massacred the Indians they encountered, seven hundred of them, then sat down for a 3-day thanksgiving celebration with the survivors.

Fact: The 52 Pilgrims (14 adult men, 4 adult women, 34 children) who survived the first winter were peace-loving, God-fearing people who made friends with the Pokanoket Indians they met in the spring of 1621. The Pilgrims and the Pokanokets lived in peace and harmony with each other until 1675, over half a century, at which point the well-armed Indians declared all-out war on the settlers.

7. **Fiction:** The Pilgrims and the Puritans were one and the same, and both were religious fanatics.

Fact: The Pilgrim Separatists were quite different from the Puritans. They were remarkably open-minded, having spent 12 years in liberal Holland before crossing the Atlantic. They had much in common, spiritually, with the Indians, made no attempt to convert them to Christianity, and were much more sympathetic to the Indians than were the Puritans, who began

389

arriving in 1630, ten years after the landing of the *Mayflower*. Once Massasoit declared himself to be 'King James's man' the Indians became subject to all the rights and protections of English law.

8. Fiction: The Pilgrims were incompetent, ignorant convicts who were expelled from England. Once they landed, they had no idea how to fend for themselves.

Fact: The Pilgrims were highly competent farmers, carpenters and tradesmen. Their leaders were Cambridge-educated. Their only crime was that they were religious dissidents, which was illegal in England at the time. They already knew the land and most of the plants they encountered. The climate was very similar to that of England.

During their first year in Plymouth, the Pilgrims constructed a village and a fort from scratch, and planted and reaped a successful first harvest, albeit with help from Squanto's corn-planting technique.

9. **Fiction:** The Indians never harmed anyone. The Europeans came to North America and massacred the peace loving inhabitants.

Fact: It went both ways. There is no question that Europeans and Indians massacred one another from time to time, but the Mayflower Pilgrims were never directly involved in a massacre.

Research shows that throughout the entire contact period (1600-1850) Indians carried out approximately 500 massacres against Europeans, and Europeans committed about 450 massacres against Indians. A total of approximately 9,000 settlers were massacred by Indians, compared with roughly 7,000 Indians massacred by Europeans.

10. **Fiction:** The Plymouth colonists wrongfully murdered Massasoit's innocent son Metacom (known as 'King Philip.')

Fact: After years of preparation, selling land and buying the latest European weaponry with the proceeds, Metacom declared all-out war on the settlers in June, 1675, bringing to an end fifty-four years of peace and friendship. His well-armed warriors killed an estimated 2,500 English men, women and children throughout New England.

King Philip's War was the bloodiest conflict, per capita, in recorded American history*. The war might have gone against the English, had not the Mohawks come in on their side. The war ended when Metacom was shot and killed - by an Indian - on August 6th, 1676.

Bax closed her eyes and thought for a while. She then added the following paragraph:

*There was in fact an even bloodier conflict during historical times, a brutal genocide which was well documented by the Jesuits. Between the years 1640 and 1648, the Mohawk exterminated their ancient enemies, the Huron, using firearms that they purchased from the Dutch in New York. Estimated at about 40,000 members in 1640, by 1648 the formerly powerful Huron had been reduced to a few scattered bands of refugees, who had fled and taken shelter with neighboring tribes. The motive for this genocide was economic hegemony as well as vengeance. The Mohawk were determined to have exclusive fur-trading rights with the French.

****

68

Skeletons In The Closet

Walking the moped up the last of the crushed coral driveway, Liz ditched the machine, leaning it against a tree. She gazed at the circus of flashing lights.

"An ambulance?" she said out loud. "Those skeletons are beyond help. What are these people thinking?" The ambulance and the four police cars completely blocked the driveway. Their emergency lights lit up the trees and the façade of the house as though this were some huge highway disaster with bodies scattered far and wide. Half a dozen uniformed men dozed in the shade under one of the giant mango trees. Liz ran up the stairs two at a time to the balcony, and collided with a large black man in a khaki uniform emerging from the wide-open front door.

"I'm sorry, officer. I'm Liz, the owner's granddaughter. Can I help you?"

"Hello my dear Mrs Alden. I am officer Andrew Jackson. We are just waiting for the lady from Archaeological Survey, and then we will see what you have here. Meanwhile your..."

"Hi, officer Jackson. Welcome. You're Gladys's cousin, aren't you? I'm Liz Nicholson, and my grandfather's name is Alten, not Alden."

"It is? Oh, I'm sorry, it says Alden House at the bottom of the driveway."

"I know. That was the original owners. The ones who... It's easy to get the names mixed up, isn't it? Maybe that's why my grandfather..." She paused for breath, and cautioned herself not to say too much. "I haven't seen the skeletons myself, but the South African workers..."

"South African workers? Hmmm. I trust they have their work papers in order? We can't have entire impis of Zulus simply showing up and moving in, you know."

"I have no idea. It did not occur to me to ask. I don't think any of them were Zulus. They just helped me clean out the cellar because none of the locals would go down there. Because of the ghosts, you know."

"So I heard. Word gets around. I wouldn't be too concerned about it, Mrs Alden. I was just asking to pass the time."

"It's Alten, officer Jackson, not Alden. My great-grand-father invented the altenator, and..." She did not finish the sentence. Officer Jackson was on to his next question.

"By the way, did you see any gho-asts down there?" Liz did not answer. She considered telling the man about the invisible Indian slave woman, but decided against it. Technically, she had not seen the ghost, although she had certainly heard her. There are times when the less said, the better. This was one of those times.

Gladys came out of the house with a tray of drinks for the men. Liz sat down on the verandah in one of the huge turquoise Adirondack chairs, the police chief contentedly fanning himself with the morning newspaper and sipping a cold beer in the chair next to her. Something told her to say nothing about the old 'bible' or the scroll, both of which were safely upstairs in her bedroom. On top of the wardrobe, well out of sight.

The cops could investigate the trunk if they wanted to, but in any case, it would be the skeletons that interested them the most. One would think.

After a while Liz left the police chief to his cogitations, or more accurately, to his siesta. The man was fast asleep. She went up and sat with her grandfather. The old man was snoring peacefully, with the Simon and Garfunkel song still on repeat. Liz flipped the player off. Outside, the surf was getting louder. You could hear the crack of each independent wave as it broke.

Almost two hours passed before a taxi pulled up behind the traffic jam of police cars. There was now an additional vehicle parked there, Dr. Ginsberg's gold Prius. An extremely large woman extricated herself from the rear of the cab and impatiently puffed her way past the traffic jam and up the balcony stairs, as the taxi backed carefully down the sweeping driveway and returned whence it had come.

*****

69

The Archeologist

It took a little doing, getting the oversized, asthmatic bureaucrat down to the cellar, but Washington saved the day by opening the exterior hatch to the rear lawn and helping the obese woman down the back way. It is not certain that the rickety stairs down from the kitchen would have survived the assault. It was the first time Washington had ever ventured into the haunted cellar, and it did not seem to worry him in the least.

The Archeological Survey official stood there puffing like a grampus, looking down at the trunk and its contents. The trapdoor stood open just behind her, and the familiar awful smell was back. Liz stood there feeling slightly nauseous.

"What is this?" the woman asked sharply. "It looks like something was wrapped up in it." The archeologist held up the decrepit oilskin wrapper that had protected the old bible for so long. Oh God. Liz had forgotten all about it.

"I don't know," she stuttered. "What is that?"

"I don't know either. But it's older than anything else in this cellar, Mrs Alden. A lot older."

"My name is Nicholson, Liz Nicholson."

"Well, be that as it may, Mrs Nicholson, we will take possession of it along with the other artifacts."

The archeologist's voice had that marvelous ring of post-colonial bureaucratic authority to it, much like that of the woman at immigration who had very nearly insisted on a strip-search when Liz arrived ten days ago. You can't be too careful these days, she had said, what with all these Islamic suicide bombers running around. Many of them disguise themselves as wealthy middle-aged American women, as I am sure you are aware.

"Take possession of...? I thought you had come to identify the skeletons?"

"And to take possession of anything of potential

archeological or historical value. Such artifacts are the property of the nation of Barbados, as I am sure you are aware."

There was that phrase again: as I am sure you are aware. Liz's hackles rose.

"I see," she said. "In that case you might want to take a look at my grandfather. He's over 93 years old. Well on the way to fossil-hood." The woman squinted at Liz suspiciously, and Liz thought better of pursuing that particular train of thought.

"Well, I'll leave you to it. You're welcome to any of this furniture, by the way, if you can use it. We haven't even looked at it in a hundred years. Washington will let you out," she said, and went upstairs to her grandfather's room. She was shaking.

*****

70

Margarita Time

Later, when the sun was going down behind the coastal mountains, and the light in the jarrah trees was magical, and the police cars and the ambulance had finally departed, taking the trunk, its decrepit contents, and seven heavy body bags full of bones and skulls with them, Liz and Barbara sat out on the verandah slurping double strength margaritas and reviewing the events of the day. After a long silence, Barbara voiced the obvious question, the one Liz had been studiously avoiding.

"Couldn't you get into trouble?"

"Fuck 'em if they don't have a sense of humor. I've got the Pope on my side. You ever hear of the doctrine of discovery, back in 1494 or whenever the hell it was? I found them. They're mine. Or at the very least, they're ours. Besides, they're part of American history. New England history. If I handed that journal and that scroll over to these people, that would be the last anyone would ever hear of them. They'd just disappear into some storage unit somewhere, and in this climate... They wouldn't have the foggiest idea how important this discovery is."

"What if you get caught at the airport when you leave?"

"I've thought of that, trust me. They might search me, under the circumstances. I'll have to put on my smuggler hat! Or deploy the diplomatic pouch."

"The diplomatic pouch?"

"It's an old trick for the well-connected smuggler."

*****

71

King Philip's War

Liz and James were assembling trays of dishes and glasses in the kitchen and taking them to the dining room in preparation for the big day. Gladys and Washington bustled about, busy with dinner. The sun had set an hour ago, but the waxing moon meant it would never get totally dark. In fifteen minutes or so, the household staff would retire to their five star slave quarters, crank up Muddy Waters, and twist the night away.

"There was something else in the trunk, James, beside the old bible. I think you'd call it a synchronicity.

Baxter has uncovered something about it in the Barbados historical records, the parish records, but I think this is an original. It has to be. It's an old rolled-up parchment document or broadside, dated June 1676, seriously water damaged. Hold on and I'll go get it."

Liz bounded upstairs. In a moment she was back, holding the scroll. James perched on the back of a red leather couch in the living room. Liz carefully unrolled the document, and read it out loud.

"*Act to Prohibit the Bringing of Indian Slaves to this Island.* That's the title," she explained. "*This Act is passed to prevent the bringing of Indian slaves and as well to send away and transport those already brought to this island from New England and the adjacent colonies, being thought a people of too subtle, bloody and dangerous inclination to be and remain here.*"

Gladys eavesdropped with obvious interest.

"Indian slaves in Barbados? From New England? 'A people of too subtle, bloody and dangerous inclination' Who'd a thunk?" James was bewildered. "What year did you say that was, Lizzie?"

"1676, immediately after King Philip's War, apparently. I mentioned it to Washington. He and Gladys had a feeling, from some of their grandmothers' stories... Did you know, Washington's name is actually Washington

Franklin, although that's a whole 'nother story? According to Bax, that name comes up when you read about the slave rebellions here. Our beloved Washington is descended from those rebels, it seems."

"Wait. Back up a little, Liz. King Philip? I thought it was King Charles in 1676. After Oliver Cromwell. I thought I knew my English history. I'm seriously confused."

"You, and about ninety-nine percent of the American population, my deah. I'll explain when we go on our walk tomorrow. Let's get this finished for Gladys, shall we? I'm hungry."

*****

72

A Little After-Dinner Reading

The extended family sat around one end of the long dining room table after dinner. Everyone was present except Washington, Gladys and Junior. The usual suspects - Liz, Bax, Jason, Jonny, Barbara, James, Scilla, and Maryah - sat sipping their coffee and savoring their dessert wines, the teenagers included. Liz wanted to take advantage of the situation. She was anxious to read something from the old diary, if she could persuade anyone to listen.

She started out by revealing the encounter with the ghost in the basement. She wasn't sure anyone actually believed her. Jason piped up.

"I've never seen a ghost."

"Well, you've come to the right place, Jason. Wait till you see the skeletons."

"Skeletons? What skeletons?" Jonny was all ears.

"We found a bunch of them in the cellar. The archeologist went off with them a couple of hours ago, but I'm sure something can be arranged. Those body bags looked heavy. I had no idea bones were so... Listen people, can we talk about something a little less morbid? I want you all to hear a bit of what I've been staying up all night transcribing. Listen..." Liz looked around to make sure she had everyone's attention, opened the tattered school composition book, and began.

"...*fend our governour to them, and they vnwilling to come. Squanto went againe vnto him, who brought word that we fhould fend one to parley with him, which we did, which was Edward Winjloe, to know his mind, and to fignifie the mind and will of our governour, which was to haue trading and peace with him. We fent to the King a payre of Kniues, and a Copper Chayne, with a Iewell at it To Quadequina we fent likewife a Knife and a Iewell to hang in his eare, and withall a Pot of ftrong water, a good quantitie of Bifket, and fome butter, which were all willingly accepted: our Meffenger*"

made a fpeech vnto him, that King Iames faluted him with
words of loue and Peace, and did accept of him as his Friend
and Alie, and that our Governour defired to fee him and to
trucke with him, and to confirme a Peace with him, as his
next neighbour: he liked well of the fpeech and heard it atten-
tiuely, though the Interpreters did not well expreffe it; after he
had eaten and drunke himfelfe, and giuen the reft to his com-
pany, he looked vpon our meffengers fword and armour
which he had on, with intimation of his defire to buy it, but on
the other fide, our meffenger (hewed his vnwillingnes to part
with it: In the end he left him in the cuftodie of Quadequina
his brother, and came over the brooke, and fome twentie men
following him, leaving all their Bowes and Arrowes behind
them. We kept fix or feaven as hoftages for our meffenger;"
Liz paused for breath. "And here's the part about the
treaty they signed at their very first meeting."

"As I understand it from the Philbrick book," James
interjected, "both sides honored the treaty until 1675, at
which point King Philip declared war and New England
turned into a bloodbath."

"King Philip. Goddamn it!" Maryah broke in indignantly. "Typical that some arrogant English king would
come over here and start a war. 1621 until 1675 did you
say? That's a long war. Over half a century." She snorted
derisively. "I wouldn't call that a war. I'd call it
genocide."

"Maryah, hold your horses a moment!" cried Bax. "Aren't you reading the *Mayflower* book? I guess you haven't got to that part yet. King Philip was an Indian, for God's sake. Philip was the name the English gave him. The King part came from his attitude. Apparently he was a royal pain. His Indian name was Metacom, so the war is also known as Metacom's Rebellion. He was the son of Massasoit. The war only lasted from June 1675 until August 1676, but it was the bloodiest conflict in American history. It killed more people, per capita, than the Civil War. It was the peace that lasted for fifty-four years. Fifty-four years of unbroken peace and friendship. Did you know that?" Bax was a little hot under the collar. Her face was red and her upper lip was tight.

"Hang on, ladies. Let me finish, and then we can all compare notes. OK, Maryah?" Liz said. "Here's something to think about. How on earth did a journal that was written in New England come to be buried in Grandpa Jack's cellar here in Barbados? Can anyone…

"Listen everyone, one more section. I just got it done this morning. This is about Chief Massasoit and the treaty they, the Pilgrims, signed with him. I really struggled with this part. The handwriting is so…

"*Captaine Standijh and mafter Williamfon met the King*

at the brooke, with halfe a dozen Musketiers, they faluted him
and he them, fo one going over, the one on the one fide, and
the other on the other, conducted him to an houfe then in
building, where we placed a greene Rugge, and three or foure
Ciilhions, then inftantly came our Governour with Drumme
and Trumpet after him, and fome few Musketiers. After falu-
tations, our Governour kifTmg his hand, the King kifled him,
and fo they fat downe. The Governour called for fome ftrong
water, and drunke to him, and he drunke a great draught
that made him fweate all the while after, he called for a little
frefli meate, which the King did eate willingly, and did giue
his followers. Then they treated of Peace, which was;

1. That neyther he nor any of his fhoula iniure or doe hurt to
any of our people.
2. And if any of his did hurt to any of ouw, he fhould fend the
offender, that we might punifli him.
3. That if any of our Tooles were taken away when our people
were at worke, he fhould caufe them to be reflored, and if ours
did any harme to any of his, wee would doe the like to them.
4. If any did vniuftly warre againft him, we would ayde him;
If any did warre againft vs, he fhould ayde vs.
5. He fhould fend to his neighbour Confederates, to certifie
them of this, that they might not wrong vs, but might be like-
wife comprifed in the conditions of Peace.
6. That when their men came to vs, they fhould leaue their
Bowes and Arrowes behind them, as wee fhould doe our Peeces
when we came to them.

Laftly, that doing thus, King Iames would efteeme of him as his friend and Alie: all which the King feemed to like well, and it was applauded of his followers, all the while he fat by the Governour he trembled for feare; In his perfon he is a very luftie man, in his beft yeares, an able body, graue of countenance, and fpare of fpeech: In his Attyre little or nothing differing from the reft of his followers, only in a great Chaine of white bone Beades about his necke, and at it behinde his necke, hangs a little bagg of Tobacco, which he dranke and gaue vs to drinke; his face was paynted with a fad red like murry, and oyled both head and face, that hee looked greafily: All his followers likewife, were in their faces, in part or in whole painted, fome blacke, fome red..."

*****

73

The Popinjay At The Wedding Feast

Tuesday, November 24, 2020

The Tuesday before Thanksgiving dawned bright and beautiful. Grandpa Jack's condition seemed to have stabilized, and it looked like he'd live through the big day, which was now just two days away. Although, of course, one never knew. Barbara's chief concern was the fact that the dying man had pretty much stopped eating, a common symptom of advanced Parkinson's disease. Eventually, that would kill him, she told Liz. Fortunately, he was still taking in a fair amount of water.

Optimistic monkeys chattered in the shrubbery. They could smell the food, and were hoping for a handout, although that was strictly against the rules. Gladys served breakfast to Liz and Barbara on the verandah. Liz's eyes were red and puffy - she had been up all night working on her transcriptions. She was making up for the lack of sleep by imbibing copious amounts of strong black coffee.

"The wedding, Barb?" Liz said. "It was ten years after Sarah's, my Mom's, accident. Layla was three. Grandpa Jack tried to make up for his neglect by spending a fortune on the wedding. 'Elizabeth,' he wrote me in a telegram, 'Whatever you want, just go for it,' he said. So I did. What the heck? If you've got it, you might as well spend it. Especially considering he had a real attitude toward James."

"James?" Barbara was confused. "Oh, your husband James, not your.... He did? What was wrong with James?"

"You better believe Old Jack had an attitude. He called it a shotgun wedding four years too late."

"I suppose that does make sense, from his perspective. So? In view of the unlimited budget, where did you have the ceremony? Gay Paree?"

"That was the question Prissy and I asked ourselves. You know her as Scilla, my little sister. We had a meeting. What was the most exotic, expensive wedding location in the world? Konya, Turkey on Thanksgiving Day, which also happened to be my birthday that year? That was James's first idea. Turkey for Thanksgiving. But the Grateful Dead had already done that. Yellowstone? India? Tahiti? Kenya? Santorini? A safari for 50 in Botswana? Fly everyone in, including the Archbishop of Canterbury to tie the knot, and the caterers and the band to keep the mob from rioting. I wanted the Rolling Stones, but I would have settled for U2." Liz laughed at the memory. "Pissy, I mean Scilla, we put her in charge of the entertainment. She wanted some band I'd never heard of called the Afghan Whigs, so that's who we got. Despite the silly name, the band was great. The guys were so much fun. If it hadn't been for the word popinjay in Grandpa's giveaway speech and the absence of my parents, it would have been the happiest day in my life."

"Where did you end up having the wedding? You didn't say."

"I didn't? We decided on Easter Island, even though it was the 4th of July. We rented an old ox-cart, with four long-horned steers, and that's what we went off in for our honeymoon. Little Layla was steering and we almost went over a cliff into the sea. We had so much fun! We took over the entire Altiplanico Easter Island hotel and three or four other places for all the guests."

"Easter Island on the 4th of July? I get it. What fun. How come your father wasn't there?"

"Where was Junior? I'll give you one guess. Golfing. Watching the young Tiger Woods in England, where else? He predicted Tiger would have a great career ahead of him. It was the 127th Open something or other. Tiger came in way on down the list, but Junior kept the faith. He was right on, needless to say."

"One more question, Liz. You mentioned the word popinjay. What on Earth is a popinjay? I've heard the word, but..."

"Washington tells me it's the local name for a parrot. There's one that keeps screaming curses at me from the tree outside my bedroom window. In Spanish, no less. But that's not what my grandfather meant when he used the term. Popinjay is a highly derogatory English insult. I'll send you a link to a definition I found online."

Maryah emerged from the house onto the verandah, walked to the top of the steps, stretched like a cat, yawned, turned and pulled up a chair.

"I thought it sounded a little uncomplimentary. Did

your James know what it meant?" Barbara turned to the new arrival. "Good morning, Maryah."

"Oh yes. I'm not sure my grandfather knew, but James certainly did. He was an educated Englishman, after all. I think it upset him for the rest of our relationship. Anyway deah, enough of me and my dysfunctional family." Liz looked across the table at her sister-in-law, who was helping herself to coffee. "What's uppermost in your mind these days, Maryah?"

"Good morning, y'all. What's uppermost in my mind, dizzy Miss Lizzie? Other than your gorgeous little sister? Pilgrims and Indians, I guess. After all, it's Thanksgiving back in the States. I'm reading this crazy book. They're all dying, one right after the other, after taking all that trouble gettin' their sorry asses to America."

*****

7 4

A Great And Strange Cry

James sat alone out on the lawn, reading Nathaniel Philbrick's *Mayflower.* The paperback was somewhat the worse for wear. He had inadvertently got it wet when a sudden surge of surf splashed up his legs the previous day, and then he'd managed to knock his morning coffee over while the book was still damp. He fired up his little electronic cannabinoid oil dispenser, exhaled, then heaved himself up energetically and speedwalked down toward the ocean, carrying the book, which had become his constant companion. He was thoughtful.

At the water's edge, he encountered an equally introspective Liz coming the other way along the beach. She lit up when she noticed who it was, standing there in front of her like that guy in the Bob Dylan song. How did the lyric go? *Why wait any longer for the one you love, when he's standing in front of you?* Liz had her notebook with her. Without so much as a by your leave, she started reading from the book.

"*A none, all vpon a fudden,*" she said ."*We heard a great & ftrange cry...*" James broke in. He had become quite excited about Liz's little project.

"Have you told your father about this? This is going to challenge his world-view, big time. You know that, don't you."

Liz was thrilled to have someone to talk to, especially someone as intelligent and cute as James was, someone who was actually interested in early American history. She was boggled by her discovery and, thus far, no one had seemed to give much of a hoot. Except the owls, and they didn't count.

"I know. That's a whole 'nother subject," she said. "But... listen to this. I opened the diary at random last night, and came across this. I call it the 'First Encounter.'

"*A none, all vpon a fudden, we heard a great & ftrange*

418

cry, which we knew to be the fame voyces, though they varied
their notes, one of our company being abroad came running
in, and cryed, 'They are men! Indians, Indians! and withall,
their arrowes came flying amongft vs, our men ran out with
all fpeed to recover their armes, as by the good Providence of
God they did. In the meane time, our firft Captaine Miles
Standi/h, having a fnaphance ready, ^T*the made a fhot, and
after him another, after they two had Indian fhot, other two of
vs were ready, but he wifht vs not to fhoot, till we could take
ayme, for we knew not what need we fhould haue, & there
were foure only of vs, which had their armes there readie, and
flood before the open fide of our Baricado, which was firft
affaulted, they thought it beft to defend it, leaft the enemie
fhould take it and our ftuffe, and fo haue the more vantage
againft vs, our care..."

"Wait a bloody minute, Liz. I've just read something
almost exactly like that. You know I'm in the middle of
the *Mayflower* book." James held the book up for Liz to
see.

"I know. That's my whole point! This is absolutely
unbelievable, James. I don't know what this is, or who
wrote it, but this has to be the real thing. The weird
thing is, this material was written in 1715, almost a
hundred years after the Mayflower. Why anyone would
be writing about... Unless it's fiction... a novel. But,
there's more. Listen to this.

"There was a luftie man and no whit leffe valiant, who

was thought to bee their Captaine, flood behind a tree within halfe a musket fhot of vs, and there let his arrowes fly at vs; hee was feene to fhoote three arrowes, which were all avoyded, for he at whom the firft arrow was aymed, faw it, and ftooped downe and it flew over him, the reft were avoyded alfo: he flood three fhots of a Musket, at length one tooke as he fayd full ayme at him, after which he gaue an extraordinary cry and away they went all, wee followed them about a quarter of a mile, but wee left fixe to keepe our Shallop, for we were carefull of our bufineffe: then wee fhouted all together two feverall times, and (hot off a couple of muskets and fo returned: this wee did that they might fee wee were not afrayd of them nor difcouraged."

"Whoa. I swear that's pretty much exactly... But first, here's something I just read. I think it might interest you. Listen!" James opened the *Mayflower* book and paged through it. He was searching for a specific paragraph.

"James, this is the real deal. It must be. I haven't read Philbrick's *Mayflower* book in years. I didn't pay a lot of attention to it back then, but what with the 400th anniversary, everyone's reading it again. Including you. I might have to..."

"And Maryah's reading it. Don't forget Maryah." James was having trouble finding the passage in the Philbrick book.

"That's right. And Maryah, to my surprise. She doesn't strike me as the reading type. But let me finish this part. I just got it transcribed in the middle of the night."

"Hang on, Liz. Here it is. Do you mind? I found this interesting. The Pilgrims went on an exploratory trip to the location of present day Boston Harbor..." James read from Philbrick's account. *This was a place where an English settlement might blossom into a major port, with rivers providing access to the fur-rich interior of New England. Not surprisingly, the Indians in the region, who had been devastated by both disease and war with the rival tribes to the north, possessed many more furs than the Pilgrims had so far found among the Pokanokets.*

"OK. Boston, before any English settlers got there. That is interesting, but what grabbed you in particular?"

"The bit about, quote: 'both disease and war with the rival tribes to the north.' I thought the Indian tribes all lived in peace and harmony before the white man came."

"So did I at first. I think my father still believes that. You'd know better than I. My late husband - another James by the way - he published a controversial article on the epidemic and the forgotten war that decimated the East Coast Indians. He called it... um... the Tarantula Wars or something like that."

"The Tarantula Wars? There are no tarantulas in

421

New England, as far as I know. They're out in the Southwest, in the desert. Your husband was an Oxford man, wasn't he? Your father told me he..."

"Cambridge, actually. But let me finish. Can I read you one more bit from the diary?"

They stood with their bare feet in the calm, clear shallows. The surf had gone flat, and for once there wasn't a surfer in sight. Where did the surfers all disappear to, in between swells? Liz read on.

"Thus it pleafed God to vanquifh our Enemies and giue vs deliverance, by their noyfe we could not gueffe that they were leffe then thirty or forty, though fome thought that they were many more yet in the darke of the morning, wee could not fo well difcerne them among the trees, as they could fee vs by our fire fide, we took vp 18 of their arrowes which we haue fent to England by Matter / ones, fome whereof were headed with brafle, others with Harts home, & others with Eagles clawes, many more no doubt were fhot, for thefe we found, were almoft covered with leaues: yet by the efpeciall providence of God, none of them either hit or hurt vs, though many came clofe by vs, and on every fide of vs, and fome coates which hung vp in our Baricado, were fhot through and through.

"So after wee had given God thankes for our deliverance, wee tooke our Shallop and went on our Iourney, and called this place, "The firjl Encounter," from hence we intended to haue fayled to the aforefayd Theeuifh Harbour, if wee found no convenient Harbour by the..."

422

Liz stopped and looked at James to see what he thought. Her body tingled. Although she had been finding the man increasingly attractive, and suppressing the attraction with due diligence, she had not fully realized what an astonishingly beautiful man her stepfather was. He turned to her. Their gazes met in a rather too intimate way. After an endless moment, they both dropped their eyes and turned away. James was nonplussed.

"S-s-sounds like the welcoming committee wasn't all red carpets and ch-ch-champagne, doesn't it?" he stuttered, blushing uncontrollably.

*****

75

Fun With Papa Jack

Junior came strolling into the dining room as though he owned the place. He looked like a million dollars, tall and suntanned and supremely self-satisfied, if a little portly and overweight. He was dressed in the finest bespoke golfing clothes money could buy, and held his noon Beefeater and Schweppes between thumb and index finger. He stopped and examined the glass, lovingly. By day's end, he would have emptied yet another bottle of Beefeater's London gin. He referred to the liquid as his 'juniper juice,' and swore by its alleged healing and anti-aging properties. There was an air of triumph about the man. Liz greeted her father brightly, as Gladys diplomatically busied herself on the other side of the room. There was something Liz wanted to share with Junior, who stood at the window with his back to her, gazing intently at the trees outside.

"Hey, Papa Jack!. Good morning. I've barely seen you since you and James got here. You having fun yet?"

"Definitely. That was a good morning. A very good morning. Two over par. Not bad for a beginner. This little island is home to two of the best golf courses on the planet. By the way, kid, it's afternoon, not morning. Can't you tell?" Still facing the window, his back to Liz, he held up the gin-and-tonic glass as incontrovertible evidence that the noon meridian had come and gone. His drinking day had begun.

"Dad, I'm not exactly a kid. I'll be forty the day after Thanksgiving. And you're not exactly a beginner. You've been playing golf for how long? Sixty years?"

"I know. Sometimes it just feels that way. Anyway, as long as we avoid the subject of Pilgrims and Indians, I think I'm going to continue having fun. I just wish your grandfather would..."
Junior did not complete the sentence. He turned from the window and looked her in the face for the first time.

"Lizzie, a question. I have a strange feeling you're up to something. You've got that look on your face you used to get as a ten-year-old. But please, whatever it is, keep it to yourself. OK?"

Liz looked down at her bare feet, wondering how best to broach the subject. The tops of her feet were bright pink, badly sunburned. She kept neglecting her feet when she applied the sunscreen to the rest of her pale white body. Junior turned again, walked away, and gazed though the big windows at the ocean beyond the ironwoods, his broad back to his daughter. He addressed the open window and the words came back to Liz mixed with the hissing of the ocean.

"It's good to see you girls. It really is. Believe it or not, I miss the two of you horribly. And it's actually not so bad to be back in the ancestral hovel, wouldn't you agree?"

"I love it here. I really do. So many happy memories. But Dad... Speaking of the ancestral hovel, this house has just revealed something beyond belief. Something to do with Pilgrims and Indians, believe it or not. Right on the four hundredth anniversary... I have something amazing to share with you... with everybody, once we're all sitting down together."

Junior's response was chillingly formal. He turned, held

426

up his hand to cut her off, then moved to the antique liquor cabinet where he mixed his second gin-and-tonic in a series of precise clatters. He had done this before. Gladys gave Liz an imperceptible eyebrow signal, then evaporated into the shadows. The housekeeper sensed trouble, as well she might. She barely knew Liz's father, but had gleaned enough from Old Jack over the years to be wary. Junior spoke at last.

"Like I said, Elizabeth, any topic of conversation is OK with me, with one very specific exception. You are well aware what that exception is. We have had this conversation before. How long ago? Ten years? Twelve?"

"More like fifteen years. But Dad, you are going to be amazed," she pleaded. "And pleased. More than pleased. I promise you. It's the historical discovery of the century."

"Historical hysterical. In the interests of hysterical accuracy, I'm going to tell you, one more time, everything there is to know about the God-awful Puritans. In a nutshell, the so-called Pilgrims were the advance party of an invading army. Nothing more. Nothing less. Religious freedom? Yeah, right. How about freedom to commit genocide? They stormed ashore, the ones who survived the first winter, men, women and children,

cannons blazing, distributing smallpox-infested blankets left right and center, raping and pillaging and putting up real estate signs. They killed 700 Indians the first day, then sat down to a joyful 3-day thanksgiving dinner with the survivors of the peaceful tribe who had welcomed them with such open arms. Roast turkey, mashed potatoes, cranberry sauce, and all the trimmings. Provided and served by the Indians. End of story. Beginning of America. Ta rah! Brandish stars and stripes flag, sing national anthem etc etc. I thank God every day that we Altens have nothing to do with those scumbags."
Liz was shocked.

"Oh Dad. That is ridiculous. You're not really serious, are you? After all these years? I mean...I'm starting to wonder... could those people, the Pilgrims, really, could any of them have been our ancestors? Could there be any family connection? I know we're German on Grandpa's side, but... What about Mom's...?"

Junior drained his gin-and-tonic in a single gulp, then interrupted her in mid-sentence.

"Note that I said hysterical, not historical. I was exaggerating for dramatic effect, but I was only half kidding. However, I *am* serious. I warn you, Elizabeth. The subject is off limits. And by off limits, I mean off limits. If we're going to get through this goddamned

Thanksgiving nightmare you have set up for us, we can talk about the weather. We can talk about global warming. We can talk about golf. We can talk about sailing. We can talk about the elections. No, on second thoughts, cancel that one. Let's see. We can talk about growing petunias. We can talk about why your goddamned husband jumped off that goddamned bridge just when his goddamned career was taking off. We can talk about how my fine young grandchildren are doing at University. Speaking of which, how are my fine young grandchildren doing at University?" Junior paused and raised his empty glass to his nose, savoring the aroma of juniper. "But no goddamn Pilgrim talk. Have I made myself clear?"

"But Dad.... That's ridiculous. Besides, James, my James, did not jump off a bridge, any more than he was abducted by aliens. He was ice fishing in Canada. It was an accident. He fell through the ice, as you well know." She threw the helm a-starboard and steered for safer waters. "It's funny how we both ended up with Jameses, isn't it?" There was no response. "Also, Dad, the boys are still at Concord. They're not yet in college. You know that, don't you? Layla's at law school out in California, which is why..."

The father glanced briefly at his firstborn daughter, then

429

continued mixing his third gin-and-tonic of the day. Junior was a creature of habit, and he had his priorities firmly in order. The clock over the mantelpiece chimed the hour. It was one o'clock. Job completed, he turned, drink in hand.

"You probably don't know this, Elizabeth, but I took a look into your husband's death." There was just a hint of compassion in Junior's voice. "Turned out the county coroner was an old acquaintance of mine from my AIM days, a Mohawk attorney named, well... Anyway, he ruled it was a fishing accident, as you know, but he never could explain the trauma to the back of the skull. Did your husband have any enemies, do you know?"

Without waiting for an answer, Junior went in search of James, who, he expected, was off somewhere as usual with his nose buried in a book. Liz yelled at her father's receding back as he walked out onto the verandah and disappeared from sight.

"Your handsome husband went grocery shopping with Maryah. They should be back any moment. Why don't you go down to the beach and check on your grandsons? They would appreciate that. They really would."

Scilla was ascending the verandah stairs as Junior went down. She stopped. The Porsche was parked in the driveway at the bottom. Her father kept his eyes carefully focused on his drink. It wouldn't do to spill the precious stuff, now, would it? After he had passed her by, apparently headed for the beach, Scilla turned and watched him pass from sight along the forest walk. Well, she thought, that's the first time I've actually set eyes on the sucker since I was a teenager. She continued up and into the kitchen. She had promised to help Liz and Gladys with the Thanksgiving preparations.

*****

76

The Priscilla Thang

It was three in the afternoon before Liz and Scilla took a breather. The day was hot and windless, and the preparations were hard work. One of the modern conveniences that Old Jack had consistently refused to install in Alden House was air conditioning. There was always a cool breeze off the ocean, he insisted. That was not the case today. The sisters sat on the verandah in sweaty silence. Liz fanned herself with a glossy tourist magazine. Scilla was the first to speak.

"So. How's it going with our dear daddy, beloved big

sister o' mine?"

"This is going to be a little harder than I anticipated." Liz stared at the condensation on her water glass. She was still upset at the encounter with her father.

"A *little* harder? Tell me about it. Did you see that? The sucker didn't even look at me. It must be the tattoos. Maybe he didn't recognize me, I hadn't thought of that. Hey, tell me, Lizzie, could anything be harder than doing anything in the whole wide world with the closed-hearted fascist we call our beloved Papa?"

"I know. It's a bitch. But Scilla..." Liz changed the subject abruptly. "Wait 'til you hear what I've discovered. Right here in this very house. There's a secret sort of cave thing down beneath the cellar. I think the slaves must have dug it. There were slave rebellions..."

"I know. You read us a whole long thing last night after dinner, remember? What language were you speaking? I barely understood a word." Scilla drained the last of her water, and put the empty glass down on the table, positioning it precisely in its earlier circle of condensation. "About the slave thing, I guess it's a possibility," she continued, thoughtfully. "The previous owners used to keep slaves, right? Back in the day. But please, please, don't say anything about that to Maryah, whatever you do. She's wildly sensitive on the issue of

433

slavery."

"Got it. It's not directly about the slaves, anyway. It's about something that somehow got into their hands, and ended up being preserved for more than three centuries. That's my theory, at least. Without them, who knows if the diary would've been lost forever?"

"Not more Pilgrim slash Indian revelations, I sincerely hope? Is that the problem with Dad? Remember the rants he used to..?"

"Oh Pissy...I mean Scilla. Seriously. Wait 'till he sees what I've discovered. He's..."

"Goddammit!" Scilla exploded. She leaped to her feet. "The next time you call me Pissy, I ...I. I don't know what I'm going to do. I'm going to set Maryah on you, that's what I'm going to do. She's a goddamned black belt, just in case you were wondering."

Speak of the Devil. The sisters were interrupted by the crunching sound of a taxi pulling into the circular driveway below the balcony. The vehicle pulled in behind the silver Porsche and stopped. James and Maryah were back from town with a significant trunkload of groceries and liquor. Maryah put her head out of the taxi window and yelled.

"Yo ladies! Care to lend a hand?"

The sisters obediently went down the stairs and lent a

hand. Maryah handed Liz a heavy bag of groceries.

"How are y'all, Liz?" she asked. "I have a question for y'all."

"A question for me-all?" Liz smiled. "I'm all ears. Fire away, dear sister-in-law."

"I been wonderin', ya know? What with it being 2020 and everything, I been reading this kinda interesting book about the *Mayflower* boat, y'know? The old ocean liner that brought all them Dutch immigrants to America. Back in the day."

"Go on."

Liz stifled a giggle, and turned to walk up the steps.

"Are y'all by any chance related to any of them folks? Turns out there was a guy named Alden on the boat. Alden, not Alten, I know, but I was kinda wondering..." Maryah heaved a grocery bag into each arm and started up the stairs after LIz. "It says Alden House down at the bottom of the driveway. What's up with that?"

A word about Maryah, in case y'all were wondering. She was an African-American punk-rock guitarist from Savannah, Georgia. She sported a shock of bleach-blonde dreadlocks, tied up on top of her head like a miniature palm tree or a bundle of corncobs hung up to dry. The matted dreads added about eight inches to her diminutive 5' 5" figure.

James paused and looked over the top of the taxi at Maryah, his arms filled with grocery bags.

"You're reading the *Mayflower* book, aren't you, Maryah? That's funny. Me too."

"Well all-righty then. Snap!" Maryah stopped and turned. "In my line of work we call that sinchronicity, with the emphasis on the sin. What d'you think about my theory, Jim? Y'know? Alden. Alten."

"What do you mean?"

"Well just for starters, what's up with the Priscilla thang? I ast you that already, in the grocery store. By the frozen turkeys."

"The Priscilla thang? What Priscilla thang?" James was confused. "I thought we were talking about transvestite hairstyles. The *Queen of the Desert* movie."

*****

436

77

Master Jack

The four of them ate their lunch out on the verandah table. Liz and Scilla reminisced about their dying grandfather, John Bradford Alden. The girls had a nickname for the old man. 'Master Jack' was Scilla's and Liz's private name for the once-indomitable figure lying in the middle of the enormous bed upstairs. The term came from a hit song written sometime in the 1960s by a British pop quintet who called themselves Four Jacks and a Jill. The song's lyrics described their grandfather, and their father, for that matter, perfectly. 'It's a very strange world you live in, Master Jack,' went the chorus line.

"What do you mean, his complaints department?" Maryah wanted to know more. In her imagination, she pictured a door at Alden Enterprises' Wall Street headquarters in New York. The sign on the door read: 'Complaints Department.'

"Grandpa was always right, even when he was wrong," said Scilla, ruefully. "Wasn't he, Liz?"

"Just like someone else I could mention. However," continued Liz, "if you didn't like things the way they were, you were always welcome to submit a formal complaint. There was a very specific procedure for that purpose."

"Well, that sounds very civilized," opined James.

"Civilized ain't the half of it," Scilla chuckled.

"Come on guys. What are y'all trying to tell us?" Maryah was losing patience. "Cut to the chase, would ya?"

"OK, so here's what you have to do if you have a problem," said Liz. "First, you write out your complaint, in detail, on the back of a nice crisp one-hundred-dollar bill. In the blank spaces."

"Step two," continued Scilla, "attach the hundred-dollar bill to the neck of a bottle of the finest

438

champagne, perfectly chilled."

"Step three," Liz giggled, "have it hand-delivered to Master Jack's office right as the sun is going down."

"Well," grinned James. "That *is* civilized. I had no idea."

"Hang on, Jim. There's one final step. He'd think about it overnight, and tell you to forget about it in the morning."

*****

78

Gettin' To Know Y'all

J ohann Bergdorff Alten, also known as Junior,
frustrated at having failed to find his handsome
husband, returned to the house in search of his other
main priority, a gin and tonic. That was much easier to
find. Carefully carrying his precious fourth - or was it
his fifth - Beefeater gin and Schweppes quinine water,
he made his way back down the verandah stairs to the
dented Porsche, where he had parked the vehicle on his
return from the golf course, telling Washington not to

put it away just yet. They were going out for dinner.

At the bottom of the steps, Junior encountered Maryah, who was standing there examining the damaged vehicle with a little knowing smile on her face. Junior did his best to evade the dreadful woman, but she headed him off with a sudden crab-like shuffle, the smile widening on her shiny brown face. Maryah was determined to get to know her father-in-law. They ended up standing at the bottom of the verandah stairs next to the vintage sports-car. To Junior's astonishment, the woman knew exactly which model it was. She went on to show some surprising business acumen as well.

"It's a '59 718 RSK Spyder, Papa Jack. Porsche only ever made ten of them. My lead singer used to have one, that's how I know. He let me drive it a couple times in LA, in Malibu. I didn't put a single dent in it. Unlike some people..." Maryah switched subjects suddenly. "By the way, Jack, are y'all really the owner of General Electric?"

"Who the devil told you that?" Junior said, sharply.

"I dunno. Definitely not the devil. A little birdie? A birdie with the word Google tattooed on its pretty little chest?" She held up her hands to emulate the quotation marks on either side of the G-word.

"The one-word answer is no," said her father-in-law. "I may be one of the larger shareholders. I'm not sure about that, but that doesn't mean I own the company."

"OK. Just wondering, Papa. Second question: How about that export-import bank thingy the Republican Congress shut down back in 2015?"

"What? How the hell..? That mistake has cost me, personally, something like half a billion dollars to date, and that was just the beginning. We had to lay off over 4,000 workers in 2016 alone."

"What about Boeing, Mr. Alten? Or should I be calling you Papa?"

"Call me Junior, for God's sake. Everyone else does. I hate it, but... Boeing? I dumped half my stock in Boeing, and a few other great American companies, beginning in 2015. Let me tell you, that hurt."

"So, Jack. I mean Junior. Oh, I get it. Grandpa Jack is Grandpa Jack and you are Jack, Junior. Scilla calls you Papa Jack. Anyway, about dumping your stocks because of the Republicans, how does that make you feel about being a Republican?"

"How does that make me feel about being a Republican? What the hell are you talking about? Republicans don't have feelings."

"So you wouldn't change if a better option came

along?"

"Change what? Parties? Are you kidding? Put it this way. Donald Trump could have saved the global economy, but no one was listening. Tell me, how do you know all this stuff?"

"I spend a lot of time on Google. Paying attention to the little birdie. Don't you?"

"Don't I what? Spend a lot of time on Google, Mary? Why would I do that? I have God knows how many employees who are paid to do that for me. I own a shitload of shares in the parent company, but I have yet to use any of their services. I guess I'm just an old-fashioned kind of guy. I've got better things to do than sit all day staring at a computer screen. Things like playing golf, for instance." He stopped and looked around. "And looking for James. You haven't come across a handsome young fellow with a strong Australian accent, by any chance? Probably with his nose buried in some ridiculous book?" Junior drained his drink and put the empty glass down on the bottom step, right where someone was sure to step on it.

"Y'all own a shitload of Alphabet stocks, Jack? Me too. Not a shitload exactly, but some. Good choice." She nodded her head, approvingly. "Well, sir, it's been an honor gettin' to know y'all. The name's Maryah, by the way, not Mary. Just in case y'all were wondering."

Maryah stuck out her hand. Junior grunted, then turned his back on his daughter-in-law and walked off down toward the beach. Maryah watched him go. She dropped her outstretched hand, picked up the offending glass, and went up into the kitchen.

*****

79

The First Discovery

Dazzling afternoon sunlight filtered through the gauze curtains. Liz and Scilla stood together in Liz's bedroom, looking down at the decrepit old 'bible.' The antique journal had sprouted a dozen or more three-by-five index cards, which stuck out every few pages. Liz picked up her shiny new exercise book and got ready to read out loud from it. The book was the fifth she had thus far filled. Scilla was decidedly skeptical.

"Where did you say you found this musty old book?

Ugh. It makes me wanna puke. Can't you smell it? And what's this crap about a ghost? Give me a break, Lizzie. What did this so-called apparition look like, moaning and groaning and dragging a length of rusty chain?"

"Well, to be honest, I didn't actually see her. I heard her. She was Indian, I mean Native American. You could tell by her voice. I saw her in my nightmare, my second night here. At least, I think it was her. I told you about it, the nightmare - on the phone. It scared the crap out of me. The girl in the dream, I think it was... I'd show you the trunk, except the goddamned authorities have confiscated it" Liz took a breath. She was still fuming about the confiscations. That was so unfair.

"I can show you the sub cellar, if you like. Washington has put a stepladder down the hole... It's pretty scary down there, I warn you. It stinks even worse than this journal does. Oh, by the way, did I tell you about the skeletons?"

"One thing at a time, Sis. Native American ghosts? Native Americans don't have ghosts, Sis. They have ancestors. And now you're talking about skeletons, Lizzie? Skeletons? Come on. What is this? Halloween is over. Give me a fucking break, Liz. Have you considered professional help? You're losing it. Either that, or you've been reading too much Stephen King."

"Reading too much Stephen King? Hardly. I'm reading my first Stephen King novel as we speak. Trying to, anyway. I'm almost on chapter two, if I can ever get through chapter one. But stop interrupting me, Scilla.

"This is more important than you can imagine. Think about it. I would never have found the bible - I mean the journal - without the ghost. And the ghost could only communicate through Grandpa Jack, once he got close to death and started seeing through the veil. That's my theory - it's what all the urgency was about. If Grandpa had died before I got here, we would have never...

"But first, Scilla, listen to this. Listen. I call it 'The First Discovery,' because they went ashore to see what they could discover. Listen: *The fame day fo foon as we could we fet a-fhore 15 or 16 men, well armed, with fome to fetch wood, for we had none left; as alfo to fee what the Land was, and what Inhabitants they could meet with, they found it to be a fmall neck of Land; on this fide where we lay is the Bay, and the further fide the Sea; the ground or earth, fand hils, much like the Downes-in Holland, but much better; the cruft of the earth a Spits depth/ excellent blacke earth; all wooded with Okes, Pines, Saffafras, Iuniper, Birch, Holly, Vines, fome Afh, Walnut..."*

"I have no idea what any of that means, Liz," Scilla

whined. She was bewildered, and not particularly interested. "It sounds like something I was forced to read in middle school. One of those God-awful old history things. OK, so it's an old book with all this weird scribbling. Look at it. I can't make head or tail of any of it. It's about a bunch of trees. Those people couldn't even spell, could they?"

"Prissy, there was no standardized spelling back then. It was pretty random. Nobody could spell with any consistency, even if you had a degree from Oxford. This is the hardest thing I've ever tried to do, but it's important. Thank God for that ridiculous Elizabethan handwriting course I took at Cambridge, remember that? The point is, do you know what this is? It's the *Mayflower*. The goddamned *Mayflower*! Do you have any idea what that means?"

"You're the library person, Liz. You love these fusty old books. You always have. Tell me something. What's the *Mayflower* got to do with a smelly old bible in Grandpa's basement in Barbados, for God's sake? The *Mayflower* was, like, New England. Wasn't it?"

"It's *not* a bible. That's the whole point, girl. It was disguised as a bible so the writer wouldn't get busted."

"Busted for what? For keeping a diary?"

"I think so. For writing. I'm beginning to wonder if

it could have been written by a woman. It wasn't considered proper for a woman to read and write, back then."

"Well yeah. At least we've made some progress since we floated across the pond. Humanity, I mean."

"Pissy, I'm going to say it one more time. Please listen. This is the *Mayflower*. It's 2020. Do you have any idea what that means?"
Scilla Barnes turned on her big sister. There was mayhem in her reptilian eyes.

"I'm warning you, Lizard Breath," she hissed, using the hated nickname from their childhood years. "It was embarrassing enough when I was four years old. Now I'm big enough to kill you with my bare hands."

"Lizard Breath? I haven't heard that in a while. Oh God, Scilla. I'm sorry. It just slips out sometimes. Maybe I really am losing it. I haven't had a real night's sleep since I got here."

"You know what, Lizard Breath? The next time it 'just slips out,' I'm gonna set Maryah on you. I'm warning you. She's a professional assassin. You probably know that. She used to work for the, well... I'm not supposed to... So watch it, sister. I'm serious." Scilla was not kidding. Liz made a mental note to be a lot more careful in the future.

80

The Demon Awakes

The ocean was calm and intensely blue. There was not a cloud in the sky. Liz and James were speeding, relatively speaking, along the undulating white sand pathway that followed the coastal clifftops. A hundred yards offshore, a humpbacked whale sent a plume of white steam into the still air. A pair of fork-tailed frigate birds circled high overhead. James was a few hundred feet ahead of Liz.

He stopped and turned, waiting for her to catch up. It was not the first time James had noticed it, but this time the realization was accompanied by something stronger. A lot stronger. This time, his whole body began to quiver. Hairs stood on end, hairs he did not know he possessed. It was a delicious and familiar sensation, but one that he had not felt in a number of decades. It was a sensation to be kept under the strictest control. As long as he kept staggering ahead, James told himself, she won't notice the bulge in his Billabongs, but he had to keep stopping and waiting for Liz. It would have been impolite not to have turned around and looked at her, and yet, turning around and looking at her was the root of the problem.

Liz had taken to joining the Aussie on his extended daily stagger while Johnny Alten, father of one of them and long-term lover and spouse of the other, the inadvertent facilitator of this newly-blossoming relationship, was off somewhere on yet another of his obsessive, gin soaked golfing missions. Liz had mentioned that she had felt like an orphan during her pre-teen years. How did James feel?

"A golf orphan? That's it! That describes me exactly."

Joining James on his walks had taken a little adjusting to, for the slender, well proportioned fifty-year-old was a walker. After all, that was his name. 'The name's Walker, James Walker,' he would proclaim, doing his finest Sean Connery impersonation. Or at least he had done so before the legal name change that accompanied the Aboriginal initiation ceremony near Ayers Rock and the dubiously legal marriage certificate that had made him an official member of the Alten clan.

James's teenage nickname back in his native Australia was 'Speed' Walker, and he was still in the habit of racing along like an endangered piping plover pursued by a voracious pitbull, his legs a twinkling blur. No normal human being could keep up with him. Back home, it was rumored that he could outwalk an ostrich, although that claim had never been put to the test, for obvious reasons. Ostriches do not live in Australia.

Liz could not recall their initial encounter, which, according to James, had been at Sarah's funeral. She had not seen anyone there, in the blur of tears and stunned confusion, so that was not surprising. The first time he and Liz had met as adults had been ten years ago in Maine, but they had exchanged barely a word at the time. The entire family reunion had lasted less than two hours.

The current phase of the relationship was less than a week old. Thinking about their brief and violent first encounter later that night, snuggled up with her sleeping father and feeling dreadfully jet-lagged in a dreamily erotic sort of way, James had experienced a powerful feeling that there was something about his stepdaughter, something special. She reminded him of someone.

Junior had re-introduced his firstborn child in his usual brusque, almost dismissive way "You remember Jim, don't you?" and Liz had responded with a polite but frosty "Hello James. Glad to meet you at last." The first

452

time James had set eyes on Liz, she had been fifteen, a weepy, scrawny, flat chested, skinny legged, foal faced virgin with glasses and buckteeth. Now, twenty-five years later, she had filled out a little, and the three children had left her with a pair of modest but perfectly proportioned breasts. Her long distance eyesight had been corrected by laser surgery. She was no longer scrawny, despite Gladys's opinion on the subject, and the protruding teeth had surrendered to the corrective ministrations of some $140,000 worth of dental modification. She had the kind of mouth, large and full, but not overly so, that hot-blooded men (and women, one has to confess) long to explore.

For a 39-year-old mother of three, Elizabeth Nicholson, widow, was rather a fine specimen of womanhood. She was one of those rare females who was destined by her bone structure and her genetics to look better and better as the years went by.

"Come staggering along the beach with me every day for the next month," Jim had mused as he drifted from the alfa state into deep, dreamless sleep, "and look out. Your girlish shape will be back with a vengeance."

But back to their initial encounter at Alden House a few days ago. "I'm glad you called me James," James had said, in response to her reserved initial greeting.

"Glad? Why would you be glad?"

"Because that is my name.

"Don't mind Jimmy," her father explained. "His middle name is Spike." Liz's father could be awfully

453

obscure at times. James added to the confusion.

"My parents were looking for something short and to the point."

"Well that clears that up, doesn't it?" she had responded coolly, and they had left it at that. James reminds me of someone, Liz had mused, as she walked out of the house and down to the clifftops in search of a certain elusive pair of teenaged boys. Now, who could he remind me of? Another James? Another island? Another lifetime? Sweet baby James? Same name, different face. Very different.

It was a while before Liz warmed up a little and accepted one of James's invitations, but eventually she capitulated, little suspecting what was to come of the offer. On the fifth or sixth excursion back into the country roads or out along the various beaches, it happened, 'it' being a singularly widespread phenomenon that paleontologists have traced at least as far back as *homo erectus*. In fact, as Liz had been led to believe by yet another Cambridge academic, at yet another faculty party, 'it' was the reason *homo erectus* was called *homo erectus* in the first place. The randy professor would have been more than happy to demonstrate, if called upon to do so.

The following synonyms seem apropos: sexual desire, sexual appetite, sexual longing, ardor, desire, passion, libido, sex drive, sexuality, biological urge, lechery, lasciviousness, concupiscence; horniness, the hots, randiness and so on and so on. Any and all of the foregoing would apply. In a word, lust, that cunning and insidious demon, which lurketh ever by the side of certain secluded by-ways, seeking to waylay the unwary passerby; lust would leap out, unbidden, and stop James and Liz in their tracks, to the quivering astonishment, delight and ultimately, the chagrin of each of them.

One would never have predicted such a development, given the explosive nature of their less than friendly first encounter. As she had done since she was fifteen years old, Liz blamed James, unjust as the accusation might have been, for the cruel, unfair and untimely death of her innocent mother. James understood, he really did, and it broke his tender heart. He knew the truth, and the truth was not what Liz had thought it was.

Liz was at first puzzled by the breakneck pace of Jim's high speed stagger, once the daily walks comenced. Was the bastard avoiding her? She had started out by viewing the excursions as an opportunity to get to know one another, and perhaps out of such getting to know, a path might be opened to the closed heart of her emotionally absent father. That is what her rational mind, rattling about in the left lobe of her convoluted brain, had told her. She never for a moment suspected that the loving, ever-evolving universe might have other, more intimate plans for the relationship.

Lying in bed the night after their first walk, however, having spent yet another fruitless evening with James's catatonic father-in-law, followed by two hours studying the confusing old diary, she found herself recalling a powerful and probably forbidden impression. Her stepfather, when viewed from astern, was quite extraordinary. He really was. He had the narrow hips and broad shoulders of a lifelong surfer. For a woman who, almost four years ago, had lost her husband, and with him, all hope of a satisfying sex life, to take such specific note of the *gluteus maximus* of a fellow human, was a phenomenon to suppress with care and alacrity.

After all, she was a New Englander, a Puritan at least in upbringing. The impression was duly suppressed, and she thought of it no more. She congratulated herself on successfully stifling the impulse to take a sneak photo with her iPhone. Besides, the man was utterly unavailable. He was married, to her own father, no less. He was completely out of bounds. Not only that, she had invested in a brand-new vibrator back at the airport in Boston, and the compact device was doing a perfectly effective if rather impersonal job.

The event, when it came, therefore, came as a colossal surprise to both of them. They had staggered much further than ever before. There was a secret, inaccessible cove that James wanted to show her. Liz was beginning to get back in shape. She could actually walk and talk at the same time. The moon was almost full, which meant, as Liz explained to Jim, who already knew such stuff but was far too polite to mention the fact, that the tides are more extreme than at any other lunar phase. The full moon was also an auspicious time for new beginnings.

In this regard, Liz had it wrong. It is the new moon that is believed to be an auspicious time for new beginnings.

New beginnings? New beginnings such as what? New beginnings such as this. This? This what? This, er, friendship. Jim stopped. Liz had it a bit mixed up. Should he correct her? He had been slowly speeding along, moonwalking almost, adjusting his pace to Liz's, while her pace had been gradually accelerating to approximate his. The ocean was uncharacteristically quiet, it being dead low tide.

"Come on!" James shouted suddenly.
Taking advantage of the fortuitous and very temporary lunar phenomenon, they sprinted forward, laughing like teenagers, as a frothing wave receded, around a little promontory at the very end of the accessible part of the beach. They found themselves in an utterly private paradise. A tiny, secret cove. There was not another soul in sight.

Little did either of them suspect, but the nearest soul was, in fact, their friend Baxter de Waal, who had spotted them passing the Ditch Witch. She had been unsuccessfully trying to catch up with them ever since. By the time Bax, red in the face and out of breath, reached the cliff face at the end of the beach, however, the tide had turned and it was no longer wise to proceed any further. Puzzled, Bax looked around, and concluded that Liz and James must have turned inland. She could not know that they were a mere fifty yards away.

Meanwhile, just around the corner in the secret

cove, James had stopped and turned. Liz, on the other hand, had failed to stop, whether intentionally or otherwise we shall never know. They collided. They looked into one another's eyes. James realized at last what it was about Liz. Her deoxyribonucleic acid, a self-replicating material present in nearly all living organisms as the main constituent of their chromosomes, was very much that of her father's, his beloved husband's.

On a deep unconscious level, he had been in love with this woman for a very long time, or at least he had been bonded with her DNA. Liz was his eternal lover, only this time in a female body. That is what had been puzzling him. He had been quivering with desire for her for decades, and he had never known it. It was more of an ancestral or genetic or even a spiritual thing than anything personal.

For Liz, it was more physical, more personal, and at the same time more universal. This James and her late husband shared the same Christian name. Making love to a man named James was nothing unusual for her. It was simply what she did, when the circumstances presented themselves. Her rational mind put itself on hold for the duration, and she surrendered to the moment. Thinking about it later, her recollection of the event was almost purely physical, although there is in fact no such thing as physical. She dissolved into a quivering, vibrating mass of ecstatic subatomic protoplasm.

As Albert Einstein had revealed to the world a century earlier, everything is vibration. There are no exceptions. The two vibrating entities gazed into one another's faces, the faces grew closer and closer, the vibrating bodies supporting the faces grew weak, they slipped to the sand as an incoming wave came up and enveloped them and washed them into the sea. They merged in a salty explosion of love and lust. At some point in a timeless time, a flock of seagulls screamed above them, but they were each screaming so loudly themselves that neither of them noticed the birds. The ocean roared. The earth shook. The sun moved, and with it, the invisible moon. The tide rose, and with it, the surf.

A long time later, they half waded, half swam, naked and amazed and increasingly terrified, back around the little promontory, carefully clutching their skimpy collection of garments, such as the collection was. Three items had survived, out of a total of four. A one-piece woman's bathing suit, medium, black. One colorful lightweight Balinese sarong, one size fits all. One faded men's T-shirt, black, with American Indian Movement logo, large. The fourth item, alarmingly, had evaporated into the cosmos. They had searched frantically for it in the inrushing water, but James's bathing suit had completely disappeared. His brand-new Billabong board shorts were nowhere to be found.

Hours had passed. They were love-struck and sunburnt. Sun-struck and love-burnt. There were no words. There was no alternative. There was no other way to get back to civilization. The surf had come up.

The tide was rising with fearsome speed and inevitability. There was no longer a beach where the secret paradise had been. Once back on terra firma on the Bathsheba side of the promontory, James resumed his terrified piping plover impersonation, his feet a twinkling blur. Liz staggered along behind him, blinded by the light, dazed but ecstatic, wondering, what the fuck? What just happened?

The beach at Bathsheba had been pretty much deserted when they had speed-walked along the shoreline, just moments earlier. Now, it was mobbed. Of all things, there was a surfing contest going on. A reggae band was playing. As he sped through the swarming tourists, aware that they could read his every thought, James was rather uncharacteristically clad. He wore a faded, soaking wet American Indian Movement T-shirt, and Liz's translucent, damp sarong.

Sarong. The alien word sarong, he realized with some alarm, rhymed perfectly with the equally alien word schlong. Not to mention Hong Kong. There was a young man from Hong Kong, who dressed in a splendid sarong. There was a limerick in the making, James realized with a nervous giggle, as he scurried homeward, wondering about his sanity. The diaphanous fabric barely concealed the fact that the wearer of the sarong was rather well endowed. In fact, the damp fabric quite possibly accentuated that fact. His receding figure was soon lost to sight in the crowd.

Liz abandoned her futile attempt at keeping up with

James. It would hardly do, she realized, for the two of them to wander happily back home, hand-in-hand. She slowed down suddenly and drifted through the crowd in a delicious but increasingly terrified post-coital daze. There was a problem. Somehow James's brand-new board shorts had vanished off the face of the Earth. Impossibly, despite the fact that the ocean was as clear as crystal, there was no sign of the navy blue Billabong garment with the dayglo orange lightning bolts down either side.

The garment had been kidnapped by the demon of lust, to be used as damning evidence when the sinners were dragged before the inevitable tribunal. The lovers had no alternative but to abandon the search, and hasten back to civilization before the tide trapped them and brought upon them their deserved fate. Their deadly, unavoidable, Oedipal fate.

Oedipal? Liz would wonder about that word later that night, in the wee hours, as she drifted off to sleep. I'm not his mother, even if my father... Well you know what I mean. Isn't it called an Electra complex, if you're a girl? Damned if I know. I shall have to Google it, Henry. She shivered with a mixture of illicit delight and utter dread, as she slipped into dreamland and slept the deep, dreamless, psychotic sleep of the evil dead.

*****

81

A Storm Is Brewing

It was late afternoon. The low sun streamed in through the bedroom windows, along with the heady aroma of frangipani and jasmine. James, fresh from the shower and dressed in khaki chinos and a light blue, collarless denim shirt, his hair combed straight back from his sunburned forehead, sat quivering by the window trying to focus on his copy of Nathaniel Philbrick's opus about the Mayflower Pilgrims and their relationship with the Native Americans. For some odd reason, the handsome but feckless and faithless Aussie could not concentrate. He kept getting distracted by the vision of an extraordinary pair of alluring, bright blue eyes set in a background of rushing white sea foam. The turquoise eyes of the goddess Aphrodite at the birth of the Universe. The eyes had brought back a long suppressed, traumatic memory, a similar set of eyes in the fifteen year-old face of his first love, shortly before the girl dumped him for another, richer, less pimply boy. James cried, as he had not cried in decades.

The sun was descending behind the coastal mountains by the time the deep rumble of the Porsche shattered the silence. Junior had returned from his second trip to the golf course, drunk as the proverbial skunk, having played a truly abysmal game. There was a direct correlation between alcohol consumption and success in golf, but, sadly, it was the opposite of Junior's oft-stated, overly optimistic opinion on the subject. He had to find someone to take it out on. Walking into the elegant bedroom, he noted, not for the first time, James's choice of reading material, and, by way of greeting, asked sarcastically,

"Hey, can't you find a more exciting way to spend your time?"

As a matter of fact, James had just discovered a significantly more exciting way to spend his time, but it was

463

not something he was about to discuss with Junior. Not at this stage of the proceedings.

James and Junior were on the verge of the first major argument of their thirty year relationship. James was anything but a wimp, despite his gentle demeanor, and he was perfectly capable of giving as good as he got. This was not the time for that, however. After a moment's reflection and a slow, deep breath, he responded mildly,

"But darling! This is the year 2020, and the *Mayflower...*"

Junior exploded. His angry roar was clearly audible out on the lawn, where Liz sat hugging her knees in one of the many colorful deckchairs, oscillating between agony and ecstasy, trying to gather her wits before going into the house and facing any of her fellow human beings.

"Whose side are you on, for fuck's sake?"

"Please don't yell at me, Johnny," answered James, softly but firmly. "What do you mean, whose side am I on? I'm not on anyone's side. There are no sides, as far as I'm aware" He raised his voice. "Get off my back, would you, John? What's wrong with you? It's only a bloody history book. I'm just trying to get at the truth, if it's Liz and her discovery you're upset about. And watch your fucking language, would you, mate? There are people in this room with delicate ears."

"Sorry Jimmy, but this is a personal matter for me. I thought you knew that. Please just stay out of it." Junior's shoulders slumped. "As you can tell, I..."

"Stay out of what, exactly? Would you mind telling me what's going on? Ever since we got here, you've been..."

"Come on, sweetheart," Junior interrupted. "It's happy hour at the Roundhouse. Let's go get a cocktail or three. We can talk there."

"Oh, now you want me to take up drinking, do you?" James retorted. "Is there no end to your corrupting influence?" The crisis was over, at least for the moment.

*****

82

The Five Wives Of Hobamok

Liz sat at her desk by the window, her notebook and her pencils untouched, staring unseeing at the open diary. She looked tired, tired and a little bit frightened, to tell the truth. She closed her eyes, took a deep breath, and found herself in a familiar, comfortable setting in a place far removed from the island of Barbados in the year 2020.

It was September or October in the year of our Lord 1627. The maple trees had turned a series of splendid and vibrant colors, reds and golds and yellows very different from the muted autumn displays of Olde England. Priscilla Alden and her Patuxet Indian friend, who was one of the several wives of a *'pniese'* named Hobamok, lived with the Plimoth colonists. The two young women had spent the cool autumn afternoon playing with their babies and exchanging stories. The women had observed Priscilla's blond little girl, just learning to talk, and Anice's black-haired baby boy, and had agreed that the children would make a fine married couple once they were suitably grown up. Just look at them. They were already madly in love.

The mothers had spoken of Squanto and the fish, how their Indian friend had showed the English, that first planting season four eventful years ago, how to fertilize the sandy, depleted soil with alewives, the little fish which swarmed in their millions up Town Brook on their way to Billington's Sea each spring, during the annual herring run. The alewife run occurred at precisely the right season every year, exactly as Kiehtan had planned it. The corn was planted each April in a series of little mounds, each containing three of the foot-long fish.

Once the corn had reached a certain height, the growing bean plants climbed up the corn stalks into the abundant sunlight, while the squash, with its broad green leaves, shaded the soil and prevented the precious moisture from evaporating into the scorching summer heat. The decomposing fish provided just the right amount of nutrient. There was a wonderful and ancient symbiosis among the three food crops, a match made in heaven. The Indians had a special name for corn, beans and squash. They called them the 'Three Sisters.'

Anice's English was much improved. She described the symbolism of the corn mound, using her hands to remind her friend how huge her stomach had been just a season or two earlier. She referred to the three staple food crops, corn, beans and squash, as the 'three sisters,' and she explained to Priscilla why the native women did all the physical work, while the men merely hunted or fished a few days a week, and went to war when necessary.

Priscilla was beginning to understand Anice and her culture in a way that the English men never could. In Priscilla's world, everyone worked, each in carefully defined gender roles. Planting a colony was exceedingly hard work, and everyone, man, woman and child, had to work from dawn until dark, except, of course, on the Sabbath. The English men, needless to say, thought the Indian men were lazy, but Anice had a very different perspective.

"We women are the givers of life. The men are our protectors. Their job is to take life. It has always been this way. It is the way of Kiehtan."

"We are so different, men and women, are we not?" said Priscilla. "The men speak of God and war and money and politics. We women think of spirit and love and food and babies."

The friends returned to a favorite subject. Priscilla wanted to be certain of the facts before writing them into her diary. Comparing their tragic histories once again, one would be hard pressed to say whose account was the more heart-rending. Priscilla, of course, had lost her entire family within three months of their arrival in New England. Her marriage to the plantation's cooper, John Alden, and the subsequent birth of her baby, had gone some way to heal her broken heart and her trust in the goodness of Providence, but the loss and the emptiness were something she would feel for the rest of her life. How, she wondered, did her stoic Indian friend feel? It was impossible to tell.

Anice had lost many of her large, extended family members in the Tarrantines War, when the armada of birchbark canoes appeared, unannounced, out of the early summer morning mist, bearing a cargo of indiscriminate and violent death. Over the ensuing two years, her entire tribe had been exterminated by the plague, which had, unseen, accompanied the fearsome painted warriors from the north with their incomprehensible chattering cries and their terrifyingly loud French muskets and their merciless carnage.

At the outbreak of the apocalypse, which had come in war canoes from the northern sea, Anice, with her mother and her baby sister, had been spirited swiftly inland to maternal relatives in a friendly village well to the west, otherwise they too would have died. Her mother had hurried back to Patuxet, and no news of her had been heard since. Long before that, however, ten winters ago, all three of her older brothers had been kidnapped by an English slave trader named Captain Thomas Hunt, with the possible collusion of her Patuxet cousin, the elusive Tisquantum.

Anice's theory was that her cousin had helped Hunt to lure the men onto his ship, at which point the perfidious captain had betrayed Squanto along with his friends, transporting all of them to Spain and selling them as slaves. If Squanto had hoped to share in the profit, he was frustrated in that desire. He too was sold as a slave, and for the second time in his young life, found himself thousands of miles from home. Whatever the facts were, it took Squanto five long years to get back to New England, and by the time he arrived back in Massachusetts Bay, the war and the plague were over, and the Patuxets were no more.

"Perchance, four of we Patuxets still live," Anice said, quietly, sadly. "Anice. One small sister. Two old grand-father. No more. Not many winter past, Patuxet two thousand warrior strong. Father of Tisquantum, brother of my mother, big sagamore. Patuxet big medicine. Medicine gone. All gone."

Anice was a first cousin to Tisquantum. To Priscilla's initial surprise, the girl had avoided the international traveler when he reappeared on the scene shortly before the *Mayflower* passengers set foot on American soil. Squanto had been a shrewd and duplicitous character, apparently. Massasoit, sachem of the neighboring Pokanokets, had been aware of this, and had taken Squanto captive before releasing him to the Englishmen. Squanto had become the Pilgrims' indispensible guide and translator, and then, without warning, he had died.

"Do you suppose he was poisoned? Who would do such a thing?"

Poisoned? Anice raised her jet-black eyebrows. Massasoit had issued a death threat on Squanto, so she wouldn't be surprised. The spirits had their ways.

"Ah, but the miracle is this, my dear Alice. At least for us. If Captain Hunt, an evil man by anyone's standards, had not captured Tisquantum..." Priscilla hesitated. She did not wish to appear callous or insensitive. "I am terribly sorry about your brothers. I did not know. Perhaps they are alive and well somewhere over the sea? Tisquantum returned, so why not your brothers? Perchance they approach even as we speak.

"But consider this, my dear. By his treachery, at risk to his very soul, the villainous Hunt preserved the life of Tisquantum in the face of certain death, and the good Lord, Kiehtan as you call Him, placed him here to greet us. We could never have imagined such a thing in our wildest dreams. An Indian who spoke English? To help us speak with the other Indians. Without Squanto's good work, how could Massasoit have spoken with us?"

"'Tis true. Often I think thus. Tisquantum voice of English. Otherwise all English killed, long ago. Every tribe think best kill English. Until you husband and Captain... how you say? Captain Shrimp... kill Wituwamat and Pecksuot and other sachem who hate English. After that, peace come to all tribe."

The Indian girl changed the subject. She wanted to hear Priscilla's mother's name, her adopted name, for the hundredth time.

"My mother's name? It was Alice. Alice Mullins. You know that very well, do you not? It is the name you are using among our people."

"Anice Murrins?"

Try as she might, the Patuxet girl could not pronounce the English letter 'l.' And so she had become Anice. Priscilla thought about the way the Indians pronounced their friend Ed Winslow's name. Winsnow.

That evening, by the light of the tall tallow candle, after discussing the afternoon's conversation with her husband, Priscilla added the following words to her journal:

"Thus by degrees we began to discover Tisquantum, whose ends were only to make himself great in the eyes of his countrymen by means of his nearness and favour with us, not caring who fell, so he stood."

*****

8 3

Happy Hour At The
Roundhouse

Reggae music and intermittent applause reverberated from the stage down at the oceanfront, half
a mile away. Sitting at the otherwise deserted Roundhouse bar, as the stars came out overhead and the birds
settled down in the ubiquitous jarrah trees, the ex-pat
British bartender pretended not to listen as Junior's
anti-English, pro-Native American prejudices became
clear. In all their time together, he and James had simply

never had this conversation.

"Listen Jimmy, I need to tell you a few things from my past. It'll help you understand something about me. You've heard of AIM, the American Indian Movement, haven't you?"

"Don't you mean the Angry Indian Movement?" asked James. "That's what my New York friends used to call it. Not that I blame them for being angry. I remember reading about the confrontations with the FBI, back in the 1970s."

"I was a big supporter of AIM, until they misappropriated a sum of money I lent them. Then things turned violent in Minneapolis and South Dakota, and a good friend of mine died under suspicious circumstances. They thought she was about to spill the beans. Another friend has been in prison ever since. The movement split into factions, and I was forced to back off."

They moved to a table on the patio outside, and sat there for a long while. Junior's misbeliefs emerged, smallpox-infested blankets and all. James was not very well informed on the early history of New England, and could not pass judgment on most of the things Junior was telling him, but he did know one thing as a result of his current reading: The *Mayflower* did not arrive in Massachusetts with a load of smallpox-infested blankets.

475

The disease that decimated the Indians had hit them in late 1616, and the epidemic was over long before the *Mayflower* dropped anchor. The subject, however, was not up for debate. Junior's mind was made up, and no amount of cajoling on James's part was going to change that.

At the root of the matter, James realized, was the fact that Junior was profoundly ashamed to be a white man. Although he was of German immigrant stock and the alleged Plymouth atrocities had been committed by Englishmen, the Pilgrims were fellow Europeans. Junior seemed determined to take on the guilt of the entire European race. He had a good heart. In racist Australia, as James was well aware, Junior was active in the restoration of Aboriginal land rights and the preservation of their sacred sites. He sat on the boards of several not-for-profit organizations dedicated to those issues.

*****

84

The Truth About Thanksgiving

While their father and stepfather were down the hill at the Roundhouse, Liz and Scilla went online and checked some of the facts about the relationship between the Pokanoket Indians and the Pilgrims, beginning with their initial meeting on March 21, 1621 and ending with the onset of King Philip's War on June 20, 1675 - the fifty-four year period of friendship and peace before it all fell apart.

Liz started out by Googling the phrase: 'the truth about Thanksgiving.' After her initial resistance, Scilla was finally showing some interest in the subject.

"I want to show you something, Scilla." Liz said. "The... Truth... About... Thanksgiving. There. Let's see. These iPads are amazing, aren't they? Everything ever written is right here at one's fingertips. Look at what I found last night. Here. Read that. What do you think?"

Among the recipes for cranberry sauce and the contradictory articles by various history buffs and the children's stories, Liz found what she had bookmarked - a series of historically-untrue, scurrilous, defamatory articles written by a number of writers, several of them individuals with the letters 'PhD' after their names. Silently, Scilla read from Liz's iPad. She burst out indignantly.

"Hey, that's not true! Look at this! The Mayflower Pilgrims were not Christopher Columbus. Even I know that. Roast bull with cranberry sauce, as that guy in Leyden would say! Bax was telling us about him. What was his name?" Scilla's sunburned forehead had a per-fectly rectangular frown between her eyebrows. "You're right. They're mixing up people and places and dates, anything to make white people look bad. There's a real situation here! Where do they come up with this crap?

It's racist. It's criminal."

"I know, girl. It's absolutely crazy. It makes me wonder about the motivation behind these poisonous articles. According to Bax, it's been going on since the 1960s. It's gotten into the school curricula, K through 12, coast to coast. Even Howard Zinn, remember him, the famous historian who was not in fact a historian? No? Anyway, he endorsed all this revisionist stuff without a second thought. Zinn famously said, 'history is opinion. This is my opinion, take it or leave it.' He'd obviously not bothered to do his homework."

"That reminds me of what you used to say to me when I was about seven. 'It's really a matter of opinion, you told me, and your opinion doesn't really matter.' That still hurts to this day, just in case you were wondering. As to your Mr. Zinn, sounds like he was listening to the wrong people," said Scilla as she finished reading another piece. "You know, sis, it's like saying, well, Adolph Hitler was a white person, and Marilyn Monroe was a white person. Therefore Marilyn Monroe murdered six million Jews. Case closed."

Liz thought about that for a moment. Had she really said that about Prissy's opinions? She had been pretty mean to her little sister, hadn't she? But Pissy was Daddy's favorite, so she deserved it. Liz went on.

"You ever read a bestseller called *1491*? Same story. These writers get a publishing contract and they apparently just fabricate stuff and everyone takes it as Gospel. The same goes for the History Channel and even National Geographic, according to Bax. They don't bother to check their facts, and nobody seems to notice."

"Jesus H. Christ. How can that be? I guess it costs money to hire a fact checker. Or you have an agenda. Look at Donald Trump, for example, the age of post-truth politics we live in. Truth isn't truth, anymore. Anyway, these writers, who's going to sue them from four hundred years ago?"

"I wouldn't have learned any of this, if I hadn't met Baxter de Waal. In the line at the bank of all places. Have you two gotten to know one another? That girl is seriously well informed." Liz picked up her notebook. "Anyway, let's take a break from the bullshit. This is way more interesting. Here's another section I just transcribed from the diary. I made the English a little more palatable. Listen.

"*...we determined to conclude of the military Orders, which we had began to confider of before, but were interrupted by the Savages, as we mentioned formerly; and whilft we were bufied here about, we were interrupted againe, for there prefented himfelf a Savage which caufed an Alarm, he very* *boldly came all alone and along the houfes ftraight to the Randevous, where we intercepted him, not fuffering him to goe in, as vndoubtedly he would, out of his boldneffe, hee faluted vs in Englifh, and bad vs well-come, for he had learned fome broken Englifh amongft the Englifh men that came to fifh at Monchiggon, and knew by name the mod of the Captaines, Commanders, & Maflers, that vfually come, he was a man free in fpeech, fa farre as he could expreffe his minde, and of a feemely carriage, we queftioned him of many things."*

"Savages? That's not exactly PC, you know. Better not let Maryah read that."

"Well, I know, but that was the commonly accepted term back in those days. It didn't have the derogatory connotation it does now. Although I have to say, behavior does have consequences. The word has come to describe certain behaviors that are regarded as uncivilised. The Indians certainly exhibited some uncivilised behavior, back in the day. Do you know what the word actually means? The original meaning?"

"I do not. Enlighten me, por favor."

"According to Henry David Thoreau, and he would know if anyone would, the word savage was originally spelled with an 'l' – salvage. It meant simply a 'person of the forest.' Salvage is the old spelling. Think about the Spanish word 'la selva,' the woods. It really only meant

non-Christian, or wild person. It was not meant to be
demeaning. Anyway, let me finish.

"He (Samofet) was the firft Savage we could meete withall; he fayd he was not of thefe parts, but of Morattiggon and
one of the Sagamores or Lords thereof, and had beene 8 mon-
eths in thefe parts, it lying hence a 2 dayes fayle with a great
wind, and fiue dayes by land; he difcourfed of the whole
Country, and of every Province, and of their Sagamores, and
their number of men, and ftrength; the wind beginning to rife
a little, we caft a horfemans coat about him, for he was ftarke
naked, onely a leather about his waft, with a fringe about a
fpan long, or little more; he had a bow & 2 arrowes, the one
headed, and the other vnheaded; he was a tall ftraight man,
the haire of his head blacke, long behind, onely fhort before,
none on his face at all; he asked fome beere, but we gaue him
ftrong water, and bisket, and butter, and cheefe, & pudding,
and a peece of a mallerd, all which he liked well, and had bin
acquainted with fuch amongft the Englifh;

"He told vs the place where we now Hue, is called Patuxet
and that about foure yeares agoe, all the Inhabitants dyed of
an extraordinary plague, and there is neither man, woman,
nor childe remaining, as indeed we haue found none, fo as
there is none to hinder our poffeflion, or to lay claime vnto it;
all the after-noone we fpent in communication with him, we
would gladly haue beene rid of him at night, but he was not
willing to goe this night, then we thought to carry him on
fhip-boord, wherewith he was well content, and went into the
Shallop, but the winde was high and water fcant, that it could

not returne backe: we lodged him that night at Steven Hopkins houfe, and watched him; the next day he went away backe to the Mafafoits from whence he fayd he came, who are our next bordering neighbours: they are fixtie ftrong, as he fayth;"

"Hold on. Wait a goddamned minute." Scilla had been paying close attention and she was excited, suddenly. "Did you just say the plague happened four years *before* the *Mayflower* got to New England? That kinda does in the smallpox-blanket theory, doesn't it? Unless the suckers killed off the Indians retroactively, four years before they arrived. Where did they come up with that idea, anyway?"

"Who's they?"

"The people putting out this disgusting stuff on the Internet. It's total dis-information. Makes me wonder about Cher."

"Cher? The actress Cher? What's she got to do with anything?"

"I love Cher. She's one of my heroes. Heroines."

"Mine too."

"I follow her on Twitter. She put out a tweet back a few years ago: 'I don't celebrate Thanksgiving because they - the Pilgrims - gave smallpox blankets to my people.' I didn't even question it. I just took it for granted, as in, of course they did. I already knew that."

483

"Me too - until Baxter straightened me out. Wow. I missed that. How many Twitter followers does Cher have?"

"I dunno. A couple of million, I would guess, if you include me."

"See? That's what I'm saying. There's another two million people who believe this crap."

"Question: is Cher really Native American? Someone told me she's actually Armenian."

"I have no idea, but there's a long history of fake Hollywood Indians, mostly Italians or Portuguese. I always thought Cher was Cherokee. You remember when she and Dad and Russell..."

"Yeah but... you know?" Scilla had no problem interrupting her big sister. She went on. "The important thing is all this horrific misinformation. Listen. You know what I'm thinking all of a sudden? It sounds just like Dad."

"I was waiting for you to say that, Sis. Exactly. You remember how involved he was with the Indians when we were kids? You remember Russell Banks, don't you? He and Vernon whats-his-name just about lived at the Fifth Avenue house when we were little. He was always nice to us, but he definitely did not like white people, unless they were giving him money, or hosting him at fancy fundraisers. He made no bones about it. I can't help wondering..."

"You mean," Scilla cut in, thoughtfully, "what if Dad got his information from the Indians, from the AIM guys?"

"Exactly. And what if the information he got was totally, completely wrong? Historically wrong?"

"Yeah. Those guys were from out West. Where did they get their information from?"

"Oral history, presumably. Their grandmothers told them what they had heard from their grandmothers, and that was it."

"Sounds like a four hundred year game of telephone to me. How could they possibly keep the facts straight? But Papa Jack, why would he get his panties in such a bunch over something that doesn't involve him. Or us, or our ancestors?

"I know. It seems totally irrational. That stops me in my tracks every time. Maybe he's just ashamed of being a white man. A rich white man."

"Could be, and not without good reason. For what it's worth, Maryah is all excited about the book she's reading. The *Mayflower* book. She's come up with a wild theory that..."

"She told me. James is also reading *Mayflower*. I'll see

485

if he has any ideas. About Dad, I mean."

Something about the way Liz said the word 'James' made Scilla look at her sister closely. Liz did not notice. She was unusually flushed and animated - and badly sunburnt. Beneath her eyes, her cheeks were actually starting to blister.

*****

85

Dinner At The Royal Westmoreland

Junior turned to James. "What time is it, Jimmy?" he asked. His brain had just re-engaged after an extended hiatus, and he had suddenly remembered the reservations he had made for the entire family at the Royal Wesmoreland's five-star restaurant.

"Not a clue, mate. Why?"

"Hey, bartender, do you know what time it is?"

It was dark before the Mercedes made its way down the driveway and turned right, in the direction of

Bridgetown, an hour away. The almost full moon was high in the sky. Washington sat at the wheel of the limousine. The entire family had been invited to join Junior and James for dinner, but Liz, Gladys and Maryah had opted out. Each of them had business that could not be put off. Barbara of course, was on hospice duty, and Maryah was engrossed in her book. So, it was just Junior, James and Scilla, plus Washington if he wouldn't mind joining the party. Scilla sensed the tension bubbling just beneath the surface, but everyone was on his or her best behavior. She was still waiting for her father to acknowledge her presence.

Back at Alden House, Liz and Barbara finished their dinner, and Gladys served Irish coffee with whipped cream.

"Take a break, Gladys. Go have some fun with that handsome young husband of yours."

"That is kind of you, but that handsome young husband of mine is working, Miss Lizzie. He had to drive your father into town for dinner."

"Oh, he's still working? Well, give yourself a break, deah." Liz's Maine upbringing was detectable, occasionally, especially with words like 'deah' and 'lobstah.'

"We'll clean up, won't we, Barb? And thanks for making the Irish coffee. It's good. Is there any more?

Do you mind? I've got a lot of work to do tonight."

After making another batch of coffee, Gladys went upstairs, while Liz and Barbara lingered at the verandah table, talking about the family dysfunction, Liz's late husband's death, the blow-up between Liz's father and grandfather a quarter of a century earlier.

After a while, Liz excused herself, and followed Gladys up the stairs. She went into her grandfather's room to say goodnight. She had a question for Gladys, but there was no sign of her in the bedroom. For the second time, Liz examined the locked glass-fronted bookcase – which, little did she guess, would turn out to contain just about everything ever written about the Mayflower Pilgrims. Did Alden know the truth, but never mention anything to the girls? Why would he keep the cabinet locked? Was it a symbol of conflict, of closed hearts?

Gladys tapped politely on the open door and entered the room, towing a fresh oxygen tank in its little cart. Alden lay there, as theatrically arranged as ever, peacefully dozing. *I Am A Rock* played on for the thousandth time. Gladys finished getting Alden ready for sleep. Liz looked up from ground level. Her knees were aching, as were some of her more private parts.

"Gladys, just the person I was looking for. Do you

know where I'd find the key to this cabinet?"

"I don't know, Missy. The master always keep it locked. Ever since I can remember. Let me ask that handsome young husband of mine."

Liz had the distinct impression that Gladys knew more than she was letting on. To her own surprise, she respected that.

"Good night Gladys. Goodnight Grandpa, I'll check in on you later," she said, and went back downstairs. She had left her second Irish coffee on the outdoor dining table.

*****

86

Girls Will Be Girls

Maryah sat alone, reading by the light of one of the flickering sconce lights that illuminated the verandah on either side of the tall mahogany entry doors. She was deeply absorbed in Nathaniel Philbrick's *Mayflower* book. Scilla had gone off to town with her father. She would have been better off getting an early night, Maryah thought. They were both still jet-lagged, and Scilla had exposed herself to far too much sun today, having fallen asleep in one of the blue-and-white striped

491

canvas lawn chairs most of the afternoon.

Liz came out onto the verandah and sat down. The almost full moon was rising above the trees. The sisters-in-law, absolute strangers that they were, had a bit of a one-on-one chat, their first ever. Maryah seemed to have a chip on her shoulder. She did most of the talking, something about invading English armies and genocide. The Mayflower Pilgims were Dutch, apparently.

"Who'd a thunk? I always thought they were..." Liz tried to get a word in edgewise, but failed. Maryah went on and on, although Liz was so distracted by her own thoughts and feelings that she could not for the life of her remember a word of the conversation once she was back in her room lying face down on the bed watching the moon shadows as they writhed across the ancient planked floor. The African ghosts of Maryah's tribal ancestors drummed and chanted in the shadows.

She got up and tried unsuccessfully to work on the manuscript, until the sound of voices alerted her to the fact that the rest of the family had returned from their dinner in the little town of Mullins, out on the West Side of the island. Carefully picking up the old journal, she went down the hallway and sat with Alden for half an hour. Alden was sleeping peacefully, so she went back to her room and continued staring at the arcane text.

She had a lot on her mind, and did not feel in the least sociable.

When Liz heard her sister and Maryah passing by her bedroom door, she had no inclination to go out and engage them in conversation. She heard their door click shut, and went back to work.

"I'll run us a tub," offered Scilla, turning to her lover affectionately. When the Mercedes returned from the restaurant in the moonlight, Maryah had still been reading on the verandah. The women reclined in the big old claw-foot bathtub, massaging each other's feet, talking about the day's events. After the meal, Scilla was saying, Junior had picked up the tab. It was expected of him, needless to say. To compensate, perhaps, he was unnecessarily obnoxious to the sweet Bajan waitress, out of the blue.

"Junior made up for his rudeness by leaving an extravagant tip. Well that fixed that, didn't it? There's nothing money won't fix. Such is his world-view," said Scilla. "The whole time, I was waiting for him to meet my eyes. I'm still waiting. The sucker didn't say a word to me all evening."

"Hmmm," said Maryah.

"Did she tell you what she found? She's all excited."

"Hmmm? What? Who's she? The cat's mother?"

"I'm sorry, baby. Liz. My sister. Liz found an old sailor's trunk in the basement. And someone's musty old diary. She's wildly excited. She thinks it has something to do with the *Mayflower* - the book you're all engrossed in."

"Mmm. I got somethin' else on my mind right now. Can't we talk about that Mayflower stuff later?"
Her gentle probing toe went to a familiar, tender spot. Scilla stopped talking and started purring.

*****

87

Deathwatch

Liz sat there staring at the old manuscript. She was a teenager in love, quivering, completely unable to make any progress, constantly distracted by endless re-runs of the day's unprecedented experience. She looked up from the journal.

"Just two nights before Thanksgiving, Henry," Liz said, feeling an odd sense of guilt at her act of infidelity. "It looks like Grandpa's going to make it." Can one be unfaithful to an invisible friend, she wondered? She took

495

a breath, rubbed her eyes, sighed deliciously and got determinedly back to work. She was on her sixth and last composition book, and that one was almost full. She would need at least half a dozen more.

It was well after midnight when there was a polite tap, and Liz's door opened quietly behind her. She turned at the sound. Barbara, fully-dressed, was standing silhouetted in the open doorway. The nurse's voice, soft as it was, carried a sense of urgency.

"Mayday, Liz! Emergency! So sorry to disturb you, but Mr. Alden is dying. I have alerted Dr. Ginsberg. This is it, I'm afraid. I was just on the phone with the doctor and I think he's right. He's on his way over." She paused. "I think you should wake the rest of the family, don't you?"

Hearing the old man moaning weakly on the baby monitor, Barbara had rushed into Alden's room to check on her patient. The dying man was groaning softly and breathing stertorously. His pulse rate was oscillating wildly and his oxygen level was way down. She paged Dr. Ginsberg.

The silent gold Prius crunched up the coral driveway in the moonlight. An owl hooted from the tree above the vehicle as Ginsberg clambered out. The doctor stopped and listened for a moment, but the sound was not repeated. He grabbed his old leather bag from the passenger seat and shuffled up the verandah stairs. Barbara was waiting at the door to let him in. Ginsberg's tone was brusque and faintly triumphant, as the sleepy family members trooped in and gathered in the master bedroom.

"This is it, people. Didn't I warn you? He's not going to make it through the night. Jack Alden has seen his last Thanksgiving. I could have... But, it's too late to think about getting him to Queen Elizabeth. I'm putting him on a morphine drip as of right now. It will make his breathing easier. It will ease his last moments. Nurse, you have what you need, do you not? I'll make the necessary arrangements with the coroner and telephone you in the morning. Good night. Phone me if anything changes, Priscilla."

"My name is Barbara, not Priscilla," said the nurse, but Ginsberg was already on his way down the stairs.

*****

497

88

Jack Bounces Back

Liz was upset. "Damn. Ginsberg was a little less than sympathetic, wasn't he? Does he care more about his own predictions than about the family? Apparently so," she said, looking around at the assembled family. Nobody answered. The death vigil began, the final countdown. Late as it was, everyone had roused themselves and gathered around the huge bed to be with Alden at the moment of his passing. James and the two teenagers brought up ten white folding chairs from the garage, where they were stacked against the back wall.

Mostly they sat in silence. An hour went by. Two hours. Liz and Barbara whispered back and forth; of reincarnation, of angels, of seeing through the veil. Liz was on the alert for strange visitations, ghosts, spirits of the dear departed coming to welcome her grandfather to the other side, but she detected nothing unusual. Silence. The owls were silent. Even Simon and Garfunkel were taking a break, thank God. Alden had settled down, and now he seemed preternaturally calm, most likely as a result of the morphine pulsing though his bloodstream.

Junior stood over at the French doors gazing out through the glass at the moonlit trees and the flickering shimmers on the distant water. James and Scilla were holding hands. They were both crying softly. Maryah sat in an armchair under a floor lamp, reading James's battered copy of *Mayflower*, which he had lent her. Her still-pristine copy was out on the verandah where she had left it when Scilla came home.

Without warning, Alden opened his bloodshot eyes, blinked twice, and glared around at the semi-circle of family members. His gravelly voice was astonishingly clear.

"What the devil's going on here? What are you all staring at, for the love of Mike?"

Flabbergasted, everyone jumped up in embarrassment and backed away from the bed, leaving the arc of empty folding chairs as mute witnesses to the premature nature of the deathwatch. They gathered near the door, ready to leave the room. Impossibly, the old Jack was back. Alden took command. He was as intimidating as ever.

"Where's the Ferrari? I want my Ferrari!" he grated.

"The Ferrari?" Liz said. "There is no Ferrari, Grandpa. Don't you mean the Porsche?"

"Grandpa, it's after midnight."

"It's later than that, Scilla. It's half past three," Liz corrected her.

"I'm getting up. How long have I been sleeping?" Alden hoisted himself up on his elbows and glared at his gathered family.

"Getting up? Right now?"

"This very minute, Elizabeth. I've got work to do."

"But Grandpa!"

"Why are you yelling at me, Lizzie? I'm not deaf, goddammit. Where's Gladys?"

Liz glanced at the hearing aid on the nightstand next to the water-glass with the dentures in it. She moved closer to the bed and spoke softly.

"It's the middle of the night, Grandpa. Gladys went to bed hours ago. She and Washington had a date. Can't you wait until morning?"

"Well OK, if you insist, but I'll need the Ferrari at first light. I've got work to do. And what the hell is this?" Alden held up his arm. A long translucent tube disappeared into it, near the elbow. "Where the fuck is Ginsberg?" he demanded.

Junior had observed the proceedings from the French doors. He moved, a tiny bit unsteadily, toward the bed. He spoke, hesitantly.

"Well hello, Dad! It's good to see you all bright-tailed and bushy-eyed again. You were getting us a bit worried there."

"Hello, son. It's been a while, hasn't it? How's Sydney been treating you? And that handsome young Aussie of yours?" Alden coughed and cleared his throat. "By the way, Johnny, I have an idea. Listen. Where's the boat? Is she shipshape? I'm thinking we should throw a party. A little family Thanksgiving cruise. Just for old time's sake, you know?"

"Dad, *Weetamoo* is at Spencer's. She's been up on the hard since last month. We were..."

"Spencer's? Fort Lauderdale? Dang! So much for that bright idea. In that case let's charter something."

"I'll look into it in the morning, Dad."

"Anyway Grandpa, we've got quite a party planned

for the day after tomorrow. Think you'll be up for it?" Liz had overcome her astonishment, and was as chirpy as chirpy can be.

"Up for it? What on God's green Earth are you talking about, Elizabeth? Why shouldn't I be? Of course I'll be up for it, or my name's not John Bradford Alden."

"Alden, Grandpa Jack? Alden? Our name is Alten, as in 'altenator.' Alten with a 't.,'" said Scilla.

"Oh God! That was a long time ago, Priscilla." Alden shook his head and sighed. "It was a joke. I was kidding. Like I was kidding about pulling the lion inside out. Speaking of pulling, someone has been pulling your leg."

"But Grandpa!" Scilla said, then fell silent. Suddenly, she remembered sitting with her teenaged big sister and her grandfather on the yacht. They were moored alongside an ancient stone dock somewhere in the Mediterranean. Cartagena, maybe? Majorca? The girls had wondered how their family had become so wealthy. Grandpa Jack was going on about how his father, their great-grandfather, had made a fortune inventing something that was even more profitable than the proverbial better mousetrap. It was a better generator. They called it the 'alten-ator'. The device was named after their great grandfather. There was one in every vehicle on the planet. There was a royalty on every unit sold...

The group had snapped out of the collective trance and gradually re-convened around the bed. Maryah eased herself up from the armchair against the wall and joined the circle. Amazement. Introductions. Finally, Alden waved them away. His customary irascibility was back in full force.

"OK, OK. Enough. That's it!" the re-born fossil shouted, "Don't you people ever sleep? Do you have any idea what time it is? I need my beauty rest. In case you haven't noticed, I'm getting to be an old man." Old Jack's diction was remarkable, although the absence of his dentures did impart a shertain comic counterpoint to the sherioushnesh of the shituashun.

There was a chorus of good nights as everyone headed for the door.

"I guess the old bastard's not quite ready for the great whorehouse in the sky," Junior muttered as the last of them left the bedroom. He and Liz stopped in the doorway and turned around, side by side. The doorway was not quite wide enough for such a maneuver. Spontaneously, Liz put her arm around her father's waist. It was the first time the two of them had made physical contact in decades. An unfamiliar sound had stopped them in their tracks. Father and daughter stared at the huge bed, from whence the offending sound was

503

emanating. An ancient creaky voice was singing a bois-
terous sea shanty, a decidedly risqué little ditty, a song
about someone called Barnacle Bill the Sailor.

"Oh no. That song is NOT for ladies' ears!" said Liz's
father.

Amid amazement and wondering laughter, the ten
of them chattered off to their rooms. In the echoing
hallway they sounded like a flock of happy chimpanzees
scuttling off to their cages. Junior and James, arm in
arm, were the last to go. Silence fell. Liz stood at the
bedroom door for a long moment.

"Welcome back, Grandpa Jack. Good night," she
whispered, gently closing the door. There were tears in
her eyes.

Without warning, an urgent and irresistible need
assailed her, a call of nature. She was overdue for the
traditional squat upon the pot, as her deceased husband
had called the daily ritual. There was not a moment to
be lost. Liz scuttled along the hallway and into her bathroom, urgently discarding items of clothing as she scuttled, and thinking about that bawdy song. It was by no
means unfamiliar to her, although she had led a relatively sheltered life. As a girl she had learned dozens of so-
called camp songs, some of them distinctly off-color, but
somehow she'd assumed that the Barnacle Bill song was

far too naughty to be part of her oh-so-respectable grandfather's repertoire. Don't assume, she thought, as she sat down with a sense of relief. Assumptions make an ass out of you and me. Ass you me.

"Bugger the mat, I can't fuck that, cried Barnacle Bill the Sailor," she sang. "Shit," she said out loud. "Now I'm going to have trouble getting that song out of my head. Ah well, it'll be a change from Simon and Garfunkel."

Dear departed James Edward 'Nick' Nicholson, PhD, had had quite a selection of naughty songs, as he called them, from his rugby days and his stint in the English army. Get him stoned and off he'd go. You couldn't stop him once he got started. James had had an entirely different vocabulary from hers. He had been profoundly influenced by nineteen fifties BBC radio comedy – the notorious Peter Sellers and his manic ilk. It was sometimes difficult to tell what Nick was raving about, in that thick Lancashire accent of his. He was a congenital lunatic, wasn't he?

Congenital? Liz rather liked the sound of that, especially now that she had found someone to congenitalize with. One of Nicholson's favorite phrases was: it's time for a squat upon the pot. As Liz squatted on the pot and reminisced, she wished she'd had time to open the window and turn on the fan, but it was a bit late for that. Her eyes defocused. She gazed blindly at the patterns in the stone floor tiles. Old Jack had had them specially quarried somewhere or other. The old sea shanty was still going through her head.

Suddenly her attention snapped into the present. The floor. She focused on one tile in particular. There was a distinctly human face there, bearing a desperate expression. "Whoa!" she exclaimed, resisting an inappropriate urge to leap to her feet and flee. She looked at the next tile. Another frightening face stared back at her. Tile after tile, it was the same. It was as though an entire collection of human souls lay there at her feet, trapped in the stone. Absurd as it sounded to her rational mind, her thoughts went to the pile of skeletons, their centuries-long rest under the cellar disturbed by a ghost, followed in short order by a sudden invasion of post-colonial bureaucracy. She had been trying not to think about the skeletons. She and Washington had agreed to let the matter lie until after Thanksgiving and after the funeral, but the Universe had had other plans for the bones.

"Jayzus!" Liz yelped. "No wonder you people think this house is haunted."

*****

89

I Dream Of Sarah

It was 4:30 a.m. on the bedside clock. Before Liz fell asleep, in that in-between state of consciousness, she fell into a lucid dream. Or was it a visitation? Her mother stood at the foot of her bed. Sarah appeared to be about forty, the same age as Liz was now, the age Sarah had been when she died. Sarah looked nothing like Liz, however. She was a much better looking woman, in the traditional sense, than her firstborn daughter. Liz was the spitting image of her father, which was not necessarily a good thing in a girl. Sarah spoke, her long-absent voice familiar and comforting.

"Hello my dear, dear Elizabeth. Listen to me. I have a few things you need to know. One, I am fine, absolutely fine. Two, there is no time. We will be together again in no time at all. Remember that. Three, it was purely an accident, my death. The AIDS came from the blood transfusion. Your father had nothing to do with it."

Liz tried to respond, but no words came out. Sarah continued.

"I am happy that John is in such a loving relationship with James. James is just adorable. Don't you agree? Oh, and one more thing. When you get a chance, ask your grandfather about his family's ancestry. It might surprise you. Don't forget, now. Until we see one another again...fare thee well, my love."

The apparition faded and was gone. Liz stared up at the ceiling. James adorable? Well, yes. Little did Sarah know! Or did she? How much do those on the other side know about the lives of the living? Do they watch our every move? Can they read our every thought? Or is that terrible omniscience reserved for God, if there is any such Being eternally observing His, Her or Its own creation? Liz lay there, wide-awake now, examining the ceiling in the dimly moonlit room. The breeze outside caused ghostly tree shadows, reflected off the polished floor, to undulate across the walls.

Was Liz feeling pangs of guilt? Why shouldn't she be? After all she was having an affair with her stepfather, wasn't she? Or was she? Does kissing count as infidelity, as incest? Wait. They had done a lot more than kiss, hadn't they? Confused, stimulated, and strangely joyful, filled with the insane joy that comes from being newly, madly in love, wondering about the wisdom of that second Irish coffee after dinner, Elizabeth Nicholson floated off into an exhausting series of alternately erotic, disturbed and confusing dreams.

Out of the drifting smoke, whooping Indian warriors attacked and burned an old New England colonial home. A young Indian woman, screaming, came running out of the flames, her hair on fire, clutching a large leatherbound bible to her naked bosom. African slaves rebelled on tropical plantations, and were shot down in cold blood by policemen of African descent. A Puritan preacher, in early Colonial finery, lectured her on the sin of self-love, before attempting to seduce her. James, the Australian James, appeared before her, naked, his manhood ready to romp. As she reached for him, her lover turned into a gigantic lion attacking her out of the blue. She reached deep into the lion's gaping maw, groping for its tail. It was too far, too deep. She woke up, drenched in sweat. A wild wind was shaking the house. The dim light of dawn lit the windows. Liz looked at the bedside clock. It was almost six in the morning.

*****

90

Liz Takes A Shower

Wednesday, November 25, 2020

It is said that Queen Victoria of England, may she rest in peace, took a bath once every three months, whether she needed it or not. Being a 21st Century American, Liz bathed even more frequently. The digital clock by her bedside read 5:45 a.m. It was just beginning to get light outside. Liz staggered up and took a shower, letting the stinging hot water wash away her weariness. She peeked in on her reincarnated grandfather. Did last night's events really happen, or was it some kind of collective hallucination? The old man was sleeping peacefully. He looked like a little boy.

She went downstairs and wandered outside, rubbing her bleary eyes, just in time to watch the sun emerge red and huge from the ocean behind the ironwood trees. It was the morning before Thanksgiving. To her own surprise, she remembered something. She hurried round back and down the path to the converted slave quarters. She had never been down there before, at least not since the renovations. An astonished and half-asleep Gladys came to the door in her nightgown. She looked at her bleary eyed mistress in consternation.

"Oh my goodness. What is wrong, Miss Lizzie? You look terrible."

"Master Jack is back, Gladys! He has come back to life. Please have Washington get the wheelchair out of the garage and up to his room, ASAP."

"Master Jack is back?" Gladys could not believe it. "Good heavens! That is wonderful news, indeed. I will wake my husband up and tell him. There is a lift, an elevator, for just that purpose."

Liz wandered down to the cliffs in a daze. The surf was rolling in, big, clean and beautiful, just the way the boys liked it. I'd better go and wake them, she mused.

They'd hate to miss it when it's this perfect. Little did Liz suspect, her boys were already in the water, and had been for some time. Two of the twenty or so bodies bobbing out there off the point were the fruit of her loins. 'Dawn patrol' had occurred an hour ago. In fact, ten or fifteen surfers had paddled out in the moonlight, long before dawn, it was so perfect. The first heat of the contest was scheduled for 9 a.m., and non-contestants wouldn't be allowed back in the water at the main Soup Bowls break until the end of the day.

*****

9 1

Junior Snaffles A Book

The early morning sun was low over the sea as Johann Bergdorf Alten emerged from the house, dressed for golf. He had an early date at the Royal Westmoreland. On the verandah table lay the *Mayflower* book, left there open but face down, by Maryah the previous evening. Jack scowled at the book, and on a sudden impulse picked it up and took it with him. He dropped the offending item onto the passenger seat of the Porsche convertible, which Washington had pulled out of the garage a few minutes earlier. Junior started the engine. The deep rumble reached Liz, where she stood on the cliffs overlooking the ocean, but she quite failed to notice the earth shattering sound. She had other things on her mind.

Maryah, too, was up bright and early. She could not wait to get back to her reading, and stood in her pajamas at the kitchen sink, filling the coffee maker. Through the window, she noticed a movement out on the verandah, and spotted her father-in-law. She saw him making off with her *Mayflower* book. Outraged, she almost ran out after him, but after a moment's indecision, she finished making the coffee and took it back to bed, wondering, what the fuck?

*****

92

Can't Do No Harm

Washington had jumped out of bed as soon as he heard Liz's voice at the door. He had overslept. He pulled the Porsche around to the front of the house for Junior, just in time. After the subsonic rumble had faded into the distance, he and Gladys exchanged a few words about the locked bookcase. The key had been in the glove compartment of the Porche, where it always was. Washington handed it to his wife.

"Can't do no harm," he said. "The old man will never know."

"I can't see why he keeps it locked, anyway. It's just a bunch of ol' books in there."

Gladys knew what she was talking about. On several occasions when her husband and Alden were off-island, she had quietly opened the cabinet and examined its musty contents. What Gladys did not know, however, was that, among the more mundane books on its shelves, the cabinet contained a priceless collection of first-edition copies of several dozen of the most significant literary publications in Elizabethan English and early American history.

Old Jack was sleeping like a baby as Washington manoeuvred the Ferrari-manufactured wheelchair up to the master bedroom, quietly wheeling it out of the elevator and parking it in its accustomed spot by the bedside.

*****

9 3

The Morning After
The Day Before

Silently, James approached Liz, who was standing as still as a statue, gazing out to sea. She was re-living certain events of the previous day, moment by delicious moment. James was wearing khaki chinos and a long-sleeved off-white linen shirt. His feet were bare. A flock of birds exploded from the trees above Liz, startling her. James spoke before she spotted him.

"Liz," he blurted. "My baggies."

518

"Good morning Jeem," she smiled, unable to restrain her joy. "Hi! I was just thinking about you. Your what?"

"My baggies. My board shorts. You know? My swim trunks."

"Oh, you mean your missing bathing suit? What a mystery."

Liz could not suppress a girlish giggle. Despite, or because of, the sleepless night, she felt ridiculously happy, happier than she'd ever been in her life. She had been standing in the same spot for the past forty minutes, under the shade of a spreading flame tree. It was going to be another hot one. She had been so still that the birds, concluding that she was made of alabaster, had resumed their daily chores above and around her, until they flew off suddenly and there was James, standing in front of her like the guy in the Bob Dylan song. It was *déjà vu,* all over again.

"Right, bathing suit. Reminds me of those huge striped shoulder-to-knee affairs men used to wear back in the day." James paused. He continued urgently, the anxiety evident in his voice. "Listen, Liz. There's a problem. He noticed."

"Huh? What d'you mean he noticed? Who noticed? Noticed what?"

"Your father. Johnny. I always rinse the salt out and

519

hang them up in the bathroom."

"Your… what do you call 'em? Your baggies? So?"

"They weren't there."

"Your baggies weren't there? Obviously they weren't. But what..?"

The missing Billabongs were the last thing on Liz's mind, on this most glorious morning of all glorious mornings.

"'No beach today?' he asked when he came to bed."

"Oh dear," Liz said. "What did you say?"

"Nothing. I pretended to be asleep. But I didn't sleep all night, after we all… Listen, Liz..."

James paused. His lower lip quivered. Liz looked down at her feet, the tops of which were so sunburned that the straps of her flip-flops hurt. She had searched every available nook and cranny in the house but couldn't find the calamine lotion anywhere.

"Let's sit down. Come." She pointed to a concrete bench on the nearby clifftop. One end of it was shaded by a large flowering hibiscus bush.

"How did you sleep, Liz?"

"Like a baby. I just woke up with a smile on my face and came down here to watch the sunrise. No. I'm lying. Actually I had some very strange dreams, but I'm damned if I can remember anything. My mother was in there somewhere. She had a message for me." Liz paused and looked at the anxious profile of her beautiful new lover. "I'm surprised he noticed. What's up with that?"

"He notices everything, not in a suspicious way or anything. He just does. Back home, he can tell if a single molecule is out of place."

"Even a little thing like a bathing suit? A pair of baggies?"

"It wasn't just any bathing suit, Liz. It was the perfect pair of Billabongs. He bought them for me a week ago, ten days at the most." His voice trembled.

"Oh. That *is* different, isn't it?"

"We had a 3-hour stopover in LA while they were servicing the plane. I had forgotten my ratty old baggies back home. I remembered them suddenly, somewhere over the Pacific. They're in the boot of the bloody MGA. 'Come,' he said, 'I'm willing to bet there's a surf shop right here in the terminal.'"

"And there was?"

"There was. We spent the next hour looking at every single pair in the place. He made me model at least ten pairs for him. Nothing doing. Then the salesgirl had an epiphany. She went into the back room and came out with a big un-opened box that had just come in from Billabong."

521

"Billabong?"

"It's an Australian surfing gear manufacturer."

"And...?"

"And there they were. The perfect pair of baggies. 'They'd last you the rest of my life, he said. Time you retired those decrepit old shorts of yours, always flapping in my face in the bathroom back home.'"

"Hmmm. I see what you mean."

"Liz, I have to tell you something."

"Why am I not surprised, darling? OK. Shoot."

She turned and looked at him. James had aged overnight. While their encounter had restored her girlhood, he suddenly looked his fifty years. There were actually lines on his face. She had not noticed them before. He had a haggard, haunted look about him that was new. He did not return her piercing look, but sat there gazing studiously out at the horizon, where a group of seabirds was diving and fighting over something in the water. Liz spoke again.

"Where *is* my Dad, by the way?"

"Golfing, of course. He just left. Didn't you hear the Porsche?"

"So tell me, dear James. You look troubled."

"Troubled? That's not the half of it. Liz, I'm..." He rotated toward her on the rough concrete surface.

"I'm...Ow!"

James yelled out loud and stuttered to a halt. He stood up suddenly. His rear end was so sunburned that it was agony to sit on the concrete slats. He walked around behind the bench and continued. It was as if he couldn't bear to look her in the eyes.

"Liz, let me finish. I have to say..." His voice broke. "I am so, so sorry. It was a huge mistake. I don't... I don't know what came over me."

"Jim stop! May I say something? Jeem?"

"Of course. Please."

"Mistake? A huge mistake?" Her voice rose. "In my world there are no mistakes. I thought we agreed on that. I have a different word for what happened yesterday."

"Liz, I was just trying to say how sorry..."

"James, please. I said stop! I beg you. Listen to me. You look like a poor beautiful dog who has lost his bone. Well actually, you *have* lost your precious baggies." She giggled. Nothing could destroy her fierce joy this exquisite morning. "You're using words like sorry, like mistake."

"But..."

"Don't interrupt, darling. Listen. Perhaps I have a different perspective. I can summarize what happened to

523

us yesterday in a single word. Are you ready?"

"A single word? Tragedy? Disaster? Betrayal?"

"I said, don't interrupt. No, none of the above. Here's the word." She stopped and turned and looked at him. He did not interrupt. Good. She went on. "Heaven," she breathed.

"Heaven? Heaven. Hmm. I'll have to think about that for a bit."

"What? It wasn't good for you?" Liz was teasing. She spoke a lot louder than she had intended. They had company. A group of surfers and their girlfriends had pulled up in a pair of rented mini-vans and stood gazing out at the perfect waves, deciding where to get into the water. They turned as a group and looked at the couple at the bench. It was pretty obvious what they were arguing about. A ripple of laughter moved through them. Liz took charge.

"Come. Let's go back to the house. I need some coffee."

In silence, they made their way up the trail through the woods, Liz leading the way. Their mouths may have been stationary, but their brains were boiling. Liz was thinking about seagulls. Could those goddamned birds have..? No. James was contemplating heaven. Yes, you're right. It was heaven, but...

Two wildly divergent perspectives on the same event. As they reached the house, there were Maryah and Scilla, hand-in-hand, coming the other way, heading for the cliff-tops.

"Hey, what are you two lovebirds doing up so early?" Scilla asked, greeting them with a sleepy yawn. Lovebirds? Pissy had always had a way with words, her big sister thought to herself.

"You missed the sunrise, guys. It's going to be another scorcher." Liz greeted them radiantly.

Maryah stopped in front of James. She had a question for him. The woman was nothing if not direct.

"James, where did Scilla's father go? Do y'all know? He took off in the Porsche."

"Scilla's father?" It took James a while to remember who Scilla was. He had other things on his mind this morning. "Oh, John, you mean. He had an early golf date on the other side of the island."

"Well, when y'all see him, tell him I have a question for him. OK?"

"A question? OK. I'll tell him. Happy to."

"It's about a book."

"A book?" Scilla was puzzled. As the two couples went their separate ways, Liz heard Maryah declaim in her loud Southern drawl.

"That book I'm in the middle of reading. Why the fuck would your father steal my book?"

"Are you sure? The *Mayflower* book, you mean? He wouldn't do that. My father may be an emotional zombie, but he's not a thief."

"He did. I saw him. He picked it up off the fucking porch table and took it with him. Fuck him. He could of asked if he wanted to read it. I was just really getting into it. These crazy religious Dutch guys were sailing across the ocean in a hurricane. Their boat was falling apart. It was sinking." Maryah's angry voice faded off into the distance and merged with the crashing of the waves. James had heard nothing. His mind was on other things. Heaven. Hell. Baggies.

The aroma of freshly perked Jamaican coffee, grown and marketed by the Marley family, floated out though the kitchen door and reached their olfactory senses as they approached the back door through the last of the trees. In the kitchen, Gladys was just picking up Alden's breakfast tray and preparing to head upstairs.

"Ah, smell that coffee, would you?" Liz said.

"Oh good morning again, Missy. Good morning Master James."

"Is there anything I can do to help?" Liz wanted to know.

"Oh no. I do it every day. I used to have to do ten or twenty at a time. This is no problem. And Barbara is up there with Massa Alden. Today is his bath day, and she is getting him dressed. We have to get him polished up for Thanksgiving."

"How is my dear grandfather this morning?"

"He's a little bit grumpy, if you must know. He hates bath day. He's worse than his beloved dog was, may she rest in peace.

"But, I mean... How is he?"

"He said he doesn't know yet. He will tell me when he has had his breakfast. I must go up before it gets cold. He does not like his breakfast cold."

"Thank you Gladys. Tell Grandpa I'll be up to see him a little later."

"I will tell him. The coffee is ready, and that there is a jug of creamy milk fresh from the farm, just the way you like it. I will be upstairs if you need me."

*****

94

Junior Recycles
A Book

Without giving it a great deal of thought – his mind was elsewhere, taken up with James and the peculiar change in him – Johann 'Johnny' Alten deposited Maryah's brand-new, partially read *Mayflower* book in a shiny green recycling container at the Royal Westmoreland resort. It was a strange, unconscious action that was to cost him dearly. The world-class golf course with its reflecting ponds and its electric green perfection and its five-star restaurant was in a little weatherbeaten beach town named Mullins, on the sheltered West Coast of the island.

Deep within Junior there was a vague sinking feeling, an intimation of impending collapse. His stomach was knotted. It felt as though his carefully constructed and maintained universe was about to implode. The earliest warning waves were arriving from some distant but apocalyptic disturbance in the galactic field, and no amount of gin and tonic could turn them back. No amount of denial could deflect the inevitable. The shit, as the Americans so elegantly put it, was about to hit the fan.

The fact that the golf course was in a place named Mullins meant nothing to Junior. You can't put two and two together if you don't have either of the twos. Apparently, he mused, sitting on the clubhouse verandah waiting for his golf date, who had left a message at sign-in that she'd be half an hour late, which turned out to be an hour and ten minutes late, Liz had made some sort of historical discovery in the Alden House cellar. An old bible or diary or something to that effect.

The document in question had been written by a person named Mullins four centuries ago, but even if Junior had known that, the information would have meant nothing to him. It was unlikely to be of much significance in any case, but in the game of historical

529

detective work it can be rewarding to be on the lookout for such synchronicities. Liz, studying a map of the island online, had spotted a place called Mullins, but she too had had no idea at that time that the 'M' in 'PM' stood for Mullins. Despite her inebriated reggae dance session at the Mullins Beach Bar a few nights back, she had yet to hear the surname Mullins, although once she did, she would never forget it.

Mullins is an old English family name that reverberates down through history, but in the year 2020 few non-academics had heard of it. The eyes of the world were firmly on the contested election results in America, although, it must be said, the 400th anniversary of the *Mayflower* landing was also getting a certain amount of airtime.

Liz, antiquities librarian and budding amateur historical detective that she was, despite the apparent *Mayflower* references she had transcribed, was still convinced that the diary or novel or whatever it was had been written sometime in the early 18th Century by an English sea captain whose initials were 'PM.' It made logical sense. After all, the slave rebellions had begun in the seventeen sixties, Alden House had been built in 1659, and those skeletons were most likely those of some of the rebels who had not survived. She was also hot on the trail of a Colonial-era plantation manager named Peter Marbury, a sympathetic, light-skinned mulatto who had overseen the slaves at the Bayley Plantation a few miles away.

On the other hand, Liz was completely flummoxed by the fact that much of the journal appeared to refer to earlier events in New England, and not at all to events in Barbados. Some of it made no sense at all. It seemed as much an account of the writer's developing friendship with a Native American woman as anything else. What self-respecting sea captain would talk about babies, for Heaven's sake? Or plantation manager, for that matter.

*****

95

Maryah Goes Hitchhiking

Shortly after lunch, the Porsche rumbled to a halt at the bottom of the stairs. Distracted by personal events, and annoyed that his golf date had wasted his entire morning before thrashing him soundly out on the links, Junior had just played one of the worst games of his life. The tall skinny Eastern European woman had beaten the pants off him, and then laughed in his face, before stalking off on the arm of a huge black man dressed all in white.

Junior eased his long legs out of the Porsche. He looked up, and there was that black woman with the insane hairstyle, in his face. She was obviously furious. Maryah's father-in-law, drunk and distracted, was taken aback. Having no idea what had offended the ridiculous goddamned woman, he proceeded to insult her. In two colorful words, he referred to her as an Afro-American female of the Sapphic or homoerotic persuasion, or at least that's how Maryah chose to remember his delicate choice of epithet, when she described the event up in the bedroom. She had no problem with the veracity of the description. It was Junior's choice of words that enraged her. Furiously stuffing her clothes into her backpack, she raged at Scilla.

"How uncouth. He called me a nigger dyke. A nigger dyke! After stealing my book. Your family is insane, Scilla. How did you turn out so beautiful? That, my darling, is the mystery of the century. I'm out of here. Tell everyone Happy Thanksgiving for me." Before the astonished Scilla could say a word, Maryah planted a kiss on her lover's third eye, swung her backpack over her shoulder, and strode out of the room, down the stairs, and out of the house. She took the shortcut through the bushes down to the road, stuck out her thumb, and hitchhiked off into the glorious, sunny afternoon.

Leaning out of the upstairs window, Scilla heard the shriek of tires. The very first vehicle screeched to a halt, very nearly causing a traffic accident in the process. It was a pickup truck packed to the bilges with tired, happy landscape workers. They had just completed a big job for the owner of the Coca Cola company, and had been given a generous Thanksgiving bonus.

"Ooh, there gonna be a party tonight," they were chanting over and over. Maryah, her blonde dreadlocks gleaming in the westering sun, clambered into the back, where the delighted men made room for her, even though there wasn't any.

Scilla watched Maryah's departure from the bedroom window, as much as was possible through the gently waving trees.

"Maryah's a big girl. I love her. My father's an asshole. I hate him," she screamed out loud. From the mango tree, a thousand mynah birds exploded into the air, squawking as though the end of the world had arrived. The mynahs seemed to concur with Scilla's assessment.

*****

96

Return Of The Billabong

Liz sat with Alden, the old diary open in her lap, as she had done two dozen times before. The sun was setting outside. She could tell by the color of the light on the jarrah trees, and the raucous sound of the mynahs coming home to roost in the gigantic mango tree. Old Jack was dozing peacefully, calm and contented. Thinking about it, Liz realized that this had been the case ever since the discovery of the old sea trunk. There was no trace of the usual trickle of drool. This was new. Could there be a connection? Was it the calm of approaching death, she wondered? Liz got up and switched off the CD player. Enough already. Go home, Simon. Go home Garfunkel.

Simon? Ah that name, come back to haunt her. As she stood there thinking about Simon Collins or Collin Simons, whatever his name had been, a familiar clattering sound came through the open door from the hallway. Two pairs of flip-flops on a wooden floor. Ah, the boys were back. They must be starving. Liz turned and went out into the hallway. Jonny was swinging a familiar object round and round on his right forefinger.

"Hi, Mom," he greeted her brightly. "Look what I found out there by the point. They're brand-new."

"No they're not," said Jason. "They've got holes in them. But they're still good. They're too big for either of us. But we thought..."

"Holes in them?" Liz's eyes widened. "Where did you find those?"

"Out beyond the lineup. We were sitting out there watching the contest. I was just paddling, getting my breath, and I saw this flash of orange. Some birds were diving. But Jonny beat me to it."

"I'll grow into them, Mom."

"No you won't grow into them, Jonny. I'll buy you your own pair when you get to be that size."

"Hi Grandpa!"

There was Junior, coming up the stairs. He carried a gin-and-tonic in his right hand.

"Hey Jason. Hey Jonny. What you got there?"

"Some really nice Billabongs. We…"

Jason stopped. His mother had her finger to her lips and her eyes were huge.

"Anyway, I'll take them. Thank you. James was wondering where they had gotten to. Come boys, I've got something you might like. It's in my suitcase."

"Can't we see you at dinner, Grandpa? We've got to shower and…"

"The concert on the beach is starting in an hour. Kelly Slater's gonna to be playing, and we…"

"If we get there in time for sound check," Jason interrupted. "we might get to meet him…"

"Aha! I see you have your priorities in order," said their grandfather, and he continued along the hall to the end suite. Liz watched him go, and exhaled at last.

Junior held the Billabongs between finger and thumb, still dripping wet and sandy, and opened the door of his bedroom suite. James was sitting in the window, doing his best to concentrate on his battered copy of Philbrick's *Mayflower*.

"Here ya go, mate," the older man said in an exaggerated and fake Australian voice, and playfully tossed the wet, sandy shorts at his lover. They landed on the book with a wet splat.

"Excuse me! Where the hell did you get that?" Junior's voice was sharp. He was pointing at the decrepit Philbrick book, which only this morning he had disposed of more than twenty miles away. James, of course, thought he was referring to the Billabongs, not the book. He stood up abruptly. The shorts slid to the floor with a slippery wet flapping sound like the slippery wet flapping sound at the end of the world, the terminal whimper... James grabbed his damp, sandy, coffee-stained book and fled out of the room and speedwalked down to the beach, where he sat in the shade of a rock, shaking. Jack watched him go in astonishment.

"What the hell has gotten into you?" Junior wondered out loud. He shouted at James' retreating back. "Hey, I was doing you a favor, man. What the fuck is going on around here?" Well might he ask.

James could not for the life of him focus on the misadventures of an uptight bunch of religious misfits four hundred years ago. He closed his eyes and leaned his sunburned back against the rock. Ow. That hurt! The shade would be gone in a few minutes and he'd have to move and a noisy rock band was tuning up their guitars and the place was getting crowded and he needed to think. What was I thinking, he asked himself for the umpteenth time? I wasn't exactly thinking, was I? Liz's glorious face, her turquoise eyes like windows to the sky, appeared before him in his mind's eye. He heard her voice.

"What are you doing down here, Jeem? I thought..." James opened his eyes. Liz was squatting before him, her turquoise eyes like windows to the sky. He scrambled to his feet and looked around in alarm.

"Hey, I was just going to sit down and join you. Are you all right? You don't look so good."

"My baggies..."

"I know. I know. I was just going to mention them."

"No, you don't understand..."

"James, stop! I do understand. Listen to me. I had just come up with a good story, and then the boys..."

"A good story? What do you mean?"

"Well, we have to explain the missing baggies, don't we? It brought back a memory. We were in Puerto Rico, my mom and my little sister Pissy and me. It was Spring Break. Just before... We went down to the beach as soon as we got off the plane. Right in front of the hotel. We were out there in the water, and Mom looked back to check on our stuff on the beach. It was gone. Towels, my mom's purse, the car keys, everything. Three local kids were running down the beach."

"Liz, now you stop. I'm sorry. Why are you telling me this?"

"So I thought... You went skinny-dipping."

"I did?"

"Yesterday. Don't tell me you've forgotten already?" Liz giggled. "No. Not really, but in this story. While you were bodysurfing in the nude..."

"I see. And when I looked back at the beach..."

"Exactly. However, that would not have explained why you were wearing my sarong. So I thought, what if..."

"Liz. Liz. Come."

Their conversation was being overheard by a tourist couple, who had been busy plonking themselves down in the shade a few feet away, and spreading out their blanket with the arrogant territorial temerity of tourists everywhere. They had just read that nude bathing was illegal in Barbados, and, good God! Here was this awful Australian... Liz and James moved down to the water's edge.

"Liz, stop. Please. I have something to tell you."

"And I have something to tell you, James. It's OK. It's all OK."

"No it's not! Jack found the baggies. I have no idea how or where, but..."

Liz interrupted him.

"That's my point exactly," she said. "He didn't find them. Jonny and Jason found them. I gave them to him."

"What?"

"Well, my kids gave them to him."

"Oh God. What is going on?" James hid his face in his hands.

"Relax darling. I told you it's OK."

This was not necessarily the best time for this rather intimate conversation to be interrupted, but interrupted it was. Junior materialized between the two of them, and put his arms around their shoulders. His voice was just slightly slurred.

"What's OK, Lizzie? You two have a conspiracy going on?"

Liz was speechless. So was James. Then a flash of genius struck. She snatched the Philbrick book from Jim's limp fingers, and held it up to her father. There was fury in her face.

"James thinks the *Mayflower* arrived with a load of smallpox-infested blankets. Did you tell him that? Do you have any idea how fucking crazy that is?"

Feigning anger, she turned and stormed back off the

beach and up to the house, flinging the offending book back at James as she left. She was quite the little actress in her spare time.

"The details about the baggies will have to wait," she muttered. James was a big boy. Let him figure it out. James caught the book in mid-flight and watched her go. His lower lip was quivering. Jack watched his firstborn daughter's retreating sarong-clad body until it disappeared among the trees.

"Jimmy, what the fuck is going on?"

"We... We..."

"Were you fighting with Liz? About Pilgrims and Indians? Oh my God."

The two of them walked off down the beach. After they had walked a hundred yards, James reached out and took John's hand, tentatively. The British tourists watched disapprovingly, as the two men's body language slowly returned to normal. Everything was going to be OK. James knew it intuitively, although he could not for the life of him imagine how or why it should be so. The end of the world was over, or at least the apocalypse had been deferred - for the moment.

Junior was sobering up rapidly, and for once another gin-and-tonic was not uppermost in his mind. He had been thinking.

"I've been thinking, Jimmy," he said. "I've been neglecting you a bit lately, haven't I?"

Junior's voice was tender. James thought about the question. Yes, it was true. Junior had been neglecting him, for about twenty years. He countered.

"Do you mind if I answer your question with a question? Are you by any chance familiar with the phrase 'golf orphan'?"

"Golf orphan? What are you talking about, Jimmy?"

"It's a Lizzie term. That's how she felt as a kid, when you and Sarah..."

"Golf orphan? Is that how she felt. Is that how you feel? Oh my God, Jimmy. I had no..." The crisis was over, or so it seemed. There was other terrain to be explored, rocky terrain perhaps, but nothing quite as dangerous as the subject of Billabong board shorts.

"Darling, I want you to think about something, if you don't mind," said James.

"Shoot. I'm all ears."

"All ears and heart." It wouldn't do any harm to remind him about the heart, now, would it? "Liz. You know? We were talking, arguing almost."

"So I gathered. What the hell was that about?"

"It was about you."

James, too, was a natural improviser. He would have

made a very competent cross-dressing vampire actress if only a certain individual had been paying attention to the once-in-a-lifetime economic opportunity before him.

"Me? What did I have to do with anything?"

"I was defending you."

"And getting yourself into trouble, I bet. Elizabeth is a tough little cookie. I should have warned you."

"But listen Johnny. She's onto something. You know she found this book, this ancient diary, in your father's cellar."

"Yes. I heard there was something. The Barbados archeological people were here. And the police. That does not bode well..."

"True. But that's not what I'm trying to say, Johnny." James stopped. This was not going to be easy. "Let's turn around, shall we? The tide's coming in, and it's almost full moon." They had reached the end of the accessible part of the beach. Fifty yards away lay the magical cove.

"It is? I had lost track. Go on."

"OK, here goes. Bear with me, please. It seems that almost everything you've told me about the Pilgrims and Indians is..."

"Listen, James. We are not going to start talking about Pilgrims and Indians, are we? For God's sake?"

544

"For God's sake, I think we'd better, John. Or at least for the family's sake. For our sake, yours and mine. I'm not sure God cares that much. Listen to me. Liz has turned around completely. She's in the middle of transcribing something that appears to be authentic. It's an eye-witness account written by someone who was actually there."

"Actually where? I'm sorry, you lost me."

"In Plymouth Colony, from the very beginning. 1620."

"What? Oh bullshit man. Don't listen to her. Liz is as crazy as a loon."

"No crazier than I am, darling. I've been reading her transcriptions."

"You've been what?"

"You heard me. It's authentic. There's no doubt in my mind. Plus, as you may have noticed, I've been reading the *Mayflower* book, Nathaniel Philbrick's account of the same events." James held up the *Mayflower* book as incontrovertible proof.

They had returned to the south end of the beach. A large crowd had gathered on the lawn in front of the bandstand, and a very loud reggae band was launching into its second song. It was getting hard to have anything resembling a serious conversation.

"Speaking of the *Mayflower* book, where did you get that? May I ask?" Junior shouted, indicating the dog-eared, coffee and water stained book in James' hand.

"I got it on the way to the airport in Sydney, before we left." James yelled. "Remember? After breakfast. You were there. It's the 400th anniversary of the *Mayflower* landing. Every-one's reading it. Even Maryah."

"Maryah? Who? Oh Maryah. My so-called daughter-in-law."

Junior turned away thoughtfully and gazed out to sea in the twilight. The glow of the about-to-rise full moon was growing stronger on the horizon. The music was loud. It was impossible to maintain the conversation, so they joined the dancers at the edge of the enthusiastic crowd.

Had she still been on the beach, Liz might have been astonished to see her overweight, stodgy, silver haired old father skanking in the sand with a beautiful androgynous younger guy. They were doing a groovy little dance number called the Aborigine Stomp, but Liz was long gone. It was dinnertime up at the old plantation manor, and she had been neglecting her duties.

*****

546

97

'Twas The Night Before Thanksgiving

Tomorrow was going to be a big day. Gladys had set up an elegant little dinner party, buffet-style, so she and Washington could get an early night. Cold meats, cheeses, salads. A huge English trifle for dessert. Scilla, Liz, Baxter, and Barbara sat around one end of the long dining room table, and, to everyone's delight, Alden had insisted on coming down and joining them. The old man beckoned to Washington, who came over and bent down to listen to the request. The factotum left the room, and moments later returned, bearing four frosted bottles of vintage *Veuve Clicquot* from the locked wine cellar off the main kitchen.

Gladys and Washington sat shyly at the far end of the table. They had been invited to join the family Thanksgiving festivities tomorrow. After all, as Liz had told them in no uncertain terms, they *were* family. Liz had noticed that, for some reason, Gladys and Washington no longer seemed to need to get out of the house as soon as the sun went down. Apparently, the archeologist had taken the ghosts away with her, along with the skeletons. Was such a thing possible?

Baxter de Waal had come over to lend a hand with the final preparations and was planning to spend the night. Alden was downstairs for the first time in months, in his one of a kind Ferrari-made wheelchair. He was astonishingly much improved, despite Ginsberg's ongoing refusal to countenance such nonsense. Old Jack was resplendent in white Sperry Topsiders, freshly pressed khaki chinos, a lime green shirt, and his favorite fuschia colored cashmere sweater.

After a while, James came in, apologized for being late, winked cheerfully at Liz, served himself some food, and sat down. Liz passed him a glass of champagne. The only ones missing were Maryah, who had disappeared off the face of the Earth, Dr. Ginsberg, of course - he'd be here on the morrow - and Junior, who had some kind of un-put-off-able golf related meeting at the Hilton in Bridgetown. He would be back later.

Also, Liz's boys were nowhere to be seen. They had taken two of the electric mopeds and were hanging out down by the contest tent, in the hope of meeting a famous surfer or two. A big winter swell, the first of the season, was moving in, and the SurfQuest website said a number of the world's greatest surfers were winging their way to the island. Kelly Slater was already there. This contest was going to be very interesting, SurfQuest predicted.

As they ate and chatted and sipped the superb champagne, Liz prepared to read some of her diary transcripts. She had made a series of notes, as she gradually put the story together. It was not easy. Aside from the atrocious handwriting, the writer of the journal had not cared much for keeping his entries in chronological order. Liz's grandfather sat there in his Ferrari, seemingly fascinated by this new development. Liz held the diary aloft for all to see.

"Believe it or not, Grandpa, this is all your fault," she began. "I know it sounds crazy, but this fake bible, it's not a bible, it's a journal, as far as I can tell, although sometimes it reads like a novel... Whatever it is, it appears to be a firsthand account of the first fifty years at Plimoth Colony, you know, the plantation that the *Mayflower* people established back in 1620. Here we are, exactly four hundred years later, and..." She stopped and looked around. To her surprise, everybody was paying attention. She went on.

"One problem I'm having with the transcription, Grandpa, is the actual date it was written. Also, we'd never have found it in a million years if it hadn't been for you and your invisible friend, the ghost." Alden's bushy eyebrows went up, but he refrained from interrupting his animated granddaughter. "This may look like an old Geneva bible," Liz continued, excitedly. "That's what I thought it was, at first, but it's not. I found it buried in the cellar of your house. Alden House. In an ancient sea chest. Right about there..." She pointed down at the floor, dramatically, remembering the seven skeletons with a shudder. "Here's a piece I transcribed in the middle of the night last night."

Everyone adjusted their chairs, turned to Liz, put down their drinks politely, and gave her their full attention. She opened the notebook, and said, by way of introduction, "The Pilgrims have received word that Chief Massasoit is dying. Governor Bradford sends Edward

Winslow and an English visitor to say farewell to the
dying sachem. Guided by their friend Hobamok, they
travelled something like forty-six miles on foot, deep
into Indian country. Can you imagine? On the way, they
are told that they are too late. Massasoit is already dead.
On hearing the news, Hobamok breaks down and
weeps. Listen.

"*In the way, Hobomok manifesting a troubled spirit,
brake forth into these speeches, 'Neen womasu Sagimus, neen
womasu Sagimus,' etc. 'My loving Sachem, my loving Sachem,
Many have I known, but never any like thee!' And turning
him to me said; 'Whilest I lived, I should never see his like
amongst the Indians,' saying, 'he was no liar, he was not
bloody and cruel like other Indians; in anger and passion he
was soon reclaimed, easy to be reconciled towards such as had
offended him, ruled by reason in such measure, as he would
not scorn the advice of mean men, and that he governed his
men better with few strokes than others did with many; truly
loving where he loved'; yea he feared we had not a faithful
friend left among the Indians, showing how he oft-times restrained their malice, etc. continuing a long speech with such
signs of lamentation and unfeigned sorrow, as it would have
made the hardest heart relent.'*"

Liz went on. "But, against all odds, Massasoit was
still alive when they got to his village, which, by the
way, was in present-day Rhode Island, a long way from

551

Plymouth. Massasoit was barely alive, but Winslow proceeds to save his life by administering an English herbal conserve, which he had brought with him from Plymouth. Massasoit recovers immediately, at which point he realizes that the English really do care for him.

"But upon his recovery he brake forth into these speeches: Now I see the English are my friends and love me; and whilst I live, I shall never forget this kindness they have showed me.

Liz paused for breath. "There's more," she went on, after glancing around the room to make sure she wasn't boring anyone. "It turns out there was a conspiracy brewing among the neighboring tribes. They had been trying to get the dying Massasoit to join them in destroying the two English settlements. Listen to this.

'At our coming away, Massasoit called Hobomok to him, and privately revealed the plot of the Massachusetts before spoken of, against Master Weston's Colony, and so against us, saying that the people of Nauset, Pamet, Succonet, Mattachiest, Manomet, Angawam, and the Isle of Capawack, were joined with them; himself also in his sickness was earnestly solicited, but he would neither join therein, nor give way to any of his. Therefore as we respected the lives of our countrymen, and our own after safety, he advised us to kill the men of Massachusetts, who were the authors of this intended mischief.

'And whereas we were wont to say, we would not strike a

552

stroke till they first begun; if, said he upon this intelligence,
they make that answer, tell them, when their countrymen at
Wessagussett are killed, they being not able to defend them-
selves, that then it will be too late to recover their lives, nay
through the multitude of adversaries they shall with great
difficulty preserve their own, and therefore he counseled
without delay to take away the principals, and then the plot
would cease. With this he charged him thoroughly to acquaint
me by the way, that I might inform the Governor thereof at
my first coming home. Being fitted for our return, we took
our leave of him, who returned many thanks to our Governor,
and also to ourselves for our labor and love: the like did all
that were about him. So we departed.' "

Liz fell silent, looking down at her lap.

"What do you think?" she asked.

To everyone's astonishment, Alden picked up the
story, his voice raspy but strong. Liz stared at him open
mouthed.

"On March 23, 1623, I believe it was, the full council
of Plymouth meets to consider their options. They
reluctantly conclude that there is no alternative but to
undertake a preemptive strike, using the same kind of
stealth and deceit the Indians commonly used. The diminutive Captain Standish takes eight men to
Wessagussett and kills the sachem Wituwamat, with the
man's own knife, mind you, after the tall, strong Indian

brags that the knife has previously killed both French- and Englishmen. They kill Pecksuot and a number of other leaders who have come to Wessagusset. Standish returns to Plymouth with the decapitated head of Wituwamat. The Indians react in terror all over the area.

"As you can imagine, modern historians question the justification for this preemptive attack." Alden continued. "Was there really a conspiracy to destroy the English settlements? Or was Massasoit manipulating the English to pursue his own ambitions, by eliminating his competition? We will probably never know. It's an open question.

"Three of Weston's men, who had foolishly moved out of the Wessagusset village, are killed three days later. After this, Weston's men abandon the plantation. In his *Good Newes from New England,* published the following year, Winslow criticizes the colony at Wessagusset for making Christianity stink." Alden stopped and looked at Liz. There was a dead silence around the table. Liz was the first to find her voice.

"Oh my God, Grandpa, that's pretty much exactly what it says right here. Listen.

"And so, by God's goodness, Captain Standish brought away the head of the chiefest of them. And it is set on the top

of our fort, and instead of a flag, we have a piece of linen
cloth dyed in the same Indian's blood, which was hung out
upon the fort when Massasoit was here. And now the Indians
are most of them fled from us...."

James had a comment. "Man! I hate to say this, but those religious, peace-loving English settlers were pretty damn violent."

"What alternative did they have, James?" Liz turned to him and countered. "Think about it. It's easy enough to understand the Indians wanting to get rid of the settlers before they got too well established. Imagine someone walking into this house right now and announcing that they were taking over. What would you do?

"But the Pilgrims, from their perspective... I mean, again, what would you do, if your entire community were threatened with annihilation? If it hadn't have been for Massassoit blowing the whistle on the conspirators..."

Baxter piped up suddenly.

"It's a miracle anyone survived at all, James. Think about the Jamestown massacre the previous year, down in Virginia. The Indians, who were peacefully integrated into the English community, rose up without warning one day, and murdered over four hundred English men, women and children. The Pilgrims used violence as a last resort. Do you have any idea how treacherous and violent the Indians were?" Bax changed the subject suddenly.

"Liz, that bookcase you were talking about. The one with all the Pilgrim books?"
Alden's bushy eyebrows shot up. Liz glanced at him, a hint of guilt on her face. Bax went on.

"Is there by any chance a copy of the Iroquois Great Law? It's a probably in a little white book. I know it's not directly Pilgrim-related, but I want to show you something, if possible. If you're trying to understand the way the Indians were before European contact, there's something that might be relevant."

"There's only one way to find out, Bax. Let's go up and look. Gladys, is the key still where I put it?"

As they got up, Alden surprised them. He swung the Ferrari around to face Bax.

"Second shelf on the left, girls. All the way to the right. And while you're about it, there's a little brown book about the Huron right next to it. Bring that one down as well, would you?"

Liz looked at her grandfather in alarm. Busted! But all she said was,

"Thanks Grandpa! A little brown book about the

Hurons? Roger. We'll be right back."

Liz and Bax bounded upstairs to the bookcase, searched briefly, and came back down to the group, who were oohing and aahing over the English trifle. They'd never tasted anything quite like it. Bax held up a small white book, and then a small brown book. She stood behind her chair searching for a particular section in the former.

"The Five Nations of the so-called Iroquois established the Great Peace among themselves, after generations of endless war," Bax said. "But, outside of the confederacy, they regarded all of the neighboring tribes as foreigners to be conquered and converted. You will accept the Great Peace, or else. Ah, here it is. Listen.

"The War Chief of the Five Nations shall address the Chief of the conquered nation, and request him three times to accept the Great Peace. If refusal steadfastly follows, the War Chief shall let the bunch of white lake shells drop from his outstretched hand and shall bound quickly forward and club the offending Chief to death.

"I found that passage a few years back when I was visiting the Mohawk reservation in upstate New York. It kind of changed my view of Native American history, as you can imagine." She turned to the old man in the wheelchair. "Is this the Huron book you were talking

about, Mr Alten? Or is it Alden? I'm sorry, I'm confused." She held up a small brown colored book titled
simply 'Huron.'

"That's the one," rasped Alden. "Gimme. And Baxter, for the record, my name is Alden, not Alten."
Bax handed him the book. Bax and Alden took turns
quoting from the Iroquois and Huron books.

"So yes, it wasn't all roses, was it?" James said.
"There's two sides to every story."

"At least two sides, James," Alden replied. "This
Huron book has some interesting information, if any of
you'd like to read it. Most historians would say King
Philip's war was the bloodiest conflict per capita, in this
country's history."

"This country being America, not Barbados, I
presume," Liz commented.

"The Civil War was the bloodiest..." Scilla said.

"No it wasn't, Priscilla. Not per capita. Over eight
percent of the English men died during King Philip's
war, versus about five percent during the Civil War.
That's a big difference. But that's not my point, actually.
There was a much bloodier war, in historic times."
Alden had everyone's attention. "I don't know how
much you all know about the northeast Native Americans before the white man came."

"Not a whole lot, in my case." Liz said, ruefully. "Growing up in Maine, I didn't even know there were any Indians in New England. I finally met a bunch of Lakota activists in New York City."

"Well, that's why I went and got the Great Law," Bax chipped in. "It was written a thousand years ago." Alden begged to differ. "Written a thousand years ago? Well, no."

Liz stared at her grandfather in amazement. She had no idea he was so well informed.

"The Great Law of the Iroquois," Alden continued, "they call themselves the Haudenosaunee, the People of the Longhouse – the Great Law was passed down from generation to generation in the Confederacy's oral tradition. There's no real way to know when or even if those events actually happened. The best guess, according to the historians, is sometime between 1142 and the mid-1300s. That document you are holding, Baxter, was first written down in the seventeenth or eighteenth century, by the Jesuits, I believe." Alden paused, breathing deeply. He continued.

"As you may or may not know, the Great Law contributed to the drafting of the United States Constitution in 1787. The Native Americans made a significant contribution to the founding of this country, to the way

our government is structured. By this country I'm referring, of course, to the United States, not to Barbados, as
Lizzie just said." Alden was looking tired. He stopped for
breath, then went on. "Well, the point I wanted to make
was this. Don't believe the people who tell you the Indians were sitting here meditating and living in perfect
peace and ecological harmony until we evil white people
came over and started slaughtering them."

"But Grandpa... Everybody knows... That's what it
says on the Internet." Scilla was still unconvinced. She
seemed to have forgotten the conversation with Liz the
previous afternoon "It's what most of my generation
believes. It's what my father believes. Everything we
were taught in school was a lie. Have you read *The Peoples' History of the United States?* What about the smallpox
blankets the *Mayflower..?*"

"Smallpox blankets on the *Mayflower?*" Alden raised
his voice. "I'm sorry, Priscilla, but that is insane. The
coastal New England Indians were wiped out by war and
disease several years *before* the *Mayflower* arrived.
I know. It's a mess out there. Someone needs to do
something about it.

"Listen to me. About the Indians' behavior toward
one another - read that little brown book. It's about as
authoritative as it gets. It was written a long time ago, by

560

an anthropologist, based on interviews he did with the Indian elders themselves. It contains the most terrifying chapter on torture that I've ever read. And it tells the story of the almost total extermination of the Huron tribe by their ancient enemies, the Mohawk."

"There was actually a Huron tribe?" Scilla was surprised. "I've never heard of them. There's a Lake Huron, isn't there?"

"Well, there you have it, Priscilla." Alden looked at his granddaughter. "The Huron tribe was something like 40,000 strong in 1640. They were many hundreds of years old. As has been well documented, they were completely gone by 1648, with the exception of a few scattered refugees. The French Jesuits were there to witness..." Baxter smiled at the old man, but she did not say anything.

"Grandpa, let me get this straight," Liz said. "I always thought it was the Pilgrims, them and the Puritans, who killed the New England Indians off. Smallpox blankets were part of the genocide. Are you saying..?"

"That's what some people would have you believe, based on the postscript to a letter written in 1783, during the French and Indian wars, a century and a half after the *Mayflower* arrived. Listen, people, I'm not saying we Europeans didn't have a huge impact on the native people of this continent. Of course we did. It was European guns that killed the Huron, for example. Guns the Mohawk got from the Dutch in New York, guns that changed the balance of power. And the subsequent treatment of the Indians by the United States has been atrocious. It still is." Alden was panting. He looked about ready to collapse. Gladys stood up and moved behind the Ferrari.

"I want to say one more thing. Please don't think I'm being anti-Indian when I point out the Indians' behavior toward one another. They have a shadow, just like the rest of us. It's true, Baxter, that the Iroquois confederacy became the most powerful military alliance in the American northeast. And they used the Great Law to dominate all of the other tribes on the Eastern seaboard. Just as the Christians used the Church and their combined power to take over half the world. Just as the Muslims did in the Middle East. Just as the United States uses the power of its union to intimidate the rest of the world right now. Think about China, and Russia. Germany. Japan. It's the way we humans have behaved to one another since the beginning. My question is – when are we going to wake up?"

Old Jack stopped and stared around at his dumbstruck audience. He looked exhausted, understandably.

This was his first time out of bed in two months.

"I think I'll go on up to bed now, Gladys," he wheezed. "I'm just a wee bit tuckered."

The party was over. Gladys and Barbara got Alden back upstairs and tucked him in for the night. Thoughtfully, the family members meandered off to their bedrooms. Baxter was spending the night. There was no shortage of space, after all. There were still ten or a dozen vacant rooms. She and Liz were the last ones up. They sat out on the verandah in the moonlight, decompressing. Bax had summarized the evening's proceedings.

"Liz, that grandpa of yours is pretty amazing. He just told your whole family pretty much everything I've been trying to get across to you this past week."

"Except for my father. Damn! I wish he'd been here to hear that."

"By the way, Liz, on a completely different subject. I've been meaning to ask. How many kids did you say you have? I'm confused. I swear you said three, back when we first met, but so far I've only met two."

"That's a tough question, Bax. I have two sons." Liz hesitated, then went on. "Two sons and an ex-daughter."

"An ex-daughter? A daughter who died? I am so sorry, Liz."

"She died to me. Not to the rest of the world."

"What the hell are you talking about, Liz?"

"Hell is right. Have you ever had someone you loved with all your heart and soul just suddenly walk out of your life? Your best friend and closest companion? Gone, like you didn't exist? Do you have kids, Bax?"

"I do not. I wish."

"Well, I had three of them. Had, past tense. Two of them you have met. They'd better get home soon, or their mother is going to start worrying about them. The other keeps me awake at night, crying."

"Tell me. Come on. That's what friends are for, Liz."

"Well, I told her the truth. She didn't want to hear it. She walked out. She hasn't spoken to me since. That was almost four years ago, at her father's memorial service in Cambridge."

"And the truth was..?"

"Well... Her paternity." Liz stopped, then took the plunge. "Only once in my life have I participated in a threesome."

"A *menage a trois*? Uh oh."

"Exactly. James and his college roommate and I - we met in Mykonos."

"James? Oh, you mean your late husband? Well that explains it. Moonlight on the water. Soft music. Perhaps a spot of opium?"

"Shut up Bax, please. Let me finish. I can't even remember the guy's name, Collin Stevens or Steven Collins or something, but the three of us pulled an all nighter. I was pretty drunk. There was some Lebanese blond hashish. A bottle of Armagnac. It was a lot of fun, what I can remember of it."

"And in the morning?"

"His name just came back to me. Collin Simons. No, Simon Collins. One or the other. God, I haven't been able to remember his name forever. Anyway, there was no way to know whose kid she was, Bax. I just told Layla the truth."

"Layla? Now there's a name for you."

"The Clapton song. The guys played it all night long, over and over. It was a no-brainer to call her Layla."

"Did you tell her all that?"

"God no. Of course not. Just the basic facts. She needed to know."

"I'm not so sure about that, considering the out-come. It must've been a difficult choice."

"Yeah."

"And Simon? Or did you say Colin?"

"I never saw him again. He packed up and left the island before I woke up. I had the worst hangover of my life."

"He screwed your brains out, then walked out, just like that?"

"Well, there's more to the story. Turns out the guy was bisexual. After I passed out, he wanted to keep going. James was not into it."

"Oh."

"James took full responsibility. He was such an honorable... I finished the semester and went back to the States for Christmas before I even realized... We stayed in touch. Four years later I moved back to Cambridge and we got married. Layla was the ring bearer. She was three."

"But you never told her? Not until..."

"Right." Liz sobbed. She had held it in for a long, long time. The tears were streaming down her face, reflecting the moonlight and the headlights of an oncoming motor vehicle. The Porsche crunched up the driveway and pulled up in front of the house. Junior came bounding up the stairs.

"Goodnight, ladies," he said, affably enough, and disappeared into the house.

"The truth will set you free, Bax. So they say. A strange kind of freedom. The truth cost me my firstborn child. Right after her father died."

"So you lost both of them?"

"I lost both of them. Layla thinks I'm a slut. Maybe she's right."

Liz stopped and thought. The week's events certainly supported that conclusion. At least she was beyond her fertile years. She sincerely hoped. She was pretty sure the first hot flashes were kicking in.

"Fuck!"

It was the best Bax could come up with. Fuck, the most expressive word in the English language, in all of its many connotations. There was nothing more to be said.

After a while, the friends got up, locked the front doors, and went up the winding staircase to bed. Halfway up the stairs, Liz remembered something. The boys were still out. She went back down and unlocked the front doors. For the second time since arriving on the island two weeks earlier, Liz slept through the night, dreamlessly.

*****

98

The Book Of Revelations

Thursday Nov 26, 2020

It was 8 a.m. and the sun was high in the sky by the
time Liz emerged from dreamland. Tomorrow she
would turn forty. Today is Thanksgiving Day in the year
of our Lord 2020, she realized, and gave thanks that her
path in life to date, rocky as it had been, had at least been
less harrowing than PM's, whoever the author of the
journal might turn out to be. Or the Indians' for that

568

matter – their life had been anything but easy, both before and after the coming of the white man.

Liz luxuriated in bed for a delicious hour, re-living some of the sensations from her magic cove adventure, and reviewing what she thought of as her hero's journey. She knew about stuff like that, having been a Joseph Campbell devotee ever since attending his wake at the New York Museum of Natural History as a precocious fifteen year-old. The high point of that event was meeting Mickey Hart of the Grateful Dead backstage, while her parents hobnobbed with the glitterati. It was one of the last things she had done with Sarah, her mother. The endless summer in Europe, New York in the fall, then the beginning of the end of the world, the fateful March vacation in Puerto Rico. Lying there, half awake, drifting in and out of the dream state, out of the blue, it hit her. The revelation dawned. Liz finally realized who PM was. What? Impossible! But it had to be. There was no other possibility.

The last thing Liz had done, before brushing her teeth and getting into bed the previous night, was to go online and Google the *Mayflower's* passenger list. She was checking to see whether the people Baxter claimed to be descended from were actually on the ship. There they were, Brewster, Hopkins and several other names she couldn't quite recall. Drowsy and bleary-eyed, she had read through the entire list of 102 names. She wasn't consciously looking for someone with the initials 'PM,' but there was in fact one person on that long list with those very initials.

As Liz drifted back to consciousness on Thanksgiving morning, suddenly, there her answer was, clear as daylight: 'PM' was Priscilla Mullins! The author of the diary was a girl. A young woman! Was it possible? Liz reviewed the series of events that had led up to the discovery of the old bible, and then her increasing obsession with it, as she got deeper and deeper into the transcription of the challenging document.

With a little help from James, she had, at last, corrected her initial error as to the date. She had not misread the Roman numerals. They really did say 1715, not 1615, but the contents could not have been from the Eighteenth century. There was no question that many of the excerpts Liz had 'tranfribed' described the journey and the landing of the *Mayflower*, and the subsequent history of the fledgling colony. The writer must have got his numerals wrong in the first place, she concluded at last. And he must have been a Mayflower passenger. He was just a hundred years ahead of his time, she had giggled to James.

It had never seriously occurred to Liz, however, although she had in fact given the matter some thought, that he might have been a she, or that she might have been a child, a teenager. Her second mistake, however logical, given the time period, was to assume that the author had to have been a man. There was only one passenger on the Mayflower with the initials 'PM,' but that person was not a man, it was a teenage girl. The author of the ancient diary was Priscilla Mullins, the girl immortalized in Henry Wadsworth Longfellow's epic poem *The Courtship Of Myles Standish.*

Liz lay there, half in and half out of her body, in a state of extreme excitement. She felt like leaping up, rushing into her father's bedroom and yelling out the news to James. That would hardly have been appropriate, however, and she restrained herself with some difficulty. She sighed. The puzzle was solved. The search was over. It was almost a letdown, an anticlimax.

It is true, dear reader, that the puzzle of PM's identity had been solved, but there was more to come. Liz had no idea there might be a personal connection. That realization called for information from an entirely unexpected source, New Zealand.

*****

571

99

Thunder From Down Under

It was just after 9 o'clock. With the exception of
Washington, who was gently buffing the old Mercedes in the garage, and the ever-faithful Gladys, everybody was sleeping in. James, the first one up on this
glorious morning, sat out on the verandah, reading and
re-reading the stunning email on his Samsung, sipping
his morning coffee, and pondering the imponderable. At
4:43 a.m., his phone had chirped, waking him from a
deep sleep. It was another message from his cousin

572

Alison in Christchurch, New Zealand, the one who was working on the Alten genealogy. The prior communications had been interesting, if frustrating. This one was a bombshell.

Liz came out onto the verandah, blinking in the brilliant light, and the starstruck friends and lovers took a stroll down to the ocean. Liz couldn't wait to share her revelation, but James was completely distracted. He was boggled. He did not know what to think, or how to break the news to her. Something else was going on, too, in James's mind. James was angry.

"The bastard!" he fumed, silently. Junior had lied to him. Old Jack Alden was a *Mayflower* descendent and proud of the fact. That much had become clear last night, and Ali's email had just confirmed it. Junior must have been misled by the bloody Indians, but that was no excuse. What the hell? He must have concocted the German ancestor story and changed the family name 'back' to Alten after his wife had died. Or was the name change earlier? Junior had then married one James Walker, whose cousin back home was updating the Walker family's genealogy. James' New South Wales driver's license said his name was James Walker Alten. So did his Australian passport. It was not. The documents lied.

573

About six weeks ago, without telling Junior, James had asked Alison to look into the Alten ancestry, going back to Germany in the 1800s, just for the fun of it, really. Once Alison got around to it, she had run into a blind alley, a dead end. Nothing. Frustrated, she had made a fresh start, initiating a brand-new online search, starting from scratch. Here were the results of the new search, the email said.

A John Bradford Alden (not Alten) had indeed been born in Brunswick, Maine, on the correct date, ninety-three years ago last month. BINGO! There was, however, a problem. It was the wrong John Bradford Alden. That John Bradford Alden had absolutely no German ancestors. Not one. In fact, it looked like... As far as Alison could tell, Old Jack, James's father-in-law, had a direct line all the way back to John Alden, the *Mayflower's* cooper. Hence, therefore and thus, she wrote, the family name was in fact Alden, not Alten. Just as it said on the old gatepost down at the bottom of the driveway.

*****

100

The Truth Will Out

On the jagged cliffs above Soup Bowls, the crowd of onlookers was growing. They were watching a spectacular swell peeling around the point. The surfers were having a field day. Liz could not make out whether any of the tiny figures out there were her sons. The echoing public address system reminded her of something. Oh yes, there was a surfing competition today, wasn't there? The contest was about to begin. The boys would not be in the water, would they? Liz turned to her companion, who was staring down at his feet, his hands in his pockets.

"You're awfully quiet, James. Is everything all right?"

"Well I... I have something to tell you."

"Oh I see. You're still in a froth about what happened yesterday, the day before yesterday, aren't you?"

"It was out of this world, Liz. It truly was. It was like a dream. What did you call it? Heavenly. It was possibly the most amazing experience of my entire life. I mean it. But there's nothing to do, but keep mum about it, don't you agree? Maybe next lifetime..."

"I'm still quivering..." Liz was about to wax poetical. James made up his mind. He interrupted her.

"As beautiful and important as that is, Lizzie darling, I've got something at least as amazing to share with you. Would you like to sit down? Come."

"Sit down? Why? What could be more...?"

"I've just had an email from down under, New Zealand, actually. My cousin Alison has been working on..."

"You told me that." Liz interrupted. "Your ancestry. The Walker family, going back to Scotland in the 1300s."

"The 1500s, actually. But no. I'm not talking about *my* ancestry, Liz. I'm talking about *your* ancestry."

"My ancestry? What on earth..? Your cousin Alison

576

has been working on *my* ancestry. You mean, my German ancestry? Whatever for?" Liz stared at James in disbelief.

"Your ancestry, believe it or not, German or otherwise. Let me see if I can get this straight. It just came though this morning, right before you came downstairs. I'm still trying to figure out exactly what it means. Here's how it started. I asked Ali if she would take a look into your father's genealogy. We won't have any descendants, obviously, but... Just for the halibut. You will not believe what she's discovered, Liz. It's a boggle."

"Stop teasing me, James. Out with it!"
The conversation was interrupted by the sudden piercing wail of emergency sirens on the road above the waterfront. Down at the far end of the beach, something was going on. People were running. A small crowd was gathering. Liz and James walked swiftly in the direction of the crowd. They broke into a run. A surfer had been pulled from the water, unconscious. It was Jonny Nicholson.

*****

577

101

Denouement

Fortunately, young Jonny was not badly injured, despite the spectacular display of blood. He had whacked his head on the reef, but had sustained no permanent damage. Sitting in the shade on the main stage next to the contest judges, Jonny's head bore a splendid blood-stained white bandage, and photos of the wounded surf warrior were already circulating on Facebook by the time Thanksgiving dinner was announced at 4 p.m.

Up the hill at Alden House, the immense table

groaned with food. The Caribbean island of Barbados was a long way from the United States of America, but you'd never know it at the old plantation manor that afternoon. Down below the house, the surf roared, and the hollow, echoing sound of the contest's public address system alternated between the announcer's enthusiastic commentary and the loud rock music. A huge stars and stripes flag flew out over the Alden House lawn. The whole 'fam damily,' as Liz liked to call it, milled about on the verandah, or sat around the immense table in the dining room. The table went back hundreds of years in the family. Long and narrow, it was designed to seat a dinner party of twenty-four. If it could only have told its story, Liz had often thought. The ancestors and the aristocrats who had sat at that table. The projects that had been launched. The decisions that had been taken. Grandpa Jack had shipped it over from one of the old family homes in Germany. Or was it England? New England? Liz was confused.

Alden was in his wheelchair, bright-tailed and bushy-eyed, chatting up Baxter as though he was forty years younger and had a snowball's hope in hell. Aside from family members Liz, Scilla, and James, there were the guests, who included the aforementioned Baxter, a subdued Dr. Ginsberg sitting there polishing his greasy spectacles with a discolored handkerchief, and Barbara, the English hospice nurse who had become a family friend.

There were a number of locals and other friends, including Washington and Gladys. Old Jack Alden was about to become the star of the show, but no one knew that yet. Washington and Gladys had, reluctantly but joyfully, agreed to join the family, so the plan, as Liz announced, was to eat Thanksgiving dinner buffet-style. Serve yourself. Everyone was busily loading his or her plate with hors d'oevres, and filling their wine glasses, opening their Lion Ales, and sitting down. Conspicuously missing were four family members: Maryah, Junior, Jason and Jonny.

The festivities commenced. Everyone was seated at last. Just as Liz stood up to propose a toast, Junior interrupted the proceedings. He staggered in from the verandah and stood there blinking owlishly, trying to focus in the gloom. As he had done every day since his arrival, he had spent the morning at Westmoreland. His golf game had sucked. It was the worst game he'd ever played, at least in living memory. Even worse than the day before. Leaving the club in a fury, he had backed the Porsche into a concrete lamppost in the parking lot, putting to shame the minor damage that Liz had inficted on the long-suffering vehicle's bulbous tail. Needless to say, Junior was intoxicated. All conversation stopped. Silence. Scilla leaned over and whispered to Liz.

"Uh oh, Sister. Looks like Dad's reverted to type." Liz nodded. Junior looked around the room aggressively, then growled in a low voice, just loud enough for all to hear,

"Priscilla, where the fuck is Mary?" You could have heard a feather fall.

"Why the fuck do you ask, Junior?" Scilla took a deep breath. "What kind of question is that? Mary's up in Heaven with Jesus, last I heard. Unless you mean the love of my life, Maryah? In that case, your guess is as good as mine. You insulted her. She walked out. End of story. I'm not worried about her. Not in the least." Scilla's voice rose. She rose to her feet.

"I'm not worried about Maryah. It's you I'm worried about. You are really losing it. Did you really steal her *Mayflower* book, the book she was so engrossed in, and then call her a 'nigger dyke' when she asked you about it? What on God's green earth were you thinking?"

"No! I did not. I thought..."

"Junior!" There was a warning note in Scilla's voice. She was not a woman to be trifled with. She had friends with black belts. Professional assassins. She looked around the room.

"Listen, people, it's OK. Maryah's as tough as nails. Think about it. Growing up black and queer in Savannah, Georgia. A nigger dyke in the deep South. Good training for joining this goddamn family, I tell you that. She might have left the Island and gone on home, but I doubt it. More likely she found herself a bunch of reggae musicians and she's recovering from an all-nighter. She'll text me when she wakes up. Right around sunset. It wouldn't be the first time." Scilla looked around the table, laughing. She cheered up a little. "You should see her. Maryah shows up at a nightclub, picks up somebody's electric guitar, everyone does a double-take; 'say whaaat?' and the next thing you know the sun's rising." There was a long silence. Everyone looked at Junior. He was trying to say something, but his mouth wouldn't work.

"I... I'm sorry. Priscilla..." Junior's voice, when he spoke at last, was slurred. His habitual tone of arrogant command was gone. "I didn't mean... The book was... I thought... I wanted to...to apologize."
Liz took charge. She had had enough.

"Dad! Please sit down. Would you mind? Sit! Look around the room. We have company, and this *is* Thanksgiving, you know. There are people in this room

582

who have no idea what a whacked-out family we are."
Scilla nodded in agreement. She picked up the thread.

"Dad, listen up. Sit down and join the party. Forget
about Maryah. She'll get over it. You're not the first
homophobic racist asshole she's ever met, believe me.
That's right. I don't care how gay and liberated you
think you are, you're as sexist and homophobic as
Donald fucking Trump when it comes to women. Talk
about a double standard! Sorry, everybody, but it's true."
She paused for breath. She looked tired and drawn
suddenly. She sat down.

"Anyway, Dad, sit down, please." Scilla went on.
"There's something much more important going on
than you and your racist prejudices. Do you have any
idea what Liz has discovered about the Mayflower
Pilgrims? Right here in this house? I was as skeptical as
you are, but it's true. There's no way that diary can be a
fake."

"Oh bullshit," Junior replied, rolling his eyes. The
magnifying lenses of his spectacles lent comic drama to
an absurd attempt at self-mastery. "Don't give me that,
Priscilla. Come on."
James spoke up.

"You might want to take a look at it, Johnny. It's an
incredible historical discovery. And there's more you

583

don't know. A lot more."

"It's straight from the horse's mouth." Liz agreed.
"Why would you deny it? What's the point?"

"Johnny, listen to me, son," Alden took charge,
firmly but gently. "The time has come, the walrus said.
Drop the bullshit. Tell 'em the truth. What have you got
to lose? Your ego?"

Slowly, Junior turned his back on his father. He
walked around the far end of the table, staggered a little,
then collapsed into an empty chair, deflated. Silence.
Junior took his glasses off and put them on the table.
The little clicking clatter was the loudest sound in the
room.

"OK! OK! I give up," he sighed heavily. "I'm out-
numbered and outgunned. It's true. It has to be, I guess."
He looked down at his feet, then up again. "Jimmy, I'm
sorry I doubted you. I'm sorry. I was wrong. Lizzie,
Priscilla, Dad, I'm sorry. I lied about the whole Alten
thing. The German thing. I made it up. I am ashamed of
our ancestors, what they did to the Indians. I know that's
not an excuse." He paused. "I hope you'll be able to
forgive me."

Dead silence. Far off in the distance, the popinjay
laughed uproariously. Junior paused, then looked at his
father uncertainly. The pleading expression on his face

hearkened back to when he was a fourteen year-old boy.

"Dad? What do we do now?" he pleaded.

Alden attempted to stand up in his shiny electric wheelchair. The machine lurched erratically, threatening to send its wildly gesticulating occupant flying. Barbara rushed around behind him, grabbed the handles, and braced herself, ready for anything. The twisted old man's ancient creaking voice was loud and clear. Everyone stared at the old man in astonishment.

"I'll tell you what we do now, Johnny my lad!" Alden shouted. "We celebrate this beautiful goddamned family and each and every one of our goddamned ancestors. Going back to the goddamned *Mayflower*. Going all the way back to goddamned Gloucestorshire, England in the 1540s. And we're going to celebrate every goddamned Indian any of us ever met along the way, living or dead. East or West. We're all human, every last one of us, warts and all. Each and every one of us is beautiful. Each and every one of us has a shadow."

Pausing for breath, he glared fiercely at each family member in turn. Old Jack had never been known for passionate philosophical outbursts. Was this a breathrough?

"Listen to me, Johnny, and every Alden gathered here today," he continued. "I'm a goddamned *Mayflower* descendant and I'm goddamned proud of it. Your mother was too. Your ancestors came over on the first boat, exactly four hundred years ago this month. They signed a treaty with the Indians four months later, on the first day they met. Both sides honored that treaty for more than half a goddamned century. Our ancestors treated the Indians with honor. That is something to be proud of. Have I made myself clear?" Alden glared around at the astonished gathering, his emaciated claws raised in supplication. "Who's going to carve these goddamned turkeys? John? You haven't lost your touch, have you?"

Silence descended. Everyone stared at Old Jack, speechless. A diminutive, enigmatic silhouette entered the room from the kitchen, unseen, followed by a tall, dreadlocked shadow carrying a guitar case. Maryah was an apparition from another dimension. She was wearing a fringed and beaded buckskin mini-dress and she sported a brand-new hairdo. The blonde dreadlocks were gone. Her skull was as clean-shaven and shiny as a brown billiard ball. Could it be real? Crowning her head was a gigantic multicolored Mohawk headdress made from dyed porcupine hair. She yelled out loud...

"HAPPY THANKSGIVING, EVERYONE!!!"
The entire group spun around to face Maryah. Barbara

turned Old Jack's wheelchair so he could see the intruders. Maryah was not alone.

"I'd like y'all to meet my new best friend, Eddy," she said. A chorus of voices rang out, tumbling over one another in their enthusiasm and relief.

"Welcome home, Maryah."

"Hi Eddy."

"Happy Thanksgiving!"

"Welcome to the family!"

"I got some news for y'all." Maryah continued. She was excited, and her voice was loud. "I was gonna keep it a secret, but I changed my mind. Y'all can take it or leave it." The apparition stopped and took a deep breath. "I ain't just any ol' nigger dyke from the deep South. I'm a Native American nigger dyke from the deep South. My grandmother is a full-blooded Cherokee. And I love this crazy family. I really, really do. I thought y'all might like to know that."

She sat down next to Gladys, signaling Eddy to take the chair next to her. Washington leaned over to Eddy, and put out his hand.

"Hey you're not *that* Eddy? Are you? Yes, you are! I'm Washington Franklin the Fourth, and I've been looking forward to meeting you for a long time."

"Hey, you're not *that* Washington Franklin, are you?

587

Your ancestor is pretty famous over at my house."
Washington's face broke into a huge, happy grin, and he
broke into song. Without hesitation, Eddy joined him.
They ad libbed the chorus from a famous hit song from
the 1980s.

"Electric Avenue. And then we'll take it higher!"
The two men laughed, instant friends. *Electric Avenue*
was Eddy's greatest hit. The tension broken, everyone
burst into applause and cheers.

Except Liz. She had just realized something. The
surf was *huge*. You could hear it roaring over the chatter
in the dining room. Future generations of surfers would
remember the legendary 2020 Thanksgiving swell that
hit Soup Bowls right on time for the contest. Her boys
were missing. They must have drowned, obviously, or
they would have been here by now. Liz leapt up and
spoke in a panic stricken voice.

"Wait a minute. Where are my boys? I've been so
busy I..." Nobody paid her the slightest attention in all
the excitement.

Jonny and Jason came bursting into the room, right
on cue. Their timing could not have been better. Jonny
looked surprisingly elegant in his blood stained turban.

"Surprise!" he yelled. "Look who's coming to
Thanksgiving, Mom! Grandpa! Great-grandpa! Say hi to

588

Kelly, everybody. He's got to get back down to the contest in a minute. He's one of the judges, but he ran up quickly to wish you all a Happy Thanksgiving."

The hulking shaven-headed silhouette in the doorway turned out to be Jason and Jonny's all-time hero, the 15-time world surfing champion they could not stop talking about. He too was carrying a guitar case. Kelly and Eddy exchanged hugs. They were old friends.

Liz banged a spoon on the water jug, insistently. It took a few minutes, but the riotous mob finally quietened down and looked at her expectantly.

"OK, family, extended family, it's turkey time. Whew. But first..." She held up the old bible dramatically. "I have a little something to share with everyone. This here book is the historical discovery of the century! Some of you already know what it is. If I could have everyone's undivided attention, I want to read you something that was written at the very first Thanksgiving, exactly 400 years ago."

"Three hundred and ninety-nine years, actually, but who's counting?" Bax corrected her.

"Oh no. Not the Bible. Mom! Please. What's gotten into you? You always said you never darkened..."

"Shhh, Jason. Didn't you hear what I just said? It's not a bible. It just looks like one. Listen to me. This is an original account of the very first Thanksgiving. It was written by someone who was actually there, and it turned up in the cellar of this house. I can still barely believe it.

"Firstly, this handwritten book is over four hundred years old." Liz went on. "Think about that. How did this precious document get here, to our house in Barbados? Here's my theory, or at least part of it. It came here in the possession of a New England Indian slave. No listen. I'm serious. I've been trying to figure it out, ever since... I think that is where it all began, in Massachusetts at the end of King Philip's War, when so many Indians were shipped down here as slaves. Listen to this. This is the final entry in the diary. It is dated June 18, 1675. It's a dire warning from a Mr. Cole." Liz read directly from the final entry in the diary, not her transcription in the exercise book.

"*Utmost urgency. Philip's men are on the march. They intend to burn Swansea. They will show no mercy to man, woman or child. Make ye haste for refuge at Taunton or Plimoth before 'tis too late and disaster overtake thee and thine...* Was there a Cole on the *Mayflower*," Liz asked. "Or did he come later? Does anyone know? Bax?"

"I'm not sure," Bax responded, thoughtfully. "But there's a Cole Hill in Plymouth, immediately above the

590

Plymouth Rock monument. Right now there's a huge event going on there. This very moment. It's on every television set on the planet."

"Except ours." Jason was nothing if not observant.

"This year, 2020," Liz continued, "is the four hundredth anniversary of the landing of the *Mayflower*. I know you all know that. That's one of the reasons I'm so boggled by this ancient diary showing up at precisely this moment in history. Listen to this. It's an original account of the First Thanksgiving. It's in Olde English, but I'll do my best to read it accurately, and then we can eat.

" 'Our harveſt being gotten in, our Governour ſent foure men on fowling, that ſo we might after a more ſpeciall manner reioyce together, after we had gathered the fruit of our labours; they foure in one day killed as much fowle, as with a little helpe beſide, ſerved the Company almoſt a weeke, at which time amongſt other Recreations, we exerciſed our Armes, many of the Indians coming amongſt vs, and amongſt the reſt their greateſt King Majſſafoyt, with ſome ninetie men, whom for three dayes we entertained and feaſted, and they went out and kilied fiue Deere, which they brought to the Plantation and beſtowed on our Governour, and vpon the Captaine, and others. And although it be not alwayes ſo plentifull, as it was at this time with vs, yet by the goodneſſe of God, we are ſo farre from want, that we often wiſli you par-*

takers of our plenties. Wee haue found the Indians very faith-
full in their Covenant of Peace with vs; very louing and read-
ie to pleafure vs: we often goe to them, and they to vs."'
James followed up with another piece of the story.

"The Pilgrims and the Indians lived in peace and friendship for over half a century. I did not know that. I thought it was nothing but conflict, right from the beginning."

"That's exactly what they did, goddammit." Alden took over. "They lived in peace for fifty four years. And this goddamned family is going to live in peace and friendship for the *next* fifty four years if I have anything to say in the matter."

"Hear hear!" cried Junior, to everyone's surprise.

"Hear hear!" chorused the rest of the family.
Liz went on with her reading.

" '...*yea, it hath pleafed God fo to pofleffe the Indians with a feare of vs, and loue vnto vs, that not onely the greateft King amongft them called Maffafoyt but alfo all the Princes and peoples round about vs, haue either made fute vnto vs, or beene glad of any occafion to make peace with vs, fo that feauen of them at once haue fent meffengers to vs to that end, yea, an Fie which we neuer faw hath alfo together with the former..."'*

Scilla stood listening with one arm around Maryah's shoulders and one around Eddy's. She was almost faint with hunger.

"That's great Liz," she said, "but guess what? It's turkey time! Let's eat. We're famished."

An exuberant, ragged cheer went up, startling the mynah birds outside. Before anyone could get a forkful of food into their mouth, however, Baxter de Waal stood up and banged her spoon on her water glass. She held up her iPhone. She was reading a text message.

"Sorry to interrupt, folks, but I have a very quick announcement to make." What now? Silence fell. "My parents are at the town dock in Bridgetown. They just got in from Maine. They've chartered a sailboat for the week, and everyone is invited to come on a little shakedown cruise tomorrow. Like my Dad, the crew is from South Africa. We're going to check out the Grenadines, then end up in Grenada."

A crew of South African yachtsmen? Why did that ring a bell? Washington and Liz's eyes met. A twinkle passed between them. James was next to delay the feast. The turkey was getting cold, but nobody seemed to mind.

"Hold on, everybody." He stood up. "Sorry, folks, but there's yet one more thing." James held up his smartphone. "I too am going to read something to you. I think you will agree it's relevant to today's proceedings. It's an email that I received this morning from my cousin down under." James broke the ancestry.com news from New Zealand.

"Do you get it? You are all *Mayflower* descendants!" James announced. Liz absorbed the news for a moment, then gasped...

"Oh my God, James. You know what that means, don't you? It means... First, let me say this. This diary was written by Priscilla Mullins. I knew that. I just figured it out this morning. Anyone here know who Priscilla Mullins was?" Old Jack nodded, but refrained from interrupting. Liz went on. "Priscilla Mullins was the only *Mayflower* passenger with the initials 'PM.' But... This is crazy, James. I can hardly believe it. This means..." She stood up and inhaled deeply. "What I did not know is that Priscilla Mullins, the teenaged *Mayflower* passenger who wrote this precious American treasure, starting back in England in 1615, was my twelve times great, great, great, great, great, great, great, great-grandmother, the ancestor from whom each and every one of us Aldens is descended. Grandpa Jack, did you hear what I just said? This is absolutely, insanely unbelievable!"

Old Jack nodded knowingly. His eyes twinkled under the bushy eyebrows, but he held his peace.

102

The Mohawk Headdress

It was by far the best Thanksgiving of Liz's life. The turkey (and the rest of the abundant feast) was beyond perfect, as was the spirit of the entire afternoon. Old Jack sacrificed every last bottle of his precious collection of *Veuve Clicquot*, twenty eight bottles in all, to the occasion. Liz sat at the long table between her father and James, sipping the champagne in a state of wordless amazement. Old Jack continued his amorous pursuit of Baxter de Waal, insisting on having the Ferrari pulled in next to her at the long table. That arrangement did not exactly work, so a compromise was reached. Old Jack took over the head of the table, with Bax to his immediate right. Bax played along cheerfully, and fortunately, she and the old man were soon deep in conversation about early New England history. From what Liz could gather, they were discussing the never-ending historical controversy about the nature of the first thanksgiving back in 1621.

Bax looked down the table and took note once again of Maryah's astonishing transformation. There was something familiar about that Mohawk headdress. Excusing herself politely, she got up and made her way all the way to the far end of the table, and then halfway back up the other side. Maryah was deep in conversation with her Eddy, her guest, who was a famous reggae musician who lived a few miles away. Bax stood behind Maryah for a long minute, then tapped her gently on the shoulder.

"Excuse me, Maryah," she said. The Mohawk headress spun on its axis.

"Oh hi, I'm not sure we ever met. Did we? I'm Maryah."

"I know. You're Scilla's partner. My name is Baxter, but everyone calls me Bax."

"Well, hi there Bax. This here is my friend Eddy."

"Hi Eddy. Pleased to meet you. I love your music. Maryah, may I ask you a quick question?"

From the far end of the table, Alden watched Bax with a degree of interest that had little to do with Pilgrims and Indians. Or Mohawk headdresses. It had more to do with the way Bax's blouse hung away from her body as she leaned forward. Liz got up and sat down in Bax's vacated seat. Mariah responded to Bax's question.

"A quick question? Of course you can, honey. What's up?"

"It's that amazing headdress you're wearing."

"It's pretty cool, isn't it? What about it?"

"Well, this may sound crazy, but I've seen it before. Where did you get it?"

"Why, I got it from..." Maryah indicated the dreadlocked man in the next chair. Eddy stood up politely.

"Bax," he said. "Why don't you sit down? I'll grab another chair."

Once the seating had been rearranged, Bax continued.

"Eddy, did I hear that correctly? Maryah got this amazing piece of headgear from you?"

"That is correct, Miss Bax. She dropped by the studio last night and..."

"I was feeling like a change," Maryah interrupted.

"So yeah, we decided to shave her head, just for the halibut." There was that word again. Halibut. Eddy laughed. "If you ever want to make a change in your life, try shaving your head. Anyway, once we got the debris cleaned up off of my studio floor, we got into a little reggae jam - this lady is hot, did you know that?"

"There's this collection of African masks and costumes hanging on the studio walls. I was checkin' 'em out while we was playin'. I saw this crazy headdress."

"Wait a minute," said Bax. "That thing you're wearing, it's not African. I swear it's Native American."

"You are right," said Eddy. "Why are you so interested, if I may ask?"

"Let me ask you a question. Where did it come from? I know I've seen it somewhere before."

"That's an easy one. We were on tour in the States two, three years ago. We played Boston, and we had the next couple of days off, so we all went out to Cape Cod."

"Don't tell me you went to Plimoth Plantation, the living history museum in Plymouth?"

"Aha. I see where you're going with this, Bax. Let me ask you a question. Did you ever meet an Indian guy, a big heavyset Native American..?"

"A big heavyset man in a wheelchair, who sits there in the gallery making the most amazing warrior headdresses out of..."

"Out of dyed porcupine hair. Exactly! We got into a really interesting conversation."

"Anything to do with thunderbirds, by any chance?"

"Now wait a minute, Bax..."

103

A Message From The Ancestors

As the sun prepared to set behind the coastal mountains, everyone walked down to Soup Bowls to watch the surfing finals, everyone except Old Jack and his firstborn granddaughter. Liz was emotionally and physically exhausted, and she had imbibed one glass too many of Old Jack's rapidly diminishing private hoard of *Veuve Clicquot*. She was as happy as the proverbial clam. The moon was high in the sky when Gladys gently woke her from an impromptu nap at the verandah table.

Gladys bore a message from Old Jack.

"Come and see me before you go to bed," he had instructed. "Don't worry about waking me. I've had enough sleep in the last month to last me a lifetime. Bring your friend with you."

Rubbing her eyes and shaking her head, Liz took the clinking jug and splashed a handful of iced water into her face.

"My friend? Any particular friend?" she asked, a hint of guilt in her tone.

"I do not know which friend, Miss Lizzie. That is all he said," replied Gladys.

Liz hurried up the winding staircase. She pulled up the antique chair and sat down by the bedside. Old Jack was fast asleep, or so it seemed to her. She sat there quietly for a while. His eyes still closed, the old man opened his mouth and spoke, his voice as clear as it had ever been. Unfortunately, his teeth were not in his mouth. The dentures rested in the glass of water on the nightstand. Consequently, Alden's diction was rather comical, as it had been on the night of his sudden resurrection.

"Lithie?" he asked. "Are you there, thweetheart? Did you bring Bakthter de Waal with you? I have a methage for the two of you. A methage from the anthethtors."

"Baxter de Waal?" Oh, and uh oh. Liz suppressed a giggle. She was relieved that the requested friend was Baxter and not James, but to be honest, she was a little concerned that the old man might be harboring improper intentions with regard to her new best friend.

"The ancestors, Grandpa Jack?" Liz asked. "Whose ancestors?"

"Yourth, Lithie. Yourth and mine. They've got a bit of a job for you, if you're interethted. And for your lovely friend."

"A job, Grandpa? A job working for the ancestors?" After doing something she had never done in her life before, to wit, putting an old man's dentures back into his toothless mouth, Liz trotted down the stairs and fetched Baxter, who was sitting in the living room, quietly studying the issue of *Time* magazine that Liz had brought with her from New England.

*****

104

The First
Thanksgiving

axter and Liz wrestled the second chair over to
Old Jack's bedside. The new friends sat down side
by side, smoothing their skirts primly. After all,
this was a job interview, was it not? They gazed expectantly at the emaciated, much-diminished figure almost
five feet away from them. Alden was dwarfed by the
huge bed, and yet his presence filled the room.

There was no immediate evidence that the old man
was aware that he had company. Alden's eyes were
closed, and his breathing was barely audible, but Liz

thought she detected the flicker of a mischievous smile playing around the edges of his mouth. A long five minutes went by. At last, the old man spoke.

"Are you there, Baxter de Waal?" Alden asked. His pronunciation was perfect. Baxter duh Vahl.

"I'm right here, Mr. Alden," said Bax.

"And you, Lizzie?"

"Elizabeth Alden Nicholson, PhD, reporting for duty," said Liz, putting her right fingers to her forehead in a cocky military salute.

"Well, thank you. Thank both of you. That was one helluva Thanksgiving, was it not?" Alden rasped. "Now listen to me, girls. I have something..." He paused in mid-sentence and took a different tack. "But first, Baxter, I have a question for you. Do you remember me?"

"Remember you, Mr. Alden? Well, we only met a couple of days ago, so I'm not quite..."

"You don't remember, do you? I thought not. Dang! I thought I had made more of a goddamned impression. Ah well. Allow me to jog your memory. It was three years ago, sometime in November of 2017. I don't recall the exact date. You and I had quite a conversation."

"We did? I'm sorry, Mr. Alden. Three years ago? November 2017? Where were we?"

"It was at the State House in Boston. Don't tell me you've forgotten. You were writing a book about all the misbeliefs around the *Mayflower* Pilgrims."

"November 2017, in Boston? Wow, Mr. Alden, I'm drawing a complete blank."

"Aha! And to think that us old and decrepit codgers are supposed to be the ones with the memory loss." Alden let out an exaggerated sigh of frustration, and continued. "OK, I can see I'm going to have to give you a few more clues. Do you remember an event at the State House, it was put on by the Mashpee people? It was a cold, rainy day. You came in late. The Indian chief was leading a prayer. We had all joined hands in a great big circle, and you sort of pushed yourself ..."

"That was you? Good heavens. It's coming back to me now," said Bax, astonished. She turned and looked at Liz, her eyes wide.

It turned out that Jack Alden and Baxter de Waal had indeed met before, three years ago this month. The occasion had been a Thanksgiving celebration put on by the Mashpee Wampanoag tribe, who live out on Cape Cod an hour's drive beyond Plymouth. The invitation stated that, since their ancestors had hosted the *Mayflower* Pilgrims at the first Thanksgiving back in 1621, the Mashpee would like to promote peace and unity in 2017 by hosting a similar festivity in Boston. Those were divisive times. It was the first year of Donald Trump's contentious presidency, and the invitation was a clear call to inter-cultural solidarity.

Baxter had driven into Boston from Plymouth, where she was working on her research. She attended the event partly in order to see what, exactly, the Indians were up to. The *Mayflower* passengers' first thanksgiving on American soil, in the autumn of 1621, was based on a

604

traditional harvest feast that the English settlers had shared with their Dutch hosts for the previous twelve years. The Plymouth celebration, an expression of inter-cultural solidarity if ever there was one, was hosted by the Pilgrims, not the Indians. The sachem Massasoit and his Pokanoket warriors, almost a hundred strong, had attended the three-day feast, and had contributed five deer to the banquet.

That was the other thing that puzzled Bax; the Indians who joined the 1621 celebration were not the Mashpee. They were the Pokanokets. In fact, Bax had found no mention of a Mashpee tribe in the primary source material she was studying. She was determined to get her facts straight for her work-in-progress, and four hundred years after the events in question it was not an easy task.

In the opening prayer circle in the flag-festooned Great Hall of the Boston State House, she had found herself tentatively holding the gnarled left hand of a wizened old man, who, it transpired, shared her concerns about the motivations behind the gathering. To the great relief of both Bax and Alden, the event was indeed oriented toward inter-cultural unity. It went off without a single reference to any of the contentious and often historically incorrect 'facts' around the early Pilgrim/Indian relationship. In fact, the entire presentation was remarkably warm and friendly.

The Republican representative from a nearby town read a statement that said 'we should nurture the seeds

that have been planted here today.' The Mashpee tribal
chairman ended his speech with a phrase in his native
language that meant 'I love you.' The statement was
addressed to the entire room.

At the reception after the speeches, Alden and Bax
were introduced to the chairman, a tall, handsome,
friendly man. They learned that he was very much a
Christian. In fact, it seemed to Bax, virtually every
Indian present was a Christian, a 'praying Indian,' to use
the long-disused terminology of the 17th Century.

Alden, his eyes sparkling with optimism, invited Bax
to join him for dinner as they walked together through
the echoing halls after the gathering had dispersed. He
had a penthouse suite at the Langham Hotel, he said, and
the view was out of this world. There was a guest room,
if she'd like to spend the night. Politely but firmly, Bax
declined his kind offer, citing an important meeting
back at Plimoth Plantation. To be perfectly honest, Bax
was considering seeing a film of rather dubious quality
at the Plantation that night, on her own, but the fictitious meeting was the best excuse she could summon up
on the spur of the moment.

*****

105

The Birthday Cruise

Friday, November 27, 2020

It was Liz's 40th birthday and it was Andre de Waal's 69th birthday. There were two messages in Liz's email inbox. Baxter de Waal was as good as her word. They were going sailing. The second message was brief, but it made Liz happier than she had ever been. "Hope you have a wonderful day, Mom. Love, Layla."

"What better way to celebrate? It's going to be a little rough out there, Liz. I hope you don't get seasick?"

Bax asked, as the latter clambered aboard the *Tokoloshe*.
"How about the National Day of Unity?" she continued.
"Did you hear? No? I can hardly believe what happened.
I got the email this morning. Yesterday was the fiftieth
year of the so-called National Day of Mourning, and
almost a thousand angry Indians converged on Plymouth, planning to totally disrupt the Plymouth 400
festivities.

"Instead, and this is amazing, a Mohawk peacemaker
in full regalia took the stage and instead of spouting the
usual divisive anger, he made a proposal to the crowd of
protestors. He asked whether anyone was sick and tired
of all the separation, all the hatred? All the racism? The
crowd stopped and listened, and took notice. The
peacemaker offered to perform an Iroquois condolence
ceremony, and once they understood what he was talking about, the whole crowd shouted YES!

"When the condolence ceremony was over - it only
took about fifteen minutes - the peacemaker had one
more proposal. He asked if anyone would like to change
the title of the National Day of Mourning to the
National Day of Unity? The crowd went dead silent,
then roared YES! They were unanimously in favor.
I can hardly believe it, Liz, but in fact, this is exactly
what all the prophecies said – that we'd all get together

some day."

With the exception of Old Jack and his only son, and the surf-obsessed boys, the extended family went sailing on the rust-streaked ketch *Tokoloshe* with Bax's parents and the familiar South African crew. The reunited father and son, when the latter returned from his first-ever Alcoholics Anonymous meeting, had a little catching up to do.

Liz was hoping to hear Bax's story directly from the horses' mouths - her parents'. In the meantime she was talking to Fritz, whose eyes had opened wide upon hearing the fate of the dreaded skeletons. The conversation had moved on to the chain of command on the sailboat.

"So, you're all equal, Fritz? How does that work on a boat like this?" she asked.

"Well yes, hey?" he answered, after a moment's thought. "We's all equal, jus' like the blerry communists. But, obviously, jus' like the blerry communists, some of us is more equal than others. Thus, Danie, he is the kapitan. He gets to wave his arms around and yell out various commands, and we ignores him completely. I am the poor blerry engineer, which means I do all the dirty work." Fritz held up his battered, grease-blackened hands.

"And the others?"

"Gerry? He took a course in conceptual nagivation."

"You mean celestial navigation?" Liz was beginning to wonder whether the Afrikaner was pulling her leg. After all, as she had discoverd on Google, the friends were a well-known comedy team back home in South Africa.

"Ag yes ja, hey. That's it. Ah gets it all mixed up."

"What about Frikkie?"

"Frikkie the fish-stick? Frikkie's the cook. He does the fishing. He's caught three so far. He caught one right as we almost crashed into Barbados two weeks ago, but not a nibble since. He's in charge of the food, and he mixes the drinks when there isn't any food. He can mix a blerry good cane and Coke. Speaking of which, can I get you another one, Miss?"

Andre listened with interest. He had never seen a sailing vessel more incompetently run, and yet he was part of the charter party for the first time in his life. He had no say in how the vessel was operated, despite the fact that he had a thousand times more sailing experience than the entire crew put together. Somehow, the *Tokoloshe* had made it this far, all the way from Cape Town.

It had been a long time since Andre de Waal had last prayed, but he offered up a sincere entreaty to Mantis, the little green trickster god of the Hottentots, and helped himself to another tepid cane spirit and Coke out of the plastic jug. In honor of the higher forms of civilization, he dropped a dehydrated, secondhand slice of lime into the drink. He wished there had been some ice, but hey, beggars can't be choosers, can they? Hey?

The vessel heeled alarmingly and the swells towered above the main mast. The deep thunder of the surf could be heard pounding against the cliffs, less than a mile away. Andre decided to intervene.

"Liz, we should let the chaps do their job, hey? Aside from anything else, it would improve our chances of survival. Tell me, Liz, how did you and my daughter... She said..."

"We... Well, it was at the bank. She told me her name and I got hysterical."

"Hysterical? What do you mean hysterical? What's hysterical about her name, hey?"
Oops. The conversation was not going as well as Liz would have liked. She steered for calmer waters.

"I'm sorry, Andre. Mister de Waal. It's a bit of an inside joke. My late husband... Well, it's a long story, but... What I was hoping you could do is to explain how Baxter got her name. She's been trying to tell me, but I still don't get it, even though I'm from Maine."

"Oh, you're from Maine, are you? I 've heard of it. Sally, Baxter's mother here, she's from Portland, at least that's where she was born."

"So, Baxter Thunderbird. That is an unusual name if ever there was one."

"Hey Baxter, come 'ere a sec." Andre yelled to his daughter, the wind whipping the words out of his mouth. Bax struggled over in her tank-top and hot pants and flopped down into the cockpit, clinging tightly to anything she could lay her hands on, which happened to be Fritz, mostly. Fritz did not seem to mind.

"You told Lizzie here how you got your name, sweetheart?"

"Well, to be honest Papa, I don't think I got all the way through the story. We kept getting interrupted. You tell it. You've had more practice than I have."

"Come on, Papa. Out with it," encouraged Liz.

"Well it's pretty simple, really. Me and Sally, we was a bit younger back in those days, we met. In Maine, by the by. We decided to have a baby. So the obvious question came up - where?"

"Where?" Liz was puzzled.

"Exactly. First things first. Where. So Sally said, I know, Mount Katahdin. She was all excited. I said, what? She said Mount Katahdin. I said OK, whatever that is, what are we waiting for? Let's do it. So we did."

"Let's do it?"

"Mount Katahdin is this big mountain way up in the *bundu* in the north woods of Maine."

"I know. I've climbed it many times."

"So you know?"

"Know what?"

"The magic. Sally said that's the spot, so off we went. We borrowed a couple of ratty old sleeping bags that could be zipped together, and a rainproof poncho. We bought some trail mix, and a bottle of good brandy, and we climbed up there."

"Up to Baxter Peak?"

"Exactemundo, baby. Baxter Peak. You know the story already, I can tell."

"Dad, come on. Give her the gory details."

Danie managed to stagger aft without falling overboard. He took the wheel from Fritz, sat down and listened in.

"So yah. There we was, up on the tippy top. It was a beautiful day when we started out, but there was a storm coming in, and all of a sudden you could barely see your hand in front of your face. The clouds were thick like pea soup. We had to crawl along the Knife Edge on our hands and knees, it was so windy. But when we finally

613

got up there in the sunshine above the blerry clouds, the place was too crowded."

"Too crowded? Baxter Peak? You've got to be kidding."

"I kid you not, Liz. There was some sort of Appalachian Trail ceremony going on. They had champagne and everything. A whole bloody film crew. So we got pretty smashed with them. Then the thunderstorm started."

Sally had perched there all this time without saying a word. She chipped in.

"The thunderstorm started. We were actually above it. The clouds were down below us, and the lightning ... We had to get down quickly, before... Anyway, we ended up more soaked than if we had been scuba diving fifty feet underwater. Sleeping bags, everything, sopping wet."

"There was a sort of cabin thing down there," Andre said.

"Thoreau Springs. The lean-to." Liz could see it in her mind's eye.

"Right. Thoreau Springs. Named after that guy, the guy with the pond, what's 'is name? We got in there and the thunder and the lightning... We were right in the middle of it. It was probably pretty dangerous, but we were young and crazy and madly in love."

"I know the feeling. So, OK. Great story. I've been up there in one of those storms. Several of them, in fact. What's that got to do with Bax's name?"

Andre and Sally looked at each other.

"Well," said Andre at last. "There we were. Alone at last, even if we was as wet and slippery as a couple of freshly caught salmon."

"It was really cold, so we got out of our sopping clothes and wrung them out and hung them up and wrapped ourselves in the wet sleeping bags... We were just beginnng to warm up ..." Sally laughed at the memory. "Suddenly, the whole goddamned film crew showed up, and everybody came racing down and tried to cram themselves in there with us."

"All twenty of them," Andre continued. "And, most important of all, their camera equipment. Half of them still had their wet bums out in the rain waiting for the next lightning bolt to strike. But eventually they realized it was ridiculous, and they decided to make a run for it. Finally we were alone..."

"So that's where Bax was... In the lean-to at Thoreau Springs?" Liz interrupted. Sally stopped and looked around. All eyes were on her. Bax had had enough.

"Mom, Dad. Enough already. We get it. That's

where I was conceived, Liz."

"Right. Right." Andre agreed. "Then nine months later, here we was down here in Grenada trying to think up a name, and Sally just said 'Baxter Thunderbird,' so that was it."

"Got it, Liz? That's me, Baxter Thunderbird."

"I couldn't imagine a more auspicious beginning. Wow!"

Fritz made his way aft again and took the helm. They had succeeded in reefing the mainsail, more or less, and the vessel had settled down a bit. Liz had been waiting to have a little chat with Fritz.

"What happened with the famous sailor's chest?" Fritz wanted to know. "What was in it, after all that?"

"It's a long story, Fritz. No Spanish doubloons, sad to say. Just bunch of decrepit old stuff going back to the days of slavery. The Barbados historical people came and took it away."

"What about the skeletons? Was I hallucinating or was there really..?"

"They were real, all seven of them. They must have died down there during one of the slave rebellions. That's my theory, anyway. The Archeological Survey lady had them bagged up and off they went as well. End of story."

"So, no Spanish doubloons, hey? What a pity. They might of come in handy, hey?"

"Not even one." Liz stood up and clung to the overhead boom. She had something to say to Fritz in private. She leaned over toward the grizzled man. "That reminds me, Fritz. Can I talk to you? I need to ask you about a little smuggling operation. Could you guys use a few bucks? A thousand dollars, maybe? You wouldn't really be breaking any laws... And you'd be doing America a huge favor."

"America? America doesn't need any more drugs, from what I hear."

"No, no. Not drugs. It's just an old book. If you wouldn't mind taking it to Grenada when you leave, I'll meet you there and give you the cash."

"An old book, hey? Don't tell me it's a first edition of *Lady Loverly's Chatter*?"

"No, it's not *Lady Chatterley's Lover*." Liz laughed. "Nothing as exciting as that. Just a mouldy old family bible that needs to get back to its rightful owners."

*****

617

EPILOGUE

Where There's A Will

A week after Thanksgiving, Liz took a quick trip to the United States, via the nearby island nation of Grenada. Somewhat to her surprise, her luggage was not searched upon her departure from Barbados. Back in Maine, she resigned from her job at the Library, cleaned out her office there, and rented a large safe deposit box in the climate controlled section of her local credit union, into which she deposited a rectangular object carefully wrapped in acid-free, museum-quality archival paper.

Back on the island, Old Jack Alden's resurrection continued unabated. He had taken out a new lease on life. Improbably, his hearing and his speech had improved dramatically, and his mind had never been sharper. It was nothing short of a miracle. Dr. Ginsberg threw up his hands in disgust, his predictions of an imminent death frustrated. He never told another patient, "You have three months to live." In fact, it is not at all certain that Ginsberg had any other patients at that point in his career.

Alden, in the meantime, raced happily around the house and the property in the solar-charged electric wheelchair, which he had designed himself. The machine, as he explained to anyone who would listen, had been custom fabricated for him in Italy by a branch of the Ferrari automobile company that he happened to own. The company made electrical components for high performance racing cars, including alternators, spelled with an 'r'.

Old Jack was like a little boy. All traces of his formerly rough nature had evaporated. In the weeks before Christmas, he and Junior sat down and went over the current status of each of the family businesses. Junior was a changed man. At his second AA meeting, he declared that he was a hopeless golfaholic. He had gone cold turkey immediately after the Thanksgiving feast, and suddenly had an abundance of time for his relationship with James. Father and son came up with a series of profitable ideas for the future, and laid the groundwork for a Barbados-based nonprofit organization dedicated to the history of slavery. Alden House was to be its university, museum and headquarters. There might just be a job there for Baxter de Waal, PhD, should she be interested in such a vocation, once she had completed her thesis.

During Spring Break of 2021, Old Jack and the Ferrari hazarded the bumpy, half-mile road trip down to Soup Bowls, to witness his great grandsons surfing. He was highly impressed with their skill. He lived in joyful harmony with the reunited family, who had collectively decided to extend the Barbados idyll until the old man finally passed. In early August, Alden made his final transition, an enigmatic smile on his face. Was Lizzie's grandmother there to welcome him on the other side? We will never know.

The funeral was held in Brunswick, Maine. When John Bradford Alden's last will and testament was read, it contained a surprising codicil, bequeathing the sum of $25 million United States dollars, or the Bitcoin equivalent thereof, to a mysterious not-for-profit entity called

'The Foundation for a New England Pantheon.'

No hint of this secret project had ever reached Old Jack's descendants. The mission of the Foundation was *"to establish and maintain a public museum honoring the ideals and principles of the early settlers of New England, who carried the seed of free government to the New World, and those of the indigenous Native Americans with whom the settlers laid the foundation for the future United States of America."*

The bequest continued: *"Accordingly, I have this day purchased the old library building at 1117 North Main Street in Plymouth, Massachusetts. The architectural renovations are to be completed by the last day of the year 2020.*

"I hereby appoint my firstborn granddaughter, Elizabeth Alden Nicholson, Chief Executive Officer of the Foundation in perpetuity, subject to her desires and approval. Additionally, I hereby appoint my second-born granddaughter, Priscilla Alden Barnes, Executive Director for the New England Pantheon Online, a 'virtual' pantheon and comprehensive historical resource to give voice and remembrance to the descendants of the early settlers of New England and their Indian friends." The codicil was dated December 31, 2017.

Priscilla Mullins' long-lost diary, after the lawsuit with Barbados had been settled to the satisfaction of all concerned and the fair copy had been delivered to the

Archeological Survey, became the most significant historical artifact on display at Plymouth's popular New England Pantheon. The journal is now known as, simply, the Mayflower Diary. After three hundred and fifty years, the book has been returned to the very spot where it was written, and the half-century of peace and friendship between the Pilgrims and the Pokanokets has been firmly restored to its rightful place in both American and English history.

*****

HAPPY ENDING #2
(the filmic ending)

ONE YEAR LATER.
PLYMOUTH, MASSACHUSETS.

FADE IN

EXT NEW ENGLAND PANTHEON DAY

JACK ALDEN'S MEMORIAL SERVICE.
Thanksgiving 2021. The inauguration of the New
England Pantheon. Newspaper/TV headlines. Banner
saying "WE MISS YOU JACK ALDEN!"

JACK ALDEN JR, LIZ, and SCILLA walk out of the
Pantheon. RUSSELL BANKS, a Native American man
in full regalia, joins them. Russell is accompanied by a
beautiful unidentified INDIAN WOMAN with an
enigmatic Mona Lisa smile.

Arm-in-arm, the five friends walk down toward Plymouth Bay and the tall bronze statue of the Pokanoket sachem Massasoit overlooking Plymouth Rock. The newly renovated *Mayflower II* ship is visible in the background.

There is a festival going on. A thousand joyful people are drumming, singing, dancing and celebrating. A huge banner reads NATIONAL DAY OF UNITY. The five friends blend into the crowd and are lost to sight.

The entire crowd slowly turns to ghosts and fades away. The Pilgrim Rock Memorial, the *Mayflower II*, the other boats in the harbor, and all signs of human activity fade away, leaving Patuxet Bay and the beautiful New England sunset exactly as it might have been in the summer of the year 1620.

FADE TO BLACK
CREDITS ROLL
MUSIC: "Electric Avenue" by Eddy Grant

THE END

Copyright © 2017 Andrew Cameron Bailey

Author's Note

I confess to exercising a modicum of artistic license concerning the geography, flora and fauna of the lovely Caribbean island of Barbados. I trust the locals will forgive me. There is no Alden House or Indian Point near Bathsheba as far as I know, although there certainly is a famous surfing break called 'Soup Bowls.' How it got that name I have no idea. There may or may not be Indian mynah birds or purple popinjays on the island, but there certainly are green monkeys and timid little ungulates that resemble alien deer.

The long-lost diary and the dysfunctional Alden family are entirely fictitious, but other than that, the historical material in this novel is based upon verifiable fact, as far as it is possible to establish such details four hundred years down the road. The journal excerpts that Liz Nicholson 'tranfcribes' are reproduced verbatim from primary source material. These first-hand accounts were written and published in the early 17th Century by eyewitnesses to the events portrayed. The writers may not have understood everything they saw, and they certainly had their cultural prejudices, but there is no reason to believe they were lying.

The critically important but forgotten Tarratines War (1607- 1619) is an historical fact, as is the pandemic that decimated the native population of coastal New England and New France between 1616 and 1618, shortly before the *Mayflower* made its historic landfall on November 9th, 1620. The origin, nature and course of the pandemic is my own hypothesis. Based upon careful historical research and evidence from a remarkable 2014 archeological and epidemiological discovery in London, England, it is as likely an explanation as any I have found.

And, finally, the 'New England Pantheon' described at the end of the book is not fiction. The idea is based upon a 1921 bequest to the City of Boston by New England's great philanthropist and historian, James Phinney Baxter. Boston has, unfortunately, failed to build Baxter's pantheon, and his money has been spent on unrelated projects, but this author would dearly like to see some wealthy, visionary Mayflower or Puritan descendant step forward and carry Baxter's work to fruition.

It is said that history is written by the victors, but

during the first half-century of the English settlement of New England, especially in Plimoth Plantation, there were no victors. There were no victims. There were merely two groups of human beings from very different cultures, living together and working as best they could to adapt to one another. Some readers will have found their basic assumptions about early American history challenged by this book. There is good reason for that. Much of what is currently believed about the *Mayflower* Pilgrims, and especially about their relationship with their Native American friends and neighbours, is historically incorrect.

To such readers I say, please open your minds and do your own research. There is a great deal of misplaced anger, blame and shame around these long-ago events, as a result of 'politically correct' revisionist history. It is time to let such things go, especially if they are not based upon historical fact. The truth will set us free.

Andrew Cameron Bailey
Barbados, November 2015

Appendix

THE PANDEMIC THAT TRANSFORMED
AMERICA (AND THE WAR THAT CAUSED IT)

By Andrew Cameron Bailey

Four centuries ago, in the sultry summer of the year 1614, the indigenous population of the northeast coast of the continent, which today's native inhabitants call Turtle Island, caught their first glimpse of the troubles to come. An English sea captain with a marvelously generic name - John Smith, no less - sailed his open pinnace into Cohasset harbor on the rocky coast of Massachusetts Bay.

Captain Smith's welcome by the Cohasset locals took the form of a shower of arrows. You have very likely heard of John Smith, as a result of his legendary (and probably apocryphal) 1607 rescue in Jamestown, by a young Indian maiden named Pocahontas. Seven years later, having escaped a lingering and painful death at the hands of the Powhatan Indians who then occupied present day Virginia, Smith was back in the American Northeast, engaged in an exploratory mapping expedition in the service of one Sir Ferdinando Gorges, a visionary and wealthy Englishman who was determined to 'plant' the first colony in the part of Turtle Island that Smith was about to re-name New England.

Sailing with Captain Smith were several other men who were destined to play a part in the impending colonization of New England. One of them was, notably, a local native of the nearby Patuxet band, a group which could muster about 2,000 warriors, according to the detailed report that Smith presented to Gorges upon his return to England. The Patuxet man's name was Tisquantum, or 'Squanto,' as his English shipmates had nicknamed him. Also on the vessel was a young sailor named Thomas Dermer. A part of Smith and Dermer's mission was to return Squanto to his home at Patuxet, today known as Plymouth, Massachusetts. Squanto had, willingly or otherwise, spent the previous several years in England as the guest (or captive, depending on your perspective) of Sir Ferdinando. Squanto seems to have liked and trusted the English, and had learned their language. Now, at last, he was being delivered home to his people.

In command of a separate vessel sailed a certain Thomas Hunt, Smith's business partner and subordinate. Captain Smith was able to get his vessel turned around and out of Cohasset, while the local warriors rained arrows on them from the high cliffs on either side of the harbor entrance. It was no easy matter.

None of the arrows found its mark, fortunately for the sailors. A few weeks later, after completing his survey and returning Squanto to Patuxet, Smith and Dermer set sail for Jamestown, at that time the only English settlement in North America. Captain Hunt was left behind, with unambiguous instructions to fill his hold with fish and beaver pelts, and then to return to England with the cargo. Squanto was to remain with Hunt, and assist him for the time being, if the former so chose.

Captain Hunt, however, was a devious fellow. He had an alternative strategy, one which he believed would bring him a great deal more wealth, a great deal sooner. Using Squanto as interpreter and go-between, Hunt was able to lure twenty or more lusty Patuxet men onto his ship. Trustingly, they came aboard, with a view to trading their beaver skins and other pelts for kettles and hatchets and knives and other European goods. As soon as the Indians, including Squanto, were below deck, the hatches were slammed, the anchor was weighed, and the ship set sail for Málaga, Spain, bound for the slave market there. Squanto's Patuxet homecoming was shortlived. Once again Squanto found himself in Europe.

It was not until late 1619 or early 1620, five years later, that Squanto was able to make his way back home, thanks once again to his friend Thomas Dermer, who was by that time a fully-fledged sea captain in his own right. As fate would have it, this dastardly act by Captain Hunt had an unexpected consequence of profound proportions. It preserved Squanto's life, and as the reader probably knows, Squanto went on to play a significant role in the survival of the first boatload of English settlers to arrive in Massachusetts Bay in late 1620.

These events took place four hundred years ago, six short years before the fateful arrival of a little English ship named *Mayflower*. The landing of the *Mayflower* in New England signalled the first tiny stirring of one of the most significant population transfers in recent centuries, a phenomenon known to historians as the Great Migration. In the half-decade between Smith's 1614 voyage and the historic landing at the place Smith's map renamed Plimoth, however, things had changed dramatically.

Two little-understood, closely-related, and profoundly devastating events had unfolded among the native tribes in the area. In 1614, John Smith had described a thriving, fully settled New England coast inhabited by tens of thousands of indigenous people. The *Mayflower's* passengers disembarked in late 1620, at the place known to the natives as Patuxet, formerly home to some 2,000 souls, to find a scene of utter desolation. There were signs of human habitation everywhere. There were skulls among the rocks on the seashore, and unburied skeletons in the woods, but the Patuxet people, Squanto's people, were gone. Something truly awful had occurred. An apocalyptic disaster had changed everything.

Whatever that awful something was, this pivotal event in New England history is still not fully understood, four centuries later. The Pilgrims, once they had made contact with the local Indians four months after their late December landing, concluded that the catastrophe was the result of an outbreak of plague which had swept the entire New England coast from maritime Canada to Cape Cod between the years 1616 and 1618.

The precise identity, nature, origin, and mode of

transmission of this epidemic is the subject of this writing. Many theories have been put forward over the centuries, many with merit, some patently absurd, all falling short of satisfactorily explaining the historical evidence. This writer offers a groundbreaking hypothesis based upon a decade of historical research and upon some very recent, as-yet-unproven epidemiological findings thousands of miles from New England. Neither the disease itself, the hypothesis goes, nor its origin, nor its mode of transmission are what we have been led to believe. The truth, if this analysis stands up to scrutiny, is stranger, wilder, and more compelling than any of the various fictions. It is a game-changer.

Here is a 17th Century account of a critical element of this pivotal but forgotten American story, in the words of Captain Smith's employer Sir Ferdinando Gorges. It is excerpted from *A Briefe Narration*, which Gorges published in London in 1658.

"...the Warre growing more and more violent between the Bashaba and the Tarentines, who (as it seemed) presumed upon the hopes they had to be favoured of the French that were seated in Canada their next neighbors, the Tarentines surprised the Bashaba, and slew him and all his People near about him, carrying away his Women, and such other matters as they thought of value; after his death the

633

publique businesse running to confusion for want of an head,
the rest of his great Sagamores fell at variance among them-
selves, spoiled and destroyed each other's people and provision,
and famine took hould of many, which was seconded by a
great and generall plague, which so violently rained for three
yeares together, that in a manner the greater part of that
Land was left desert without any to disturb or appease our
free and peaceable possession thereof..."

The history of humanity, for better or worse, has been one of unending migration, invasion, and inter-cultural exchange. Ever since *homo erectus* left Africa 70,000 years ago and began to populate the rest of Planet Earth, we humans have rarely been content to stay in any one place forever. Always, the unknown, the far horizon, has beckoned, and we have never failed to answer the call. We got to Australia 50,000 years ago, they say, across uncharted waters. Today, we are looking to the stars, the place the Aborigines say we came from in the first place. It wasn't necessarily that our current home was overpopulated, or that we'd exhausted the local resources. It was often the spirit of adventure that drove us, the urge to push the boundaries of our current understanding, as well as the compelling human desire for freedom from conflict and oppression and the vision of a safe and prosperous home for future generations.

By the end of the most recent Ice Age, *homo sapiens* had pretty much settled the entire planet. New migrants were more likely than not to encounter human communities already established in the places they migrated to. That could and did create problems, one of which is the subject of this dissertation. But first, an example, a relevant example as we shall see, of a place that has been invaded countless times: the British Isles, the tiny group of islands where this writer happened to be born in the midst of the most recent invasion attempt - World War Two.

For thousands of years, every couple of centuries, boatloads of warlike foreigners, Angles or Saxons or Romans or Vikings or Celts or Normans or whatever the latest invaders called themselves in their gutteral, incomprehensible languages, swarmed over the narrow English Channel to the British Isles and made themselves at home, no ifs, ands or buts.

"We're here. Get used to it!"
The original Ancient Britons, the tribal ancestors of today's Welsh population, adapting as best they could, became a minority in their own homeland. They're still angry about that, just as the current generation of Native Americans is today an angry minority in its own homeland. These days, having repelled later invasion attempts

by the Spanish, the French and the Germans, among others, the United Kingdom, at least on the surface, is a reasonably well-integrated, ever-evolving mishmash of multicultural bloodlines, and the blending has been, to a great degree, beneficial. The United States of America, the greatest meltingpot experiment in human history, is a direct outgrowth of those early invasions of Britain.

Each time a major migration (or invasion, depending on your perspective) occurs, the inevitable result is a cross-cultural exchange with profound and often positive consequences for humanity as a whole. The new immigrants learn from the locals, and the locals learn from the newcomers. Genes, DNA, ideas, cosmologies, art, fashion, language, music and technologies are exchanged, each side adapts to the other, and the net result is an evolutionary technological, cultural, and spiritual advance for our species.

Unfortunately, there is occasionally another, unseen, unintended and unexpected transfer that takes place at the same time - an exchange of dangerously infectious or contagious microorganisms. For instance, one of the more significant and least-understood consequences of Columbus's 1492 journey to the New World, at least for the rest of the world, was that he and his crew returned to Europe carrying a devastating new malady: syphilis.

Within twelve short years, the Spanish Pox, as syphilis was known, had spread as far as China. Over the
subsequent centuries, syphilis has become a much more
treatable malady, but throughout the 1500s, 1600s,
1700s and 1800s the disease was a rampant, slow, painful
and almost certain killer. Syphilis, a New World disease
going back at least 1,800 years, has been responsible for
countless millions of extremely unpleasant deaths all
over the world, up until the discovery of penicillin and
its widespread use beginning as recently as 1928.

The foregoing is a controversial and little known
historical fact, but it has been proven beyond doubt by
recent medical analysis of New World skeletal remains.*
A much more notorious transfer of disease travelled in
the other direction, from the Old World to the New.
From 1492 on, relentless waves of Europeans brought
smallpox, bubonic plague, measles, and numerous other
deadly maladies to the native peoples of the Americas,
with devastating results. This investigation specifically
addresses one of the most historically contentious
transfers of disease from Europeans to Native Americans: the pandemic that is believed to have reduced the
native population of coastal New England by as much as
75 - 90% between the years 1616 and 1618.

What exactly was the terrifying, voracious, deadly

disease that decimated the New England coastal tribes, beginning in 1616 and ending by 1619? Where did it come from? How was it spread? Who was to blame? Was anyone to blame? There is a great deal of speculation, confusion and misinformation concerning these questions. Right now, in the opening decades of the 21st Century, you may be surprised to hear that there is a great deal of anger, blame, shame and guilt around the issue, four hundred years after the fact. It would appear, for instance, that there are lot of Americans of both Native and European descent, who blame the *Mayflower* Pilgrims for the epidemic, and would like the Pilgrim Fathers, all fourteen of them, to go down in history as cruel, rapacious, murderous invaders who proceeded to massacre the indigenous population upon arrival, while simultaneously, intentionally or otherwise, delivering a deadly epidemic to the shores of New England.

This widely believed but utterly incorrect viewpoint is not supported by the historical record. Not remotely. In fact, it is an absurd fabrication. Whatever the disease was, the historical evidence indicates that the pandemic began sometime in late 1615 or early 1616, peaked around 1617, then tapered off and ended by early 1619, almost two years before the Mayflower passengers came ashore at a haunted and abandoned place on Massachusetts Bay that the former inhabitants had called Patuxet.

The English settlers called the place Plimoth, the name given to it by John Smith six years earlier. The inhabitants of Patuxet, 2,000 warriors strong in 1614, had become virtually extinct by 1619, with the exception of the afore-mentioned Squanto, and perhaps a handfull of scattered survivors who had fled and taken refuge inland. What could have killed all of these people with such devastating efficiency? A smallpox epidemic? Leptospirosis? Measles? Yellow fever? Influenza? Bubonic plague? Or could it have been something else, in combination with an epidemic disease?

As Alice Park writes in her December 2014 *TIME* article on AIDS, a disease with African origins that has thus far killed an estimated 36,000,000 people worldwide: "Every epidemic, however devastating, has a beginning and an end. The Black Death that spread from China to Europe in the 1300s peaked over five years. The Spanish influenza pandemic of 1918 ripped through nearly every country on the planet, leaving an estimated 50,000,000 dead in its wake. But nearly as quickly as it came, it disappeared after about 12 months." Park goes on to say: "However dark the circumstances seem at the start, history teaches us that eventually there is an end."

Like the pandemics described by Park, whatever the

639

New England disease was, it started, peaked, and disappeared over a period of approximately two years. The timing of that cycle is critical to this hypothesis, but first we must ask a question; how do infectious diseases develop into pandemics? Every potentially epidemic disease, in order to spread, requires a 'vector' in order to propagate its lethal legacy. The virus or bacterium needs an agent, a carrier. In the case of HIV/AIDS, the virus is transmitted, human-to-human, by sexual contact, blood transfusion or the sharing of hypodermic needles. Other 'social diseases' such as syphilis and gonorrhea, like AIDS, are spread by sexual contact. Christopher Columbus, his randy crewmen, and their sexual behavior were, as we have seen, the unwitting but very effective vector for the rapid spread of syphilis from the New World to the Old.

The Black Death, commonly called bubonic plague, was the cause of the most lethal catastrophe in recorded history,** It originated somewhere in present day China, and was spread by the ubiquitous rats and fleas that infested medieval communities. Smallpox was spread by physical contact with the bodily fluids of an infected person, whereas measles, influenza and many other infectious diseases are spread by coughs and sneezes. These airborne or pnuemonic diseases are delivered invisibly, and are very difficult to avoid. Highly relevant to this investigation, current research is revealing that, hundreds of years before the *Mayflower*, there existed a second, hitherto unsuspected form of Black Death, a far swifter and more deadly one than the rat-and-flea-borne bubonic strain.

There was (and still is, potentially) also a *pnuemonic* or airborne version of the plague. Historical evidence for this was recently unearthed during one of the largest construction projects in human history. Excavating for a 2014 extension to London's underground transportation system, the workers came across a mass grave containing the skeletons of twenty-five 14th Century Londoners.*** DNA analysis of genetic material from the remains has shown that between 1348 and 1349, 60% of London's population perished over a very short period. They were killed, it would seem, by a *pnuemonic* form of plague. Ongoing research from this discovery may provide a critical contribution to our understanding of what occurred hundreds of years later in New England, in the years immediately preceding the arrival of the *May-flower*.

"*Evidence taken from the human remains found in Charterhouse Square, to the north of the City of London, during excavations carried out as part of the construction of the*

Crossrail train line, may support a theory held by some scientists that only an airborne infection could have spread so fast and killed so quickly.

"The Black Death arrived in Britain from central Asia in the autumn of 1348 and by late spring the following year it had killed six out of every 10 people in London. Such a rate of destruction would kill five million now. By extracting the DNA of the disease bacterium, yersinia pestis, from the largest teeth in some of the skulls retrieved from the square, the scientists were able to compare the strain of bubonic plague preserved there with that which was recently responsible for killing 60 people in Madagascar. To their surprise, the 14th-century strain, the cause of the most lethal catastrophe in recorded history, was no more virulent than today's disease. The DNA codes were an almost perfect match."

The recent Ebola epidemic in West Africa is only the latest in an ever-unfolding series of devastating pnumonic diseases, the control of which is vastly complicated by the realities of modern transportation and human mobility. The Ebola vector is simply any infected or exposed human being. Anyone coming in contact with a carrier (or his breath, or his bodily fluids) is at great risk personally, and becomes a potential carrier. Other current examples of potentially deadly epidemic diseases include Asiatic flu, swine flu, bird flu, yellow fever and West Nile disease (transmitted by mosquitoes), SARS and most recently, the Zika virus (also transmitted by mosquitoes.) Many of these viruses originate among domesticated animals in central Asia, just as they did hundreds of years ago. The viruses are often spread by the annual migrations of birds, an extremely effective method of worldwide transmission, and one against which it is almost impossible to defend. This is a global biological phenomenon that has been in motion for countless thousands of years, and it will not end any time soon.

To return to the New England pandemic of the early 1600s, let us ask ourselves a few key questions. What *do* we know about the 1616-1618 outbreak that so dramatically reduced the indigenous New England population, and how does that knowledge accord with commonly accepted beliefs on the subject? Challenging as it may be to unearth the epidemiological truth four centuries after the fact, a little historical detective work, combined with the latest medical research, sheds an entirely new light on the subject, light that effectively does away with a number of the most commonly-held theories and beliefs on the subject in 21st Century America. Remember, we are looking for two factors: a highly contagious, rapid acting, deadly pestilence, and a distribution mechanism that might have enabled that pestilence to spread over hundreds of square miles and annihilate tens of thousands of people, very, very swiftly.

This writer has spent a great deal of time analyzing just about everything that has been written (at least, in the English language) about the earliest contacts between Northeast America's indigenous peoples and Europeans, with a particular emphasis on Plymouth Colony and the relationship between the so-called *Mayflower* Pilgrims and the Pokanoket Wampanoag Indians, with whom the English settlers shared more than half a century of peace and friendship.

In the autumn of 2014, I sat in on a conference of leading academic historians at Plimoth Plantation, the marvelous living history facility in Plymouth, Massachusetts, carefully listening to each of the sixteen panelists to see what is currently being said, and just as importantly, to see what is not being said. I had recently developed the theory presented here, and was interested to see whether anyone else had noticed what I had noticed, in particular the experts in the field. Apparently nobody had, or if they had, no one was talking about it.

In the course of my research, it had not taken me long to realize that, in order to truly understand the events that unfolded at Plymouth after the historic landfall in November, 1620, it is essential to know what had preceded that event. Why, for example, was Patuxet (a.k.a Plymouth) uninhabited in 1620, whereas Captain John Smith had described a thriving community there, possibly 2,000 warriors strong, as recently as 1614? How did the famous Squanto, a Patuxet native, come to be almost the sole survivor of his people? What was the relationship between the local native groups and other, earlier European visitors? What were the socio-political structures within and among the various native tribes across all of the North East? How were the indigenous people of the Eastern seaboard reacting and adapting to ever increasing European contact? These and many other questions cannot be fully answered merely by investigating colonial Plymouth and its immediate surroundings. We must expand our horizons.

We need to go deeper in time, and wider in space, much deeper and much wider. At least half a century deeper in time, and a radius of at least several hundred miles wider in space. The events at Plymouth in late 1620 and early 1621 did not take place in a vacuum. Massachusetts Bay in the early 17th Century, like most other inhabited locations on the planet, was part of a populous, adaptive, ever changing, interactive network of indigenous communities, some coexisting peacefully, and many in the throes of intense competition and even, at times, brutal war. The Massachusetts tribes were connected, by trade and political alliances, with hundreds of other native groups, north into present day Canada and Nova Scotia, to the west deep into Iroquois country, and south through present day Rhode Island, Connecticut, New York and all the way down to Jamestown, Virginia, where the first struggling English colony had been established in 1607.

We can't understand the history of Plymouth and the 17th Century Cape Cod natives without a pretty exhaustive study of the Iroquois Confederacy, in particular the Mohawk; the Massachuset Federation, headed by the great sagamore Nanapashimet; the Narragansetts, the Mohegans and the Pequots; and most importantly, the major tribes to the north; the Abenaki Federation, in particular the Penobscot, and the Mi'qMak. We also need to understand the profound impact of French fur trading around the mouth of the St. Lawrence and St. Croix rivers, which began in the late 1500s. More than anything, we need to know about the Tarrantines War. Excuse me? The what?

The reader may not have encountered some of the words, names and events in the foregoing paragraph, especially the last one. Don't feel too bad. Not every professional historian has, either. A couple of months ago, for example, I asked a leading Plymouth-based historian what he knew about the Tarrantines War. He looked at me blankly. 'The what?' he asked. I told him that, in my humble opinion, the Tarrantines War was the most significant event in pre-*Mayflower* New England history. He was unconvinced. Oddly, given the importance I ascribe to the event, I have, with one exception, yet to meet an historian in or around Plymouth who knows anything at all about this forgotten inter-tribal conflict, inspite of the abundance of information available simply by Googling the phrase 'Tarrantines War.' Try it!

The one exception, in my experience, to the universal ignorance of this pivotal event in American history, is a Cohasset, Massachusetts historian whom I met briefly at a 2014 event called 'Captain John Smith Day,' a celebration of the 400th anniversary of John Smith's brief and tumultuous visit to Cohasset. To my great surprise, the historian brought up the subject of the Tarrantines War unasked. She obviously thought it was important. There was no time to explore further, but she did offer one very interesting piece of information. She said, and I quote, "The Indians will not talk about the Tarrantines War." Interesting, I thought. Very interesting. Nobody in New England is talking about one of the most significant events in early New England history. Not the historians, and not the Native Americans. How could that be?

Let's play a little game of Imagine. Imagine you are an indigenous person belonging to the Patuxet band or tribe, living, as have your ancestors for many generations, relatively peacefully and abundantly on the shores of present day Plymouth Bay in the year 1615. Your name is not Tisquantum (or Squanto) because Tisquantum had been abducted the previous year, along with some twenty other young men, and transported to Spain to be sold as slaves. Other than occasional raids by the neighboring tribes, predictable autumn scavenging sorties by seafaring warriors from the north, and the occasional visit from a European explorer or fishing vessel, life goes on pretty much as it always has. The crews of two visiting French vessels have recently come to an unfortunate and painful end at the hands of some of your immediate neighbors.

Your people are a semi-autonomous part of a loose federation of tribes and bands headed by a sachem called Massasoit. This Pokanoket or Wampanoag Federation is in turn part of the larger, more powerful Massachuset Federation a little to the north and west. The leader of the Massachuset Federation is the powerful grand sagamore Nanapashimet. You have some powerful enemies, including the Narragansett and the Pequots to the south, the Iroquois to the west and various others. Your leaders pay an annual tribute to these powers in the form of corn, squash, beans, dried fish, and animal skins. Every autumn you have to keep a sharp eye out for seafaring Mi'qMak raiders from the north, when they materialize each harvest season in search of food and attractive young females. Your village is portable. It is designed to be dismantled and moved at a moment's notice, a phenomenon which astonished the French explorer Samuel de Champlain when he explored your coast a decade ago.

As we have learned, the English ship that captured Tisquantum and the twenty young men in 1614 was skippered by John Smith's associate, the treacherous Thomas Hunt. There had been other recent visitors from over the sea. In the past couple of years, as mentioned above, two French ships had paid visits to the area, with dire and terminal consequences for the crews of each. The first vessel was shipwrecked, its crew captured, used as slaves, passed around from tribe to tribe for their general entertainment, and eventually tortured to death. The second ship had come seeking furs to trade, but was overrun by Indians and burnt. The second crew met a similarly horrific fate to those on the earlier shipwreck. We know this because, against all odds, one Frenchman survived to tell the harrowing tale, and his story was later corroborated by one of the Indians who had led the raid on his ship. The French survivor was redeemed in 1620 by Captain Thomas Dermer, when the latter delivered the kidnapped Tisquantum from Europe to his home at Patuxet. As is well established historically, Tisquantum came home in the summer of 1620 to find his people gone and Patuxet an abandoned ghost town. Just a few months later, in mid-December, the *Mayflower* hove into view.

Let's continue our 'what if?' scenario. What if, four or five years earlier, in the year 1615, in the midst of this period of relative peace and stability at Patuxet, long before the *Mayflower* made its fateful appearance, an unprecedented, horribly unwelcome surprise materialized from beyond the northern horizon? What if, out of the blue, an armada of birch-bark war canoes, infinitely faster and more maneuverable than your ponderous hollowed out log *mishoons*, each carrying a dozen terrifying warriors in full war-paint, appeared on the Patuxet shoreline? What if the seafaring invaders were familiar, because they were the same fearsome, well-armed raiders who came down from the north every autumn, right when your crops were ready for harvest? The ones who emerged from the autumn mist firing their terrifying French muskets, chasing you away, and helping themselves to your crop of beans and corn - and as many of your young girls as they could capture - each and every year?

What if this time, however, the situation was different, very different? Horribly different? What if, this time, the canoes appeared in the spring, out of season, catching you unprepared, bringing sudden, incomprehensible, indiscriminate death and destruction? What if the raids continued for the next several years, all the way until 1619, when these northern warriors, the Tarrantines, finally succeeded in killing a person you had heard of, but knew very little about; the Massachuset grand sachem Nanpashimet, hiding out in his secluded, inaccessible fortress near present day Medford, Massachusetts?

And finally, what if, in addition to unprecedented death and destruction, the war canoes were also delivering something invisible, something deadly; lethal doses of the bacterium *yersinia pestis,* carried in the bodies and on the breaths of hundreds of the bloodthirsty invaders? What if the Tarrantine warriors were, in fact, the unrelenting and unwitting vectors for a disease epidemic unprecedented in North American history?

If this scenario comes close to describing what actually happened during the Tarrantines War, can you imagine a more effective distribution mechanism for a pandemic - sustained hand to hand slaughter, and all the other body-to-body activities that accompany war, going on year after year after year? There is no way the innocent villagers of the Patuxet community could have known what hit them. Like many of today's historians, the Patuxet knew little about the Tarrantines, but the Tarrantines War was about to change their lives and the lives of every indigenous band and tribe within fifty miles of the New England coast, all the way from north-eastern Maine to the tip of Cape Cod. The war was about to change the future history of Turtle Island, of North America. In the case of the Patuxet, the war and the accompanying epidemic was about to terminate their very existence. The fearsome Tarrantines themselves, as the deliverers of this terrible fate to the tribes of New England, were far from exempt from its consequences. They too lost 60-70% of their tribal members between the years 1616 and 1618, after which they ceased to be nearly as much of a threat to their southern neighbors.

By the time the *Mayflower's* passengers set grateful

eyes on Cape Cod on November 9th, 1620, there had been a profound demographic change throughout New England. Captain Smith's detailed 1614 ethnographic description spoke of a situation that simply no longer existed. Were the *Mayflower* passengers aware of the change? Did this information, if they were in possession of it, affect their decision as to where to plant their colony? It is entirely possible that Captain Thomas Dermer had reported on the changed circumstances at Patuxet before his unfortunate demise at the hands of the Capawack (Martha's Vineyard) Wampanoags. If the Pilgrims had access to that report, which seems quite likely, the information may have influenced their decision as to where to settle, but that question is beyond the scope of this investigation.

My primary focus, as the reader knows by now, has to do with the nature, the genesis and the distribution of the epidemic that decimated the coastal tribes of New England between 1616 and 1618. To reiterate, I am seeking to answer the following questions: *what* was the disease, *where* did it come from, and *how* was it spread so rapidly? What is the historical truth, and what are the most common current misbeliefs around the subject? Of contemporary socio-political significance, what is the situation on the ground in present day New England?

What do the people there believe, and why?

For many decades, the disease was most commonly believed to have been smallpox, but as we now know, the historical evidence does not support such a conclusion. There are numerous historically inaccurate and occasionally absurd theories that have entered the modern worldview, including the widely held and unpleasant misbelief that the *Mayflower* arrived carrying a load of smallpox-infested blankets as poisonous gifts for the Indians they expected to encounter. Biological warfare, no less, back in 1620.

The Hollywood actress Cher, for example, appears to be one of these believers. She sent out this 2013 Thanksgiving message to her 2,000,000 Twitter followers: "I do not celebrate Thanksgiving because they (the Pilgrims) gave smallpox blankets to our people." Apparently, children are taught this and other inflammatory untruths in school, as 'politically correct' revisionist history has crept into our curricula. Difficult as it may be to believe, I have encountered this same story at the college level, being taught as history in a Massachusetts university in very recent times. Just a month ago, I was in California interviewing a retired college professor on an entirely different subject, when he went into a rant about smallpox blankets. Roughly three out of every four people I have asked, believe the blanket story in one form or another.

A great deal of this fraudulent misinformation originated with the published writings of a tenured University of Colorado Native American studies professor named Ward Churchill, who has subsequently been discredited and dismissed from his academic position. Churchill has also been dismissed from the Indian tribe in which he fraudulently claimed membership, but again, this is beyond the scope of this paper. The details are easily discovered. Simply Google Mr. Churchill's name. The unfortunate fact is that his poisonous work has received wide attention and has entered the worldview of countless Americans.

Let's dispense with this nonsense and move on, shall we? Let's look at the facts, at least as far as the *Mayflower* is concerned. The pandemic raged between 1616 and 1618. The *Mayflower* arrived in late 1620. There is *no* historical evidence of smallpox on the *Mayflower*. The epidemic occurred several years *prior* to the arrival of the *Mayflower*, and the disease was *not* smallpox. The first recorded outbreak of smallpox in New England occurred in the Boston area in 1633, when Indians from present-day New York came north on trading journeys, carrying smallpox that they had contracted from the

Dutch. The first known discussion of the possible use of smallpox-infested blankets occurred in 1763, 143 years after the landing of the *Mayflower*, up north in present day Maine, during the French and Indian Wars. So much for that absurd and inflammatory hypothesis!

Other preposterous misbeliefs continue to be spread, especially around Thanksgiving-time. Pilgrim historian James Baker calls such misinformation 'gratuitous nonsense.' There are other, less kind terms that could be applied. Leyden, Holland based scholar Jeremy Bangs calls it 'roast bull with cranberry sauce.' The phrase 'malevolent propaganda' comes to mind.

Myth has enormous power, more power than historically verifiable truth, sad to say. People believe what they want to believe, and resist anything that does not fit their belief system. Historically correct or otherwise, the current consensus among many native people (and many non-natives) in and around New England (and all across the country, apparently) is that the English brought smallpox to the Indians, intentionally or otherwise, and that is what caused the demise of such a high percentage of the native population.

Having said that, in a recent meeting with a Wampanoag tribal leader at Plimoth Plantation, I heard a different story. I was told: "The disease came down from the north." "Aha!" I thought. He went on to explain that the disease was not smallpox, but leptospirosis, an obscure illness spread by rat urine and particularly dangerous to dogs. On examination, this diagnosis, which was the subject of a CDC study, seems improbable. How did so many rats suddenly come down from the north, and how did leptospirosis, which has no known epidemic history in human populations, suddenly kill such a high percentage of the coastal natives?

So, what *was* the disease, and where *did* it come from? If it indeed came down from the north, what was it, and how did it get to Patuxet? Perhaps a pattern is beginning to emerge here? Detective work in general, and historical research in particular, has a lot to do with the detection of patterns. If, for example, one sees something coming down from the north, and then lo and behold, discovers something else also coming down from the north at precisely the same time and in precisely the same geographical location, the alert investigator might begin to put two and two together. Elementary, my dear Watson?

As suggested earlier, the most likely candidate for the disease is *pneumonic* plague, the airborne, fast moving and exceptionally infectious, lethal, bacterial illness that some scientists believe killed 60% of London's population back in the mid-14th Century. Apparently, bubonic plague can become pneumonic when, as with the Londoners of 1348, the victims are malnourished, and their immune systems are compromised as a result. In the midst of the protracted inter-tribal war that prevented the New England Indians from growing their staple crops, was the indigenous population malnourished? What about the raiders themselves, who depended on the labor of the southern tribes for a large part of their sustenance? New England was starving! There is no question about it, is there? It seems clear that all of the conditions were ripe for a pandemic of the kind I am describing. The various other candidates - smallpox, measles, leptospirosis, yellow fever - do not stand up to examination.

One has to give serious consideration to influenza, the bird-distributed disease that, in the malnourished aftermath of World War I, killed an estimated fifty million people worldwide. As recently as 1993, an outbreak of Bejing Flu killed 60,000. For a long time, though, based on the few written accounts that have come down to us, I was convinced that the disease could only have been bubonic plague, but I was stymied by the 'established fact' that bubonic plague requires rats and fleas as its vector, and that the process would take far too long to fit the bill, despite firsthand reports that the native wigwams were indeed flea- and louse-infested. I just couldn't picture the rats in those war canoes. A few fleas perhaps, but not rats. Where would they hide?

Compelling support for the plague-versus-smallpox theory comes from the testimony of one Phineas Pratt, an English settler who escaped in 1623 from an impending massacre at Wessagusset, a shortlived colony not far from Plymouth. Pratt later wrote about his experiences, and clearly distinguished the 1616-1618 outbreak from the later smallpox epidemics around Boston in the early 1630s. He called the earlier epidemic 'the plague' as distinct from the 'small pox.' The Europeans at the time certainly knew the difference between the two diseases. The rat-borne bubonic plague theory remains and will continue to remain problematic, but the emerging 2014 research concerning *pneumonic* plague unexpectedly offers a viable explanation for the humanitarian disaster that hit New England between 1615 and 1619.

So let's, as a thought experiment, accept two things as true: first, that the disease was indeed pneumonic or airborne plague, and second, that it came down from the north. By 'the north' I refer to present day northern Maine and the Maritime Provinces of Canada, in particular New Brunswick and Nova Scotia.

The remaining question, then, is this: if we have correctly identified the disease, what was the mechanism by which it was delivered and distributed? I propose that we already have the answer. It was delivered by sea, transported by high-speed birch-bark war canoe, in the context of a multi-year inter-tribal conflict called the Tarrantines War. In that war, wave upon wave of war canoes came down from the north, year after year, in precisely the same time frame as the pandemic. Do we have a match? It seems likely. If so, two questions still remain: who or what were the Tarrantines, and exactly where did the plague originate?

Let's address the second question first. I propose that the disease originated, having crossed the Atlantic in the form of rat-borne bubonic plague, among French fur traders in the area of present day Quebec, around the mouth of the St. Croix River. Is there evidence for an outbreak of plague, possibly airborne plague, at that time in that area? There is. I have not found statistics for the French, who were probably not malnourished and may have had some acquired immunity, but an estimated 60 - 80% of the native Eastern Etchemin and Mi'qMak (a.k.a Tarrantine) population perished during a series of epidemics (the historical record calls the disease simply 'the plague') between the years 1615 and

1618. The plague that decimated the northern natives so swiftly, whatever it was, seems to have been identical with the pestilence that destroyed a correspondingly large percentage of the coastal population to the south, during the identical time period.

To wrap up our hypothesis, then, the final questions are; who were the Tarrantines, where did they live, and what possessed them to attack the coastal tribes to the south of them? The word Tarentyne or Tarrantine does not sound Native American, does it? It is not.

Tarrantine was the European name, possibly of Basque origin, for a confederation of the Eastern Etchemin tribes and the Mi'qMak, the seafaring raider people of Nova Scotia. Because corn will not grow so far to the north, the Mi'qMak had, probably for centuries before the advent of the French fur traders, adopted a survival strategy involving annual raiding parties, in high-speed birch-bark canoes, which swept down the coasts of present day Maine and Massachusetts each autumn, returning with a bounty of corn, squash, beans, furs and fair young maidens.

Once the French arrived in the latter part of the 16th Century, and the fur trade began, things started to change. The Mi'qMak (Tarrantines) of Nova Scotia were the first tribe to ally themselves with the French, who proceeded to trade them modern European arms, and to teach them how to use the new weapons. Needless to say, this gave the Mi'qMak an enormous advantage over the neighboring tribes.

Unfortunately, the Tarrantines were not the only natives interested in trading with the French. There were the Mohawks inland, who had already established a trading monopoly, apparently by exterminating the competition far up the St. Lawrence River in the region of Lake Champlain. Much closer at hand, though, the Mi'qMak's traditional enemies, the Mawooshen Alliance of Western Etchemin, in particular the Penobscot immediately to the south of the St. Lawrence, were in direct day-to-day competition for the French fur trade.

Ongoing, small scale clashes between the Mi'qMak and the Penobscot ensued in 1607, culminating in the killing of the Bashaba, the grand sagamore of the Penobscot, and his entire family, in 1615, a very significant date for our hypothesis. This event signaled a major escalation of the Tarrantines War. Of critical relevance to our story, the Mawooshen had a powerful ally to the south, the Massachuset Federation, which encompassed all of the tribes in and around Massachusetts Bay, including Massasoit's domain in present day Rhode Island, Massachusetts Bay and Cape Cod.

Fatefully, Nanapashimet, the grand sagamore of the Massachuset, dispatched a large war party north in support of the Penobscot. Their campaign was successful. They killed a large number of Mi'qMak warriors, captured a number of women and children, and returned to Massachusetts with their captives.

This bold and supportive act on the part of the Massachuset was the beginning of the end for Nanapashimet and his entire federation. It was rather like walking up to a hornet's nest hanging from a branch in the forest, punching a hole in it with your fist, and then turning around and walking off as if nothing had happened.

Revenge was not long in coming. An armada of war canoes swept down the coast, indiscriminately slaughtering anyone and everyone the warriors encountered. Nanapashimet and many of the other tribal sachems fled inland, leaving their people confused and leaderless, easy prey for the raiders.

Unbeknownst to anyone concerned, and this of course is the central point of my hypothesis, the war not only killed thousands of innocent people directly, and completely destroyed the Massachuset Federation, but I believe it also delivered and spread one of the most devastating disease epidemics in all of human history.

The disease stopped where the warriors stopped. It never reached the Narragansett, for instance, just a few miles to the south of Plymouth. It never reached the Nauset, at the very tip of Cape Cod. It did not travel very far inland, other than in isolated outbreaks, most likely triggered by terrified refugees fleeing the invaders and carrying the disease with them.

Today, hardly anyone seems to have heard of Nanapashimet, or of his once-powerful Federation, or of the Tarrantines War, for that matter. How can that be? The events related above seem to me to be very significant, given their profound and pivotal effect on the future of North America, but somehow they have either been forgotten or suppressed. The Massachuset Federation was utterly destroyed. It was erased from history. Some northern Maine historians acknowledge that the Mi'qMak (a.k.a the Tarrantines) did indeed wage war on their southern neighbors, but propose that the warriors 'ran headlong into the epidemic' down south, turned around and brought it back north with them, triggering the demise of 60-80% of the Mi'qMak. I believe that scenario to be the opposite of what really happened, as I have set forth above.

Knowing nothing about infectious disease, and never having encountered anything like the ferocious, all-devouring plague in their midst, how could the Patuxet, or any of the dozens of other coastal groups, have known what caused the epidemic, where it came from, or how it traveled? If my theory is correct, the answer is that inter-tribal competition over fur trading rights with the French triggered a paradigm-shattering event that changed the future of New England. Had things been different, had there been no Tarrantines War, had there been no epidemic, Squanto would have returned from his European sojourn to his thriving Patuxet friends and family, and the *Mayflower* would have arrived later that same year, coming ashore in a fully occupied, fiercely defended region, where their chances of planting a successful colony would have been slim to non-existent. A number of earlier settlement attempts had failed, often because their presence was fiercely opposed by the native inhabitants. There is no reason to think New Plimoth would have been any different.

As it turned out, however, when the Pilgrims debarked on December 16, 1620, Patuxet was abandoned. Squanto, who would appear on the scene some four months later, was living in a state of captivity - and virtual slavery, apparently - at Massasoit's Pokanoket headquarters at Sowams, present day Mount Hope,

Rhode Island, some forty-six miles from Plymouth. Of the one hundred and two *Mayflower* passengers who came ashore that icy winter afternoon, fourteen adult Englishmen, four adult women, and thirty-four children survived the first bitter winter. Fully half their number perished, killed by the 'general sicknesse,' which was probably scurvy exacerbated by the unfamiliar local microorganisms in the water they drank.

A week after the spring equinox of 1621, Squanto, who had developed a fondness for the English and had learned their language, was on hand to broker a mutual-protection treaty between Massasoit and the Plimoth settlers, an agreement which the Pilgrims and the Poka-nokets would honor for more than half a century. Providence does indeed move in mysterious ways. The Pilgrims, as well as the Puritans who began arriving *en masse* a decade later, can be forgiven for seeing the hand of God in these events.

Finally, we must ask ourselves a challenging but un-avoidable and currently relevant question. It is apparent that the Tarrantines War has been expunged from the oral history of the Indians, as well as from the written history of this very well researched part of the world. If what I was told by the Cohasset historian in the summer of 2014 is in fact true, and the present day Indians for some reason will not discuss the conflict, the obvious question is: why not? Do they actively refuse to address the subject, or do they simply not know about it? Could it be that to acknowledge the very existence of that purely indigenous conflict would be to change their entire history, as handed down in the oral tradition of the native population?

In the American North East, hundreds of years after the event, there continues to be enormous bitterness, anger and blame and unhappiness among the Indians in the never ending aftermath of King Philip's War, the 1675 bloodbath that brought a sad and avoidable end to the half-century of peace and friendship between the English settlers and the Indians of New England. The Indians started the war. They had their reasons. They came close to victory, but in the long run they were defeated, not because the English had superior weapons, but because the Indians lacked unity.

Contrary to popular belief, the Indians were significantly better armed and trained than the settlers, who were farmers, not warriors. King Philip - Massasoit's son Metacom – was able to arm his warriors with the latest European firearms by selling land to the settlers and spending the proceeds on illicit weapons. Philip, in fact, lost his war because many of the Indians chose to side with the English. The Massachusetts phase of the war ended when Philip was shot and killed, by an Indian, in the late summer of 1676. In Maine, the bloody conflict initiated by Philip continued sporadically for another eighty years, with a great deal of instigation from the French.

In New England today, among the descendants of the tribes encountered by the Pilgrims and the Puritans, there is still a very active antipathy towards white people, especially those of English descent. Given the subsequent suffering of the Native Americans from coast to coast, this is more than understandable. On the other hand, if the old adage is true, and the truth will set us free, then it is essential for future generations that the historical facts be acknowledged, challenging as it might be to face one's ancestors' shadows. Propagating untruth and hatred is not the way to move forward.

If the foregoing hypothesis is correct, and an epidemic of pneumonic plague, originating with French fur traders, did indeed come down from the Maritime Provinces, and was delivered to all of New England as a consequence of a sustained inter-tribal conflict called the Tarrantines War, it is no longer possible to blame the English in general, or the *Mayflower* Pilgrims in particular, for the grisly fate that befell the coastal tribes between 1616 and 1618. An entire world-view has been built on the historically incorrect idea that the English were responsible for the disaster, intentionally or otherwise.

If instead, the natives themselves were responsible in large part for their own demise, this information will inevitably be controversial. It is going to be challenging to face, and there will be resistance. It is understandable that the Tarrantines War might be a forbidden subject, but the truth *will* set us free, if anything is going to set us free. There is no alternative, if we are to heal the rift between red and white, if we are going to eliminate the untruths being taught to our children, if we are to assuage the ongoing guilt and anger dividing us.

Consider this: it is incontrovertible that syphilis is a New World disease. It travelled back to Europe with Columbus in 1492. I don't think anyone is angry at the Native Americans for that unfortunate fact. It was simply a horrible, unexpected consequence of human exploration. It is equally incontrovertible that the *Mayflower* Pilgrims had nothing to do with the New England pandemic of 1616 -1618. And yet, irrationally, countless Americans of all ethnic backgrounds blame the Pilgrims for a crime against humanity of which they were entirely innocent. The Pilgrim-Indian story and the Puritan-Indian story were in fact a great deal more positive than they appear from the recent 'politically correct' portrayals, which began, perhaps, with Washington Irving's 1819 *Philip of Pokanoket* and Nathaniel Hawthorne's 1850 *The Scarlet Letter*, and appear in many cases to have been distorted and exaggerated for political purposes.

Here, as an example, is an excerpt from John Winthrop's description of the manner in which the Puritans behaved toward their Indian neighbors during Boston's first smallpox epidemic in 1633:

It wrought much with them (the Indians) that when their own people forsook them, yet the English came daily and ministered to them; and yet few, only two families, took any infection by it. Among others, Mr. Maverick of Winnissimet is worthy of a perpetual rememberance. Himself, his wife, and servants went daily to them, ministered to their necessities, and buried their dead, and took home many of their children. So did other of the neighbors. John Winthrop (1633)

In the fateful summer of 1614, the fierce Cohassett warriors succeeded in chasing Captain John Smith away with their bows and arrows. By 1675, however, it was too late to get rid of the newcomers, even with the finest European weaponry money could buy. For better or worse, the English had come to stay. The Puritans, it is worth repeating, were nowhere near as unpleasant as they have been portrayed to be, and the first generation of Pilgrims, William Bradford, Edward Winslow *et al*, were pretty much impeccable in their treatment of their Indian friends and allies.

The *Mayflower* journey was not a military invasion, nor was the Great Migration of Puritans a decade later. What both the Pilgrims and the Puritans recognized, however, was that their successful, conflict-free settlement of New England would have been infinitely more difficult - and bloody, if not impossible - had it not been for the 1616-1618 pandemic which preceded their arrival.

Like most of today's historians, the English settlers had no idea that the epidemic was triggered and spread by an indigenous inter-tribal feud, although the *yersinia pestis* bacteria causing the New England pandemic had its origins among the rats aboard a French fur trading ship. All the settlers knew was that the Massachusetts Bay area had been cleared of much of its previous population. Given the terrifying precedents set in other settlement attempts, the 1622 Jamestown Massacre being just one of numerous examples, they were understandably grateful for that fact.

©2017 Andrew Cameron Bailey

SUGGESTED READING

There are countless books available on the *Mayflower* Pilgrims. One of the best is *Mayflower*, by Nathaniel Philbrick. For those readers who would like to dig deeper, here are some primary sources. The material is available online at www.MayflowerHistory.com.

1. Books Written by *Mayflower* Passengers

A Relation or Journal of the Proceedings of the English Plantation Settled at Plymouth by Edward Winslow and others (London, 1622). These are the Pilgrims' journals for the first year at Plymouth.

Good Newes from New England by Edward Winslow (London, 1624). These are the Pilgrims' journals for the second and third year at Plymouth.

Of Plymouth Plantation (Volume 1 and Volume 2) by William Bradford (written 1630-1651, first published 1854). This is the most complete first-hand history of Plymouth, written by its long-time governor.

First Conference Between Some Young Men Born in New England and some Ancient Men who Came out of Holland by William Bradford (manuscript, 1648).

Third Conference Between Some Young Men Born in New England and some Ancient Men who Came out of Holland

Concerning the Church and the Government Thereof by William Bradford (manuscript, 1651.)

Poetry of William Bradford (various poems, 1640s and 1650s).

Hypocrisy Unmasked by Edward Winslow (London, 1646).

New England's Salamander Discovered by Edward Winslow (London, 1647).

Glorious Progress of the Gospel Amongst the Indians by Edward Winslow (London, 1649).

2. Books Written by Pilgrim Associates

The Sin and Danger of Self Love: A Sermon Preached at Plymouth in December 1621 by Robert Cushman (London, 1622).

The Works of John Robinson: Pastor of the Pilgrims (Volume 1, Volume 2, and Volume 3) edited by Robert Ashton, plus his *Manumission of a Manuduction* (1615, the only one known to be missing from the 3-volume *Works*).

New England's Prospect by William Wood (London, 1634).

673

New English Canaan by Thomas Morton
(Amsterdam, 1637).

History of New England, 1630-1649 (Volume 1, Volume 2)
by John Winthrop.

The Works of Captain John Smith
edited by Edward Arber.

*Declaration of the Affairs of the English People that First
Inhabited New England*
by Phineas Pratt (manuscript, 1662).

New England's Memorial
by Nathaniel Morton (Cambridge, 1669).

Biographies of William Bradford and Edward Winslow
by Cotton Mather, excerpts from *Magnalia Christi Amer-
icana* (Boston, 1702).

General History of New England, by William Hubbard
(17th century manuscript, first published 1815).

Chronological History of New England in the Form of Annals
by Thomas Prince (Boston, 1737).

ADDITIONAL RESOURCES

Pilgrims Then and Now by Gary L. Marks.

Indian New England 1524-1674 edited by Ronald Dale Karr.

The Times Of Their Lives: Life, Love, and Death in Plymouth Colony by James Deetz and Patricia Scott Deetz.

Indian Deeds: Land Transactions in Plymouth Colony 1620-1691 by Jeremy Dupertuis Bangs.

Thanksgiving: Biography of an American Holiday by James W. Baker

The Identity of the Tarrantines, With an Etymology By Frank T. Siebert, Jr., Studies In Linguistics, Volume 23, 1973

Bradford's Indian Book; Being the True Roote & Rise of American Letters as Revealed by the Native Text Embedded in Of Plimoth Plantation by Betty Booth Donohue

ABOUT THE AUTHOR

Andrew Cameron Bailey is an Englishman who
grew up in South Africa, where he studied physics,
chemistry, mathematics, photography, filmmaking,
anthropology and literature. He sailed a 90-foot yawl
from Italy to the United States in 1969, and arrived on
Thanksgiving Day of that year, so he calls himself a
latter-day Pilgrim. He lives in the Colorado Rockies
with his life-partner, Connie Baxter Marlow,
who is a *Mayflower* descendant.

67833054R00376

Made in the USA
Columbia, SC
01 August 2019